The War in Vietnam— 1991!

The first rocket over the berm awakened Major Rebecca Carnes. Six more landed with their terrible *whoop* WHAM! in the midst of the firebase before she managed to roll out of the cot.

The smell of flesh dead so long it was liquescent mingled chokingly with explosive residues.

A great explosion shocked the night orange. A flying object hit Carnes and flattened her against a half-collapsed sandbag wall. It was a human leg. The sight had the unexpected effect of steadying her.

Suddenly blue light and a sound like frying bacon enveloped Carnes. Outside the aura, all noise and motion stopped. An oval bubble formed before her. Tracer bullets hung in midflight.

The bubble split vertically. A man stepped out. "Major Carnes? We have a proposition for you."

★　　★　　★　　★

DAVID DRAKE & JANET MORRIS
ARC RIDERS

ASPECT

WARNER BOOKS

A Time Warner Company

WARNER BOOKS EDITION

Copyright © 1995 by David Drake and Janet Morris
All rights reserved.

Aspect is a trademark of Warner Books, Inc.

Cover design by Don Puckey
Cover illustration by Jean Targete

Warner Books, Inc.
1271 Avenue of the Americas
New York, NY 10020

Ⓦ A Time Warner Company

Printed in the United States of America

First Printing: June, 1995

10 9 8 7 6 5 4 3 2 1

DEDICATION

To Doctor John Miesel.
It's always handy to have a biochemist around.
—*David Drake*

To Uncle Ray, who would have been amused.
And to Bill Lewis (even-numbered pages)
and Bob Gladstein (odd-numbered pages).
—*Janet Morris*

Prologue: ARC Central

"Come on, Roebeck, I don't need a load of grief after an operation like this was," Jalouse growled. Jalouse's displacement suit had a panoramic display, so he didn't have to turn to see his five teammates in the capsule. Still, the sight of his armored figure swinging slowly around, displaying the battle damage, was a useful reminder of how rough a time he'd had—and how little he was asking.

"Oh, let him go," said Tim Grainger. Chun Quo pursed her lips and stared at her personal display, pretending that she didn't have an opinion.

"Come on," Jalouse repeated. "I'll be down in Debrief in ten minutes. Unloading me in the control room instead of the docking bay won't hurt anything."

The shimmering ambiance of plasma discharges and auroras had faded from TC 779's screens, leaving only the bare plates and girders of the dock. The bay door was a touch-sensitive unit, accepting a high leakage rate in order to speed operations. The black-and-yellow chevrons on the leaves had been scuffed almost entirely away by equipment entering ARC Central. The personnel airlock directly into the transfer control room was almost never used.

"Transfer Control to Capsule Seven-Seven-Niner," said a

bored voice that Jalouse heard both through his helmet earphones and over his suit's audio pick-up from the speaker in TC 779's cabin. "You're cleared to Berth Seven. How do you intend to proceed? Over."

"Hold one, Control," Roebeck said, grimacing as she reached for the airlock switch. "Go on, then, Jalouse. But I don't know why she can't meet you in Debrief like anybody else."

The inner hatch cycled open. Jalouse entered the lock. "Thanks, Nan," he said.

"Because he's afraid his wife'll be in Debrief, too." Pauli Weigand chuckled from his seat opposite the hatch. "We've had enough excitement on this operation already."

The inner lock closed. The outer membrane opened and Jalouse stepped onto the slotted emergency walkway. ARC Central was insulated from the world around it by hard vacuum.

A derrick slid into position above the capsule, in case Roebeck wanted to hand control over to the mechanical transporter. The operator could see that somebody'd gotten out of TC 779 here, against regulations; but the ground crews didn't make trouble for ARC Riders—and anyway, Sonia herself was the supervisor on this shift.

"Transfer Control to Seven-Seven-Niner," said the voice, which Jalouse now heard only through his earphones. "Do you have a problem?"

Jalouse stepped into Central's lock. The hatch closed behind him. He felt the clang through his boot soles, and the strip-lights on the paneling above quivered at his armored weight. Somebody else in a displacement suit was coming along the walkway from the other direction.

"Jalouse?" Weigand called over the team's intercom. "Bet you can't get out of your suit in ten minutes, much less into hers."

"Wise ass!" Jalouse muttered as pressure built in the airlock. Hell, they'd never been in love. Grimacing, Jalouse poked the switch to open the inner door and raised his faceshield as he stepped into ARC Central.

Sonia wasn't waiting on the other side of the airlock.

Neither was anything Jalouse had ever seen in his life.

Instead of the worn paint and control panels of Transfer Control Room Two, this chamber was hung with silk brocade. From the ceiling beamed the face of an Oriental whom Jalouse didn't recognize in the instant he had to give to the decor.

A dozen people in one-piece taupe coveralls sat stiffly at desks. For an instant, they gaped in amazement as great as that of Jalouse himself. Machine pistols were slung from their straight-backed chairs.

"   *R*   *o*   *e*
b   *e*   *c*
k   —" Jalouse said. His gauntleted left hand grabbed his helmet faceshield down. The plate wouldn't seat.

"Invasion!" screamed the translation program in Jalouse's suit as the strangers gabbled in some language that sure-hell wasn't Standard. "Invasion! Kill him!"

Jalouse pressed the switch of the airlock behind him. It didn't open. One of the strangers fired point-blank into the ARC Rider's chest.

Bullets ricocheted in all directions. Jalouse stumbled sideways, over a desk, and fell. He pointed the weapon he carried slung, but it was a plasma discharger. If he fired it here without his faceshield clamped, the hostiles elsewhere in ARC Central wouldn't have to do anything but sweep up his ashes.

Short, screaming people in coveralls leaped to their feet to get a better shot at the invader. One of them spun and fell, his face torn by a keyholing ricochet. The slamming, sparking impacts bruised Jalouse even though they hadn't yet penetrated his armor.

During the operation, Jalouse had used the pair of acoustic grenades that should have hung from his equipment belt. Fifty-fifty the detonation wave would have pulled his head off anyway when it inevitably lifted his helmet.

"   *K*   *i*   *l*

ARC Central

N an Roebeck tilted her seat as the transportation capsule shuddered and clucked. The electronics were aligning themselves in the limbo that was neither *when* nor *where*, preparing to displace again.

Roebeck could have saved an apparent ninety seconds by maneuvering the capsule in the sidereal universe to its berth. With the amount of traffic around ARC Central, though, it was both simpler and safer to let the software displace the vehicle . . . and anyway, Roebeck didn't feel like doing any unnecessary work right now.

The operation had been a bitch. Central's preinsertion intelligence had a gap in it that could have gotten somebody killed. Would have gotten Dor Jalouse killed, except Chun Quo had noticed the anomaly in the hostiles' wake, and Tim Grainger was a fast triggerman even by the standards of the ARC Riders. Grainger pulsed the *second* hostile vehicle, frying the circuitry of the coil gun maybe a half second before penetrators would have chewed the rest of the way through Jalouse's suit.

Roebeck turned her head slightly as she stretched. Weigand and Chun were chatting, while Barthuli was already reviewing clips of the raw data the team's sensors had gathered during the operation. That left Grainger to himself, as usual.

4

Quiet, composed; not obviously uncomfortable, but still looking like a well-mannered goat that had wandered into a luxury apartment.

Tim Grainger had been born at the beginning of the 21st century. The rest of the team, Jalouse included, was from the 26th, where ARC Central was parked in a huge vacuum chamber isolated from the rest of the Earth except via temporal displacement.

In a manner of speaking, all the ARC Riders were displacees. The teams used technology from far up the line—how far, most Riders didn't want to guess—to operate outside of their own periods. The fact remained that Grainger was an outsider even to the general outgroup.

"Got anything planned for your downtime, Tim?" Roebeck asked. She was team leader, so it was her duty to make her personnel comfortable.

At the corner of Roebeck's mind was the awareness that, because of her position, she was as much alone as Grainger. Roebeck's comfort was somebody else's duty, she supposed, though they were making a piss-poor job of it.

"My orange tree ought to be ready to flower," Grainger said. His smile suggested that he knew what Roebeck was trying to do—and appreciated it. "If it's going to, that—"

The capsule slid into normal spacetime. The alarms went off.

The display across the forward bulkhead was set to show the hangar in which the capsule was settling. That remained as the background, but the color was washed out to highlight the emergency dump from Jalouse's suit in the center of the image. A red strobe lit the cabin, and Roebeck's four team members muttered exclamations as they lunged for weapons and gear.

On the display, a woman screaming "Death to the intruder!" jumped onto a desk. She fired a machine pistol point-blank at the sensors on Jalouse's helmet. The projected image fuzzed and speckled as Jalouse toppled backward.

"Open the—" Grainger shouted. He had a fléchette gun/EMP combination in one hand and was pulling down the facemask from his headband with the other. There'd be no time to suit up fully.

The expression of the woman facing Jalouse from the display went blankly farcical. One of her fellows managed accidentally to shoot her in the nape of the neck. The high-velocity bullet flicked out one of her front teeth as it exited.

Roebeck's hand threw the switch that did the only thing which made sense under the circumstances. Transportation Capsule 779 shunted toward its most recent previous temporal location, out of danger.

Out of an ARC Central that wasn't the base the team had left for the just-completed mission.

Aboard TC 779

Displacing from 2522 AD to circa 50,000 BC

Grainger turned to Roebeck. "Nan?" he said, certain of what she'd done but hoping he was wrong. He wanted the vehicle to shunt into realtime on the dock outside the admin wing again so that the five of them could charge in to rescue Jalouse.

Charge in to get their asses blown away, was more like it. Roebeck was responsible for the whole team, not just Jalouse in his immediate difficulties. If their ARC Central had been replaced by a hive of hostile strangers, then she and her people were the only chance their timeline had of displacing the different present to which the transport capsule had returned.

"We didn't really return after all, did we?" Barthuli said with a smile, as if he were reading Roebeck's mind. Maybe he was. The analyst was too strange for Roebeck to rule out any possibilities.

"Suit up," Roebeck said, pushing between Grainger and the still-seated Chun. "Me and Pauli, then the other two of you. They may be waiting there, too."

She nodded to Barthuli. "Gerd?" she added. "Watch the controls, will you?"

The locker containing the displacement suits was at the rear of the cabin. There wasn't enough room in the capsule for more than two riders to don the suits at a time. Pauli Weigand was already latching his closed around him.

"We're running back to 50K, aren't we?" Grainger demanded at rising volume. "We're just going to run off and leave Jalouse!"

Weigand stepped forward in his armor to face the hatch. Displacement suits were miniature temporal vehicles, though they lacked the sophistication and spatial displacement abilities of a transport capsule. For the moment, the important things were the protection the suit gave the person wearing it and the load of weaponry its powered muscles could handle.

"We're not running anywhere," Roebeck said. They were running and she knew it, but they *had* to run. "We're backing out of an ambush. When we figure out who's responsible for the problem, we'll deal with them."

She locked her suit closed. Anonymous within its scarred, rounded surfaces, she stepped to Weigand's side.

Grainger sighed. "I'd hate to lose Jalouse," he said. He raised himself on the crossbar and slid his feet down, into the legs of his fitted suit.

Jalouse had survived the operation because Tim Grainger did exactly the right thing in next to no time. For Jalouse to die in the first moments following the team's return to the apparent safety of ARC Central would be worse for Grainger than for the rest of them.

Worst of all for Dor Jalouse, though.

"We haven't lost anybody yet," Roebeck said. "We're regrouping, then we'll see what we can do."

"It's our job to fix things," Chun said as her armored form joined Weigand and Roebeck. "This is no different."

This was a lot different.

"It's all clear outside," Barthuli said from the front of the cabin. "Of course, we may not have sensors to track intruders subtle enough to cause a change at Central."

The analyst sounded interested, but not in the least concerned. Roebeck knew she was lucky to have somebody as skilled as Barthuli on her team, but he still got on her nerves in a crisis.

Barthuli had become an ARC Rider because of his genetic predisposition to Alzheimer's disease. At some point—which could be *any* point, from the present moment on—his splendid mind was going to begin unraveling into psychosis. Barthuli intended to see as much as he could in whatever time he had, and he'd decided the field operations of the Anti-Revision Command provided the best opportunity of doing that.

The trouble was that Barthuli's world view was unique. Fate had condemned him to something worse than death in his own terms, so matters that seemed of incalculable importance to the rest of the team didn't touch him emotionally. The vanishment, the *destruction*, of the timeline in which Barthuli was born was to him only an opportunity to glimpse additional realities before his intellect drowned in spasms of memory loss and mindless rage.

"I'm going to open up," Roebeck said, warning the others a moment before she activated the outer hatch through the keypad on her suit's left thigh. With an electromagnetic pulse generator clipped beneath a fléchette gun, Roebeck followed Weigand into a continent empty of all human life save their own.

50K was a temporal direction rather than a specific time. Anyone who carried out time displacement activities without being a member of the ARC was a temporal violator, a revisionist. Central targeted the revisionists, and the ARC Riders solved the problem.

Sometimes violators were killed in the process of being stopped; normally (and by choice; a truly civilized society is a squeamish society) they were captured. Rather than imprison the captives in the 26th century, revisionists were freed, unharmed but without tools or even clothing, at around 50,000 BC. Males were dumped in North America, females in Australia; in either case, tens of millennia before humans populated those continents.

The period chosen was in the middle of a major ice age, but the glaciers had been in temporary retreat for thousands of years. The dumps were made in what was locally the late spring, giving the violators as much time as possible to adapt to their new surroundings before winter closed in.

And the dumps were made at intervals of a century, preset into the mechanisms of the transportation vehicles themselves. This wasn't primarily to protect the ARC Riders involved, though some separation was necessary for that reason: the later version of a person who revisited the person's own timeline vanished.

It was barely possible that captives might find the exiguous remains of a dump from a hundred years earlier. There was no chance at all that the groups would join forces and somehow manage to reenter the time stream. Those from up the line who ran the Anti-Revision Command may have been squeamish, but there was no question about their ultimate ruthlessness.

Roebeck viewed their surroundings without noticing anything that shouldn't be present. They'd settled onto a prairie, as expected. The ground looked flat as a table until you noticed the treetops in the middle distance. Ten meters or more of trunk were hidden by a combination of slope and the banks of the stream which the trees fringed.

Roebeck had made twenty-three displacements to 50K, so she knew the terrain. Sixteen of those trips had carried captives, naked and terrified, to what would be home for the rest of their lives.

As Barthuli had said, hostiles who were able to escape Central's detection could also fool TC 779's sensors. Roebeck raised her opaque faceplate with her left hand and scanned the landscape again, this time letting her Mark One Eyeball gather the information.

There was still nothing anomalous. The grasses and associated flowering plants were waist high for the most part, though occasional sere canes of the previous season's growth waved three or four meters in the air. A mixed herd of horses and camels cropped vegetation; some of the animals were within a hundred meters. The brown-black forms half a kilometer to the west were giant bison. Dust rose as beasts hooked dirt over themselves with their long horns.

All as it should be, in the days before men. The hissing and actinics of the capsule arriving must have startled the animals somewhat, but they had settled back into their routine by the time the hatch opened. Suited humans didn't disturb them.

Spring or not, the wind on Roebeck's bare cheeks was chill and harsh. Sometimes she wondered how many captives survived their first week in 50K, but the process wasn't one she could've changed if she wanted to. Anyway, temporal intruders would end the unborn lives of billions if they weren't stopped.

But the wind was very cold.

"Clear," said Weigand from the other side of the vehicle.

"Clear/Clear," echoed Chun and Grainger from the positions they'd taken to bow and stern.

"Clear," Roebeck agreed. Whatever had happened at ARC Central, the folks responsible hadn't managed to follow Transportation Capsule 779's flight into the distant past.

"Now," she added softly, "let's check the recordings and figure out just what was going on up there."

North America

Circa 50,000 BC

"To begin with," Barthuli said as he reran the dump from Jalouse's suit, "the personnel in what should have been Transfer Control Room Two were speaking Japanese. Rather, a language that differed from 19th-century Japanese in a fashion similar to the differences between Standard and 19th-century English."

The image on the display was enhanced to glassy cleanliness. This halfway stage between reality and iconic representation disturbed Roebeck at a gut level more than the static of the raw transmission did, though she'd never admitted that to anybody else. Anything that she told others about herself was a handle fate could use against her.

Grainger carried a piece of the bullet that smashed his rifle—but not his face as he sighted the rifle—during some action back in his home time. Weigand wore one blue and one brown stocking at the start of every mission. Chun had an unfailing silent routine that could have been prayer, mantra, or who knew what. Jalouse didn't touch—literally touch—a woman from the time they were warned for an operation till he'd boarded the vehicle.

No Rider and nobody at ARC Central really knew how the capsule mechanisms worked. The technology was from up the line. A savage doesn't have to understand electricity to flip a light switch, but the need to use forces he doesn't understand might make the savage more, not less, superstitious.

Even Barthuli might have a talisman. Though perhaps not.

"The physiognomy of the office staff fits a Japanese matrix better than any available alternatives," Barthuli continued, "though I wouldn't put much stock in that. The interesting thing is that there's no sign of the mid-20th century growth spurt driven by an improved diet on the home islands. Of course, these twelve individuals may not be a random sample."

Barthuli had slowed the movement on the display for better detail. It was like watching a ballet performed underwater. Sparks and chips of furniture pirouetted deliberately as staff members fired, their faces distorted in terrible hatred. Perhaps that, like the delicacy of the bullet damage, was merely an artifact of slow motion.

"We're assuming there's been a temporal revision," Chun Quo said crisply. Her very dispassion was a sign that she was aware of the Oriental ancestry she shared with the folk trying to kill Jalouse. "Is it possible that there's been some kind of political change at Central? That the staff has been replaced in a . . . a coup?"

"No," said Barthuli approvingly. He cut the displayed image from the firefight in Transfer Two back to the docking bay as seen when TC 779 settled into her berth. "But that brings up a very interesting point. Notice the other vehicle?"

A transportation capsule rested in a cradle two berths over. The vehicle was probably undergoing routine maintenance, because several of the skin panels had been removed. No personnel were in view.

"The nose is too blunt," Weigand said.

Barthuli beamed. His fingers touched controls. The image became a blue schematic rotating slowly against a white background. The analyst overlaid it with a second schematic, this time yellow, as like to the first as raindrops are to one another.

And as different. Where the exterior of the capsules was identical, the schematic was green. At least 90 percent of the outlines remained blue and yellow.

"The second image is that of a 700-series capsule, of course," Barthuli said. "Quite a remarkable convergence. I could have shown the same similarity in the bay itself or the geometry of the transfer control room. But it's not the same Central we left, no."

"The clerks' reaction," Grainger said. "Do you suppose they were expecting us—somebody like us? Or is the social structure such that people are always armed and ready to go off like bombs if the unexpected occurs?"

"No society could be that paranoid," Weigand said. "Those people were afraid somebody'd show up to undo the revision their organization made."

"If you'd been raised with me on Sunrise Terrace," Grainger said with a wan smile, "you wouldn't be so sure of limits on xenophobia."

"What I found particularly striking," Barthuli said, "is the close similarity of the physical plant, despite the obvious divergence from the social system of our timeline. I'm not sure those up the line would be concerned about the changes. They may not have been discommoded in the least."

"*We've* been discommoded," Roebeck said, ending that discussion. She went on, "Our data banks have a full download for the late twentieth alone, is that correct?"

"1971 through '91 in full detail," Barthuli said. "Twenty years before that at second order. For the rest, we have only the normal baseline."

The team's just-completed operation had been against a pair of 23d-century revisionists who had gone back to 1991. They weren't dabblers who might have distorted timelines by inadvertence. Rather, they'd consciously intended to change the past by using mind-control devices on the US national security advisor. For the mission, TC 779's data bank had been prepared with information regarding the temporal area of operations at the highest level of detail of which ARC Central was capable.

"The first thing we need to do is to enlist someone from this timeline's 1991, since that's when our capsule's database is most complete," Roebeck said. She was stating a course of action, not asking for opinions. It struck her that she was the highest official of *her* Anti-Revision Command on this timeline; she smiled inwardly.

"We'll compare the local's timeline with ours," she continued. With the keyboard she began to adjust the gross parameters of the next immersion in the timestream. TC 779's artificial intelligence would determine the precise settings in accordance with Roebeck's generalities. "We'll spot the divergence, and then we'll cure it."

"Cure the bastards who caused it, too," Tim Grainger said in a voice as emotionless as a shard of broken glass. The conversation had brought Grainger's mind back to the milieu in which he'd grown up. It always took him a while to return to an even tenor when he'd been thinking of the Sunrise Terrace enclave.

"What if the split took place later than 1991?" Chun Quo asked. "We won't have any kind of details then."

"We'll assume that's not the case," Roebeck said, bending over her task. "If it is, then we've got a problem."

"If it is . . ." Barthuli said. He smiled as he bent his tongue around a phrase that was neither his nor that of the time horizon in which he had been born. "If it is, then we're shit outa luck."

Yunnan Province

Timeline B: June 29, 1991 AD

T he first rocket over the berm awakened Major Rebecca Carnes. Five more had landed with their terrible *whoop* WHAM! in the midst of Fire Support Base Schaydin before she managed to roll out of her cot.

The ground bucked every time a warhead detonated. The gooners were launching their rockets in pairs. The six-foot rip across the top panel of the tent hadn't been there when Carnes went to bed at midnight. Through it she saw the green tracking flare of another rocket an instant before it impacted.

That blast toppled one side of the tent's three-course sand-bag wall and knocked all the breath from Carnes' lungs. The canvas vanished as rags flapping on the shock wave.

Carnes lifted her face from the dirt. She'd gone to bed fully dressed, though she'd loosened the laces of her boots to keep her feet from swelling during the night. She'd been using her flak jacket as a pillow. The protective garment was an old one with interleaved layers of ballistic nylon and aramid fiber, but it was better than nothing.

Carnes reached up just enough to grab the jacket. The barracks belt and holstered revolver slid down also. She hooked the belt around her waist after she'd put the jacket on.

Carnes didn't know how to shoot. She was a *nurse*, for chrissake! She'd never even taken the revolver out of its holster since the supply sergeant tossed the weapon onto the pile of gear she had to carry to the helicopter waiting to fly her to her new command. The weight was a comfort of sorts, now.

The bombardment ceased or paused. Fifty or more rockets had struck; this was no mere harassing attack. Carnes raised herself on one arm to see what was happening around her.

By virtue of being the only officer of American citizenship present, Major Rebecca Carnes was in titular command of the battalion of Argentinian mercenaries making up the remainder of the firebase complement. A few of the Argentinians spoke English. None of them would speak to Carnes, at least not after she made clear within the hour of her arrival that she'd as soon have slept with the dogs subsisting on the battalion's garbage as with any of the Argentinians themselves.

The mercenaries might have been less dismissive if Carnes was male, but probably not. The assignments office in Hanoi hadn't told her what happened to the AmCit officer she was replacing, but she'd already gotten the impression the fellow hadn't died as a result of enemy action.

That was how Rebecca Carnes was going to die, though. She knew enough about combat to see that. She'd arrived at her "command" less than eighteen hours before the Chinese overran it.

The Tactical Operations Center was a trailer buried in a trench by the same team of US combat engineers who'd bulldozed up the earthen berm to create the firebase six months before. The engineers had done a good job.

That was just as well, since FSB Schaydin had been the last mission for most of them. They'd been ambushed while withdrawing by road. Carnes, looking out the side window of the CH-47 helicopter, had seen the burned-out lowboys and construction equipment as the bird made its approach carrying her and a sling-load of supplies.

Machine gun fire and the dull *crump* of grenades replaced the howling rockets. One of the warheads had plowed up a grave that must have predated the firebase. The stench of flesh dead so long it was liquescent mingled chokingly with explosive residues.

Carnes stumbled toward the TOC. She supposed she belonged there, but she knew also she was drawn by the fancied protection of the dirt covering the trailer. That wouldn't save her, but she didn't suppose much of anything would.

The attackers had chosen the night of the new moon. The only light came from explosions and the green-white tracers—Chinese tracers—snapping across the firebase. Very occasionally an Argentinian shot back, but the red sparks of the US ammunition were smothered by storms of return fire.

A great explosion shocked the night orange. A flying object hit Carnes and flattened her against a half-collapsed sandbag wall.

The base existed as a gun emplacement for four World War II–vintage howitzers which were supposed to support the infantry patrolling the surrounding hills. A Chinese grenade or satchel charge had detonated the ammunition bunker in a single volcanic blast.

Carnes couldn't breathe. She knew she'd only had the breath knocked out of her, but knowing that didn't permit her to move.

A white star cluster shot up from a bunker across the firebase. The flare was meant for signaling rather than illumination. Even so, its momentary light permitted Carnes to see that the object which had hit her was a human leg, complete to the ankle.

The sight had the unexpected effect of steadying her. Carnes had entered the US Army as a nurse in 1968. Her first tour in what was then the Vietnam War had been at the 93d Evacuation Hospital. She'd seen enough severed limbs then that she could never again feel horror at the sight of one; only sadness, and that when the living had been tended to and there was time to be sad.

Carnes stood and resumed her course toward the TOC. She stepped carefully over the leg; not because she was queasy but rather out of respect.

The radio tower adjacent to the buried trailer twinkled like a Christmas decoration with the reflections of tracer bullets. Argentinian officers would be begging higher command for support. US resources in southern China were stretched to—or beyond—the breaking point. Even if help was available, it couldn't come in time to save the situation now.

Fifty yards from Carnes, the fuel tank for the firebase generator ignited with a *thump*. A column of flame shot skyward from a pool that spread sluggishly across the ground. Two figures ran out of the blaze, their identities shrouded by the flames.

A man silhouetted by the burning diesel fuel hunched, then flung a heavy parcel down the ramp to the entrance of the TOC. It was a satchel charge. Two seconds after the Chinese sapper threw it, the bundle exploded.

Overburden covering the trailer bulged upward, then collapsed in a smoking, square-edged crater. Loose earth covered the mangled bodies of whichever Argentinians had been in the operations center when the charge went off.

The sapper got to his feet again. Carnes was still standing, though the blast had numbed her eardrums. The gooner saw her and reached for the automatic rifle slung across his back.

Carnes unsnapped her holster's retaining strap. She tried to draw the revolver. It stuck to the leather. She had to tug twice, the second time with hysterical strength, to get the weapon loose.

The gooner was only five meters from her. He jerked back the bolt handle to charge his rifle. The clang of metal tinkled like an ill-tuned bell to Carnes' shocked hearing. She pointed the revolver at the soldier, wondering if she should instead have run.

The trigger didn't move, no matter how hard she pulled it. For a moment Carnes thought wildly that the safety was still on. A scrap of information from training twenty-odd years before returned to her: Revolvers don't have safeties.

The weapon she'd been issued had languished, God knew how long, in some arms locker. A logistics system scraping the bottom of its resources dragged the revolver out to equip an officer who was equally useless in the combat role in which she'd been placed.

The Chinese soldier aimed his automatic rifle. Carnes threw the revolver at him. The awkward missile didn't come within a meter of the man.

Blue light and a sound like bacon frying enveloped Carnes. Outside the aura, all noise and motion stopped. An oval bulk formed before her. She wondered if this was death.

The only thing that moved in the landscape was the object solidifying from the air before her. Tracer bullets hung in midflight, sparks of light filtered blue by the surrounding haze. Fine hairs on Carnes' arms and the back of her neck prickled as the building static charge made them rise.

Carnes lifted her right hand to prove that the general paralysis didn't extend to her. The object forming had lost almost all of its insubstantial shimmer. It was smoothly ovoid, some three meters by five along the primary axes. A large bubble formed on the surface facing Carnes.

The bubble split vertically. A man stepped out. "Major Carnes?" he said. "My name's Tim Grainger, and we have a proposition for you."

Carnes choked. She'd been holding her breath without realizing it. Gasping, she began to laugh. Her bruised ribs hurt her. She knelt and leaned over to relieve the pressure on them, still laughing.

Grainger didn't look surprised, though that didn't necessarily mean anything. Carnes suspected he was the sort who made a point of not displaying any emotion until he'd thought it through. He was a lightly built man of medium height. His hair was brunette, and his complexion probably a deep tan. Carnes couldn't be sure under the present light conditions.

Grainger wore a one-piece garment which covered him from wrists and neck to a pair of seamless, lightweight boots. Its fabric was thin enough that the man's bone structure was visible through it. The surface of the coveralls mimicked the pattern of its surroundings so perfectly that sometimes Grainger appeared to be a disembodied head and hands.

Carnes got control of her laughter. She didn't know whether it had been hysteria or relief. Maybe the gooner had shot her. Instead of her life passing before her eyes, she'd imagined a stranger in a weird outfit and the degree of calm interest that high-school guidance counselors show.

"I accept your proposition," she said. "Am I dead?" She stood up. Though the spasm had passed, the whole business still struck her as funny.

Grainger frowned for the first time. "This isn't in your imagination," he said. "Your agreement will commit you to certain things. We're ... time travelers; from a timeline that should have occurred but didn't because of something that happened within your lifetime. We want to go through your memories and find that nexus of change so that we can reverse it."

"I said I accept," Carnes repeated. She was tired and she hurt and she'd been on the point of death. Anger as violent and irrational as the laughter of a moment before made her voice shake.

"Look!" she shouted, gesturing toward the frozen chaos around her. "If I don't volunteer, that gooner kills me, right? I volunteer!"

Grainger smiled. The expression had a murderous chill that Rebecca Carnes had seen before, when men who'd come in from the bush talked among others of their kind. The survivors talked, the ones who returned again and again with everything but perhaps their souls.

"Gooner," Grainger repeated in a soft voice. He wasn't speaking to Carnes anymore. "Welcome back to Sunrise Terrace, Tim Grainger."

"I'm sorry," Carnes said. The anger was gone. She didn't know what she'd said, but she knew wounded men, and she knew the wounds the surgeons didn't see.

She reached out her hand.

Grainger shook his head. "Wait," he said. "If you come with us, you'll never be able to return to your own time. With luck, this timeline won't even exist for you, for us. You'll be comfortably maintained in the 26th century, or you may—if you want to and if you meet the requirements—be permitted to join the ARC Riders."

He smiled again, this time wryly. "They took me. I'm from 2025. But we have to have your informed consent before we take you aboard."

"I'll come with you," Carnes said. "I'd probably come with you even if the . . . the soldier on the other side of your ship wasn't about to kill me."

"Ah—" Grainger said. "In the interests of precision, I'm *not* telling you that Chinese soldier will kill you." He saw her surprise and added quickly, "Major Carnes, you'll die here if you stay, I don't mean that. But you may not be killed by these bullets or any particular bullet."

"I'll *come* with you," Carnes said with soft emphasis.

Grainger extended his hand and took hers at last. "Watch the lintel," he warned as they stepped together into the misty object from which he'd appeared.

The bulge clam-shelled shut behind them. The walls around Carnes were suddenly as real as those of a submarine's pressure lock. An inner hatch split open before them.

A man, a woman, and two figures in suits as rigidly confining as medieval jousting armor waited within. The woman nodded welcome or approval.

The front quadrant of the inner hull showed the firebase in three-dimensional detail, as clearly as if the wall were glass. The flashes and chaotic movement resumed.

The Chinese sapper goggled over the sights of his rifle, staring at where Carnes had been and no longer was. He began shooting. Tracer bullets vanished when they should have struck the wall of the time machine. They reappeared on the opposite side of the display, flickering away into the darkness.

"We're out of phase with the horizon," the woman said. "We can observe, but we don't exist here in a material sense. I'm Nan Roebeck, by the way. I'm team leader."

The image of the firebase went white, then opalescent. Grainger's jaw tightened, but he said nothing.

"What happened?" Carnes asked. "Why did . . ."

She thought she was starting to see objects outside again, though they might have been eddies in the glowing fog.

"A tactical nuclear weapon," the other man in the compartment said. He was much older than Grainger, sixty or more against Grainger's apparent thirty-five. "Northern Command couldn't relieve your position, so they decided to use the only resources they had available to turn it into a killing ground for the attacking forces."

"They nuked us?" Rebecca Carnes said. She backed against the bulkhead for its support. Otherwise her knees might have buckled. "Our own people nuked us?"

"It was the first use," Grainger said. His face was calm, and his voice was too calm. "That's why we chose you. If you'd refused . . . well, we counted one hundred and nineteen nuclear explosions when we scanned this timeline. Someone would have accepted our offer."

Roebeck was keying commands into the flip-up panel before her. "I'm going to take us back to 50K," she remarked generally.

Carnes stared at the display. The roiling hell outside the time machine had cooled enough for its emptiness to become apparent. "Our own people," Carnes repeated in a whisper.

When she thought about it, though, she knew that the folk who had made the decision to go nuclear weren't "hers" in any sense. And she wasn't sure that they were human in her terms, either.

North America

Circa 50,000 BC

Roebeck's controls gave an electronic chirrup. The queer pulsing within each of Carnes' muscles ended. The sensation hadn't been unpleasant.

The forward display had been blank for the previous minute and a half. Now it showed high grasses whipping in the snow-laden wind. The time machine had landed in something close to a blizzard.

Roebeck frowned; Grainger became very still.

One of the armored figures stepped past Carnes. The lock opened, then closed behind, him/her.

"It could be a late storm," the other figure said in a woman's voice. The words came from chest level, though Carnes didn't see any sort of speaker plate there. "It doesn't necessarily mean that we've lost our zero."

The older man shrugged. "There may have been some drift. Operating at 50K puts us at the long arm of the lever, so to speak. We'll have to recalibrate each time we return to our operating levels, but we'd do that anyway. I doubt there's a significant problem."

The first armored figure appeared on the display, shrouded in snow. The second figure stepped through the lock in turn.

"All clear," a male voice reported from the display itself.

"We've gone to the far past, where we can prepare without interruption," Tim Grainger said to Carnes. At some point he must have been in much the same situation as she was now. Remembering that, he was explaining events in a fashion that the rest of the team didn't think to do. "Fifty thousand BC, 50K. We can't be sure hostiles haven't followed us. Pauli and Quo are making a physical check."

Carnes nodded appreciatively. She didn't have enough context for the words yet to claim that she understood, but the fact of Grainger's effort made her more comfortable. She was still trying to understand how the US government could launch a nuclear attack *on her*.

"I'm Gerd Barthuli," the older man said, extending his hand. "I look forward to working with you. Chun Quo and Pauli Weigand you will meet when they take off their displacement suits."

Grainger glanced at Roebeck. The team leader acknowledged the unspoken question with a nod but continued to work at her keyboard. Sometimes Carnes caught a hint of color and motion in the air above the keys. There was a display there, but normally it was visible only to the system's user.

"We're field operatives for the Anti-Revision Command," Grainger said, accepting Roebeck's nod as approval to go ahead. "ARC Riders. Central spots indications of unapproved time travel and sends us—one of the teams, there's more than just us—to deal with it. Only this time something went wrong. Central was gone when we returned to it."

"*Our* Central was gone," Barthuli corrected with a vague smile. He was doing something also, but his fingers moved on a flat plate with no keys or apparent markings.

Weigand and Chun returned to the hatch. On the other side of the display, an animal with snow in its shaggy fur stared at the time machine. Its legs were braced to run. Carnes thought the creature was a horse, but the light wasn't good enough for certainty.

"Our Central," Grainger agreed, smiling also, but with a touch of something else in the expression. "Someone revised the past without being noticed by ARC Central. We were down the line from the nexus, dropping prisoners here in 50K, so we weren't affected. We're going to use you—your memories—to determine the target, since Central can't guide us in this time."

The hatch passed a woman, Chun, with snow clinging to the raised faceplate of her armor. Chill air entered with her.

Oriental names place the family first, followed by personal identifiers. That was one of the less traumatic things Rebecca Carnes had learned during her tours in Southeast Asia.

"We're a little early in the year, I'm afraid," Chun said to the company as she walked to the locker in the back of the compartment. "The grass has started to grow, but it can't be later than March."

The hatch opened again. Weigand, a blond man with a long jaw and deep-set eyes, entered. He smiled at Carnes in friendly fashion. Weigand was a very big man, even apart from the armor's added bulk.

"You know . . ." Barthuli said. He looked neutrally toward a corner of the ceiling. "We might be able to hide more effectively in a populated era than we can back here. They might expect us to run to 50K."

Grainger said, "We've lost Jalouse already, Gerd. We've got more important things to worry about than your sightseeing." He spoke without heat, but equally without any flexibility in his tone.

Barthuli nodded. "Yes, I suppose that is what I was thinking about," he admitted.

"I wish . . ." Chun Quo said. She opened the chest plate of her displacement suit. She was stocky, short, and—to Carnes—very young. Certainly no more than twenty-five. ". . . that we knew where they came from."

Chun gripped the horizontal bar in the locker and lifted her legs from the suit's lower half. "Then we'd know what technology we're going to be up against when we meet them."

Grainger looked at Carnes and said, "A nexus of change can occur anywhere. The people responsible, though, come from 1900 AD to up toward the middle of the 25th century. By 2500, there's a unitary society in which nobody would think of tampering with time. Before 1900, there wasn't the technology available to build displacement devices."

"I wonder about the lower terminus sometimes," Barthuli said.

Weigand looked surprised. "Why?" he asked. He spoke in a tenor, a lighter voice than Carnes had imagined but smooth and beautiful to hear. "I grant that Da Vinci visualized a helicopter in the 16th century, but he didn't *build* one. There wasn't an engine that could power a helicopter for another four hundred years."

"Yes, but that's a technocentric assumption," Barthuli argued. "If time displacement requires modulated magnetic fields, perhaps 1900 or so is the earliest possible venue. But that's *if*, not a certainty."

"The people we're looking for," Chun said as she pulled a seat—somehow—from the bulkhead and sat beside Carnes, "aren't using techniques that ARC Central recognized in time to stop. Either the revisionists' experimental equipment was so sophisticated that it left no more temporal wake than a 700-series capsule does, or—" she shrugged, "mental manipulation? Sacrificing a black cock at the new moon? Barthuli's right—they could have come from anywhen."

Grainger reached behind Carnes and pulled out a seat for her. "Sorry," he said. "I wasn't thinking."

Nan Roebeck stood up. "No, sit here," she said to Carnes. "We need to hook you to these inputs."

Carnes obeyed the team leader without comment. Like her, Roebeck was in her early forties, but the two women had few other similarities. Roebeck was rangy and big-boned; Carnes was six inches shorter and had always had a weight problem, especially when subsisting on the military's high-carbohydrate meals. Of course, when Carnes was a teenager, she'd been a cheerleader and Roebeck was probably an ugly duckling. . . .

"I've programmed a four-displacement sequence," Roebeck said. "I want to be able to get out of here instantly if we have visitors, and I don't want it to be any easier than it has to for them to follow."

Did they have cheerleaders in the 26th century?

"Do you think that'll happen?" Chun asked.

"I don't know what will happen," Roebeck said. She looked down at Carnes. Weigand was taking apparatus, including a skeletal helmet, out of a cabinet in the central console. Barthuli was busy at his . . . control board?

"This doesn't hurt much," Grainger said. "A headache, maybe. But it has to be done."

As the helmet settled coolly over her temples, Rebecca Carnes wondered if the people who'd decided to nuke her firebase had said something similar.

Nan Roebeck and her fellows watched the display:

Quang-tri Province, South Vietnam

The eastern sky was dark, but dawn would arrive as suddenly as a knife thrust. The US advisor bent over an acetate-covered relief map spread on the hood of a jeep. Flanking him were the commander and chief of staff of a Vietnamese armored regiment. The regimental sergeant-major held a penlight as the American's fingertip indicated the route of advance for the last time.

The gasoline engines of the regiment's M41 tanks and M113 armored personnel carriers were already turning over. A tank rotated its long, coffin-shaped turret 30 degrees to the right. The squeal cut brutally through the snarl of the unmuffled power plants.

The Vietnamese colonel shouted agreement. He shook hands with his chief of staff, then with the advisor.

The chief of staff got into the jeep and lifted the handset of the radio there. He began to speak, gesturing with his free hand.

The colonel stepped quickly to an APC whose double whip antennas were bent forward and clinched to the front of the vehicle where they wouldn't be so obvious. A crewman reached down to help his commander mount from the side, using the tread itself as a step.

The American advisor boarded the lead tank and settled himself into the turret's right-hand hatch behind the .50-caliber machine gun. He put on the plastic helmet waiting for him on the cupola and checked its radio and intercom switches. Then he turned and waved back to the Vietnamese colonel.

The colonel saluted. The tank's six-cylinder engine roared, sending the vehicle forward with clangs and screeches. Eight other tanks fell in behind the first. The regiment's integral artillery batteries were firing a preparation onto the hilltops flanking the advance.

The shells were falling into North Vietnam.

Washington, DC

Timeline B: March 31, 1968

The President of the United States polished his glasses against the cuff of his shirt and replaced them on his nose. He picked up his sheaf of notes, cleared his throat, and nodded to the director.

The red light on the TV camera came on. Speaking directly into the lens in a high-pitched voice, the President said, "My fellow Americans. I was informed this morning that troops of the Republic of Vietnam, responding to an attack on their positions from across the so-called Demilitarized Zone, have pursued elements of the North Vietnamese Army into the bases from which those treacherous attacks were launched."

The President glared into the camera. The notes in his hand flapped as he pumped the heel of his right hand three times against the lectern without striking it hard.

"The communist aggressors . . ." the President continued on a rising note, "have not learned the lesson that the people of America are resolute in the defense of freedom. They will learn that lesson now. I have directed American armed forces to act in support of our South Vietnamese allies in the exercise of their right of hot pursuit. I warn the aggressors not to interfere with this fully justified defensive operation. If enemies challenge American resolve, they will feel our might in a direct way."

There was a palpable intake of breath from the assembled White House press corps. A print journalist dropped his tape recorder clattering to the floor. A young woman from one of the wire services prayed or cursed with a silent movement of her lips. Tears ran down her cheeks.

"As a palpable warning to the enemies of freedom," the President said, "I inform them that as of this date there are no more sanctuaries. Even as I speak, troops of America and of our allies have crossed the boundaries that our adversaries have scoffed at since their invasion began in 1956. We are striking at the bases of the communist aggressors in Cambodia and Laos, destroying the matériel stockpiled to subvert the government of the Republic of Vietnam."

The President tried to shuffle the next page of his notes to the front. He dropped the page instead. He flung down the rest of the sheaf and said, "And I issue this warning to the leaders of China and the Soviet Union: watch where you step. If you become directly involved in this attempt to conquer a member of the free world and an ally of America—watch out! There's a bear trap ready to snap, and there's room in its jaws for you as well as for your lackeys in Hanoi!"

The President turned abruptly and walked away from the lectern. Several of his aides, shaken by what they had just heard, were taken by surprise. They had to jump to get out of the way.

The press was in bedlam. The camera continued to roll, focused on the empty lectern.

Cambodia,
Fishhook Region

Timeline B: April 17, 1968

The men in the mechanized company could hear the Command-and-Control helicopter circling above them, but they couldn't see the bird through the jungle's triple canopies. The ten vehicles below were ACAVs—armored personnel carriers converted from transport to combat duties by the addition of M60 machine guns behind gunshields on the right and left flanks, and a steel cupola around the .50-caliber machine gun mounted forward. At Table of Organization strength, there would have been seven more tracks.

The captain in the fourth vehicle finished giving his orders. He took his commo helmet off to rub his forehead. His platoon leaders were a lieutenant, a platoon sergeant, and a staff sergeant. Personnel were as short as equipment. Both had been tight even before the Tet Offensive.

"We'll be lucky if we get a hundred yards into that shit," said the soldier manning the cal fifty. The vehicle lurched beneath them as the driver began to back ten meters to the closest thing the company had found to a trail on this heading.

"If he wants us to break trail, he ought to give us Rome Plows, not ACAVs."

The captain put his helmet back on. The man in the cupola had been his track commander when he was a lieutenant leading a platoon. With promotion and company command, he'd brought the man along. They went back seven months together; a lifetime in Southeast Asia, and much longer than some lives lasted in the theater.

"The colonel says there's a blue line"—stream—"half a klick north," the captain explained. "He says there's a major trail along it—if it's the right blue line. Ours is not to reason why."

The driver was an experienced man. He turned the vehicle cautiously, clutching partial reverse power to the right track while braking the left track lightly.

"When we find more fucking empty jungle," the TC said, shouting over the engine noise, "what do we do? Laager here for the night? Intelligence couldn't find their ass with both hands."

The captain shrugged.

By applying full reverse power to one track and full forward power to the other, an ACAV could spin on its central axis—until it threw one or both tracks. As worn as the equipment was, and as badly overloaded as they were on running gear designed for the weight of an APC without the additional weapons and ammo, both tracks would slide off the road wheels in a matter of seconds.

The captain didn't want to be riding a thirteen-ton aluminum box down a trail that was probably worn by pigs. He wanted even less to be standing on that vehicle while the crew tried to make it mobile again. He wished he was in the CnC bird and the colonel was down here in the bush.

That wasn't fair. The colonel was being pushed by people who had *no* idea of conditions. Going after sanctuaries was well and good, but you don't order an invasion off the top of your head, which was what had been done this time. Everybody was still bleeding from Tet, and if intelligence had a clue as to where these wonderful sanctuaries were, it sure hadn't filtered down to the line companies.

The ACAV rocked slowly along the trail, its engine howling in low gear. Branches grabbed at the barrel of the right-side wing gun and spun it back. The gunner lost his steel pot as he tried to realign the gun with his sector of responsibility. The captain tried to catch the helmet, but it went over the side.

He thought of calling the driver to stop, but if the dinks *were* in the neighborhood that'd be handing it to them on a plate. He shook his head at the gunner, who shrugged and nodded.

Normally the company commander wouldn't be on point, but trying to reorder the line of march in this jungle would make things a worse ratfuck than they were already. Even now the three vehicles that had been in the lead would need to reverse as much as a hundred meters. The captain was waiting to hear that one or more of them had thrown a track.

The commo helmet crackled, the preliminary to the colonel putting his oar in again. The captain grimaced, composing his situation report—"Proceeding north as ordered, *sir*"— when the first B-40 rocket laid a smokey trail out of the bush and struck the ACAV's bow.

The anti-tank warhead burst with a sharp crack. The splash-board and the two duffle bags secured behind it blew apart. The vehicle itself was undamaged, but the startled driver stalled the engine. The cal fifty and the right-side M60 began slashing the jungle forward. There were no targets, only green and black and the rocket's gray exhaust trail.

The captain leaned forward to aim his M16 between the cupola and the right gunshield. The second B-40 hit the cupola. The track commander screamed as gaseous metal disemboweled him. Smoke grenades hung on a wire inside the cupola. Six of them went off simultaneously, pluming their varied colors in the still jungle air. AK-47s opened fire from both sides of the trail.

This time intelligence had been right about the presence of the enemy.

TROOP STRENGTH IN SOUTHEAST ASIA
TO RISE BY 250,000
Student, Other Deferments Canceled

Cleveland *Plain Dealer*

Timeline B: September 24, 1968

Durham, North Carolina

There were over three thousand people in the Quadrangle framed on three sides by pseudo-Gothic buildings constructed when the university expanded in the 1930s. The fourth side was Chapel Boulevard, stone-railed and level on a causeway above the sloping ground. A few cars, trapped in the Quadrangle parking area by the start of the demonstration, provided seating for scores of students.

The leaders were on the steps of the chapel, a cathedral-styled building with tall spires and a rose window. The banner drooping across the triple archways read END THE WAR!, the legend framed by peace signs.

An extension cord into the chapel powered a portable PA system. The amp was cranked up so high that electronic howls punctuated the phrases of anyone using the microphone.

One of the student leaders, wearing a denim jacket over a checked shirt, had a bullhorn and knew how to use it. When he saw the four olive-drab trucks pass through the police cordon at the head of Chapel Boulevard, he pointed with his right arm and hand and began the chant: "Hell no! We won't go! Hell no! We won't go!"

The trucks stopped some fifty yards from the back of the crowd. Troops got out, wearing steel helmets and carrying World War II–vintage Garand rifles. They were National

Guardsmen, nearly 150 of them. One of the trucks wouldn't start at the armory where the unit assembled, so the men were packed into the remaining vehicles.

The demonstators turned by stages. Those in the back and—guided by the pointing arm—the front of the crowd were aware of the presence of the troops sooner than those in the middle.

"Hell no! We won't go!"

Campus administrative buildings were locked. Banners and a Viet Cong flag hung from windows of the dormitories farther from the Quadrangle. Some of the professors who had been supporting the demonstration discreetly from the side-lines drifted away as the Guardsmen deployed.

People standing at what had been the back of the crowd were the less committed. Many of them were sightseers rather than real demonstrators. Some edged to the side and started to walk away by their only practical route—up the sidewalks flanking Chapel Boulevard.

A young student pushed out of the center of the crowd and screamed "Kill the pigs!" as he hurled an empty beer bottle at the troops almost eighty yards away from him.

Two Guardsmen fired simultaneously. A woman screamed, though no one had been hurt by the shots.

At least a dozen more Guardsmen fired in a ripping volley. Demonstrators surged away as if flung by the muzzle blasts of the powerful rifles.

There was a score of bodies on the ground. A lieutenant ran forward and turned, trying to shout something to his troops. A Guardsman shot him from fifteen feet away. The lieutenant slammed to the pavement with a look of agony on his face. Blood pooled beneath him as his body thrashed.

"Fucking Commies!" screamed one of the Guardsmen as he raised his reloaded Garand to his shoulder again. "Fucking Commies!"

He shot off the eight-round magazine as quickly as he could pull the trigger. His eyes were closed in terror. Two of his bullets blasted stone from the chapel tower, forty feet in the air.

New York City

Timeline B: July 12, 1969

The usual anchorman was not at his desk when the CBS logo dissolved. The presenter who replaced him had been an assistant producer until a few hours earlier. He looked nervous, perhaps because he had very little experience in front of a camera.

"Good evening," he said. He cleared his throat. "The following report is made in accordance with the Emergency Censorship Regulations as issued by the White House this afternoon."

The presenter cleared his throat again. He continued, reading the words off a TelePrompTer, "By authority of the Constitution, the President has today assumed full responsibility for the administration of the country during the present emergency. The President has authorized the call-up of military reserves in all categories. National Guard units in all states have been transferred to federal control. All National Guard personnel are ordered to report to their normal—"

The presenter began to cough. He tried to drink from a glass of water that had been out of line with the camera. Another cough sprayed part of it across his shirt front.

He gripped his desk with both hands for a moment, wincing. When the spasm passed, he continued, "That is, to their normal assembly points, where they will receive further orders."

The wall behind the presenter had been showing a view of the Earth from space since the beginning of the broadcast. Now it shifted momentarily to the words FBI RAIDS in red block letters against a white background; went blank; and returned to the image of the cloud-swept planet, all within ten seconds.

"I am instructed to inform you," the presenter continued, "that although the rumors that congressional leaders are under house arrest are untrue, the new emergency regulations give the President sweeping powers to detain persons acting against the interests of the United States and the safety of American personnel serving in Southeast Asia. The President will not hesitate to use these powers if the cause of freedom demands it."

For a moment the presenter was silent. His eyes were open but focused a thousand yards away. Then he smiled as brightly as a plaster mannequin and continued, "In other news today . . ."

Boston, Massachusetts

Timeline B: December 13, 1969

After the third knock, the brunette girl called "Who is it?" from beside the hall door. Her blond apartment mate stood in the curtained doorway of her separate bedroom. Both girls wore knee-length white nightgowns.

"Jane Marie LaBrett?" a male voice called from the hallway.

"I'm Jane LaBrett," the blond girl said, stepping gingerly into the living/dining room. The illuminated display of the clock beside the television read 3:12. "What is this, please?"

She was trying to keep her tone cool and superior, but there was a quaver in her voice as it reached the "please."

Voices murmured in the hall. The door bulged inward and split with a loud crash. The sliding bolt at the top of the panel still held, though the latch had sprung when one of the men outside kicked the doorknob.

A Boston policeman slammed his shoulder through the broken door and entered the apartment. Another policeman, two soldiers, and a man in civilian clothes followed him. The soldiers carried rifles. They grabbed the brunette with their free hands.

The civilian held a flashlight in one hand and a sheaf of 8×10 photos in the other. He shined the flashlight in the face of the brunette, then down to the top photograph. It was a grainy blowup of the blond girl's head. The lower edge of the sign she'd been carrying was visible at the top of the frame. Her mouth was open as she shouted.

"No," said the civilian, pointing his flashlight at the blonde. "The other one."

The blonde clutched at the doorjamb and began to scream. The policemen moved to her. The curtain tore away in her hands as they dragged her out into the front room.

The brunette shouted, "What are you doing? What are you—"

She tried to grab the photographs out of the civilian's hand. He fended her off with his elbow. A soldier raised the butt of his rifle to strike her. She cringed. The soldier wiped his face with his left sleeve. He looked sick.

"Jane Marie LaBrett," the civilian said. "By authority of Section 3, Part 79(b) of the Federal Emergency Regulations, you are hereby inducted into a penal company of the armed forces of the United States, to serve at the pleasure of the government for the duration of the emergency."

The civilian stepped out of the doorway so that the policemen could pass with the blond girl. She was weeping uncontrollably. Though she did not resist, her feet hung limp as the men dragged her.

The civilian started to follow them. The brunette shrieked, "Who do you think you are, you bastard? What do you think you *are*?"

The civilian turned and looked at her. He was in his late twenties. Seven years before, CIA had recruited him from the same Ivy League university the girls attended.

"Take this one, too," he ordered the soldiers. The brunette tried to lunge away, but one of them caught the nightgown. It held long enough before tearing that both men got good grips on her arms.

"So far as you're concerned, *miss*," the civilian said in a voice like a snake sliding on stones, "I'm the Lord God incarnate!"

DRAFT EXTENDED TO WOMEN
Measures Proposed in 1944
Now Put Into Effect

New Orleans *Times-Picayune*

Timeline B: February 13, 1973

Tasman Sea: Aboard the USS *Bonhomme Richard*

The two turbine engines of the CH-46 helicopter were mounted on the tail, just above the boarding ramp. The twin rotors were still motionless, but even at idle the jets sounded like all the demons of hell.

Three of the Marines in the corporal's fire team were newbies who'd never boarded a Sea Knight before. Two of them strode blank-eyed up the ramp, but one hesitated midway. The corporal had been expecting something like that. He put an arm around the kid's pack and walked him up as if they were best buddies.

The lieutenant commanding the platoon didn't have any experience, either. Besides a rifle, the lieutenant carried a .45 in a shoulder holster, *two* long-bladed knives, and enough ammo for a squad. The corporal didn't know which scared him worse: the newbies he commanded or the macho dickhead who commanded him.

The *whop* of blades faintly audible over the engine noise indicated the helicopters farther forward on the *Bonnie Dick*'s flight deck were preparing to lift. It was a fuck of a long way, over water and over land, to Canberra. The corporal hoped to hell that if the birds got separated, his wouldn't arrive first to land on the grounds of the Australian parliament building.

The newbie put his mouth close to the corporal's ear and shouted, "Will they be shooting at us, Corporal?"

Who the fuck knows? "Hell, no, kid," the corporal shouted. "You'll have to wait for Nam for that. And with a little luck we'll get some time in Sydney. Best R&R city in the world, if you like round-eyed pussy!"

LEFT-WING COUP FOILED IN AUSTRALIA

US VESSELS STEAM TO AID GOVERNMENT

Plotters Would Have Withdrawn Australia From War

New York Times

Timeline B: July 20, 1976

South of Ha Trung, North Vietnam

The seventeen bodies were laid out in a row between the firebase berm and the pad where the civilian's black-painted helicopter waited, its turbine at idle. The battalion commander, a twenty-eight-year old lieutenant colonel, nodded to the civilian and said, "We killed more, but they dragged the bodies off. There's at least a hundred blood trails."

The civilian bent, reached into the breast pocket of one of the corpses, and pulled out a letter that the soldiers had missed. He glanced at it and smiled wryly.

"Sir?" the colonel asked.

The civilian turned his head. He carried a well-worn M45 submachine gun, a "Swedish K," slung from his right shoulder. The barrel looked unusually fat because an integral silencer replaced the normal heat shield. "His mother hopes he's keeping well," he said. "He's not going to keep at all in this heat, is he?"

He crumpled the letter in his fist and threw it back down on the body. "They're Chinese," he said in a conversational tone. "I suppose you knew that? First time we've seen them in formed units."

"We thought they might be," the young colonel said. "We didn't know for sure."

The civilian resumed his walk down the line. If you squinted, you could imagine the bodies were so many empty sacks.

"That's why they came straight on the way they did," the civilian said. He was a man of fifty. His clean fatigue uniform was without any markings or identification. The round-brimmed boonie hat he wore was so old that the sun had bleached it nearly white. "They haven't learned what our fire-power does when they try to pull that."

The soldier nodded. The battalion's own six artillery pieces hadn't been able to fire because the attackers were too close, but neighboring units had brought a barrage down to within fifty meters of the berm. The shells fell like the wrath of God on the massed communist troops.

"They will learn, though," the civilian continued. "The VC did, and the NVA did. I wonder if the Russians will be next?"

The soldier looked at the civilian. He assumed the man was joking, but . . .

"Do you think they can hold out much longer, sir?" he asked. "We're killing, we've killed—" He spread his hands. "And the air strikes."

"I don't know how much longer it'll go on, Colonel," the civilian said, answering a question different from the one the soldier had asked. "It's already gone on longer than I dreamed it could. Well, analysis was never my job."

He barked out a laugh.

"There's a Taiwanese battalion taking over this AO"—area of operations—"in ten days," the lieutenant colonel said without emphasis. "They're supposed to be good troops."

"Yeah, they're good," the civilian said. "And the Koreans. The Pakistanis aren't that bad. The South Americans, though, I'd as soon have Thais. Beggars can't be choosers, I guess. It's a seller's market for every police state willing to export its soldiers."

He turned his face toward the northern horizon. "And I tell you, son, there's a shitload of Chinese where this lot came from."

Superior, Minnesota

Timeline B: May 30, 1987

The bartender and his two male patrons were all in their sixties. There'd been a power cut earlier in the evening, but now the lights and television worked again. The bartender stood in a corner, polishing glasses in front of the BLATZ ON TAP sign. On the television above him the President was saying, "... pulling together in this final stretch, so that ..."

"They aren't going to draft me," one of the patrons boasted. He was a regular. He didn't know the man three stools down the bar. "My brother-in-law, you know? He's in the military governor's office."

The other man looked at him by turning only his head. "You think they're looking for you, huh?" he said. His tone wasn't quite as unfriendly as the words could have been spoken.

He slid his empty glass toward the back rim of the bar. The bartender ran another draft from the pump.

"... veterans are therefore being directed to report ..." the President said.

"They're getting pretty damn deep in the barrel," the regular said with a cackle. He pointed toward the TV. "If he ain't careful, they'll be taking him!"

"He's dead, you know?" the stranger said. "That's not really him up there."

He laid a $2,000 bill on the bar beside his refilled glass.
The bartender made change from the cash drawer, two ragged
hundreds. The stranger stuffed the violet scrip into the brandy
snifter that served as a tip jar.

"Go on," the regular said. "Sure that's him!"

"Look how jerky the picture is," the stranger said. "Words
don't quite fit together, the lips don't move with the words—
they're cutting bits from old speeches and putting it together.
He's been dead four, maybe five years."

"Go on!" the regular repeated. "They can't do that. Charlie,
they can't do that, right?"

The bartender smiled and resumed polishing glasses.

"It's true," the stranger said morosely. "Four, five years.
It's MacNamara running everything, but you never see him."

Four motorcycles and a limousine roared down the street
at high speed. Four more bikes followed a moment later. The
limousine's windows were blacked out and there were no insignia on the vehicle. The motorcycle guards wore black
Gendarmerie uniforms.

The regular grimaced. He cupped his beer glass in both
hands and stared into it to avoid looking anywhere else. "Go
on," he muttered. His hands trembled. "Go on."

North America

Circa 50,000 BC

"I feel," Rebecca Carnes said without opening her eyes, "like I went skydiving without a parachute. And landed on my head."

She heard her own voice through a curtain of pain. Someone was splitting her skull with the back of an ax. She hadn't hurt this terribly since the time she broke her knee in an auto accident.

Cold light washed through her, dissolving the hot, sticky haze. There were a few nodes of quick agony. Carnes' limbs thrashed. She opened her eyes and saw four images for a moment before her optic nerves locked into synchrony.

She was lying on the floor of the time machine. The transport capsule, she should learn to call it. A rolled-up garment cushioned her head.

The five ARC Riders watched her with expressions of concern or pity, depending on individual temperament. Roebeck was packing away the headset. Tim Grainger held a bottle with a nipple, ready to offer Carnes when she sat up.

"Anybody get the number of the truck that hit me?" Carnes asked, attempting a smile. Weigand, the blond man, helped her rise—all the way to her feet, when she found her body obeyed normally except for the terrible shivering that wracked it.

51

She didn't feel cold, so why . . .

"It'll pass in a few seconds more," Grainger said, giving her the bottle. It contained water with a dash of something tangy. "There's no permanent nerve damage." He smiled. "Trust me."

Chun extended a seat from the bulkhead behind Carnes. She sank into it gratefully and sucked down more of the water. The spasms of trembling passed, as Grainger had promised.

Carnes smiled wanly at him. "Did you get anything?" she asked the company at large.

"We got everything we needed," Roebeck said. She was looking at the montage of images cascading over the display.

Barthuli fingered his control plate, manipulating the scenes as he watched them. "Or at least within one red cunt hair," he said, smiling in satisfaction as he used jargon from a former age with the precision he demanded of himself in all things. "The rest we can get, based on what you've brought us."

Carnes shivered again, this time from a thought. Looking at the bottle she clutched with both hands, she said, "I, ah . . . I guess I've ended the world by helping you. My world, I mean?"

"It's not—" Weigand started to say.

"Wait," said Roebeck sharply. The tumbling montage vanished into a black screen as deep as starless vacuum. "Gerd, would you run us some of the data we gathered while we were sorting?"

"We were looking for someone like you to help us," Grainger explained. "We hung just out of phase and combed the timeline."

"You were born in Jacksonville, Florida, Major Carnes?" Barthuli said as his fingers moved. "But you've at least visited Tampa, have you not? I can provide a quicker example by using Tampa. This is from sixty-eight days after you left the timeline."

The display bloomed with a view of a sprawling city. The image was so clear that Carnes felt a touch of vertigo. It was as if she rode in a helicopter's cargo bay five hundred feet in the air, looking down through the open door.

The bay was mirror smooth. Across it, and almost as dead flat as the water, were the Gandy and twin-span Howard Frankland bridges, connecting Tampa to St. Pete.

Carnes hadn't been to Tampa in twenty, at least twenty-*five*, years, but she hadn't forgotten—

The white flash expanded into an opalescent dome at supersonic speed, devouring every visible structure. The bubble vanished, leaving a shock wave that spread like a fiery doughnut. The column of glowing debris in the center mounted crookedly until it belled out into a mushroom.

"It was really quite a small device," Barthuli said, offering without emotion a point he found of interest. "Only about fifteen times as powerful as the one dropped on Hiroshima."

"The Soviets . . ." Carnes said. Her stomach lurched. She thought for a moment she was going to lose the water that was the only thing in her digestive tract.

"No," Nan Roebeck said. Her voice was emotionless also, but in her case that was out of conscious kindness to Carnes. "There was a succession fight after a palace coup against the governor of the Southeast Military Region. One of the parties believed her rival was in Tampa."

"Atlanta went the same way within the hour," Weigand said softly. "It didn't end the fighting, of course."

Roebeck made a quick gesture. The screen returned to satiny black.

Barthuli looked over his shoulder and said, "Within thirty days there were nuclear strikes on Soviet and European Union cities as well, though we don't have enough information to determine why. Neither grouping had any direct involvement with what was happening to the United States, so far as I can tell."

"Anything that happens within the time matrix," Roebeck said, "is eternal. If a timeline is revised, it doesn't vanish. It continues, but in a part of the matrix that someone in the revised timeline can't reach. You won't be destroying your timeline."

She put her hand on Carnes' shoulder. "But I want you to understand exactly what timeline we're going to revise. Revise back."

"Yes," said Rebecca Carnes. She drank the rest of the water to give her mouth something to do while her mind spun.

She lowered the bottle and looked around at her new companions. "I'd already have been dead before"—she nodded—"that, I guess. That's something to the good."

She cleared her throat. "What else do you need from me?"

Chun and Barthuli were both busy at separate control devices. "Probably nothing," said Roebeck, watching over the Oriental woman's shoulder. "You'll have to stay with us, though." She smiled wearily. "There'll be no place we can safely leave you until we return to Central."

"More water?" Grainger asked. "Or would you like something to eat?" He grinned. "The ration packs taste fine. It's just that after a while, they all taste the same."

Carnes chuckled. It struck her that after watching a city die a few minutes ago, she'd have said that she'd never smile again. "Some things never change," she said.

She looked at the main display. The analyst was moving images so quickly that Carnes couldn't be sure if each was a single scene or a montage of many scenes.

"I don't understand how what I know could be that important," she said after a moment. "I was an army nurse for four years. I didn't see or do anything important. When I got out, I worked in Oakland and then Memphis, until they recalled all veterans."

"Your knowledge, the knowledge in your mind," Weigand said, "is a fractal of the history of your time. To build your knowledge into a totality is simply a matter of the right algorithms and sufficient computing power."

"More computing power than anybody in my day dreamed of," Grainger said. "Much less dreamed of packing into a space the size of this transport capsule. The power's necessary for temporal navigation, of course."

Carnes nodded understanding. Bitterly she continued, "I wasn't that sorry to leave Memphis, to tell the truth, though running nursing at the 96th Evac in Son Tay wouldn't have been my first choice. And then they told me I had to take over an Argentine firebase. There had to be an AmCit officer in command of each foreign battalion. It wasn't just me—they were taking clerical supervisors, navigators, anybody with the right rank. It was crazy!"

Grainger shrugged. "Getting involved in a land war in Asia was crazy," he said in a quiet voice. "I can't imagine how the people making US policy could be so stupid. And it happened on our timeline, too, it just stopped sooner."

Chun looked up from her keyboard. "I can't imagine anything so stupid as war," she said.

On the main screen hung the image of a child wrapped in blazing napalm, running toward the viewer.

"Oh, war," said the man from 2025. "That I understand very well."

North America

Circa 50,000 BC

"We've found the nexus," Barthuli said, "but my instinct tells me it's a double nexus." He smiled as he added what was for him a joke, "And the computer agrees to point nine certainty."

The ARC Riders shifted slightly so that no one blocked another's view of the forward display. On it, tanks advanced across a dry, hilly landscape. Dust rose in yellow clouds. Carnes found that the image she saw wasn't distorted, despite the angle at which she sat to the concave display area.

"In this timeline," Barthuli explained, "a force from the Army of the Republic of Vietnam invaded the North on March 31, 1968. That's a revision from our database. Our background for this period isn't of the maximum detail, but I believe it's sufficient for the purpose."

"So we stop the invasion and we're back where we want to be?" Weigand said.

"I don't believe so," said Barthuli. "The incursion was trivial. In the normal course the People's Army of Vietnam would have snuffed it out—did snuff it out, as a matter of fact. The event was only important as a spark. Political decisions being what they are, the spark could have been as easily invented from the whole cloth, the way the Gulf of Tonkin Incident was."

Attempts to hurry Barthuli wouldn't make him angry, but neither would they speed his delivery. The analyst had decided in his own mind the most efficient way of imparting the information he thought necessary. The opinions of others on the question were of only casual interest to him.

The display shifted. A balding man in a brown suit delivered an address to journalists assembled in a briefing room. Even without sound, the speaker's passion was as obvious as the shock on the faces of his audience.

"The response which the US President made to this incursion," Barthuli continued, "was excessive." He smiled dryly. "Even given the gentleman's demonstrated tendency to see world events as a large-scale Gunfight at the O-K Corral, with himself as Wyatt Earp. It's my belief that the same organization which effected the ARVN incursion was responsible for the President's reaction to it."

"There could be separate elements, two or more," Chun said. "Or just one. The events are in close succession, but obviously the party responsible has very sophisticated time-displacement apparatus."

"I don't see how Central could have missed them," Weigand said. "Unless . . ."

His tongue touched his lips as if in response to their sudden dryness. "Gerd said early on that this might not have affected those up the line. Do you suppose Central only responds to changes that affect them?"

"Jap revisionists," Grainger said, as much to himself as to the others. He cleared his throat and looked up in embarrassment. "Japanese revisionists, probably from the 23d century. When the world started to come together after the bad years, the crazies got squeezed together in the cracks. Folks who dreamed of a world on which Japan imposed peace and unity, not just a world of peace and unity for all."

Weigand nodded slowly. Chun's moue was another form of agreement.

"We don't know who they were," Roebeck said sharply, asserting her leadership for the first time in the discussion. "We don't have causes, only effects. We're not going to guess, we're going to learn."

Barthuli beamed approval.

"Sorry," Grainger muttered. "Sure, I know that."

"We're going to get that information by observing the events leading up to the incursion," Roebeck continued. "We'll learn who the players are, then we'll move to Washington and stop them from affecting the President."

"Letting the invasion go ahead?" Weigand asked.

"Otherwise we spook the hostiles at the main target," Grainger said. "This isn't the sort of operation we can execute without some risk."

Roebeck nodded. "Gerd says the incursion would normally have been absorbed into the detritus of time. I accept his analysis."

She looked from Weigand to Barthuli and smiled coldly. "I would accept Gerd's analysis that the sun here will rise in the west tomorrow."

Barthuli looked down and toyed with the collar of his one-piece garment.

Roebeck eyed the company. "Let's go do it, shall we?"

Quang-Tri Province, South Vietnam

Timeline B: March 1968

It was deep, velvety nighttime outside the transport capsule. Weigand swore under his breath.

"I'm taking manual control," Roebeck announced calmly. The keyboard split at her touch. She moved the halves left and right on the console so that her arms splayed at what was for her a more comfortable angle. "We'll go up twelve."

"I've got the star sight," Chun said.

The capsule trembled as it displaced a second time; the screen blanked.

"We were supposed to arrive by daylight," Grainger explained to Carnes in a low voice. "Our inertial navigation system is off—and probably drifting rather than just out a fixed amount."

He shrugged. "Normally it's reset during after-mission maintenance at Central. This time . . . that didn't happen."

"Ready," said Roebeck from the controls.

A daylit landscape of hills and scrub vegetation bloomed on the display. "Sun sight," Weigand said.

"Four hours, thirty-six minutes high," announced Chun Quo. "Spatial displacement was accurate to the limits of testing."

"Right," said Roebeck, taking a deep breath. "Now if everybody will keep quiet for a few minutes, the computer and I will get us where we want to be."

Her fingers moved. The display blurred, shifting both in space and—judging from the quick successions of dark sky with light—in time as well. When Carnes raised her head slightly from where she sat, she saw apparent cross-wires of golden light superimposed on the rippling images. Occasionally the gold darkened to bronze or even coppery red.

"I could—" Barthuli said.

Roebeck turned her head and stared at the analyst without speaking. The display continued to scroll.

Barthuli stiffened. "Forgive me," he said. "I was in error."

He turned his back to the display so that he wouldn't be tempted to interfere again.

"Now . . ." Roebeck said. The display went frosty gray. "I think we're getting there. . . ."

With the brilliance of a lost-wax casting appearing from a shattered mold, a permanent regimental camp sprang in full detail from the grayness. The flag limp in still air before the headquarters building was the red-striped yellow of South Vietnam. A berm and concertina wire, both overgrown by brush and creepers, surrounded the encampment. Flatly conical metal roofs shielded sandbag bunkers from the brutal sun, like so many farmers in straw hats.

Regimental headquarters was a rambling building with stucco walls and a red-tiled roof, a relic of the French presence in Indo-China. Four M41 tanks squatted in revetments at the building's corners.

Roebeck took her left hand deliberately away from the split keyboard. Her right index finger moved a spherical control with the caution of a bomb disposal expert. The display's viewpoint approached the headquarters building as the sun slid toward and beneath the horizon.

Following the banquet held in the central courtyard of the headquarters building, drinking had gone on to a late hour. Not all the dishes had been cleared. Rice and sauces lay spilled among overturned bottles.

Half a dozen Vietnamese officers sat on the ground in a

circle, singing and raising glasses to drink at intervals in the song. One of them faced outward. Several other Vietnamese sprawled on or beneath the tables.

Three Caucasians with Military Assistance Command-Vietnam patches on their left shoulders walked carefully from the table. The man in the center was drunk and apparently singing quietly. He was dressed in ordinary jungle fatigues with the oakleaf collar tabs of a major or lieutenant colonel. The name tape over his left breast read JACKSON.

The men supporting Jackson were not drunk. They wore tiger-stripe fatigues of the type issued to rangers and special forces. One of the men was in his forties; the other was short, intense, and no more than twenty-five years old.

Carnes leaned forward when she saw the younger man's face. She opened her mouth to speak, then swallowed the words.

The men entered a room in the building's left wing. The oldest closed the louvered door behind them. Roebeck eased a control forward, her eyes on the display.

The viewpoint slid through the walls of stuccoed masonry, into a ten-by-twelve-foot room that served both as office and sleeping quarters. The apparent illumination level didn't change, though neither the gooseneck desk lamp nor the bare bulb under a reflector in the ceiling were on.

The young man lowered Jackson into a deck chair. It was constructed of polyethylene fabric and aluminum tubes stressed for the weight of Orientals rather than Caucasians.

The older man set a pocket lamp on the floor. When he turned it on, it bounced an amazing volume of light from the back wall. The man opened one of a pair of matching cases and began setting up the apparatus within. He connected the two cases with a flat wire thin enough to be spider silk.

"Twenty-third century mind control technology," Weigand said with satisfaction. "As expected."

"And if either of them is Oriental," Grainger said in a form of apology, "I'll walk back to 50K."

The younger man bound Jackson to the chair with swaths

of something sprayed from a dispenser. The material was so clear that it existed only as a reflection in the light.

"They could be hirelings," Chun said, accepting the apology. "Perhaps even locally recruited agents. Certainly the likelihood is that those who benefitted from the revision also caused it."

On the display, Jackson's head lolled to the side. His eyes were closed.

"I disagree," said Barthuli calmly.

The younger man stepped away from Jackson and looked toward his companion. The older man donned a helmet with an opaque faceshield, probably a display.

Chun glanced at Barthuli. The analyst said, "Analyzing the potential effects of a revision requires computing power an order of magnitude greater than that necessary merely for time displacement. One can expect to affect a given area of events . . . but causing middle- and long-term results of a predetermined type is quite another thing."

The older man manipulated a control box. A small parabolic antenna mounted on a post from the open case pointed toward the sleeping advisor. The dish waggled minutely, then locked into position.

"Same thing we were dealing with on the last mission," Grainger said to Carnes. "Different flavor, is all. Hostiles in 1991—our 1991—were using a cruder version on the US National Security Advisor to keep him from making up his mind while the Soviet Union came apart."

"Of course it was really hard to tell with Scowcroft whether the mind control device was having any effect," Weigand added, grinning slightly.

"We know this one works," Roebeck said softly as she continued to watch the process.

"We're not quite in phase with this timeline," Grainger explained. Nothing visible was changing on the display, but if the team leader wanted to see it out, no one would gainsay her. "We're close enough that we can induce images from lightwaves passing through the region we almost occupy."

Carnes nodded slowly. She stared at the display as intently as Roebeck did.

"I can't read the nametag," she said. "The fellow against the wall. Can you—"

Roebeck's index finger didn't seem to move, but the image closed to a head and torso view of the younger man. The tape on the tiger fatigues read WATNEY.

"It may not be a real name," Roebeck cautioned. "He certainly isn't a real MACV advisor."

"It's the name I knew him by in Son Tay when I was at the 96th," Carnes said tightly. "He's a recon specialist. He's so much younger here that I wasn't sure. . . . And he's . . ."

She turned to Grainger and said, "Could I have some more of that water, please? I'm—"

Grainger fished a bottle from a rack concealed in the wall behind him.

Carnes took the water, but she'd managed to swallow the catch of memory from her throat without it. "He's been wounded at least a dozen times. When they brought him in in 1990, he was . . . I don't know how he survived. Three abdominal wounds. It had been eighteen hours before the medevac bird reached him, let alone before they got him to us. But he always survives."

"That's happened to him before and he goes back out?" Chun asked.

"Oh, he's crazy, of course," Carnes said with a faint smile. She took a sip of water. "To function in the environment, you have to be. A war zone, I mean. Watney is . . . beyond the norm. He wants to die very badly, but he *won't*, even when almost anybody else would've let go."

The ARC Riders looked at the face on the display. The features were of a chiseled regularity that was handsome beyond doubt, but not really attractive except on a statue. Watney's mouth was unusually broad, though the lips themselves were thin. The face appeared calm; the pale blue eyes were windows onto a soul that blazed like the core of a reactor.

"There's one thing, though," Carnes added. "The Watney

I know wouldn't be working for the Japanese. He hates Orientals more than almost anything else in the world."

She gave the others a lopsided smile. "He hates them almost as much as he hates himself."

North America

Circa 50,000 BC

Though the sun was bright in a clear sky, the snow was so dry that wind scudded veils of it over the drifts.

"You know," said Weigand in a voice that was several shades too calm, "I'll be thankful when we make a few more trips back here and the settings precess into warm weather. I'd really like to lie back in the grass and let the clouds sail by."

"I can't hop forward a few months," Roebeck said. She was manipulating her controls and didn't bother to look up. "At 50K, the minimum setting is a hundred years."

"Less a month or two," Grainger joked. "Myself, I get nervous when the trees are closer together than the people are. It isn't a situation we got familiar with on Sunrise Terrace."

He sobered. "I guess we've lost Dor," he said in a flat voice. "We can't go back to when it happened since we were there already. And when we fix the problem, that whole timeline won't have happened. He'll be gone with it."

"First we have to cure the problem," Roebeck said as she worked. "Tim, why don't you and Pauli set up a weather screen outside the hatch. We're going to be here awhile before I'm comfortable with the settings. Some extra space will come in handy."

"I'll take the other side," Chun said. "If Pauli sets the fields, at least one of them is going to be repelling warm air right out into the blizzard—like last time."

She opened a locker set into the floor of the vehicle. Grainger reached into the opening and began handing up what looked like bricks of gray putty.

"Nan?" Weigand said. "Could I—we can't displace the capsule, but maybe I could take a suit up the line? I'm really getting . . ."

"Sure," Roebeck said, though Carnes saw the team leader's neck muscles stiffen. "Back in an hour, right?"

"Right," the blond man agreed with obvious relief. To Carnes—because she was a stranger—he said apologetically, "I'm not claustrophobic, you know, but being cooped up for too long . . ."

"Can I come with you?" Carnes asked suddenly. If Weigand hadn't brought her directly into the conversation, she wouldn't have spoken.

Roebeck's expression went blank. Grainger raised an eyebrow in amusement.

"Look, I'm here," Carnes said as she rose to her feet. "If all I learn is how not to be in the way, that's something."

Chun stepped into the hatchway, carrying a good dozen of the gray blocks. Grainger followed with a similar load. They'd pulled on gloves but otherwise wore only their tight-fitting coveralls.

Heating—and cooling, chances are—in the fabric itself, Carnes realized.

Roebeck nodded. "Quo?" she said. "All right if she takes your suit? I think it'll fit without major adjustment."

"Go ahead," Chun said, turning her head. "It'd take hours to put together a suit from the spares, and *then* it wouldn't fit."

"I'd like to go also, Nan," Barthuli said.

"I may need you later," Roebeck said.

"We'll be here three days, wouldn't you guess?" Barthuli said. "We'll be back in an hour."

Carnes joined Weigand at the suit locker. He tilted up the faceshield of the suit Chun had worn, then opened the one-piece breastplate. The pivot point was along the left side; Carnes couldn't see any sign of hinges even when the unit was fully open.

"The first thing to remember," Weigand said, "is that a displacement suit is a tool. The controls are extremely simple so that the suits can be used fast in an emergency. If you tell the suit to do something that will get you killed, the suit will do exactly what you told it. Do you understand?"

"Yes, I do," Carnes said. She met and held Weigand's eyes until he nodded with a slight grin.

Visible outside on the display, Grainger and Chun placed blocks about five feet apart on the drifts. The snow was so deep that the ARC Riders had to shuffle paths through it by main force.

"The controls are on the left wrist," Weigand said, lifting the arm to show Carnes the hemisphere and adjacent dimple on the underarm near the integral gauntlet. The displacement suit's surface gleamed like enameled metal, but the limb bent as flexibly as cloth in Weigand's hand. "Don't touch them till we get outside and I tell you what to do."

"I understand," Carnes said.

"All right," Weigand said. "Put the suit on. It's easiest to do that if—"

Carnes gripped the horizontal bar with her arms crossed. She lifted her thighs to her chest, twisted, and wriggled her feet into the lower portion of the suit.

Weigand laughed. "Yes, that's the easiest way for somebody your height, all right." He flexed his long right leg, stepped into his suit, and used the bar to raise him enough to complete the job with the other leg.

"Now," he said, "I'm going to close the suit over you. Walk outside in front of me. Don't do anything until I tell you to. We'll talk normally on the laser intercom. Do you understand?"

"I understand," Carnes repeated. She kept her voice calm and low-pitched so that she *sounded* responsible. She remembered being taught to drive by her father, who, for all his faults, had never let her forget the potential lethality of the vehicle she was controlling.

Weigand closed the breastplate, then the helmet, over her. The interior of the suit formed itself to Carnes' body about as firmly as a blood-pressure cuff on the first pump. There was a vague feeling of constriction. Carnes realized that if the suit slipped as she moved, it would in short order chafe sores in her skin.

The suit had no odor at all, neither human nor from chemicals in the construction. The air she breathed seemed cool, perhaps only because it was below blood temperature.

"Now walk to the hatch," Weigand directed. "I'll cycle it for you; just walk forward."

Carnes' view was as sharp as that of her ordinary vision. She knew she wasn't seeing optically through transparent material only because her field of view was wider by a few degrees than that of her unaided eyes.

She took a step and bumped the bulkhead with her shoulder. The suit weighed about ninety pounds, which wasn't a problem because it was spread so evenly over her body. Its bulk would take a little getting used to, however.

The bulkhead vanished a moment before Carnes would have walked into it. She saw the landscape outside the vehicle as if through a bubble of smoked glass. She stepped forward again, noticing the greater inertia of her suited limbs, and her foot came down in snow already disturbed by Chun and Grainger.

"Come on up beyond the line of the generators," Grainger said, beckoning. "It'll be pretty sloppy out here by the time you get back. We'll have melted the snow, but the area won't have dried out."

"I'm right behind you," Weigand said. "Just keep walking."

At the words, Carnes turned her head instinctively to look over her shoulder. To her surprise, she could do just that. The helmet didn't move. Her head rotated without hindrance from the firm padding and her field of view slid sideways as well.

"Tim and Quo are setting up a sorting field," Weigand explained as they passed the line of gray blocks. "It'll repel high-energy molecules on the inside and pass them in the other direction. We'll heat the area and it'll stay comfortable, despite the winter beyond."

Weigand's suit no longer made him anonymous. His size was a giveaway, and the sheen of his right forearm differed from that of the remainder of the suit's surface. The piece had had to be replaced in the recent past. . . .

They stopped in the lee of a drift from which poked thick stalks of milkweed. The open pods were now packed with snow. Barthuli was following them from the vehicle.

"The suits' default setting will displace them onto solid ground," Weigand said. "If you displace to a horizon where the ground is flooded, you'll be underwater. That's not a major problem. If you displace into a glacier, that's where you'll be: *in* a block of ice, and no way to move to reset. Ice is less dense than flowing water. Do you understand?"

"Yes, I understand," Carnes said, swallowing her impatience. Weigand's plodding approach made her forget what she had just seen and lived through. She wondered if that was part of the ARC Rider's intention.

"Suits can't displace geographically," Weigand continued. "They can't hover at the junction of now and becoming, the way transport capsules do, though they can be set completely out of phase for concealment. And they operate on a one-for-one duration with base time—that's the time horizon from which you displace in the suit. If you go forward a year and stay a week, you return a week later than you left."

"I understand," Carnes said. It struck her that the suit itself wasn't simple: the controls were. The parameters of use were deliberately limited because it would be impossible to work within more sophisticated ones while wearing gear as confining as the suit was.

"Most important," the ARC Rider said, "it's really easy with a suit to displace to a horizon where you've already been. You don't have a capsule's database to request confirmation. If you do that, you're gone."

"I understand."

Chun and Grainger had gone back inside the vehicle. They'd laid their blocks in an ovoid, with the capsule's hull forming a chord across the base of it. The snow within slumped as it warmed and compacted.

"Now, I could carry you along simply by holding you in contact with my suit," Weigand said, "but we're going to treat this as a training exercise. To prepare the suit for displacement, press the tit twice. Do that now."

Carnes deliberately thumbed the raised control. At the second touch, a pale orange mask overlaid the top half of her field of view. On the mask was the opaque legend 50K.

"We're going upline," Weigand said. "The equipment won't displace farther back than here anyway. To do that, you'll put pressure on the top of the hollow spot. You'll see the display shift. Try that now."

"Try 10,000 BC," suggested Barthuli, who was also adjusting his suit controls. Presumably to Weigand—the suits were impassive, even though Carnes was beginning to recognize individual characteristics—the analyst explained, "There's no European penetration, and we're well clear of both ice sheets and any likely operational area. And I've never been there."

"One forest is a lot like another forest," Weigand grumbled, but he added, "All right, Minus 10K. I just want a place that's warm enough I can wiggle my toes in the dirt."

Carnes pressed the concavity as if it were a rocker switch. 50K vanished, leaving only the mask. She jerked her thumb away from the control.

"No, keep going," Weigand ordered sharply. "There's a disjunction where the log scale changes."

Carnes obeyed. Numbers, initially in the high forties but descending, chased themselves across the orange field like the altimeter of a diving aircraft. On the landscape beyond the display, a thirty-inch depth of snow was melting into a pond. Water drained out along the path the three people in armor had tramped beyond the enclosure. The runoff froze as it gurgled down the track.

When the display had scrolled to −11,000, Carnes relaxed her pressure on the control. Even so, she overshot to −9851 before she managed to raise her finger completely. Without asking Weigand, she pressed the opposite curve of the dimple. The numbers dropped to −10,066 in the first spurt. She brought the display home with a series of quick taps, each adding a year.

"All right," said Weigand. He must have been reading an echo of her display, because he didn't ask whether she'd succeeded in the initial exercise. "Now change the scale by pressing the hand side of the hollow once."

The legend −10K shrank to a quarter of its former size and displaced to the upper left-hand corner of the field. A large zero was centered on the display.

"Bring it up to 50.5," Weigand ordered. "That's noon on the last day of June."

"What are you going to do if there's a thunderstorm?" Barthuli asked.

"Get wet," Weigand snapped.

As a matter of pride, Carnes ran the display to 50.5 without having to backtrack. She took her right hand away from the controls so that she didn't touch anything by accident.

"We're all ready," Weigand said, a statement and a warning. "To displace, you'll press the tit twice more. Do that now."

Barthuli vanished as suddenly as the lightning flashes. Weigand remained, his right thumb poised on his own controls.

Carnes pressed the bump twice. The mask and the landscape both vanished. For a minute and a half that seemed much longer, she was alone with her thoughts in soundless blackness.

Then there was light and life.

North America

Circa 50,000 BC

Grainger entered the cabin of the transportation capsule and glanced at the display. "The major's going to want to join the team," he said. "I think she'd be an asset."

"She's at least forty years old," Chun said as she seated herself beside Roebeck and took off her gloves. "From her period, there'll have been a lot of irreversible damage done."

Chun's tone was cool. She was attempting to avoid the appearance of argument by putting herself on a plane of detached appraisal.

"I think we can wait to decide whether we'll recruit her until there's a Central to recruit her at," Roebeck said as she worked. Her tone was neutral rather than harsh, but she expected them to take her point.

"I'll get some hardware ready," Grainger said. "Knowing they're from the 23d gives us an idea of what to expect in the way of defenses."

"Quo, I'd like you to check out the spatial navigation system," Roebeck said. "Maybe the temporal system lost its zero and spatial didn't, but I don't want to trust that without running it down ten places to the right of the decimal. Okay?"

Chun lifted the pair of control wands she preferred over a keyboard and switched a holographic display to hang in the air before her. "We'll have to recalibrate temporally before we insert in the target horizon," she said. "I'll have it set up for a simultaneous spatial check, too."

"The Defense of Freedom speech in that timeline was in the White House press briefing room," Roebeck commented, "but we don't know where the President was at that moment in ours. The geographical data may already have started to diverge."

"A pity the previous mission wasn't into 1988 instead of 1991," Chun said. "We're so close to having full data."

"It could as easily have been 1605," Grainger said with a laugh. "Then where would we be?"

"The same place we are now," Roebeck said. "Working until we fix this mess."

Grainger stood at the arms locker, considering options. The most effective way of eliminating sophisticated weapons and equipment—without blasting a hole in the landscape at the same time—was through electromagnetic pulses. The only defense electronics had against EMP was a Faraday cage or magnetic shielding of superior flux density.

The problem with EMP was that while it was almost certain to destroy a time-displacement device, it wasn't certain to prevent a hostile from killing you. If the fellow was using a gunpowder weapon with a flame or impact ignition system—let alone a knife or a bow and arrow—your pulse wasn't going to modify his activities.

Acoustics, gas, and tanglefoot projectiles all had their uses, though at short ranges they were apt to involve the shooter as well as the target. It wasn't just a throwback to his upbringing on Sunrise Terrace, where ruthlessness was a reflex, that caused Grainger to favor a weapon firing hypervelocity fléchettes (though there was also a nonlethal option clipped beneath the barrel).

"I'm going to run three test displacements," Chun said, "spatial only. Am I clear?"

"Go ahead," Roebeck said, nodding. She was building alternative scenarios for the Washington operation.

The Anti-Revision Command had an agent in place in Washington on the target horizon. The whereabouts of this agent—a local whose duties were simply to provide a safe house in a high-impact horizon—and all agents were held in every capsule at maximum detail. The team would have to intersect the agent before he or she (he, in this instance; a man named Calandine) was affected by the revision . . . and they couldn't be absolutely sure that nothing had occurred before the change showed up on their relatively coarse general database for the period.

The transportation capsule hummed as it pretended to be displacing spatially while remaining in the present temporal horizon. Outside, long, sere grass lifted as the weight of snow melted from it. Weigand and the two he was baby-sitting—Roebeck already regretted letting Barthuli go along—had displaced in their suits.

Everything flared white. The transportation capsule rang like a cracking bell as it jounced up from the soil.

Roebeck's hand hit the square red button on the bulkhead before her. Reflex—*displace instantly in an emergency*—drove her muscles to the action intellect would have taken had it not been short-circuited.

Nan Roebeck didn't know who the hostiles were—not yet. But she knew somebody had just fired a plasma weapon point-blank into TC 779.

North America

Circa 10,000 BC

The tech types at Central claimed everything was the same, whether someone displaced in a transportation capsule or a suit. The engine was identical; it was only the shape of the envelope that differed.

Pauli Weigand didn't believe that. When a TC came to rest, the horizon slid into place with a smooth, seamless feeling like that of a key turning in a well-oiled lock. A suit, though—

A suit *paused* momentarily. You were nowhere for that instant, not on a horizon or crossing horizons. Weigand was sure he would never have existed if his suit failed at that point.

Nothing went wrong this time. The horizon appeared as it always did when you displaced by suit, crashing into existence like a safe falling to the sidewalk. Oaks and hickories dotted the slope in front of him, while the rolling plains behind were different only in detail from the terrain on which TC 779 sat in the snow.

It was early summer here. Insects buzzed among the shoulder-high grasses and the mix of flowering plants with them. The sky was saturated blue between puffs of cumulus clouds, none of them threatening rain, and the bird overhead was a hawk rather than a vulture.

Barthuli and Major Carnes were already part of the landscape. Barthuli being Barthuli, he'd unlatched his suit without bothering to check his surroundings.

Weigand's display was layered: a 70-degree wedge at 1:1, normal vision, on the upper half of his display and below it a full 360-degree panorama compressed into the same 70-degree band. He turned to his right. A prairie chicken exploded from cover almost underfoot.

Weigand let his heart settle again. He put the wide-muzzled gas/tanglefoot projector back on safe.

There was nothing large or dangerous in the immediate vicinity. It would still have been nice if Gerd had had sense enough to look before he opened himself up.

"The suits appear to hold their zero despite long displacement," Barthuli said as he helped Weigand lift his legs from the armor. He smiled. "At any rate, the three of us arrived as near to simultaneously as we set out."

"Are the mechanisms of these suits different from the one in the ship?" Carnes asked. The front of her suit was open to the summer air. "Moving in them feels different to me."

Weigand beamed and went over to help Carnes from her armor. She didn't know that when the power was off, the suit would remain as stable as if fixed to bedrock until the operator released it.

"It's solid," he said as he offered his arm as a brace. "Don't worry about it falling over as you climb out."

"Central denies there's a difference, Major," Barthuli said, "but Pauli disagrees. I don't see why those up the line should lie to us, but that sort of thing does happen, of course."

The analyst drew a headband and a palm-sized recorder/computer from his armor's equipment pouch. "Where do you think you're going, Gerd?" Weigand asked in sudden concern.

Barthuli pointed up the wooded hillside. "We should be very close to the Mississippi River here," he said. "I'd like to know how considerable its flow is on this horizon, with the ice in final retreat."

Weigand grimaced and shook his head—in despair, because he already knew how the argument was going to come out. "Gerd, we may be ten klicks to the west, here, and we've got to get back to—"

"I'm just going to check from the hilltop," Barthuli said. Weigand noticed that both of them talked as if the other party were a child. "If I can't see the river from there, I'll come back. We have an hour, you know."

Weigand wiped the sweat from the back of his neck. He'd wanted weather warm enough to get out of the displacement suit—needed to get out of the displacement suit—but as usual, he'd forgotten how hot it could get in an uncontrolled climate.

"Look, these aren't the back slopes of bluffs like you'd find along the river here," he said. *Nan should never have let the analyst come along*, he thought—and smiled bitterly, knowing he was passing the buck for what was really his responsibility. "It's just another hill. And I don't want you to get out of my sight!"

Barthuli shrugged. "Then come along," he said in a reasonable tone. "A walk will do all of us good."

Carnes' eyes shifted from one man to the other as if she were watching a tennis match.

"I'm not going to leave the suits!" Weigand said. He shook his head again and added, "You've got your acoustic pistol, don't you? As a matter of fact, take the gas gun."

He held out the fat-barreled shoulder weapon. After all, he'd known from the first syllable that you couldn't argue with Barthuli.

"I've got enough to carry," Barthuli said. "Yes, I've a pistol, though I can't imagine there'll be much need for it. You know how rare dangerous animals are."

He looked at Carnes. "Would you like to come, Major?" he asked. "I'm quite confident we'll see the river. On this horizon the continent is still rising as the weight of ice lessens, so the view won't be as spectacular as it would be in your day or our own. But it will be there."

The analyst nodded to Weigand at the conclusion of what was undeniably a rebuke.

"May I go?" Carnes asked Weigand. At least somebody seemed to think he was in charge.

"Keep an eye on him," Weigand said. "And don't dawdle. And Gerd, this is really serious, so be careful. We're going to need you, and I *don't* want to explain to Nan that a pack of wolves ate you. All right?"

Barthuli nodded. "Yes, of course. We'll be very careful not to trip over tree roots, which I think you'll find is the greatest danger we encounter."

He unlatched the pouch on the hip of Carnes' armor and drew out the acoustic pistol there. "Come along, Major," he said, handing the nonlethal weapon to her. "We don't want to worry anybody."

Rather than a parent, Weigand thought as he watched the pair start up the hill, Barthuli sounded more like a spouse humoring his/her dithering mate.

Eurasia

Circa 50,000 BC

Grainger swung for the hatch. He was holding a fléchette gun/EMP generator vertically against his upper chest. He didn't have the stock shouldered because he didn't know which way he'd have to aim when he jumped outside.

"Suit up!" Roebeck ordered. "Chun, take over!"

"Fuck my suit!" Grainger shouted. "You back me up in yours!"

Two displacement suits remained in the capsule's locker. Grainger and Roebeck could have traded equipment in an emergency, but Chun was too short to wear either of the available suits without great discomfort.

Roebeck lowered herself into her armor with a care that would save time in the long run. Grainger was right, though: they wouldn't have a long run or any run at all if the hostiles caught the team inside the vehicle a second time.

The ninety seconds before displacement was complete wasn't quite enough time to don and power up a cold suit. Better that Grainger be outside, if the hostiles arrived at the same time and place, than that he be suited up to go outside later by the few seconds that they may not have.

The transportation capsule vibrated to stasis in a broad valley. The nearer wall of the valley sloped gently. The other, a kilometer distant, was for the most part a sheer escarpment.

Grainger was through the hatch in a single sinuous motion. He sprinted away from the vehicle so that he wouldn't be caught by whatever weapon the hostiles directed at it in the instant before Grainger nailed *them*.

Roebeck locked her faceshield closed and felt the tremble of her suit's systems coming on line. Her vision, momentarily grainy, sharpened. She hadn't a clue about where they'd displaced to. The emergency program was intentionally random. The quirk this time was that the displacement was spatial rather than temporal because Chun Quo had shut down the latter system to run her tests.

The hostiles had attacked TC 779 with a plasma weapon. That was Roebeck's weapon of choice also in a hard-kill situation, which this assuredly was. She snatched the fat twenty-five kilo tube from the arms locker as she passed on the way to the hatch.

Nan Roebeck was a civilized person from a civilized time. She had killed before, once. She still dreamed of the distorted face of the revisionist dropping three hundred meters into the Aegean as his EMPed microlight lost power. Specialists at Central said they could excise the memory from her profile, but she'd refused the offer. If she forgot what she'd done, it would be easier for her to do it again.

She would kill now, without compunction or hesitation. It was necessary to save the mission, to save *her* time. The hostiles had used a plasma discharge, therefore there had to be an aperture in their protection that passed charged particles.

If a concomitant of defeating the hostiles was that they be incinerated alive—so be it. Regrets were for the survivors.

Roebeck ran twenty meters clear of the vehicle and stopped. With the plasma weapon resting on her right shoulder, she touched her left hand to the helmet controls and set her display to highlight movement in a 360-degree arc about her.

She saw clouds, birds, and tree limbs waving in the slight breeze. A rhinoceros, a tonne of shaggy animal, flicked its ears in concern toward the transportation capsule. The animal was less than 200 meters away, but she hadn't seen it until the optical software rimmed it with magenta light.

Grainger squatted beneath a clump of alders. He was poised to EMP anything that appeared behind their vehicle and, knowing Tim Grainger, to rake it with fléchettes as well.

But there were no intruders in the landscape with them.

"Okay, Tim," Roebeck said. "Suit up while I watch things here. Then we'll trade places—but I want you in armor."

"Right," said Grainger with the momentary hesitation that meant he'd considered the order rather than simply obeying it. He rose to his feet and trotted to the vehicle, smiling faintly.

The ARC Riders were individuals, with individual virtues. If they'd been automatons stamped from sheet stock, Roebeck's team wouldn't have had the flexibility that made it so effective.

Still, Nan Roebeck sometimes wished that Grainger was quicker to accept "because I said so" as sufficient justification; and that Barthuli understood that anybody else's desires could possibly be important.

Roebeck walked toward a gray outcrop from which a fig tree sprouted. She wouldn't be on guard here for long, but she'd find a good location anyway. Metal ores in the granite might blur her suit's outline for a few instants. That could be critical. . . .

It would have been easy to stumble because her viewpoint was set on panorama with movement highlighted. Roebeck had trained herself to move normally despite her distorted vision.

Anti-Revision Command equipment was wonderfully versatile, but that didn't matter unless the personnel were comfortable using it. Roebeck had familiarized herself with *all* aspects of the hardware. The lives of her team and the success of a mission might depend on her ability to use some obscure capacity of her suit.

Grainger actively disliked wearing armor. He preferred to trust his reflexes and instincts, though intellectually he knew that a suit's sensor suite multiplied his human senses at least a hundredfold. He wore his suit grudgingly. He knew how to use its systems, but he had to think before he engaged them.

Confinement bothered Weigand. He couldn't like a displacement suit any more than he could have liked a pillow smothering him. He was a top systems engineer and second only to Roebeck herself as the team's jack of all trades, but he mentally cringed every time he had to put his suit on.

As for Chun, she knew the equipment inside and out. She'd once entered two separate settings by disconnecting her suit's preselector circuit, then displaced to within 31 hours of a calculated third point by riding the harmonics of the original pair. Roebeck hadn't tried to duplicate *that* trick, partly because she couldn't see any use for it—but largely because she didn't believe her grasp of the concept was subtle enough to avoid disaster.

But Chun Quo's bone-deep aversion to conflict was a danger to the team in a confrontation. She refused to handle lethal weapons, which was acceptable; but she invariably hesitated before using any weapon, however harmless, and that could get your friends killed. Chun couldn't have changed her behavior if she wanted to—and she assuredly didn't want to.

She was right, of course. Roebeck's electromagnetic pulse hadn't hurt the revisionist, just shut down the controls of the engine that kept him stable in the gusty wind currents. He'd had nearly thirty seconds to scream as he tumbled down toward water which was rock-solid at the speed he hit it.

Barthuli found displacement suits interesting, the same way he was interested in Acheulean hand-axes. The analyst's unworldliness was deceptive, though. In a crisis, he could react as quickly as a switch makes contact. The trouble was that with Barthuli, you could never be sure *how* he would react.

Dor Jalouse was the team member who'd loved his suit for the power and anonymity it gave him. No ARC Rider could be lazy or stupid, but Dor was something of an underachiever. He would use the suit's systems to access information just to save physical effort, and he took a childish pleasure in walking through closed doors in his armor. He always completed his tasks, though perhaps close to the deadline, and he knew his systems almost as well as Chun knew hers.

Dor Jalouse would have been the perfect Rider to be on external guard right now. Unfortunately, he was lost, and—as Grainger had said—lost forever. When Roebeck corrected the revision, she would saw off the branch of time to which Jalouse clung.

The grass in this valley was still green, though the beeches scattered in clumps had turned largely golden. The team had been lucky when TC 779 displaced. Another blizzard would make work on the capsule difficult.

There would have to be work. The plasma bolts had flayed off three square meters of the outer skin forward of the hatch. Some, perhaps all, of the electronics in that section of hull would be damaged.

The emergency displacement had seemed normal, but that didn't prove anything. Most of the spatial circuitry lay along the inner hull while the temporal hardware was attached to the outer skin. Until Roebeck knew where the program had intended them to land, she couldn't assume that even the spatial portion of the equipment was working properly.

Grainger stepped from the vehicle, graceful despite the burden of his armor. He'd used the suit's load-carrying ability to add a tanglefoot projector and a plasma weapon to his armaments.

"I've got the duty, Nan," Grainger called cheerfully on the intercom. He hopped to the top of the outcrop beneath which she'd sheltered.

Rather than set his suit as Roebeck did to highlight movement all around him, Grainger simply raised the magnification a moderate degree and turned his head constantly. The sensors had an alarm function that would flash Grainger a vector to anything the suit's artificial intelligence believed was threatening, but the triggerman had no intention of trusting a machine to do his job.

"You might echo the main screen," Roebeck suggested as she headed back to the capsule. "If nobody's appeared by now, they probably can't track us. Judging from the timing, I suspect they homed on the displacement suits' wake."

"Assuming our sensors are all working and the hostiles aren't hovering just out of phase, waiting for an opportunity," Grainger said. "You check on what happened back there, chief. I'll stay here and make sure it doesn't happen again."

Roebeck wanted Grainger's eye—a very good eye indeed—to go over the recording of the attack on the capsule. He was right, though. There'd be time for that later, when they were sure that TC 779 was capable of spotting hostiles lurking a few angstroms from the present. Until then, Grainger's whole attention should be on the safety of the capsule and the surviving team members.

Roebeck lifted her faceshield when she entered the cabin. The atmosphere had a burned tinge which she hadn't noticed before. She hoped that didn't mean a bolt had penetrated both hulls.

Chun noticed the pinch of Roebeck's nostrils. "One of the osmotic exchange panels was damaged," Chun explained. "I didn't notice the telltale in time to shut it off before it had started shifting ozone. We're over capacity, even . . ."

Even with one panel removed, the capsule's air system could provide enough oxygen for a full crew of six. From the way she'd failed to finish the thought, Chun must have wondered whether Weigand's trio was now as completely lost as Jalouse was.

Chun looked up with concern hidden beneath a mask of calm. "I don't think the revisionists we're after were responsible for the attack, Nan," she said.

"Well, I didn't expect that they were," Roebeck said as she slid into the seat from which she could most comfortably watch the display. "Granting a suit displacing makes more of a blip than a capsule does, it's not *much* of a blip. It'd take apparatus as sensitive as Central's to target us that way."

"Yes," said Chun simply as her wands dipped. "Central has sent a team of ARC Riders. To stop us."

The display brightened into an enhanced, slowed-down image of the attack. The computer projected a three-dimensional hologram in which TC 779 was the center of the scene. The information displayed was melded from sensor recordings, enhancement, and backgrounds stored in the database itself.

A second transportation capsule winked into existence ten meters from TC 779, just beyond the "patio" Roebeck's team was clearing of snow. The intruder hovered a meter in the air. Differences in design between the attacking craft and a 700-series capsule from the team's timeline were too slight to note with the naked eye, even though Roebeck had seen them highlighted when she went over the recording of their entry into the wrong Central. A hatch in the center of the vehicle blinked open.

Two figures waited with weapons shouldered in the hatchway. Their armor flared at the joints but was otherwise identical to the team's own displacement suits. Their weapons slashed incandescent tracks toward the hull of TC 779.

The capsule wasn't in a posture of defense, but the standby magnetic shielding instantly shot up to maximum density. Plasma repelled by the shielding splashed off like water being hosed against a smooth boulder. Snow flashed to steam. Grass and even the turf itself, rich in organic compounds, erupted in smoky red flame.

The plasma, nitrogen atoms stripped of their electron shells, was of minuscule mass. Accelerated to nearly the speed of light by positively charged coils in the fat barrel, that mass caused the weapon to recoil violently.

Instead of firing short bursts, the two figures kept their fingers on the triggers. The gun muzzles lifted; their streams of hellfire exploded deep trenches across the snowbound prairie. Momentarily a third plasma weapon fired from knee-level behind the two standing figures.

"Lousy technique," Roebeck muttered. If the gunmen had pulsed rather than streaming their plasma, and if they'd both focused their bursts on a single aiming point—the hatch was the obvious choice—they'd have holed TC 779's cabin and incinerated its occupants before Roebeck could displace.

"What?" Chun asked.

"If they were my people, I'd burn them both new assholes," Roebeck said. "Can you imagine Grainger and Jalouse letting a target like that get away? We were fish in a barrel, and they missed us."

"You're offended by a murderer's bad craftsmanship?" Chun asked coldly. She didn't comment on the fact the error had been committed by the team's enemies. That didn't affect the moral question.

"Sure I am," Roebeck said. "We *work* for the ARC, remember."

"Not this one!" Chun snapped.

Roebeck shrugged. "If it could happen here, it could happen to ours. But not to *my* people."

Chun's tight mouth suddenly broke into a broad grin. "Yes," she said, "I'm shaky from what happened, too. . . . But I prefer to cling to a myth of universal human decency rather than one of invincible skill in a crisis."

Roebeck choked, then bent as a gust of laughter clamped her ribs. "Quo, I swear by every god I've come across in fifty missions, I've never been closer to the hostiles handing me my head. And it's my own fault. I should have known that we'd have Central on the other side. What we're going to do is a revision from where they stand, after all."

"We were thinking of the group from the 23d," Chun said. "Gerd probably realized that the new timeline's ARC Riders might take a hand, but he must not have known that Central could track suit displacements. Otherwise he'd have said something."

Her face went still as she considered what she'd just said. She was suddenly less certain of the statement than she would have been if some Rider other than Barthuli were the subject of it.

"Sure, he'd have said something," Roebeck said. "We don't know that the hostiles can really track the wake of displacement suits, either. They spotted the point of displacement, but that doesn't mean they followed Weigand to wherever he was going."

The greatly slowed action on the display came to an end as TC 779, a patch of its hull glowing, vanished from the image area. As a coda to the recorded event, the capsule's computer postulated a doughnut of vaporized hull metal continuing to lift on the heated air.

"Let me offer an argument for humane behavior," Chun said, flicking the recording backward by jumps. "How would you have arranged an attack like this, Nan?"

Roebeck pursed her lips. "Full team?"

Chun nodded. She'd stopped the display about midway in the attack.

"Jalouse and me in the port with EMP generators," Roebeck said. "If the target isn't shielded, it's fried and harmless. If it's got magnetic shielding, and I'd assume it did, the generators are still more efficient against a given flux density than plasma at the range in question."

"And EMP generators have a broader field," Chun said.

"Right," Roebeck agreed. "Jalouse and me jump from the hatch, clearing it for Weigand with a plasma weapon. His size helps stabilize the recoil. And Grainger with the fléchette gun he favors—I want a mix of stimuli hitting the hostiles as quickly as we can. We don't know what their defenses are, even if the capsule does look a lot like one of ours."

"Tim would complain about being in the second wave," Chun said, acting as the Devil's advocate.

Roebeck shrugged again. "The first two use EMP generators because we can jump clear of the follow-up pair while using them. As you said, the pulses are a broad cone. There's no way to aim a high-recoil weapon with useful accuracy while you're leaping through the air."

Roebeck grinned wryly. "Barthuli's backup with another plasma gun," she concluded. "I'd say an EMP generator, but Dor and I'd be in the cone if he had to use it. And you're at the capsule controls."

"A good decision," Chun said expressionlessly, "as I'd expect from you. Now, look at what the hostiles did."

The display froze on the hatch of the attacking vehicle and changed scale downward. As the image expanded to approach 1:1, the figures in the hatchway lost individuality. The computer was enhancing detail beyond the limits of the recorder's resolution.

"You would be willing to kill on an operation of that sort," Chun said. Her wands moved and outlines resolved still further. Two more armored figures sharpened from the shadows within the cabin.

"Yes, I would," Roebeck said. She had her morality, Quo had a different one. That was life. "I'll kill now if I have to."

The hostiles behind the first pair also carried plasma weapons. Roebeck remembered the brief pulse somebody had fired between his fellows' legs. With hardware as notoriously difficult to control as a plasma weapon, the shooter was lucky his burst hadn't cut down one or both of the personnel in the hatchway.

"But that wouldn't be your first priority?" Chun prodded. Her wands let the scene crawl forward. The hostiles began firing, but the pair behind them were crowding the shooters for room to aim their weapons. "Killing, I mean?"

"Good God, no!" Roebeck said. "First priority is *always* the mission. Even for Tim. It's just that, you know it yourself, Quo. Sometimes things can't be as clean as you'd like them to be."

"It's easy to be moral when you know somebody else will pull the trigger for you, you mean?" Chun said.

"I didn't——" Roebeck said.

"Then you should have," Chun interrupted harshly. "Because it's true, and I know that as well as you do."

Chun took a deep breath. "But look at the hostiles," she went on in a settled tone again. She flicked her head sideways to indicate the display. The control wands prevented her from making normal hand gestures.

It wasn't just recoil that threw the plasma beams into a crazy-eight. The pair of hostiles inside the cabin was actively jostling the shooters in front of them.

Roebeck watched, this time in full detail, as one of the backup team dropped prone to get a shot. Plasma began to scatter as soon as it left the muzzle, so even the half-second the third weapon fired was enough to overload the environmental systems of the pair in the hatch.

"They went berserk," Roebeck said. "Just like the clerks or whatever in the transfer room when Jalouse walked in. They had us cold, and they didn't nail us because they wanted to *kill* so bad."

"Barthuli may think the revised timeline is almost identical to ours," Chun said. "*I* think there are points of distinction more significant than coincidental likenesses of vehicle and room design."

That was closer to open confrontation than Roebeck had ever expected to hear from Quo. The fact Barthuli wasn't present to hear the statement was beside the point: Quo wouldn't say anything behind a person's back that she wouldn't say to his face.

"You know . . ." Roebeck said aloud, "I think Gerd would probably agree with you."

She should have said, "will agree." She couldn't give up hope for the trio's safety, not yet.

"I checked the arms locker," Chun said, answering the question just forming in Roebeck's mind. "Pauli took a projector with a mix of gas and tanglefoot rounds. The others have only the acoustics in their integral survival pouches. They weren't expecting trouble."

Roebeck swore softly. It was all up to Weigand's trio if they returned while the hostile vehicle was still at the North American 50K site. Acoustics and gas shells would be useless against hostiles in armor. The tanglefoot mixture could net and hold against even a displacement suit's powered muscles, but chances were there'd be more than one target to deal with.

Pauli *might* be fast enough . . . . But he might not even realize the waiting vehicle wasn't TC 779.

"Perhaps they'll displace again," Chun suggested.

"Carnes won't be able to, not fast enough," Roebeck said.
"She probably won't know there's a problem. Barthuli . . ."

She smiled grimly. "I'm not sure Gerd would even try to
escape. There's a whole new timeline for him to explore, after
all."

"They might kill him out of hand," Chun said. "They probably would."

"Again," Roebeck said, "I'm not sure Gerd would care."

She closed her eyes and forced herself to imagine the bat-
tle that might be taking place *now*, only a continent away.
"Pauli could escape. If he was alone, that's what he'd do. But
I made him responsible for the other two."

Roebeck leaned the seat of her console back so that her
eyes opened to the cabin's familiar ceiling. "On the good side,
I wouldn't stick around the site of an attack where I'd let the
targets get away. That's the one place they—we—know they
are to hit back. But as you pointed out, I don't think like their
team leader."

"Nan?" Chun Quo said quietly.

Roebeck turned her head toward her.

"We're shorthanded now," Chun said. "We may have to
do things that usually there'd be somebody else to do."

She placed her control wands carefully into the holder in
her chair arm. "I can administer antibiotics to disease bacilli,"
she said. "And in this case, I can do whatever is necessary to
save *our* timeline."

"You think shooters as good as Tim and me'll want you
getting in the way?" Roebeck said. The only way to handle
Quo's offer to compromise her honor was to turn it into a
passing joke. "But I'll keep your application on file."

She coughed to clear her throat. "Now let's see what we've
got left in the way of a transportation capsule."

"We don't have temporal capacity at the moment," Chun
said, "but I think that's repairable. If we—"

"Hold on," Roebeck interrupted gently. She spread the intervals between keys so that she could use her board with gauntlets on. "First things first. I want to know whether we can spot the hostiles if they wait out of phase."

It took her a minute to bring up a three-dimensional graphic. It showed magnetic and optical anomalies in a hundred-meter circle of the capsule during the period since they'd displaced here.

"We can't check our sensors without another set to compare their data with, can we?" Chun said in puzzlement.

Time and space are relative approximations rather than constants. At no two points in space *or* time is the velocity of light, for example, precisely the same. By cataloging the local pattern of variation, the transportation capsule's computer could determine—by relatively gross changes in the flow—that another vehicle was nearly in phase with their horizon.

But that presupposed TC 779's sensors were still giving readings accurate at a sufficient level of subtlety.

"We can check what we're receiving now against similar time slices from before the attack," Roebeck explained. "The raw data won't be the same, but if the *pattern* is the same, then we can be reasonably sure that our robot friend here will warn us if somebody's peeking to line up an attack."

"If I'd thought of that," Chun said, "I could have done it myself." And faster by a good deal. "But I didn't think of it."

Roebeck grinned, aware both of the flattery and the basic truth beneath it. "Take a look and tell me what you think," she said.

Chun lifted out her wands. Instead of using a separate mini-screen, she echoed the data on the main display. She color-weighted four graphs, averaged each separately, and projected the totals as individual quadrants of the display. All four were in the yellow-green/middle-green range.

Human color vision could detect variations in shade that were a matter of a few angstroms—a few hundred millionths of a centimeter. Only the most sensitive electronic devices were capable of finer discrimination. Chun used her eyes as a shorthand method of measuring the sensors' current output against electronic perceptions before the attack.

She nodded to Roebeck. "We can call Tim in," she said. "We'll have warning before another vehicle locks on to us."

Roebeck stood up and bent backward to stretch. "I'm going to see what the damage looks like," she said.

"You'll learn more from the display," Chun said.

"I'll use the display," Roebeck said. "I want to *see* what happened, too."

North America

When they entered the shade of the trees, Rebecca Carnes felt fear close in around her .

There wasn't anything wrong with the forest itself. A squirrel scolded from the opposite side of a tree bole, implying that there was nothing more dangerous around than the two time travelers. The woods were where the enemies in Carnes' mind lurked, though. They were preparing to rake her with automatic rifles and rocket-propelled grenades, then melt away into the deeper darkness. . . .

"Mr. Barthuli?" she said.

She didn't know what the proper form of address might be. The ARC Riders didn't appear to be terribly rank-conscious. A good thing, as far as Carnes was concerned. She'd met army nurses who were more concerned with being officers than in helping their patients. Carnes' stomach turned at people who worried about status when there was a job to be done.

The analyst turned his head. "Major?" he said. He was a slender, not unhandsome man with the features of a bird of prey. His expression was friendly whenever Carnes looked at him, but she always had the impression that he stood behind a sheet of thick glass.

"I don't know how to use this gun," Carnes said, holding up the pistol Barthuli had taken from her armor. It felt light and flimsy, as if it were no more than a plastic shell. It seemed to have two parallel barrels, cast in one piece with the weapon's receiver and smooth grips.

She stopped walking. "I . . . had a problem with a gun just before you picked me up," she went on. "I hadn't checked it. I don't like to make the same mistake twice."

"Pauli fusses like a mother hen," Barthuli said. "Sometimes I think he's worse than Nan herself."

Though the analyst sounded dismissive, he turned the weapon slightly in Carnes' hand so that they were both looking at the left side. The dial there was milled on the outer edge and about an inch in diameter. Rather than increments, 90 percent of the dial's circuit was marked with a color band that changed clockwise in the order of the optical spectrum.

"Tim Grainger didn't say anything, but I think he worries, too," Carnes said reflectively.

Barthuli nodded. "Tim's afraid that one of us will need help and he won't be present to give it," he said. "I believe he thinks of us as his family, his clan. He doesn't really have friends, though I can't imagine a friend who'd do more for any of us than Tim would."

The analyst smiled at Carnes through a psychic barrier no one would ever be able to penetrate. "I don't have friends, either, of course, Major. But that's a flaw in me."

"I prefer Rebecca," Carnes said. "Though you can call me whatever makes you comfortable."

Barthuli chuckled. "It won't work," he said, "but it's kind of you to try. Now—"

He pointed. The red end of the color band was vertical. The gray dividing segment was counterclockwise of it, with deep violet beyond that.

"The weapon creates a difference tone of ultra-low frequency at the point of aim," Barthuli explained. "Minimum setting is 160 dB, which is generally sufficient. Simply point the muzzle and pull the trigger."

He indicated a standard trigger.

"To increase the output, rotate the dial." Barthuli's hands were unexpectedly large, though shapely. The tip of his index finger rolled the dial upscale, then back to its original setting. "But I really don't imagine we'll need to be armed. Shall we proceed?"

Birds flapped noisily in the foliage overhead. Carnes hadn't been able to hear them when her feet and her companion's shuffled through the dead leaves.

"Sure, I just wanted to—" She'd almost said *be prepared*. She wasn't prepared. "To know, that's all."

They resumed walking toward the top of the hill. It was farther than it had seemed from where Weigand waited with the suits, but a slab of bare rock beneath a huge oak suddenly announced that they'd reached their goal.

Barthuli hopped onto the slab. He moved his gray box in an arm's-length panorama.

Carnes assumed the box was some sort of camera. She kept a comfortable distance from the analyst, so as not to interfere—and not be bumped by the gadget. She'd noticed that photographers were generally oblivious of their immediate environment.

For that matter, she'd noticed that photographers often didn't *see* a scene until they viewed their print or videotape long afterward.

In the present case, that would have been a terrible shame. The landscape was beautiful with a touch of weirdness that Carnes couldn't identify for some moments.

She and Barthuli stood on a bluff a hundred feet above the river flowing swiftly in the near distance. The water winking beyond the treetops was a cloudy blue-white from the influx of melted ice that fed it only a few hundred miles to the north.

Though the limestone bluff was steep, trees of varying size

had found crevices to spout in. Their foliage, leaves and needles both, blurred the details of the slope.

The floodplain was narrow and willow-choked, even now at low water in the summertime. Or was it low water, when meltwater fed the stream rather than runoff from rains in the upper tributaries? The eastern margin, in the far distance, was hazy but clearly lower than that here on the west side of the river.

"I've never seen so much land without anything human in it," Carnes said. "Something felt wrong about what I was seeing. It's just that."

Instead of commenting, Barthuli touched unseen controls on the edges of his gray box. The air before him shimmered, though Carnes couldn't see the interference patterns as images from where she stood.

"Do you know, Rebecca?" the analyst said. Carnes hadn't heard so much animation in his voice before. "Do you know, I think you're wrong!"

The pine to their immediate left grew from a ledge forty feet below them. Barthuli took Carnes by the hand and pointed her whole arm past the ragged top of the tree. A wisp of gray smoke rose fitfully, dissipating long before it reached the clouds. The source was lost in the willows and alders close beside the river.

"I scanned for anomalies," Barthuli explained. He gestured with the gray box as he released Carnes' hand. "I thought the hunting bands were too thinly scattered for us to have a real likelihood of locating one, but it seems our luck was with us."

He placed the camera in a pocket of his coveralls and eyed the immediate slope. Gripping an inch-thick sapling crowned with oak leaves, he slid down sideways to an outcrop four feet below the top of the bluff.

"Wait!" Carnes said. It had taken her a moment to realize what Barthuli really intended. "Barthuli, we can't possibly get down there and back up in an hour. For pity's sake, we ought to be starting back right now!"

The analyst let himself skid to a considerable pine tree a dozen feet lower. He stopped himself by grabbing its trunk, then sidled past a sheer drop of twenty feet to a more accessible slope. Carnes could see only the top of his head.

Barthuli paused and looked up at her. "Rebecca, I won't have another chance to see this culture. They should be Clovis hunters, you know—virtually identical to the folk who originally crossed into the continent over the Bering Land Bridge?"

"Gerd," Carnes said, hugging her torso at diaphragm level as a protective reflex. "*Please*. We've got to get back, to Pauli and to the capsule."

Barthuli shrugged. "Rebecca," he said, "lives aren't eternal. I'm perhaps more constantly aware of that than others of you, but it's true for everyone. Never give up a chance to learn, while your brain can accept the knowledge. Please, come along with me."

"Gerd, people depend on you!" Carnes said.

Barthuli shrugged again. "Tell Pauli that I won't be any longer than I need be," he said. He slid down to another pine and vanished behind its trunk. Carnes could hear twigs crackling for a short while.

She turned and started back to where Weigand waited with the armor. After a moment, she broke into a run.

Eurasia

"The hostiles weren't very good, were they?" Grainger said as he and Roebeck viewed TC 779's external damage with their faceshields up. "They got buck fever and missed an easy one."

The initial jet of plasma struck to the left of the hatch. It had dug a fist-deep gouge through the outer skin and hull core. The cavity was of greatest diameter at its maximum depth, where it belled out like the top of a thundercloud. The inner plating had reflected the bolt rather than absorbing the energy.

"I was thinking that," Roebeck agreed. "We've got to assume they'll still have a full complement if we run into them again, though."

Grainger shrugged. "Numbers within reason aren't a problem," he said. "So long as you're quick and keep your muzzle down."

He smiled. The expression made him look boyish for the moment before his face settled back into its normal grim lines.

Where the bolt first hit, damage was total. From that near-puncture, the stream of plasma trailed to the left and upward, doing greatly diminished harm: after the first instant, TC 779's automatic defenses had wrapped the vehicle in a dense magnetic flux. The shielding repelled the stripped nitrogen atoms the way static-charged hairs are flung away from the scalp.

The outer skin showed the track of the plasma beam as orange-peel crinkling. Occasionally the scar deepened to a crater. These were spots where there'd been a preexisting flaw, or a flux eddy had permitted a portion of the charged particles to strike the metal directly.

The other shooter fired later than his partner—only by a temporal hair's breadth, but enough that his beam struck after the capsule's shielding had risen to nearly full intensity. The plasma blasted a divot as broad as a soup plate from the hatch just off-center, then slid left at a flatter angle than that of the first weapon. Where the second track crossed the first, it blew away a chunk of the ceramic core. A penumbra of circuitry beyond the region of total destruction was crumbled.

"We're lucky the hatch still works," Roebeck said. "I know the theory about changing it to manual operation, but I wouldn't look forward to trying it."

"For a target like this, I'd have coupled the triggers so the weapons fired together," Grainger said. "And pulses, for Christ's sake, not close your eyes and mash the trigger!"

"They had three firing for a moment," Roebeck said. She squatted to view the vehicle's underside. "I don't know whether the third one simply missed, or our shielding deflected the beam completely because it came in too low."

"Cowboys," Grainger muttered. His gauntleted right hand caressed the grip of his fléchette gun.

"The most serious damage is . . ." Chun said over the helmet communicators. A beam of red light from a lens on Roebeck's left shoulder illuminated the point where the two plasma tracks crossed. ". . . here. Other places we've lost circuits, kilometers of them, but it's nothing we can't bypass for now. Here we lost the temporal bus."

"Is the spatial bus all right?" Roebeck asked in a thin voice. All her emotions were filtered gray by the fear Chun would reply *no*.

"It's on the other side of the vehicle," Chun said. "It didn't receive any damage at all."

Roebeck felt her muscles relax. The world brightened around her again. She'd known they were looking at weeks of work, maybe months, in replacing circuits and building shunts. TC 779 wouldn't have anything like its normal delicacy of maneuver. Chances were the apparent duration of displacements would lengthen, maybe double, because the vehicle had to generate some fields in sequence rather than simultaneously.

But time it took to repair the capsule didn't matter; the team would be that much older when they confronted the revisionists and perhaps the hostile ARC Riders, that was all. The physical labor of the repairs mattered even less.

Nobody joined the Anti-Revision Command because the work was less demanding than the 26th-century norm. ARC Riders were expected to do whatever the job required. If that meant (as it occasionally did) living for months in a community where the life expectancy—for those who survived infancy—was less than thirty years, so be it.

Roebeck chuckled. Thirty years was probably a close approximation of the life span of the humans on this horizon—where she'd be trapped unless they did get the vehicle temporally mobile again.

Without a bus, there would have been billions of connections to make before the computer could distribute commands. The three of them couldn't have done the job in ten lifetimes.

"Until . . ." she said aloud.

"I have a routing plan for repairs," Chun said. "Whenever you'd care to see it . . ."

There was a touch of asperity in her voice. Quo simply couldn't understand why anybody would need to look at an actual object when the combination of computer and display would provide the information in infinite detail and clarity.

"Okay, we're coming in," Roebeck said. The repairs couldn't be done by the computer, though. She wondered how many Maxwell Field sorters remained in the locker. Probably none, and the weather here wasn't likely to remain this comfortable throughout their stay.

"Nan," Grainger said quietly. "Take a look."

She turned, expecting to see Grainger pointing. His left arm remained at his side, while the right crooked his gun/EMP generator to his armored chest. "On the hill there," he said.

Roebeck followed the line of Grainger's eyes to a knoll five hundred meters down the valley. Rock grayed the mantle of long yellow grass. A flat-topped tree twisted from a crevice. Roebeck thought it might be a fig. "What do you—" she began.

"Lower your faceplate and use some magnification," Grainger said. "I caught the movement."

Roebeck obeyed with a smooth, slow motion, much as she would have positioned her hand to snatch a fly from a tabletop. She locked the visor in place and boosted optical magnification by ten powers, enough that the edges of her field of view precisely framed the knoll.

"I don't . . ." she said, and then she did see the face looking at her through a screen of sere grass blades. "Yes."

At ×100 magnification, she could see blue eyes glinting from beneath heavy brows. There was no facial hair, but the figure's forearms—the woman's forearms—were covered with a russet pelt.

"ARC Central isn't going to like this," Grainger said with a joking lilt. "Us in a human-occupied location, and we haven't parked the capsule out of phase."

A child's face peeped over the female's shoulder. The watchers were as still as the stone on which they crouched.

"I don't know about you," Roebeck said, "but I'd be more than happy if I could displace straight to Central and take my punishment. Since we can't . . ."

She raised her faceshield again. "Let's see what Quo suggests, and then figure out how we're going to execute the plan."

She gestured Grainger inside the vehicle. As she followed him, she looked back toward the knoll. The faces had vanished.

North America

Circa 10,000 BC

Pauli Weigand glanced up at the trees, pursing his lips to try again to raise Barthuli on the radio. He saw Major Carnes jogging toward him with a set expression. She was alone.

Carnes hadn't taken a headband with her. That was Weigand's mistake, the way a lot of things were Weigand's mistake, but it didn't bother him for the moment. Now there was trouble, so he had a job to do.

He checked his shoulder weapon. There was a tanglefoot round in the chamber. That was as good a choice as gas, because he didn't have a clue yet as to what the problem was. Maybe a bear? There were bears here, he knew.

Weigand pulled on his boots. He'd been digging his bare toes into the ground, and traces of rich loam still clung to them.

"Barthuli went down to the riverside," Carnes said, breathing through her mouth between gasped phrases. "He says there's a camp of Indians down there and he wants to see it!"

"I swear, Gerd's got no more sense than a, aw, I don't know what," Weigand said. "He's all right, though?"

"He was fine when he went behind the trees," Carnes said. She was getting her breathing under control. "I'm sorry. I couldn't make him come back without . . ."

Without shooting him, probably, and Major Carnes wasn't the first to think about shooting Barthuli. "It's all right," Weigand said, smiling ruefully at Carnes. "Not a thing anybody can do when Gerd gets an idea. But he's everything you could ask for otherwise."

Weigand considered putting his armor on. If he wore the suit, he'd be completely safe from anything Stone Age locals could do. It wouldn't make the hill any easier to climb, though, and if the river had cut the other side steeper, he'd have a devil of a time going down.

That wasn't the real downside, though. Weigand would be safe and so would the major if she suited up, whether she came along or stayed back here. Barthuli *wasn't* in armor, though. If the locals decided that the stranger had brought a couple demons into their village, things might get terminal before Weigand could cover the area with gas.

"I don't even know there's Indians down there," Carnes said carefully. "Barthuli showed me smoke, but he was just guessing that it came from a campfire. He called them Clovis hunters."

Weigand nodded. "You can make a lot of money betting on Gerd's guesses," he said. The only reason it'd be a tragedy if Barthuli got his head stuck on a stick, or whatever "Clovis hunters" did, was that the guy was so *damned* good at his job. The team could get another analyst, but there wasn't a chance he'd be the artist Gerd Barthuli was.

Besides, Weigand liked the guy, though he was about as spooky as anybody you were likely to meet.

"Gerd," he said, the name keying the commo set. "Weigand to Barthuli. Let's talk, Gerd. Weigand to Barthuli."

No answer. An unusual degree of hollowness on his earphones, though, suggesting the set's AI was blanking a great deal of static.

Weigand checked the multisensor hanging on his belt for a spectrum analysis. The holographic readout flashed into the air before him. He swore.

"What's the matter?" the major said sharply. She pressed her right hand firmly against her ribs, above the flap of the pocket which her acoustic pistol bulged. Carnes' loose cotton uniform had been in bad shape when the team picked her up. Weigand wondered if they had a set of coveralls on TC 779 that would fit her.

Weigand waved at the hill. "All this rock is full of lead and zinc ore," he explained. "There's no way I can punch a signal through it. Or Gerd, either, not that I'd be real confident of him trying to call us. He didn't ask before he went off on his little junket, after all."

He raised an eyebrow toward Carnes. "Might be best if you stay here in your suit," he said. "I'll go fetch Gerd back, and—"

"No," Carnes said simply. She took the acoustic pistol out of her pocket and held it like a prayer book in both hands.

Weigand nodded. "All right with me," he said. "You know how to use that thing?"

"I point it and pull the trigger?" Carnes said.

"Pretty much," Weigand agreed. Hell, they were already near the end of their time. Nan wasn't going to like this, but it'd turn out all right in the long run. "Don't hold the trigger down longer than a few seconds at a time or it'll start to get hot from harmonics. It won't hurt the gun, but you can burn the hell out of your hand that way."

He adjusted two electronic controls on the inside of his armor's backplate, then did the same with the other two suits.

"What are you doing?" Carnes asked. She didn't sound frightened, but there was a bright edge to her voice that hadn't been there before she went up the hill with Barthuli.

"I'm setting the suits to shift out of phase with sidereal time," Weigand explained. "I doubt locals could hurt them, but you can never tell. Besides, we don't want to find bird nests in them when we come back."

Or a rattlesnake, but he didn't say that aloud.

Carnes looked at the wooded slope. She deliberately put the pistol back in her pocket. "How do you call them back when we return?" she said, her eyes still toward the hillside.

"They'll return for two minutes every four hours,"

Weigand explained. "You're right, when they're out of phase, there's no communication with them at all."

Carnes grinned stiffly and started up the hill. Weigand's longer legs brought him quickly in step with her. As he strode, he switched the magazine from tanglefoot to gas cartridges. Hard to know how many locals they'd be facing.

And ARC coveralls were great, but they wouldn't stop a flint spear.

Eurasia

Circa 50,000 BC

Roebeck leaned against the ledge of rock and looked down at the distant capsule. Grainger was at work, tracing connections. She could see only the top of his head because he was on the hatch side of the vehicle. Chun was inside, probably asleep.

A vulture circled above the valley's farther rim. Roebeck had climbed to the ledge to catch the morning sun, but the thin cirrus haze combed much of the heat from the wan light. The rock was still cold from the night just past, though the hoarfrost had sublimed with the dawn.

Roebeck sighed. This wasn't a great place to relax, but she didn't need sleep and she certainly wasn't ready to resume work. Might as well view the landscape. When the weather deteriorated, as it surely would within the next weeks and months, she wouldn't have even this.

The Riders paced themselves individually. Chun was painstaking and slow; she worked fourteen, even sixteen hours out of twenty-four, though she knew as well as Roebeck did that she'd accomplish more in the long run if she took longer breaks.

Grainger was very fast when he was on, but he worked the way a natural pianist plays: for the flow of music, not the individual notes. He'd have checked his own work if necessary, but his talent wasn't in that area. Instead, Roebeck went over Grainger's work before each spell of her own. It was a good way of bending her mind into the necessary rote pathways.

Roebeck was the steadiest of the three. She put herself on a rigid schedule, five blocks of two hours each, with an hour off between shifts. She didn't work during the ten hours of darkness. Miniature floodlights illuminated the entire hull, but Roebeck's circadian rhythms were in their down-phase at night.

She could live on her nerves when that was necessary. It wasn't necessary now, so she paced herself for greatest efficiency.

Roebeck pulled the facemask down from the headband and scanned the valley for large life-forms. After a moment on optical, she switched to the thermal imaging and directed the microprocessor in the band to highlight anomalies. This ledge was forty meters above the valley floor where TC 779 rested. Roebeck climbed to it up a scree of rock cracked from the cliff face by successive thaws and freezing.

A family of giant fallow deer, six of them, moved in a straggling line toward the head of the valley where mist overhung a pond. An animal would pace ten or twenty meters forward at a time while the others waited or browsed. Occasionally one of the deer would break into a bounding run, amazingly clumsy to watch. The stag was last of all, poised like a splendid statue among a stand of cedars near the rock wall.

The team hadn't seen any large carnivores thus far during its stay, but common sense and the cautious behavior of prey animals indicated some were present in the valley. Even the rhinos were skittish, though the smallest of them—the offspring born the past year—weighed half a tonne by now.

Despite the weight, Roebeck carried a fléchette gun with attached EMP generator every time she left the vehicle. The real purpose of the weapon was to deal with the hostile ARC Riders should their transportation capsule appear, but a burst of fléchettes would discourage wolves or a lion as effectively.

For preference, Roebeck would use the acoustic pistol she carried in a shoulder holster. For absolute preference, she wouldn't do anything at all to disturb the balance of events that would have occurred without the team's presence.

One school of thought held that the further back in time one went, the greater the capacity of the temporal fabric to close over rents torn in it by humans. Those on the other side of the debate pointed out that a revision occurring in the distant past acted on an enormous temporal lever. An event here could be magnified into an asymptotic rush of change, overwhelming history and perhaps the very existence of humankind.

Grainger took the first view, though he didn't care very much. Tim was permanently adrift from his own horizon, so the question of what happened to other times was of only academic interest to him. Chun fiercely believed that the risks of causing disruption on this horizon were logarithmically greater than they would be in a historical period.

Roebeck didn't have a strong opinion of her own, save that she intended to keep the debate theoretical. It frightened her to work in the presence of humans and *not* have proper data on what to avoid. She wasn't sure even Central had such data. Jumps this deep into the timestream were beyond the capacity of revisionists working with experimental hardware. Those up the line might not have seen a reason to gather information on a distant preliterate period, since the investigation itself could disrupt the horizon.

"Nan?" Chun said, communicating through the intercom in Roebeck's headband. Chun's exceptional calm bespoke tension to those who knew her well. "The humans are back. They're moving toward us along the cliff."

"Quo, I see them," Roebeck said. Though she hadn't until Chun relayed the warning from the artificial intelligence overseeing the capsule's sensors. Roebeck knew exactly where to look, because the mother and her young daughter made a similar trek every morning.

The local humans—the Neanderthals—carried digging sticks. The child was naked. The mother wore a deerhide with the hair-side against her back and the forelegs tied over her shoulder. Occasionally she or her daughter dropped potential food items into a bag of similar material, though for the most part they seemed to devour their finds on the spot.

The pair was three hundred meters from TC 779 but somewhat closer to Roebeck because they were working along the cliff-edge scree. Roebeck knew the Neanderthals were aware of the presence of intruders on their horizon; she'd caught them watching her, watching the capsule, many times in the past—

But only from hiding, or at a distance that they probably thought shielded them from the Riders' observance. The vehicle and its inhabitants fascinated the Neanderthals, but they refused to acknowledge its existence openly. Day after day they eased closer to TC 779, but they only viewed the capsule sidelong.

"Nan, I think we ought to displace," Chun said. "We don't know what effect we could be having on these humans."

"They're Neanderthalers," commented Grainger, wholly visible now as he lifted off a section of hull plate from near the bow. "Not on the direct line, are they?"

The curved metal caught sunlight in a brilliant shimmer. The hostiles' plasma had damaged circuits even where particles didn't fully penetrate the outer hull. The team couldn't trust the computer's own assessment by pair matching between identical circuits, because many times both pairs had been destroyed.

"I don't believe our information is that complete," Chun said, calm where another person would have snapped. "I've set up a course to Australia, where—"

"No," said Roebeck. "No, I'm sorry, Quo. The risk's just too high. By now we can be fairly certain that the hostiles haven't tracked us. I don't intend to risk that concealment until we're ready to displace to the target in 1968."

The child scrambled up a pine tree. She began breaking

cones off twigs to toss to her mother. Slender branches crack-led, waggling up and down beneath her weight.

As if by chance, the child turned so that she could look to-ward Roebeck through a spray of short needles. When she saw Roebeck was watching her, the tiny face ducked down again.

Do they know we're human? Roebeck wondered. Do they *think* we're human?

"Have either of you seen a male?" Grainger asked. "I've only seen those two, but that's not a viable group."

"There aren't any other humans in the valley, so far as our sensors can tell," Chun said. "There's no sign of fire, and an all-spectra sort during the period we've been here has shown only the two individuals—day or night."

The mother chirped to her offspring. The child chittered a response and moved back from the tip of a swaying branch. Were the sounds words or merely signals like the growl of a dog to an intruder in its territory?

"The skins indicate hunting," Roebeck said, thinking aloud. "This female doesn't have either the tools or an ap-parent desire to bring down game so large. I'd say they were outcasts from a larger grouping. Or, more likely, survivors."

The child dropped to the ground in three startling leaps and retrieved her digging stick. She moved with her mother toward the loose rocks.

"Well, don't worry about our causing problems up the line, then," Grainger said. "We could teach these two to smelt iron and it still wouldn't matter. They don't have a prayer of mak-ing it through the winter."

Roebeck watched the pair of Neanderthals overturning stones. They crowed in glee whenever their fingers snatched a tidbit from a crevice.

Tim was obviously correct in his assessment, which should have made Roebeck more cheerful. She, too, worried about the unplanned effects the team might cause here.

Instead, though, Roebeck had to stifle her desire to tell Grainger to shut up until he had something useful to say.

North America

Circa 10,000 BC

Rebecca Carnes was wearing canvas-sided jungle boots, designed to drain water away from the wearer's foot. They didn't do a lot for mud, though. She thought she'd seen her share of mud in Southeast Asia, but this Mississippi Valley bottomland provided black muck that set new standards for clinginess. It was like walking through a basin of Super Glue.

"We should've gone up as far as we needed on the high ground," she said to Weigand ahead of her. "Then straight down. Instead of tramping along through this."

"The only thing that pleases me about this," Weigand replied, "is thinking that Gerd had to walk through it, too. Hold up a moment."

Carnes was glad for the pause. Weigand pulled the facemask over his eyes and scanned the overgrown terrain ahead of them. There was no visible sign of Barthuli—or anybody else—passing this way, but filters and the processing unit in the headband detected and enhanced minute changes in the infrared spectrum. "We're on course," Weigand said.

"If we are," Carnes grumbled, "we ought to be able to smell woodsmoke."

They slogged forward. The soil was too wet and too frequently flooded to support large trees, but the alders and willows grew in dense screens. She and Weigand didn't have machetes. They had to squirm through, bending slender trunks and trying not to tangle their feet in the root mats.

A sprained ankle here would be a serious problem, though Carnes supposed Weigand would be able to deal with it. The big man hadn't struck her as solidly competent until she'd blurted the trouble with Barthuli to him.

There was buzzing ahead, as if they were nearing a step-down transformer. Could water sound like that, bubbling through rocks?

"Pauli?" Carnes said.

Weigand stepped out onto a sandbar. It was a hundred yards long and twenty wide, nestled on the inner curve of a river bend. At the farther end of the sand were a score of skin-clad humans around the corpse of a mammoth.

The beast's stripped upper ribs arched against the background of river haze. Over them hovered in the order of a million flies. The noise Carnes heard as they approached was the wings of the insects sharing tons of mammoth flesh with the hunters who'd killed the animal.

One of the encampment's dogs noticed Carnes and Weigand. Probably the animal saw motion, since not even a dog's nose could make headway against the stench of the camp; though Carnes had smelled worse. Human flesh is almost liquid in its sticky, *gripping* odor, when it's had time to ripen before a bomb or a dozer blade reopens the grave.

There were ten or a dozen dogs, nondescript animals that averaged in the 40- to 60-pound range. The beasts had varied markings, some of them gray but others brindle or spotted. They didn't look like a pack of wolves as they leaped to their feet and charged the newcomers, yapping fiercely; but neither did they look anything like friendly.

The humans rose to their feet. A male hefted a spear with a white quartzite blade as long as Carnes' hand. She'd drawn her acoustic pistol. Weigand had his out as well, though he held his gas gun by the grip in his left hand.

"Don't shoot the dogs unless you have to," Weigand murmured. "It won't hurt them permanently, but I don't know how the owners will react if we send their pets off dribbling shit and screaming."

Then he added, "Gerd, you've got a lot to answer for."

Barthuli, recognizable in his blue coveralls and obviously unharmed, stood up. He'd been sitting cross-legged among the local males. He waved the piece of meat he'd been eating and said over the intercom, "Pauli and Rebecca, the dogs won't hurt you. Don't act as though you're afraid!"

"Who's acting?" Weigand said. "Major, go on ahead and I'll follow directly behind you. I'll keep them from snapping at you from behind."

Carnes strode forward, though her first thought was, *And who keeps them from hamstringing you?* Weigand's coveralls were tougher than her worn pair of jungle fatigues, and there wasn't much use in arguing with a man determined to be gallant. Besides, somebody had to be in the rear.

The dogs, yammering like White House reporters, parted before Carnes but darted in from the side. Pauli's long arm swung the gas gun back and behind him. The thick barrel smacked a dog hard enough to send the beast yelping off in agony.

After that the pack gave the two strangers more room, though the dogs accompanied them in a snarling circle all the way to the encampment. The eight adult males remained standing, but only two of them bothered to keep weapons to hand. The women and children resumed their tasks, watching Carnes and Weigand frankly.

An older, broad-chested man wore a lynx skin around his neck by the hind legs. The rest of the hide hung down in front of him like a pectoral. The beautiful, mottled pelt was shedding, and the tied legs were black with grease. The man raised his right arm high in the air, palm outward, and spoke a short sentence.

"The language isn't in our translation programs, I'm afraid," Barthuli called. His chin and tight mustache gleamed with oils from the slab of meat he'd been chewing. "With the capsule's AI, I think we could manage something, though."

Weigand dropped his pistol into a side pocket and raised his arm in deliberate mimicry of the band's leader. The gas gun was pointed down alongside his left leg.

"We wish you good luck and good hunting," Weigand said in a voice of solemn grandeur. He spoke as though the native hunters could understand his words. "We are leaving now, taking our companion with us. We will trouble you no more."

He bowed deeply to the leader. The gesture might have been unfamiliar, but the meaning was intuitively clear.

Several children fed a fire in the center of the camp. Nothing was being cooked over the flames. At intervals an old woman levered out hot stones with a pair of sticks. She rolled the stones into pits in the sand, lined with hides and filled with water in which gobbets of meat floated. The stones shattered loudly and gushed steam when they hit the water.

"Try some mammoth, Pauli," the analyst offered, motioning with his piece of meat. "And you, Rebecca. It reminds me of horse, though it's not so stringy."

Carnes shook her head curtly. Apparently Barthuli's love of the unfamiliar extended to food products. Carnes had spent five years total in Vietnam and southern China without sampling dog meat. She had no desire to try mammoth; from an animal which, judging by the odor that permeated the camp, was riper than the Department of Agriculture would have approved.

"Gerd," Weigand said pleasantly. He clasped the analyst around the shoulders, giving him and the band's leader a broad grin as he did so. "You're coming back with us now. Either you smile and walk out of the camp with me, or I gas the whole lot of them and carry you out over my shoulder. Do you have a preference?"

Carnes was impressed. From Weigand's tone, he could

have been commenting on how pretty the flower arrangement looked. She didn't in the least doubt he was ready to carry out the threat, however.

"We'll go," said Barthuli. He turned and also bowed to the hunting band's leader. "I'm very sorry I put you to this trouble, Pauli. And you even more so, Major Carnes."

A girl wearing only a deerhide apron sidled up to Carnes. She looked twenty, but her bare breasts were too firm to have suckled children, and Carnes assumed the age of marriage in this culture was puberty. The girl rolled the rip-stopped poplin sleeve of Carnes' shirt between thumb and forefinger, marveling at the slick feel of the cloth.

Carnes smiled at her. The girl wore a necklace of clamshells and galena ore strung on sinew. The mother-of-pearl contrasted pleasantly with the metallic sheen of the crystals of lead and zinc sulfide.

Carnes reached into her hip pocket, where she carried a handkerchief. The bit of cloth would be a wonder to this child—

"Major Carnes, *don't* do that, please!" Weigand said. "Come along with us now."

Carnes broke away from the girl and bowed.

She was blushing with shame. Pauli was right. Carnes turned and trotted ahead of the two men. One of the dogs barked. For the most part the pack had gone back to quarreling over scraps of meat, despite the tons of it available on the carcass itself.

"I'm sorry," Carnes said without looking around to meet Weigand's eyes.

"We've all done worse," Weigand said calmly. "But don't let Gerd here convince you that there's no rules and no need for them, all right?"

Carnes glanced over her shoulder when she reached the willows. The band of hunters had resumed its previous occupations, sated and logy with the meat of its kill. The girl waved; then Carnes was slogging again through mud and brush, an age away from the native hunters.

If she'd been thinking, she would have remembered to go straight up the bluffs and avoid the worst of the swamp; but whatever works . . .

Eurasia

Circa 50,000 BC

T he storm came over the western rim of the valley, blotting the sun. A gust of wind tried to lift the newly manufactured roof. Roebeck grabbed the curling edge and held it down.

"I think we got this up just in time," Grainger said, dropping his load next to the hopper which fed the extrusion device. He dusted his hands and stretched. The tree he'd dragged here didn't look like much—a sapling nowhere more than ten or twelve centimeters in diameter. Multiply that by six meters, though, and you have a significant weight even in cellulose.

"Almost up," said Chun, raising her voice over the wind howl. "Another minute should do it."

She moved the nozzle in careful circles. Roebeck could see she wasn't going to slim down the pillar she was extruding from the ground anchor to the hook in the corner of the roof which Roebeck now held.

Chun had calculated that six 50-millimeter pillars were needed to support the roof if the construction material was coarse cellulose. Therefore the last pillar was going to be 50 millimeters in diameter all the way up, even if the delay meant the three of them would still be outside when the violent storm broke.

"You can go in, Tim," Roebeck said.

He shrugged. "No problem," he said. He looked at his hands and added, "I've got sap on my gloves. One of you had better cycle the hatch for me."

The first raindrops hit with cracking, slapping sounds so sharp that Roebeck thought for a moment the drops were hail. Roebeck's coveralls shed the water like polished brass, but the smash of huge, cold drops on her face was thoroughly unpleasant. She turned her head away from the storm, wishing Chun would get on with it.

The transportation capsule carried basic equipment to construct shelter and camouflage outside the vehicle. The operators loaded matter into a hundred-liter hopper. The extrusion apparatus reduced the hopper's contents into its molecular constituents. The matter was processed in the belly of the device, then sprayed out to solidify a centimeter or two beyond the nozzle.

The operator could program the apparatus to duplicate the appearance of any object whose parameters were known to a sufficient degree of detail; alternatively, she could use the nozzle freehand as Chun was doing now. If you wanted more than a visual match, of course—a wooden boulder or a granite tree—you had to to dump the correct contents into the feed hopper.

The apparatus didn't care what raw material it started with. The dissolution process was electrostatic, not mechanical: diamond would work as well as wet clay. For that matter, the device could operate on the carbon dioxide in normal air, though that material's relatively low density meant the process took forever.

Roebeck had given in to the weather on the previous morning and agreed the team would need shelter before they completed their task. The loss of the Maxwell Field generators irked her more than she'd been willing to admit. By sorting gases according to energy—temperature—and weight, the Maxwell Field would have kept the team warm and dry without the need for a physical barrier.

The rain slashed down. It'd taken a day to erect the roof, and already Roebeck could see they team would need walls as well on the two windward sides. All because those *bastards*—

Roebeck barked a humorless laugh.

"Nan?" Grainger said.

"No problem," she replied. Roebeck knew perfectly well the depth of her anger about the field generators was emotion transferred from the loss of Pauli, Gerd, and the major . . . which she wasn't willing to look at straight on.

The real enemies were the revisionists who'd split the timeline. It would give Roebeck a great deal of pleasure, however, to put the hostile ARC Riders stark naked out the hatch of TC 779, to make lives for themselves in 50K. She suspected Grainger, at least, had similar thoughts; though Tim's hopes more likely involved a view through the sights of his fléchette gun.

"All right, you can let go now," Chun said, lowering the extrusion nozzle. She stepped back to take a look at her handiwork. A roe deer—a yearling doe—blundered from the storm, caromed off the new pillar, and knocked Chun down with a cry.

The animal was terrified and exhausted. Its tongue lolled loosely from its mouth, and the fur of its breast was black with frothy sweat. The deer managed to keep its feet after shouldering Chun aside. Staggering and splay-legged, it resumed its course out the back of the sheltered area. Roebeck first thought the beast was drawn by the floodlights, but it seemed oblivious of their presence.

Lightning ripped the sky. A pine growing from the cliffside a hundred meters away split in a shower of sparks; the crashing thunder reverberated down the valley.

Grainger released his sticky palm from the grip of his acoustic pistol. He frowned in irritation and embarrassment toward the deer, which had halted with its legs braced, twenty meters from the vehicle.

Roebeck bent to help Chun. Chun got her feet under her unaided and warned, "I think she broke the brace. Grab—"

Roebeck turned and saw the three giant hyenas as they sidled into the area lit by the floods reflecting off the capsule's hull. Each beast weighed more than a man, and their long jaws were as powerful as lions'.

Grainger screamed a curse as pine pitch on his hand slowed his draw to that of a mere expert. Roebeck drew her pistol as well. Chun screamed, "Don't! Don't shoot unless—"

"It's just acoustics!" Grainger said, but he poised with his finger on the trigger instead of shooting. The post broken by the deer's shoulder gave way. The corner of the roof whipped up and back in another gust of wind. Rain sparkled in the light as it lashed the ten meters of soil between the team and the beasts of prey.

The hyenas stood several meters apart. The beast in the center weighed well over a hundred kilograms. It giggled, a sound compounded of madness and malice.

"They're meant to catch the doe!" Chun explained. She stepped to Grainger's side, still holding the extrusion nozzle. "If we frighten them off, then—"

"Then nothing!" Grainger snarled, but still he didn't shoot.

The hyenas simultaneously broke to the left, putting the vehicle between them and the humans. The beasts' stunted hindquarters gave them a clumsy, shambling look as they trotted, but they had run down the roe deer in the course of this night.

The deer tried to move again. It only stumbled. The hyenas surged into view around the capsule they'd skirted. One of the hyenas grabbed the deer by its left hind leg, just above the hoof. Bones snapped beneath the crushing teeth. Another hyena clamped its long jaws onto the deer's throat, choking the bawl of despair.

The third hyena, the largest of the pack, began tearing at the victim's anus and genitals, flinging bloody spray in its enthusiasm. The free hind leg continued to thrash wildly.

Roebeck reholstered the acoustic pistol. "I'm going in," she said deliberately. "If you want to fix the roof now, feel free, but I think it can wait till morning."

The front of the storm had passed. The rain fell heavily, but despite its drumbeat on the shelter roof, Roebeck thought she could hear the slurping of the predators' feast.

North America

Circa 50,000 BC

Through the fabric of his displacement suit, Pauli Weigand felt the initial shudder of phase synchronous. "A thousand one," he counted with his eyes closed. "A thousand two."

Nan was going to be angry about the delay of almost four hours. She had a right to be angry. He'd been in charge and he'd let Gerd wander off when he knew what the analyst was like.

But that was all right, as long as Weigand wasn't stuck in a timeless nowhere.

"A thousand—"

Harmony between his suit, himself, and the time horizon. Weigand opened his eyes. He saw the other two suits, Gerd and Major Carnes. Good. He'd made sure they were on the way back to the capsule before he displaced himself.

TC 779 wasn't present. Bad. That it had been here recently was clear from the pattern burned deep in the soil by plasma which the vehicle's magnetic shielding repelled. Real bad.

"Gerd, record it!" Weigand ordered. He ejected the magazine of gas cartridges and replaced it with one of tanglefoot rounds. That left a gas shell in the chamber. Rather than extract it, then have a loose round to fool with, Weigand pointed the muzzle at a 45-degree angle toward the gray-white sky and fired.

The *toomp!* of the gun at least let Weigand pretend he was capable of doing something useful. If the gas shell didn't hit a really unlucky bird, it would land two klicks downrange. When it dispersed its contents over ten square meters of snow, it might possibly knock some voles or rabbits unconscious in their tunnels.

Tanglefoot cartridges weren't much of a choice against hostiles armed with plasma weapons, but they were the best Weigand had available. You use what you've got.

"Carnes, come close to me!" Weigand shouted. She'd drawn her pistol, indicating she understood the problem, but acoustics would be as useless as gas. What the three of them needed to do was get the hell out of here. Weigand would have to carry Carnes with him when he displaced, or the best she'd do was become separated from the two ARC Riders forever.

Weigand switched his suit to spot and vector him to anything electronic; anything alive that weighed over 50 kilograms, and anything metal over a hundred grams. Immediately his visor streaked with dozens of pale green lines as though the optics had shattered.

He swore and clicked off the electronics parameter. He hadn't thought about the Maxwell Field generators, abandoned around the ellipse they'd mostly cleared of snow before the heat source on TC 779 vanished.

TC 779 had displaced, not vanished. If the revisionist attack had destroyed the vehicle, there'd have been more sign than trenches burned across the prairie. Nan, Tim, and Quo were fine, preparing even now to wax those revisionist bastards' asses.

Which is what Weigand and Barthuli were going to do, too. Standard operating procedure required every member of a separated team to carry on with the mission. The mission took absolute precedence.

But first Weigand had to get his people out of here. The

location had drawn the hostiles once. They could be back anytime, any *time* at all.

Carnes was standing beside him, just out of contact. A *really* good teammate. Weigand turned up the inside of his wrist so he could get to the controls, then set his suit to revert to the previous setting.

The wrist controls were as flexible as international Morse code, another two-element system. It took a while to get the touch, and a lot longer to execute a complex instruction set flawlessly. Weigand wasn't about to tell a completely green hand how to set her displacement suit to revert.

Several Maxwell Field generators had melted in the splashing ions. One seemed to have burned; it'd taken the direct charge of a badly aimed beam. The generators' gray plastic casings were almost as inert as basalt. At the temperature of nitrogen plasma, the unit disintegrated to its constituent atoms, some of which flared as they recombined with the oxygen of the air.

The same thing would happen to a man, even a man in armor, if the beam hit him squarely. Him or her.

Weigand wiped the displacement readings from his display. "All right, hug me," he said. Carnes was a solid person, too smart to act on assumptions that she'd pulled from thin air.

With his naked eye, Weigand could tell that the attack on the vehicle had occurred some while in the past. Snow melted by plasma and TC 779's heater, preparing the area sheltered by the Maxwell Fields, had refrozen into solid ice. The ambient temperature was in the order of −50°C, cold but not cold enough to flash-freeze boiling water at normal pressures.

"Gerd, are you ready?" Weigand asked. Bad as he wanted them to clear the area, Weigand knew the team would need as much information as possible to plan what to do next.

The recorders integral to the displacement suits were gathering data, but the specialized rig Barthuli panned across the site was more subtle and detailed by an order of magnitude.

The analyst had unlimbered his flat gray case as quickly as Weigand reloaded with tanglefoot rounds.

"I suppose I've reached the level of diminishing returns," Barthuli said. Weigand could imagine the slight smile Gerd would wear as he spoke the words. "Human life isn't long enough to assemble all the possible information, of course."

"All right, then we'll revert to 10K," Weigand said. As he spoke, he turned his head within the helmet, covering his surroundings with direct vision as well as the compressed panorama and the suit's own—vastly more capable—multispectral sensors. "Major Carnes, here we go."

Weigand pressed the tit on his left wrist. The horizon around him vanished into limbo, while he wondered what in hell he was going to do next.

Eurasia

Circa 50,000 BC

Tim Grainger stood and stretched. His face bore a broad, slow grin. "You know," he said, "I think we've got a working transportation capsule again." Then he added, "I think I'll put my armor on. Usually I'd worry about it turning to a straitjacket if they EMPed us, but that doesn't"—his smile went as hard as the steel maw of a power shovel—"seem to be the first likelihood with this bunch. Our opposite numbers."

"Nan, I'd like to run one more cold check on the system," Chun Quo said from her usual seat. "Could I—"

"Quo," said Grainger as he unslung the fléchette gun he'd carried even in the vehicle since the attack in North America. "There's billions of possible circuit combinations. We can't check a significant proportion of them, but we've checked a hundred and twelve without a glitch of any kind. Statistically, another hundred and twelve isn't going to change anything except the length of time our hair grows here in 50K."

Roebeck eyed the display. Bright sun gleamed from snow on the bushes and grass tufts. The ground had remained warm while the snow fell during the night. The white fluff remained unmelted only where it was elevated from the soil.

"You've got an hour," Roebeck said to Chun. "I'm going for a walk."

Grainger grimaced.

Roebeck raised her eyebrow toward him. "She doesn't complain about you keeping *your* security blanket with you all the time we've been here, Tim," she said.

Grainger looked startled, then genuinely amused. He patted the receiver of his fléchette gun and said, "You've got a point there, chief."

Instead of donning his displacement suit, Grainger flipped out a seat beside Chun's. "Let's both of us run checks while the lady mistress is gone, Quo," he said.

Roebeck smiled as she went out the hatch, carrying another fléchette/EMP combination. Tim and Quo were a good team.

The wind had died when the snowfall began, and the air remained as still as marble. Roebeck ducked beneath the eaves as she walked through the open end of the shelter.

She filled her lungs with the clean, unfiltered air. Roebeck wore gloves, but the air wasn't uncomfortably cool on her face and she didn't feel the need to switch on her coveralls' supplemental heating element. The fabric formed a nearly perfect insulating layer when conditions called for it.

She wouldn't miss this site, though she'd found it a pleasant one for the most part. Geologic and evolutionary change was so slow that TC 779's dump sites in 50K seemed static from one century to the next. This Eurasian valley was an interesting variation on the plains to which revisionists were consigned.

And the valley wasn't, of course, empty of human life.

Roebeck knew she'd come out looking for the Neanderthal mother and daughter. Chun could probably have told her where the pair was at this moment—assuming they were still in the valley—but Roebeck had been too embarrassed to ask.

Roebeck had been a crèche child—so was Quo, so were most of their contemporaries. She didn't miss the lack of *a* mother, *her* mother, in her development . . . but there was a fascination in watching a child interact with the woman who had given birth to her.

She walked toward the cliff, cradling her weapon in the crook of her left arm. The EMP generator made the combination muzzle-heavy and hard to sling, not that Grainger seemed to have much problem with his similar rig. At this point there was small chance of the hostile ARC Riders hitting them a second time, but Roebeck wasn't about to take a risk with the team's safety. She'd already lost half their personnel by being complacent.

The cliff had weathered into meter-high steps mounting from the scree which formed the tailings of the process. Roebeck had climbed that way a score of times. The ledge midway up was deep enough to be a comfortable seat.

She noticed a wink of red on the lowest step. She moved toward it, choosing her footing carefully on the slope of shattered rock.

The object was a garnet the size of her thumb, chipped laboriously from the hard matrix in which it had formed. It was no more than a curiosity in Roebeck's day; crystals of any shape and material were as cheap as any other rock. To those who placed it here for the stranger to find, however, it was an object of unique beauty.

Roebeck raised the garnet to the sun, seeing shadows wake and ripple in the ruddy depths. She looked about her again.

Two pairs of eyes watched from a clump of cedars only fifty meters away. The Neanderthals were lying on their bellies to peer through interwoven branches at the base of the four-meter trees. Beyond the cedars was a mixed copse of hard- and softwoods, nearly a hectare in extent. The wings of birds flashed among the trees in the morning light.

Roebeck slipped the garnet into one of the pockets at the waist of her coveralls. She thought for a moment, then took off one glove. She reached up to the flattened starburst on the left side of her collar, the insignia of the Anti-Revision Command. Hers was silver, not gold like the others', because she was team leader. Pressure from her bare thumb and index finger released its grip on the cloth.

A rounded boulder, an outcrop rather than a straggler from the cliff face, domed the soil about halfway between Roebeck and the cedars, though not quite in a direct line. She sauntered toward it, turning her head slightly to continue looking at the faces beneath the cedars.

She smiled, though she wasn't certain the expression would have the same meaning to Neanderthals.

Branches crackled in the copse. The gathering volume of noise ended in a damp thump and silence. Snow loosened by dawn from a treetop swept lower limbs clean as it fell, a miniature avalanche.

The abrupt changes of temperature would make this slope of the valley dangerous. Rock split as it warmed and expanded during the daytime. Water which seeped into the cracks froze overnight and further shattered the fabric. Slabs would fall without warning, crushing anyone who happened to be in their way.

Roebeck wouldn't have to worry about that after today. As for the Neanderthals, well, it was their world to adapt to or die. And eventually everything died. An ARC Rider knew that well.

She held the starburst high so that it winked brightly, then set it on the boulder. Nodding to the Neanderthals behind their screen, Roebeck walked a dozen steps away and sat down on a tussock of grass. The cap of half-congealed snow crunched beneath her, but the coveralls were waterproof.

She waited, watching the cedars.

Roebeck half expected to hear a complaint from Chun. The vehicle was only two hundred meters away. Chun and Grainger were certainly watching their leader on the display. Chun, at least, would be sick with fear and anger at what Roebeck was doing.

She had a right to be. At best, Roebeck was acting unprofessionally; at worst—and Roebeck didn't believe this, not really, but Chun did—she might be causing a revision more overwhelming than the one that had cut the team off from its own timeline.

Roebeck grimaced and started to rise. She'd retrieve the starburst, leave the garnet in its place, and TC 779 would go on about its necessary business.

The Neanderthal child wriggled out from her hiding place. She didn't seem to touch the branches, though they appeared too tightly interwoven to pass a squirrel.

For a moment the child stood, as motionless as the trees behind her. Her face broke into a toothy grin, though again Roebeck couldn't be sure the expression was equivalent to a modern smile.

Roebeck smiled back anyway. The child scampered to the boulder. Roebeck had seen her wearing a cape of plaited grass in recent days, but this sunny morning the child was nude again.

The Neanderthal stared at the insignia from a distance of two meters, shifting her position so that her shadow didn't fall across the glitter. Her mother continued to watch from the cedars.

The child leaped for the starburst and caught it in her hands. The movement was startlingly quick; the act of someone who had learned to snatch birds from low branches or go hungry some mornings. Poised to run, she stared at Roebeck. Her eyes were the same startling blue that Roebeck had first noticed in the mother.

Roebeck nodded and continued to smile. The expression was becoming a strain, but she was afraid to relax it lest the Neanderthals misunderstand.

The child put the insignia in the corner of her mouth and bit down on it with molars that could crush a walnut. Roebeck blinked in surprise. The starburst was beryllium monocrystal, proof against even Neanderthal jaws. It just hadn't occurred to her that the child would test the object in that particular way.

Roebeck stood up very slowly. She held the fléchette gun crossways with one hand at the butt and the other on the muzzle, letting her arms hang full length. The Neanderthals would think the weapon was a club, but they should understand that Roebeck wasn't handling it in a threatening way.

The child stiffened. Her mother croaked a command or warning to her. The child turned her head toward the cedars, chirped a phrase that lilted by contrast with her mother's demand, and looked at Roebeck again. Wearing a big grin, the girl dabbed the starburst against the side of her neck—the place it had ridden on Roebeck's collar.

Even though Roebeck was erect and facing in the right general direction, she hadn't seen the hyenas slinking toward her through the copse. The first warning to Roebeck and the Neanderthals came when the three powerful beasts lunged the last twenty meters toward the child.

Two of the hyenas came from the right of the clump of cedars while the other passed to the left. They were spread on a broad front to cut the child off if she fled to either side. They didn't notice the mother until she burst from cover with a scream of despair and a meter-long hickory club.

The child bawled in fear and ran, back toward her mother and the jaws of the oncoming hyenas.

Roebeck shouldered the fléchette gun. The range was a little long for acoustics and anyway the lethal weapon was already in her hands. She squeezed off a burst at the biggest of the three brutes, firing over the child's head.

The coils surged, at each pulse vaporizing a fléchette's aluminum driving band into a conductive vapor and ejecting it from the bore by magnetic repulsion. The aluminum combined with air in a white flash at the muzzle. The needle of orthocrystaline tungsten snapped toward the target at a dozen times the speed of sound.

The hyena spun and snapped at the air, then came on again. Tiny flecks of blood sparkled on the yellow and black of its spotted hide.

The fléchettes were meant to pierce heavy armor. In flesh they merely punched a pinpoint hole. The wounds gaped momentarily from hydrostatic shock, but the plasticity of muscle slapped the temporary cavities shut again.

When the fléchettes hit bone, the bone cracked. Where they hit organs of low resilience like the spleen, the tissues ruptured from the shockwave and began spilling the animal's life out into its body cavity. But for all their lethality, the dense needles had almost no stopping power.

Roebeck hosed the right-hand hyena, an easier shot because the Neanderthal child wasn't at risk from the projectiles. Recoil lifted her weapon and torqued it to the right, but Roebeck managed to rip both spine and cranial vault when the beast's spasmodic leap kept it in the path of the tungsten stream.

The Neanderthal mother swung her club horizontally, using both arms and all the strength of her shoulders. The hickory struck the left-hand hyena's flank. The club split like a marrow bone with a shower of splinters and a crack worthy of a lightning bolt. The hyena spun sideways, its pelvis crushed by the blow.

The center hyena leaped like the cat it resembled as closely as it did a dog. It knocked down the child with its forepaws and had her face in its jaws before Roebeck could swing the heavy fléchette gun back on target.

The Neanderthal mother screamed. Roebeck screamed, because she couldn't shoot without raking the child as well.

The hyena leaped up on its hind legs, snapping its empty jaws on the air. It turned a backflip and landed on its side several meters away. Its four limbs flailed without rhythm or direction.

The *whack* of the single tungsten fléchette that had decorticated the beast echoed flatly from the valley wall. A spray of brain tissue and bone chips stained the snowy grass in a direct line from where the hyena's skull had been—and back to Tim Grainger, standing beside the vehicle 200 meters away with his gun at his shoulder.

The mother snatched up her offspring and mopped saliva from the child's face with one hand. The girl blubbered, but she wasn't seriously injured. Though the long canines had punctured her scalp, the fléchette jellied the beast's brain an instant before the jaws crushed down with full force.

Grainger aimed and fired again. The third hyena had been squirming forward despite its shattered hindquarters. The animal twitched and relaxed with a sigh. Its staring eyes were bulged, driven almost from their sockets by the shockwave that slammed like a maul through the brain and optic nerves.

Roebeck knelt down. She felt so weak that she had to plant the butt of her fléchette gun on the soil like a third leg to prevent her from falling over.

"Nan, are you all right?" Chun Quo called over the communicator. Grainger ran toward the scene with his weapon held at high port, close to his chest. "Were you hit?"

Nan Roebeck had just revised the past. She didn't know, she couldn't guess, what that meant for the timeline from which she sprang.

"Quo, I'm fine," Roebeck said, letting the vocative autokey her headband to transmit. "I'm woozy, that's all. I'm fine."

All Roebeck knew for sure about what had just happened was that she'd do it again, whatever the cost, to keep from watching hyenas devour a child in front of her.

The Neanderthal mother trotted for the woods, carrying her daughter. Her eyes were on Grainger, and she slanted slightly away from his approach.

The child squirmed out of her mother's arms and ran back. Roebeck thought the child was coming to her. She stood up, swaying with the effort.

The child dropped to her knees and scrabbled on the bloody ground where the hyena had seized her. Her mother grabbed her around the waist and snarled through bared teeth.

The girl raised the starburst emblem and cooed in delight as her mother carried her into the forest. She waved toward Roebeck.

Grainger halted beside Roebeck. He was breathing hard from the run and trying not to show it. He wagged his fléchette gun in ironic salute and said, "Not really the tool of choice for the job, but she'll do in a pinch."

Roebeck embraced the gunman. "Thanks Tim," she said. "Nice to know that if I screw up, I've still got friends."

Then she said, "Now let's go see if there's still a 1968 for us to straighten out."

North America

Circa 10,000 BC

Rebecca Carnes wished she could scratch her right side. The jacket of her fatigues was bunched up over her hip, and it itched as if a mouse were crawling over her. A third figure appeared on the meadow. The displacement suits didn't move into sight, they just *were*. It was like a trick with mirrors, where a minute change of angle switched the visible scene entirely.

"Don't take your armor off!" Pauli's voice commanded. He was holding his fat-barreled weapon ready. Carnes supposed it was a grenade launcher, but guns weren't her line of territory.

What Rebecca Carnes had learned in a war zone, then found to be true in civilian life as well, is that nobody really knows what's going on while it's happening. She'd been at Long Binh with the 93d during the 1968 Tet Offensive. The night was a zoo of orderlies running into the wards shouting the alert status, constant explosions she'd thought were outgoing artillery (some of them had been incoming mortar rounds), and attempts to get the patients onto the floor for safety—then back in bed when somebody claimed the alert level had dropped to yellow again.

Carnes had done what was in front of her, without having the slightest notion of what the situation really was. The next morning they'd found a VC with a satchel charge, shot dead within fifty feet of the barracks Carnes normally slept in, not that anybody'd gotten much sleep *that* night. The whole thing was a razor's edge from catastrophe, and she hadn't known any more about it than she had at Firebase Schaydin during her last night in her own time.

More to the point, the Long Binh base commander hadn't known what was going on, either; and if the commander of US forces in Vietnam did know, he'd sure worked hard to obscure the fact. His statements were so far out of touch with reality that Carnes had suspected he'd landed on his head once too often while he was a paratrooper.

Since she'd come to that realization, chaos didn't frighten Carnes the way it once had. She'd do her job if she had one and try to stay out of the way if she clearly didn't. She was willing to attempt something even if she wasn't sure what the right *thing* was, but she was well aware of how easily blind motion could make a bad situation worse.

Right now, Carnes was keeping her mouth shut and obeying orders. If somebody dropped with a bullet through the lungs or had a foot blown off by a mine, she'd be back on the job in an eyeblink.

"I have a scenario, Pauli," Barthuli said. "Any time you're ready to examine it."

"You've run this through already?" Weigand demanded. He sounded as much angry as amazed.

"A matter of giving the correct instructions to the equipment," the analyst said in mild reproof. "Processing time is minuscule, you know."

Carnes heard Weigand sigh. Pauli had fallen into the common human trap of believing merely mechanically complicated things were difficult. It bothered him that Barthuli could solve what was basically a mathematical problem almost instantly. Pauli was their leader. He thought he should be able to solve his problem—how to rejoin the rest of the team, how to change time back to a pattern Carnes had never known— at least as quickly as the analyst could re-create a past reality. Instead, it/they remained an intractable mass in Weigand's consciousness.

Barthuli had a handheld computer as advanced from the Crays of Carnes' day as her own brain was improved from whatever it was that guided bacteria. Matters that could be reduced to number crunching were easy—like landing a man on the moon as opposed to solving poverty, where the very terms slipped like water through the nets of analysis.

It took enormous skill to repair a soldier's bullet-ripped heart, lungs, and spleen, but it was mechanical skill: *surgeon* meant literally "manual laborer." Bringing back the mind of a man found catatonic, alive and unmarked in the midst of a dozen mangled corpses—that was a job for genius or for God, and Rebecca Carnes hadn't believed in God since her first tour in Nam.

"Yeah, sure, run it," Weigand said. "Sorry, Gerd. I'm jumpy."

Weigand shifted his weapon closer to his body. It looked to Carnes as if the big man was prepared to fight but no longer expected he'd need to. The prairie and nearby woods were much the same as when the trio left them a few minutes earlier. The only change she could see was the score of shaggy buffaloes grazing on the next rise.

A picture formed—flashed—in the air an apparent meter from Carnes' eyes. Her own armor must be projecting the image, since Barthuli and Weigand were facing in different directions.

Two transportation capsules—identical as far as Carnes could tell, except that the hatch of one was open—stood in near contact. Beams of ravening light ripped from the open hatch and splashed the other capsule.

The target disappeared. Seconds later, the hatch of the remaining capsule closed and that vehicle also vanished. Only then did Carnes recognize the background as the scarred, snowclad prairie to which the three of them had returned in 50,000 BC.

"How did you do that?" she demanded. "We weren't there. How did you get pictures of what happened?"

Barthuli's helmet didn't move, but she suspected the analyst's head had turned toward her as he said, "It's one possible scenario of what happened, Rebecca. There are certain verifiable facts: the type of weapons used, the location from which they'd have had to be fired in order to give the pattern of reflection damage to the surroundings. The rest is supposition—by my computer, merely a machine, as to the most probable series of events that would give rise to those facts."

"But it *isn't* probable, is it?" Weigand asked, trying to come to grips with an image he hadn't expected. "The revisionists couldn't have a capsule like ours."

"The revisionists we've been tracking couldn't have plasma weapons of the type involved in this attack," Barthuli said. "These are standard—ARC standard—atmospheric nitrogen weapons, not the laser-pumped tritium guns that some vehicles mounted in the mid-23d century. Remember, the modeling program"—he lifted his tiny sensor pack/computer between his gloved thumb and forefinger to call attention to it—"has the benefit of a full spectral analysis of the vestiges of the attack."

Weigand's left hand rose to his helmet, then fell away without touching the faceplate. He'd forgotten he was wearing a displacement suit; he'd been about to rub his eyes with his palm.

"Sure, Central's still there," Weigand said with a pretense of calm. "It's just not our Central."

He cleared his throat. The intercom system reproduced the sound perfectly. "I'm not sure what to do next," he said simply. "Gerd—"

"We needn't rush into this," the analyst said. He was temporizing. He didn't know what the right move was, either, though he didn't sound particularly concerned about the matter. "If the other Anti-Revision Command could determine the point to which we'd displaced, they'd have attacked us also."

"Maybe I'll think better if I'm out of this armor," Weigand muttered. His hand moved toward but not *to* the latch of his breastplate.

"The other ARC Riders don't matter to you, do they?" Carnes said. "I mean, if you correct the change Watney and his friends made, the future beyond them vanishes. Right?"

It wasn't so much that pieces were falling together in her mind. Rather, extraneous bits had fallen away, no longer camouflaging the real needs. Emergency medical personnel learned very quickly to focus on critical matters, ignoring things that weren't life-threatening and could be passed until there was leisure to deal with them.

"Yes, but we can't go knocking around Washington in 1968," Weigand protested. "We don't even know who we'd be looking for."

"These suits can't hover out of phase, Rebecca," Barthuli added. His tone was too dry to be patronizing. Perhaps he didn't remember that Weigand had explained all that to Carnes before her first displacement.

"The other, ah, hostiles will spot us long before we've located our target," Weigand said.

"You don't know who we're looking for," Carnes said with a tight rein on her temper. It had been a long, hard day for her, that was the gospel truth. "But Kyle Watney does, and I know how to find Watney in 1991. If he's alive, at least. He'll be coming back to the compound in Son Tay."

"Rebecca," Barthuli said, "that's very good. I didn't—I might not ever have considered that. Of course, there's still the matter of transportation. Our suits can't displace geographically, and we're in North America, not Southeast Asia."

Pauli Weigand slung his weapon so that he could slap his armored palms together in triumph. "Don't worry about that, Gerd!" he said. "You just give us a setting that won't get any of the three of us in the way of our former selves. I'll take care of transport when you get us to the right horizon."

Carnes thought the big man was going to clap his hands again. Instead, he put his arm around her shoulder and patted her, hard enough to make the suit ring like a shell hitting armor.

"Now we're moving!" he said.

Lincoln Memorial, Washington, DC

March 15, 1967

Grainger couldn't get over how different from his memories of the district, circa 2025, everything seemed in this 1967 Washington as he hiked uphill toward Memorial Bridge and the Lincoln Memorial beyond.

On the Ides of March, one year and two weeks before the President of the United States was to make the speech that plunged his country and his world into a nuclear nightmare, all looked prosperous and orderly inside the Beltway under a bright spring sun. There was no sign on this horizon of the infrastructural stresses that would make Grainger's native Washington a cultural war zone crumbling underfoot, eroding visibly as it struggled to fund vast entitlement programs for its insatiable underclasses.

Here and now, federal green spaces were being cut with martial precision. The air was filled with the sounds of mowers and the smell of fresh-cut grass, masking the dull roar and exhaust fumes of an endless stream of gleaming internal-combustion autos. Young red tulips planted by the thousands along Memorial Bridge and its traffic arteries bloomed in the grass like tears shed by a bloody god. Across the bridge, the columned portico of Lincoln's resting place gleamed bone white.

Hide in plain sight, Grainger thought. His coveralls set to mimic sixties government issue, he hiked uphill toward the bridge and his rendezvous point. Behind was Arlington National Cemetery, where the capsule waited, displaced, with Roebeck and Chun safely out of phase.

He checked his chronograph: five minutes had elapsed since he'd left the capsule. Ten to go until pickup.

Nan Roebeck's initial orders had been to displace TC 779 straight to the safe house. Grainger's skin had crawled at the thought. There were too many unanswered questions to assume that the safe house was in any way safe.

Grainger had made his case to her while TC 779 was still out of phase: "Let me go meet this Calandine, our supposed agent in place, on neutral ground. Use our comm to ring him on his horizon's phone, set a meet at a specific time and place. Then we risk one of us to take a baseline—not all of us if something's changed."

"Everything's changed," Chun Quo reminded him implacably, with her control wands moving nervously as if she were knitting. Every time the wands clicked together, the sound grated on Grainger's nerves. She was an inscrutable Oriental Fate knitting his shroud. Those wands controlled all their fates in real time—or the person controlling the wands did. One mistake now and—

Grainger didn't like Orientals. It was a societal prejudice, one he'd brought with him from his own time into the ARC Riders. The US Department of Energy from his native horizon had an agenda of economic espionage and industrial warfare against Asian countries inside its International Programs element, where he'd worked.

In his day, you competed with the Asians or you were absorbed by them, turned into slave labor in a milieu where non-Asians could only rise so high. The US was just barely holding the line when he'd opted out of his horizon, in 2025, despite his enviable position among one of the most powerful and aggressive of Western elites, the Department of Energy hierarchy.

Amid the flood tide of ravenous underclasses created by the bankrupt US educational and welfare system, the US government had been staying afloat—barely—by empowering the ivory-tower-supported best of the best, subject to no rules but one: win, at any cost. Maintain national security through innate or imported technological superiority. Buy it. Steal it. Reverse-engineer it. Protect it. Field it aggressively in service of the remaining US and friendly Occidental elites who could still read, write, think, and act globally.

Grainger had done a lot of Asians in his time. Personally and through field assets. He'd been consciously ignoring Chun's Oriental background since he'd joined the ARC Riders, as much for his own survival in a new milieu as for the good of the team. But this revision—this mission; the berserker Orientals at the new Central which had supplanted his own—made Orientals the enemy. He knew it. Chun knew it. And Roebeck knew it.

And now they all had to ignore it, for the sake of the team. Or the team wouldn't be a team much longer. Attrition rate in this unit might already be more than was survivable. Losing your home base usually was.

In the sanctity of the out-of-phase TC 779, Roebeck had said, "Tim, I still like the first plan. Chun delivers you and me to the safe house in DC. We make a surprise entrance, giving no warning to anyone who might want to conceal a changed affiliation." She'd smiled mirthlessly. "We wear our suits for the insertion, take a look around. Chun waits out of phase as a safeguard against another attack. If it seems safe, we get out of the suits and stash them out of phase, too, gather some ground truth, get our legs on this horizon."

It made a sort of rudimentary sense, if you trusted Chun implicitly. Now that they were about to commit to a time horizon very close to the one in which Grainger had been raised, he couldn't prevent old instincts from coming to the surface.

"You're the mission commander," he'd reminded Roebeck coldly. "I'm just giving you my recommendations."

Chun said, "You just don't want to wear your suit, and you

know it. Any excuse . . ." Chun trailed off when he glared at her.

"Fuck my suit," he retorted. "It's immaterial to this discussion."

Everybody knew what subtext was material.

"Tim," Roebeck said warningly.

"Look, Nan," Grainger pleaded, shifting in the suddenly constraining environment of TC 779. "We don't have any way to judge whether this agent in place, Calandine, has been compromised. We can't be sure of any mission supports that Central set up on this horizon, let alone what amounts to a sleeper agent—not his affiliation or anything else. Remember, it's their Central that's policing this timeline. It's their timeline, so we've got to assume it's their safe house. You can't even be sure whose technology is superior on this revision, let alone who's on what side." There, it was out in the open. Sort of. "We nearly had our clocks cleaned back there in 50K, remember."

Nan Roebeck was the strategist, the team leader, not Grainger. Tim Grainger was—always had been—an operator, and his concerns were tactical. Had to be.

Tactically, it didn't make any sense to expose yourself to an arguably superior enemy force without some credible intel or at least some recon. He wanted to do that recon, and do it alone. He did *not* want to do it *en masse*, with the two women and a vehicle that was more important to the team survival than any of their individual lives.

He especially did not want to do it with Roebeck, leaving TC 779 in Chun's hands, trusting Chun with both their lives and with the mission's success. Not when Chun, who was as Oriental as the revisionists who'd created this timeline, just might let her heritage cloud her judgment while she waited out of phase in a vehicle that was everybody's last best hope.

He stared at Roebeck, willing her to see his point of view. He couldn't be any more blatant than he had been. He wouldn't.

Roebeck stared back, willing him to see her point of view. Unit cohesion was everything at a time like this. He could destroy this mission as easily as any revisionists by under-mining her leadership or the shared purpose of the team.

Finally Roebeck had nodded, her eyes too bright. "You're not sure it's safe to displace directly into the safe house. I can credit that. But displacing *anywhere* may be our most risky action, and we have to do that to function. Remember what happened—"

"We know what happened, but not how—not what signature they're using to find us, not for certain," Chun Quo said. "We only *think* we know what not to do. If we're wrong and we do the wrong thing, we give them a homing beacon."

"We can't sit still forever," Nan told her. "We have to act. They'll react. We'll be ready." She shrugged. "That's the job."

Chun wasn't finished. "Tim, if you do this your way—without a displacement suit—that's your style and nobody's arguing it's not correct for this environment—and we displace again to pick you up, then displace again into the safe house . . . who's to say we're not leaving enough signature for the Orientals"—she said it flatly—"from their Central to fix our position?"

Grainger felt as if Chun had slapped him across the face. She'd been the first to say "Orientals," not him. He just wanted to get out of there. "Nan, give me fifteen minutes with this guy. You monitor the realtime events from here. Chun can grab me off the pavement if it gets too dicey. I'll agree with the agent on a time up the line to displace to the safe house. I mean, what if he's got someone else using it today?"

"You mean, what if the enemy—if Central's people are using it. Yes, I see." Nan Roebeck's long-jawed face squared off. "But I can't risk not being able to get to you. . . ."

Chun Quo was clicking her wands impatiently. "I'll get him. Minute 16 from mission start. Or any minute you like better, Nan. Just try to make it to the designated pick-up co-ordinates, Grainger, so I can pick you up the easy way for the inevitable hot wash to come." A "hot wash" was what you did after everything went wrong in an exercise that surfaced operational problems and procedural errors. Chun smiled sweetly. "Can't lose our only remaining white male."

"Let's get these time frames fixed for insertion and extraction," Roebeck snapped. So they'd decided. Or Nan Roebeck had. She was still that good.

Now he was roaming the 1967 afternoon, because Roebeck was that good, watching for a man who'd lean against the plinth of the statue on the left. Whatever she really thought, Nan Roebeck had let him go alone. She'd stayed with the ship.

Grainger checked his chronograph. He had nine minutes before pickup. His facemask membrane was up on his forehead, obscured by a sweatband tied over it. The sweatband looked like indigenous nonanachronistic cloth from this time, but it was transparent in all EM wavelengths. TC 779 could record what he saw. The other ARC Riders couldn't talk to him or hear him in real time while they were out of phase. Effectively, he was on his own.

The walkways on the bridge were full of jogging soldiers and strolling flower children in fringe and bell-bottoms. The soldiers and the flower children were so wary of each other, he moved unremarked among them.

Eight minutes left. The statues of gilded horses, men, and women across the bridge had been given to the US by the French, Grainger remembered. The man waiting under the scant shadow of the left-hand statue on the Lincoln Memorial side of the bridge was wearing the blue blazer and chinos of his spookish kind, and studying a pro forma map of Virginia. He was sporting the agreed-upon red socks under his penny loafers.

Grainger walked up to the stranger slowly. Grainger wasn't wearing any identifying insignia—best not to pick a polarizing affiliation, best not to make himself an easy target if the agent had switched sides. This close to the Lincoln Memorial, the air smelled of carbon monoxide and marijuana. Seven minutes.

The golden horse statues, each with a naked man astride and a naked woman beside, stared down protectively on the soldiers who jogged in formation in white T-shirts and running shorts, spraying perspiration on the brightly clad civilians as they passed.

The man who should be Calandine ignored everyone until Grainger walked up to him and said what he'd agreed to say: "Excuse me, does that map show you how to get to Pentagon Mall parking?"

The man squinted at him, got sunglasses from his breast pocket, and put them on slowly. Then he said what he'd agreed to say: "I'm going to take a cab there now myself. I can drop you."

"Great. Thanks. I have to meet my cousin." Having recited the last bit of rote formula, Grainger relaxed one notch. He took his hand out of his pocket, where it had been curled around the reassuring grip of his acoustic pistol, and scratched the band of his chronograph. Six minutes. His wrist was perspiring.

Somewhere on the bridge, flower children and soldiers were exchanging angry words. Calandine looked over his shoulder. "Better catch that cab before they start rounding up those kids. District police and National Guard will close off the area at the first sign of trouble."

The dark-haired Calandine touched his sunglasses, stepped off the curb, and waved. A blue and white cab, which had been idling on the shoulder, rolled into gear and pulled up in front of them.

Calandine opened a rear door and motioned Grainger inside, then got in the front seat. The driver didn't wait for directions, but drove across the bridge and toward Arlington National Cemetery.

Five minutes. UFO mythology was alive and well in the sixties, so if worse came to worst, Project Blue Book would have another entry when Chun and Roebeck showed to pick up Grainger—even if it had to be in the middle of a highway.

Calandine opened a briefcase that he hadn't carried into

the cab. "Here you go. Credit card. Local currency. You can use the card to get traveler's checks if you run out of money, but we don't think you will." The wad of greenbacks wasn't more than half an inch thick, but the denominations were high—and therefore traceable. "House keys. Car keys. And my card, with all my phone numbers on it." Calandine grinned and showed front teeth trimmed with gold.

"Who's 'we'?" Grainger wanted to know as he took the lot. Nobody who goes to the trouble of providing himself with a driver and cab as cover, and sits in the front when you're in the back, is feeling real trusting, or leaving anything to chance.

"Traveler's Aid," Calandine said, and looked at his watch pointedly. "You've got what—four and a half minutes to find that particular gravestone you like so much. You can speak freely here." The "cabbie" was driving into Arlington National Cemetery, as if to cut across to the Pentagon. All as arranged, so far.

"You're the one who ought to have the questions," Grainger said softly. "Can I go to the site now, instead?" It was so hot in the cab that perspiration was trickling down his neck.

"Sure." Calandine touched the driver's shoulder. "Take us to 12th and E." There was no hesitation in the agent's response.

"Never mind, I guess I better make my milestones." Just checking.

The field agent took off his sunglasses and peered at Grainger before peevishly redirecting the driver back onto his original course, which caused a minor traffic accident among the other autonomously piloted ground vehicles. Brakes squealed. Someone cursed in Spanish and showed a fist as Calandine's cab veered around a dilapidated car now stalled across a lane and a half, with a smaller red car conjoining its left rear bumper.

Two minutes. Calandine said, "I'm a busy man. You people are putting some strain on our arrangement as it is. Don't push it. There's nobody near your site to bother you, if that's what this is about. You need anything more, don't hesitate to call."

You people?

The cab stopped. Grainger said, "Walk me over to see my dead uncle, cousin."

Calandine got out of the front seat; Grainger got out of the rear seat. The briefcase beside the cabbie was propped open by the snout of a revolver.

When both men had slammed the doors closed, Grainger said, "What if I call this number?" Grainger tapped the front of the other man's government-issue calling card, which had an eagle-headed seal in the left upper corner. "What happens?"

"Somebody answers, who's sitting in that office at that desk, and answers to my name. That's the way it works. I say 'Hi, Cousin,' and you're connected."

"Thanks for reassuring me. If you see any of my people around, you be sure to let me know. Leave a message at the site. Consider it part of your job."

Calandine's face, previously indeterminate, now looked closer to fifty than forty. "You expecting anybody else?"

Grainger shrugged and looked off into the distance, over the marble teeth of death, row upon row of military gravestones stretching to the horizon. He could see the Kennedy eternal flame, still burning up on the hill. "We're having a family reunion, with a couple of lady friends. And maybe a surprise party. So you wouldn't want to drop in unannounced."

"Son, I know my job. Let's hope you know yours. Things are getting real dangerous around here. Gonna have worse than martial law—gonna have anarchy. Gonna round up all those hippies and ship 'em off to detention camps. President ain't gonna serve out his term. Heard it from a friend of mine in the . . . FBI." Then he brightened. "You want a gun—I mean now, before you pick up the firepower at the . . . site?"

Then Grainger thought he had the man pegged. A patriot. "We'll get these dogies settled down." He wiped the perspiration from his eyebrows with the back of his hand. "Hot for March."

"Gonna get hotter," the traitor said.

"I've got one more minute," Grainger reminded Calandine, "and depending on how much you trust your buddy, you might want to remove him and you from the scene of what's about to happen—something you're not going to write a contact report about."

Calandine grunted, and hurried to climb into his federally provided undercover car. Its door slammed. It roared away with a belch of pollutants. Grainger promised himself a better look at Calandine's file, then realized that no data from Timeline A could be trusted.

It didn't matter. Somewhere in the distance, police sirens were screaming closer. The argument on the bridge must have gotten more serious.

"Here I am, Chun," Grainger murmured almost prayerfully as he stepped onto the grass of the cemetery, his hand thrust in his pocket and gripping his acoustic pistol. "Come and get me. Next stop, 12th and E. And ladies, for better or worse, we've got us a penetration agent."

Northeastern Iowa

Timeline B: August 4, 1991

The white steeple visible over the treetops to the northeast marked a church in the nearest community, seven kilometers away. Three kilometers due west, the tops of paired silos built of concrete staves indicated the closest farm. Weigand waited with his team at the T intersection of two gravel roads which, with the utility lines that paralleled them, were the other major signs of human occupation.

The fields were fenced, but the three-strand barbed wire wobbled on posts that should have been replaced long since. The land was either meadow or fallow, more likely the latter. Grass grew rank, and the purple heads of bull thistles stood in frequent majesty two and three meters above the ground.

Barthuli was in his element. He sat cross-legged on the shady side of a telephone pole, gorging his recorder/computer with information through a resonance tap directed at the line above him.

Any database tied into the communications net on this horizon was open to the computing power available in the Riders' basic kit. A rural phone line, connected to the rest of the country through an obsolescent electromechanical switch, was sufficient to give Barthuli greater access than the President or the directors of intelligence services had.

Weigand had thought of telling Barthuli to find them a route to Son Tay, but after consideration he'd kept his mouth shut. They didn't know yet what they'd really need, and the analyst worked best when everybody else left him alone. Weigand was lucky to have Gerd along.

"This is as hot as Memphis," Rebecca Carnes said; not angry, just making conversation. She mopped her brow with a sodden green handkerchief, spreading the sheen of sweat a little more evenly. "*And* as humid. I thought it was supposed to be cold up north here."

"Gerd, any news on when they're going to pick us up?" Weigand asked. To Carnes, lying in the mottled shade beneath a clump of blackberries growing along the fenceline, he added, "You're all right, aren't you? Should you . . ."

He didn't know quite what he was going to offer Carnes. Her clothing didn't mediate skin temperature the way the Riders' coveralls did. The emergency rations, liquids included, were in the suits and locked out of phase for another nine hours. Carnes had been eating berries the red-winged blackbirds had missed, but Weigand didn't imagine a few tart nibbles did much to cool her down.

Carnes shook her head and gave him a tired smile. "I'm fine," she said. "I drank as much as I could hold before I got out of my armor."

Barthuli had waited for Carnes to answer first. He said, "Nothing's changed, Pauli. As soon as your request came in over the link with the regional command in Chicago, the sergeant on duty at Guard headquarters in Dubuque called the district administrator's office. He was told that someone would be down immediately."

Barthuli shrugged and added, "I gather the offices are in the same building. I don't have listening devices planted, so unless the communication is by some form of electronic media—"

He opened his hands, palms upward.

"They wouldn't just ignore orders from Region without querying them," Carnes said. Her tone didn't sound as certain as the words themselves were. Her eyes were closed. "Of course, they could screw up."

Weigand had been afraid that when his team displaced to 1991, they'd find themselves in a heavily populated area. They'd avoided that, heaven knew. Weigand hadn't seen so much as a domestic animal in the three hours he'd been on this horizon.

After a quick survey of the immediate area, they'd walked their armor into a patch of woods 400 meters from the cross-roads. Weigand set the suits to remain out of phase on a twelve-hour cycle and reappear for only ten seconds between intervals. Ten seconds was too short a time for anybody to return the equipment to normal operation by hand. A remote signal from Weigand or Barthuli could accomplish the job instantly.

Weigand had left the gas/tanglefoot gun with his suit. His and Barthuli's coveralls, even with the color rotated to a dirty off-white, were going to arouse comment. He didn't want a piece of unfamiliar weaponry as well. For that matter, Carnes said her uniform wasn't going to look like anything in normal use within the continental United States.

Carnes sat up abruptly, catching her hair in thorny black-berry canes. "I see dust," she said. She nodded her chin because she was using both hands to free her hair and couldn't point. "On the horizon."

Weigand pulled the facemask down from his headband and stood. He was embarrassed that Carnes had seen the movement first. He'd been too busy worrying about what he'd done wrong and what he should do next.

"Two vehicles," he said. He increased magnification and dialed in enhancement because of the dust. "A sedan and a light truck painted green, with a machine gun. There's something stenciled on the door."

The roads were graveled with soft yellow limestone, the Niobrara chalk laid down in the Cretaceous Period a hundred million years ago. There was very little breeze today. The leading vehicle, the sedan, kicked up dust which drifted evenly to both sides of the road. Without enhancement by the mask's processing unit, the truck following fifty meters behind the sedan was no more than a shadow in olive drab.

Four people in chalk-yellowed uniforms bounced in the back of the truck, holding on to the side panels instead of sitting down. At high magnification, they looked grimly determined. Weigand wondered if the machine gun on a pintle in the middle of the truck's cargo compartment was too dusty to fire.

"They've seen you, Pauli," Barthuli said. "They're reporting in. The officer in command is a Captain Kawalec."

He paused. "Now they've seen the rest of us, too."

As Barthuli sat beside the utility pole, he browsed data both through a pinhead-sized link in his mastoid bone and optically via holographic projection. The sensor pack controlled the display based on prioritized key words the analyst had given it.

Weigand had used the same phone line to tap into the Midwest Regional Headquarters of the Federal Emergency Control Authority—the military government. In the name of the regional administrator, he'd faxed an order to the National Guard HQ nearest to where Weigand's team arrived, directing the local authorities to pick up three officials at a rural location and provide them with full facilities.

The message itself was simply a matter of downloading a recent order of suitable format, modifying the contents, and sending it via the command link with the proper verification codes. Given the team's equipment and training, there was nothing tricky to the job.

The problem was determining where Weigand and his team were, in terms that the local authorities could understand. The Global Positioning Satellite system existed on this timeline, though in a truncated fashion—three units of the satellite constellation were malfunctioning and should have been replaced. Access to the system was tightly restricted, however. A district HQ wasn't equipped to handle information in terms of precise latitude and longitude.

There were no identification signs along either road for as far as the ARC Riders could see at top magnification. Gerd had finally solved the problem by getting the local road numbers from the computer in the county deed room.

The oncoming vehicles slowed half a kilometer from where Weigand stood by the road. The truck pulled around the car. One of the soldiers clung to the pintle and the grip of the machine gun. There were two more soldiers in the truck's cab, and a driver as well as a passenger in the sedan.

"We're playing this one by ear," Weigand said, watching the vehicles rather than his companions. "Major, I expect you to do most of the talking, but I'll tell you now, I'll step in if I think I should. Ultimately, it's my responsibility."

"Ultimately," Carnes said firmly, "it's all of our asses, Pauli. But I hear what you're saying."

The worst problem the team faced for the moment was that only Carnes had hard-copy identification. The team could create any ID desired, given access to a suitable output device, but right now all they had available was a considerable acreage of meadow and woodland.

The transportation capsule could duplicate local IDs from air or sawdust, but that equipment wasn't part of a displacement suit's kit. If the Dubuque authorities offered the team the "full facilities" the fax demanded, Weigand was sure he could cobble something impressive together with the local tools. For the moment, Weigand and Barthuli had to depend on the compartmentalized security of a police state to baffle the locals. They also had to hope Carnes wasn't listed as a deserter.

The truck pulled up. The left rear brake grabbed and made the vehicle shimmy. The soldiers in back held on to the sides in fear of being flung from the bed. The man at the machine gun swung from the grip like a pendulum, pointing the barrel skyward. The sedan halted behind and a little to the right so that the truck blocked the team's direct line of fire toward the other vehicle.

Major Carnes strode to the cab of the truck. The driver—both vehicles' drivers—and one of the soldiers in the back were women.

"Who's in charge here?" Carnes demanded in brittle anger. Weigand could imagine her dressing down a roomful of orderlies partying on duty. "I was informed a Captain Kawalec would report to me at 1330 hours at the latest. The latest!"

She tapped her watch—it was after 3 PM—as she stared at the sergeant in the truck's passenger seat. "Where's Kawalec, and where have you *been*?"

An officer got out of the back of the sedan, put on his saucer hat, and straightened his tie. His shoulder patch was the red-on-white EA of the Emergency Authority. A circled numeral in the middle indicated Military Region 3.

Kawalec was at least fifty years old, bald, and overweight. Weigand supposed if he'd been a more prepossessing specimen, he'd have been overseas—or at least somewhere other than a backwater like this. "May I see your identification, please?" he said. His voice shifted keys in the middle of the demand.

Carnes glanced at Weigand and raised her eyebrow. Weigand looked stern and said, "All right, Major. You can show him your ID."

Carnes unbuttoned her left breast pocket and removed a plastic wallet with a military crest embossed on the flap. She held it open in her hand, smiling grimly at Kawalec over the hood of the truck.

The captain swallowed. He started to step around the truck. His face suddenly contorted and he shouted at the driver, "Back this damned thing up! Are you good for nothing?"

The driver shifted into reverse with a clang. The truck backed twenty feet, its transmission whining. More dust rose and drifted. The tires had a coarse, all-terrain tread, but they were worn to the belt in patches.

Captain Kawalec wore a green dress uniform. The trousers were summer-weight polyester, but the coat was of wool. No wonder he was red-faced and overheated.

Carnes continued to hold her wallet, ready to show the identification to Kawalec but not offering it to him. He came to her, wiping his face again. Despite the heat and dust, the sedan's windows were open. Either its air conditioner didn't work or fuel was in too short supply for the district to afford the mileage cost of air-conditioning.

Kawalec tried to take the wallet. Carnes didn't let go of it. She was good, really good; a first-class prospect for the Anti-Revision Command.

Kawalec bent over to read the warrant in the card pocket, then straightened with a frown. "I don't see what you're doing here, Major," he said in a peevish voice.

"No, you don't," Carnes said. "What *you're* doing here, Captain Kawalec, is carrying us into Dubuque, where you and your superiors will provide us with absolutely everything we request."

"Or else your successors will," Weigand said. He deliberately looked up the road as he spoke to Kawalec, denying the captain the courtesy of eye contact.

"I need to see your identification also, Mr. . . ." Kawalec said, the last syllable rising in interrogation.

"No," Weigand said.

Weigand stood at ease with his arms linked behind his back, apparently bored but not impatient. Barthuli was standing also, holding his recorder/computer at waist level, where it had an angle on the telephone repeater above. The analyst was still auditing the information his unit gathered. His expression was pleased and interested—which in his case wasn't acting.

Kawalec looked from Carnes to Weigand, then back to Carnes. Carnes buttoned her wallet away, pointedly closing the discussion as far as she was concerned.

"I'll have to get orders," Kawalec said. He swallowed again.

"You've already gotten orders," Carnes snapped. "The length of time it's taking you to execute them is not going unremarked."

The captain scuffled back into the sedan. He spoke in an undertone to his driver. Both of them rolled their side windows up before Kawalec took the handset of the dashboard-mounted radio. The flex connecting handset and transceiver was so short that Kawalec had to lean over the front seat to use the unit.

Barthuli and Carnes watched Kawalec, though the analyst's smile suggested the vagueness of a person who was really paying attention to something else. Weigand surveyed the landscape, looking grim.

The sergeant had gotten out of the cab to talk with the four soldiers in back. He continued to stand beside the vehicle. The machine gunner was wiping his weapon with a rag he'd taken from an ammo box containing cleaning supplies. There were only thirty rounds of ammunition in the belt hanging from the gun's loading gate. Two of the soldiers had bolt-action rifles while the third, the woman, carried a civilian-pattern shotgun with a blued barrel. The troops muttered to one another and watched the team from the corners of their eyes.

Kawalec blinked. His eyes stared and his lower jaw drooped. He gave the handset back to his driver and reached for his door handle.

"Watch out," said Barthuli as he did something with the instrument in his hands. The truck's fuel tank blew up, covering the six soldiers in blazing gasoline.

Carnes ran toward the sudden inferno. Weigand grabbed her with his left hand as he drew the acoustic pistol from his pocket with his right. He knew what had happened; *why* would have to wait.

Kawalec was shouting unheard to his driver. Weigand aimed and fired. The side window in line with the driver's head shattered into fragments the size of sand grains. It was

safety glass and bulged in both directions from the plastic
film separating the parallel layers.

Barthuli had his pistol out also. He slipped his
recorder/computer into the special pocket in the front of his
coveralls while with his other hand he shot the machine gunner. The fellow's legs and torso were covered with gasoline
from the ruptured tank, but he still held the weapon by the
grip. The twin hypersonic pulses of Barthuli's weapon inter-
sected on the gunner's forehead. The 10-hertz difference tone
knocked him backward unconscious, as if a mule had kicked
him in the face.

Kawalec ducked in the backseat and squirmed to the door
on the other side of the sedan. He hadn't been carrying a
weapon, even a handgun for show.

The driver was logy but still upright. Weigand fired again.
She flopped sideways unconscious, now that the window
glass was out of the way.

Weigand ran toward the car, but he had to drag Carnes with
him. The nurse screamed in fury and hammered his chest to
get free so that she could help the people burning alive.

The only thing Carnes could do was get caught in the blaze
herself. The team had no firefighting equipment, not even
blankets with which to smother the flames on the shrieking
victims.

It was beyond that now anyway. To survive, people with
third-degree burns over most of their bodies needed better
medical help than this horizon, let alone this region of it,
could provide. Weigand's heart was frozen in a cold white
rage at what had happened, but it *had* happened and you went
on from there.

Kawalec scrambled out the far side of the car. He ran, still
hunched over so far that his hands dabbed the gravel as he
moved. Weigand leaned onto the trunk of the sedan, took a
deep breath, and threw Kawalec down on his face with a slug
of focused sound.

The air stank of gasoline and hot metal and the flesh of
people whose limbs twitched but who had lost the ability even

to moan. One of the soldiers had managed to crawl five meters from the vehicle before he collapsed. Grass and blue-flowering chicory burned in an expanding circle from his body.

Carnes stopped struggling. Weigand let her go. "I'm very sorry," he said. He couldn't meet her eyes. "I would have stopped it if I could."

Gerd Barthuli had blown up the truck because it was the most efficient way to eliminate six enemies. The fact that those enemies were human beings hadn't affected his decision in the least.

Not for the first time, Weigand wondered if that was because Barthuli himself wasn't human.

Northeastern Iowa

Timeline B: August 4, 1991

Rebecca Carnes knelt and watched the truck. The tires burned with low orange flames, intensely saturated. The pall of black smoke mounted a thousand feet before it drifted into a smudge.

Cartridges cooked off with vicious cracks, flinging sparks and bits of brass in all directions. For the most part the explosions were empty fury, but the round chambered in a dead soldier's rifle could have been dangerous. The bullet blew a jagged, fist-sized hole in the side of the truck and screamed over the empty fields. It would have killed anybody who'd been standing in the wrong place.

At times like this, when people were dying and there was nothing she could do about it, Carnes sometimes wished she'd been standing in that wrong place herself.

Kawalec and his driver were unconscious but not seriously injured. Weigand was stripping the captain. Carnes walked over to help him.

"The fuel tank of the car contains seven gallons, Pauli," Barthuli called. He squatted beside the sedan, looking at his gray box rather than the vehicle's gauges—which wouldn't be accurate to that degree anyway.

"I don't understand what happened," Carnes said. She had Kawalec's shoes and trousers off before Weigand had gotten the captain out of his coat. Carnes had plenty of experience in stripping unconscious men, though often enough that had been a job for blunt-ended shears ripping through the bloody, shrapnel-ripped remnants of what had been clothes.

"Barthuli, give the driver a red dose," Weigand ordered harshly. "*One* dose, for God's sake, and don't damage the spinal—no, I'll do it myself."

Weigand got up. Carnes swung to her feet and followed in perfect harmony, as if the big man were a doctor on rounds. "What's a red dose?" she asked, her tone sharper than she'd meant it to be.

"It'll put them out for an hour," Weigand said in weary anger. "And they'll lose all personal memory."

He took a thimble-shaped object from a pouch on his coveralls. It was scarlet and the surface was scored with three lines so that it could be identified in the dark.

"They'll retain language and it won't affect their motor skills in the least," Weigand continued. "But you bet, the amnesia's irreversible on this horizon."

He opened the sedan's front door. It wasn't locked, but the hinge caught. Weigand jerked the door so hard that further bits of side window shivered onto the ground. Carnes hadn't realized how strong Weigand really was, because he normally controlled his movements to display only minimum force.

"Major Carnes," Barthuli said with a formality that Carnes thought the analyst had gotten past earlier. "The captain there"—he nodded toward Kawalec—"received orders from his superiors to kill us immediately."

"What?" said Carnes in amazement. She stepped back, looking instinctively toward Weigand to see how he reacted.

Weigand, grim-faced, pretended to ignore the discussion. He set the flat end of the thimble against the base of the driver's skull, among the wispy brown hair. There was a hiss. The driver twitched, then lay flaccid with her tongue lolling from her mouth.

"The sector commander believes we're part of a plot by the state's military governor to take control of the district,"

Barthuli said. His face wore its usual faint smile. "The Emergency Authority and the state office are in separate chains of command."

"Yes, but *kill* us?" Carnes said, still trying to metabolize the statement. "That's crazy. Without talking to us, *any-thing*?"

"You haven't been in this country for three years, Major," the analyst said. "I'm afraid the deterioration of the polity during that period, particularly during the last twelve months, has been precipitous."

Weigand lifted the driver's limp body from the sedan. Shards of glass glittered like a dusting of jewels on her sweaty fatigue uniform.

"My God," Carnes whispered. "In the war zone we knew things were bad, the shortages of everything." She grinned like a skull. "Or they wouldn't have given nurses line com-mands, not that I commanded much. But back here . . ."

"Before Kawalec could give the order to his troops to kill us," Barthuli continued, "I—"

"Barthuli, shut *up*," Weigand ordered. His voice trembled with a rage that Carnes had thought wholly absent from the big man's personality. "You're going to make it worse, and it's plenty bad enough!"

"I'm sorry, Pauli," the analyst said calmly, "but she has to know. She's one of us now, so she needs to be fully informed."

"Needs to know that she's dealing with a moral imbecile?" Weigand shouted. He cradled the driver in his arms as though she were an infant he was shielding from wolves.

"I won't quarrel with your choice of terms," Barthuli said. He turned to Carnes. His tone had been emotionless, but there was sadness and even pain in his eyes.

"Major," he said, "my equipment here"—he tapped the pouch containing his recorder/computer—"can emit tuned microwaves. They're of relatively low power, but they were sufficient to my purpose. I treated the vehicle's fuel tank as a cavity resonator and induced a static discharge within the tank. Since the fluid level was low, and it was gasoline rather than diesel fuel, the spark caused an explosion."

Weigand put the driver down in the shade of the blackberries. He squatted beside her. "We didn't have to kill them!" he said. "We could have reacted before they did. They weren't trained, they didn't—I don't know if any of their guns would have fired!"

"Major," said Barthuli, "I acted in the quickest, most efficient fashion that occurred to me to save our lives. You have to expect me to do that the next time, anytime a situation of the sort arises. Afterward, I may agree that there were better ways of dealing with the problem . . . though I don't know that I do in this case."

He turned his sad gaze toward Weigand. "Skillful though I know you are, Pauli."

"But they were going to kill us?" Carnes said.

"Oh, yes," Barthuli said. "The orders were clear, and the captain was clearly going to carry them out. Try to carry them out. He was terrified of us from the first, you know."

"Terrified of the unknown," Weigand said tiredly. "Well, that's the usual thing. Sorry, Gerd. You're probably right. The chance of a bullet going the wrong place was unacceptably high."

He stood up. "You want to get her clothes off, Rebecca?" he said. "You're better at it than I am. I figure her uniform will fit Gerd, and you can wear the captain's. That puts us a little better off than we were."

Weigand turned his head toward the truck. The rubber and paint would burn for hours. Sheets of metal pinged against one another from differential rates of expansion. "None of that lot were big enough to fit me."

"There's an airport seventy miles south of here. An aircraft is scheduled to leave for Chicago tomorrow noon," Barthuli offered. "From there, it should be practical to arrange transportation to Son Tay. To the war zone, at any rate."

Weigand nodded. "Yeah, we'll do that. Let me borrow your access, Gerd. I don't want anybody looking for this vehicle."

"We'll want to take the displacement suits," Barthuli said. "That means we won't be able to leave before midnight."

He handed his recorder/computer to Weigand. Weigand squatted cross-legged with the device balanced on his ankles. He spread his hands as if over a keyboard. Light quivered above the device.

Carnes looked at the sedan. It was a full-sized Ford, twenty years old and painted institutional gray except for the right fender—a replacement in metallic blue. They could put two suits in the backseat and one in the trunk, she supposed, though she wasn't sure the trunk lid would close then. A pity the truck hadn't survived.

She turned and looked at the man who'd made it as far as the ditch. The charred exterior of the corpse had cracked in a few places to expose raw, red muscle. She'd never gotten used to that sight, neither when it was a GI dragged from a blazing helicopter nor a VC who'd been napalmed.

She'd have saved them if she could. But they'd been about to kill her, even though they weren't aware of that at the moment they died. Carnes didn't know where the morality of the situation lay; but what was done, was done.

"What's happening now?" she asked Barthuli, her eyes on the motionless Weigand. She spoke in a low voice so as not to interfere with whatever was going on.

"The device responds to neural commands," the analyst said, also whispering. "That is, the intention to type a command enters that command without physical input. It's the system I prefer."

He cleared his throat. "As for 'what' in the larger sense, I suspect Pauli is instructing the district data bank—perhaps regional as well—that when the identification of this vehicle is entered"—his toe touched the sedan's rusted permanent license plate—"the information transmitted is something quite different, and innocuous to us."

Carnes watched Weigand, her eyes narrowing in surmise. "You can do that with any computer, then?"

Barthuli nodded. "Any computer to which we have access," he agreed. "On this horizon. Effectively anything that's attached either to a communication line or to an outside power source."

"We'll stop at a driver's license bureau before we go to the airport," Carnes said. The pieces became gleamingly visible in her mind, as though layers of ice were melting away from a sudden truth. "Nobody in a license bureau is going to argue with us, but their equipment is the same as we'd get in a military installation. They'll take photographs which we can laminate in place of the originals of this pair's IDs."

She waved the driver's wallet to emphasize it, then frowned. "There's a problem with the names, though. The driver's Joyce Shilts. That gives us two female IDs and only one male. They may not check height, but first names . . ."

Barthuli shrugged. "Joyce Kilmer, who wrote "Trees," was male enough to be killed in combat in the trenches in World War I," he said. "We'll give that one to Pauli, whose masculinity is least in doubt."

"All right," she said, beaming. "And you'll fix it so that any query to these identification numbers will come back with a highest security classification hold! Mine, too."

Barthuli's smile broadened. "Yes, Rebecca," he said. "Pending Pauli's approval, of course, that's exactly what we'll do."

Arlington National Cemetery

March 15, 1967

C alandine had been expecting someone. Grainger had showed up. Taken Calandine's pledge of allegiance. All Grainger's old agent-running instincts were beginning to surface. Only the "we" bothered him. When Grainger rang that number, somebody up the river would pick up an extension in the Old Headquarters Building at CIA and say hello. But what if the "we" to whom Calandine had reaffirmed allegiance by the act of handing money and keys to Grainger wasn't the "we" that counted Tim Grainger as part of its active duty service roster?

As TC 779 shimmered into real time, Grainger decided to suggest to Roebeck that they all get a good night's sleep out of phase before parking themselves and the suits in some 1967 basement.

Maybe after he'd slept he would believe that he had gotten some answers out of this exercise. Right now, all he had was more questions. Where was Barthuli when you needed him? Nowhere on this horizon, that was certain.

Roebeck nearly pulled him inside. She was big in her suit, loaded for bear. She hugged him.

"Piece of cake," he admitted ruefully as the lock closed behind him and his ears popped from the pressure differential.

Chun never once looked away from her station until the TC 779's integrity was restored and they were safely displaced.

By the time they were out of phase, Roebeck was levering herself free from her suit and Grainger was sitting quietly at his station, just breathing air that smelled like home.

"Nice job," Nan Roebeck said generally. "At your soonest convenience, Chun."

The safe house. He hadn't thought to tell Nan he wanted to wait. . . . Now it was too late.

Roebeck was watching him closely. "If we had Barthuli, perhaps we could analyze what happened back there more thoroughly." She finished racking her suit and eased behind her command console.

"I miss him, too, especially now that we're trying to figure out Calandine," Grainger told her.

"The National Guard and the DC police cordoned off the bridge you were on when the fighting broke out. There was shooting. Some civilians were hurt, perhaps military as well. The protesters were gassed and beaten, taken away in vans. It's all over the local airwaves. Some sort of crackdown on the libertines—drug arrests, incarceration." Chun was talking as she worked the displays.

"We were lucky you weren't caught up in it," Roebeck said softly.

"I smelled the marijuana, but this . . ." Grainger watched the displays of violence, horses and riot shields and teenagers with blood all over them. It hadn't seemed that bad when he was there. "What do they say started it?"

Chun merged the video, it swirled, and an announcer was telling the audience that the incident had begun when a young girl spat on a soldier. There was, miraculously or suspiciously, footage of the event. And footage of the girl, screaming, her hands to her cheeks, when the shooting broke out. Grainger's trained eye couldn't detect the original source of gunfire, no matter how many times Chun ran the sequence for him.

"So what now?"

He knew what now.

"The safe house," Roebeck said implacably. "We'll suit up and power up, but nothing more. Even leaving the suits out of phase on their own is a last resort. In a completely controlled media, you can't believe anything but what you actually see with your eyes. What we saw was the beginning of the roundup of the dissident youth."

"As Calandine predicted."

"As Calandine informed you. He knew," Chun said from forward.

"And that makes him what?" Grainger asked Chun.

Chun didn't answer.

"Well informed," Roebeck said, and motioned to the racked suits. "Too well informed not to be a player."

"Wired, you mean," Grainger muttered.

"We will reenter Timeline B in, what, Chun?"

"Thirty-five seconds."

Then he had to deal with his suit. Roebeck wasn't taking no for an answer. He didn't like the hard suit's weight. He had a horror of being EMPed in it, knocked flat and left helpless like a beetle or a turtle on its back. But the boss was right. There was trouble out there that only a hard suit could get him through alive. Bad trouble. Waiting for them. And it would still be waiting whenever they popped out of phase to deal with it.

Grainger hated nothing so much as walking into an ambush, but that was what this job was about—had to be, given mission parameters and who was in control of the timeline. The only question was when that ambush was going to find them.

And his only function was to make sure that, when the ambush did find them, they were ready, willing, and able to do whatever was necessary to survive it, even if that meant shooting up 1967 in ways that wouldn't otherwise be thought of for a couple hundred years.

Travis Air Force Base, California

Timeline B: August 12, 1991

Pauli Weigand rose from his fold-down canvas seat along the aircraft's side and stretched. The jungle fatigues fit him, but the cotton felt rough to his unaccustomed skin.

The C-141 had touched down just after midnight local time, but the big transport taxied for what seemed like forever before it reached its fueling berth. Two dozen men and women wearing a variety of uniforms walked toward the lowered rear ramp with caution born of fatigue and stiffness.

A truck drove up to the aircraft, bathing the cargo bay with its headlights. Weigand glanced at his companions.

Major Carnes looked as though she'd been awake for a week. Her skin was dull and, though she'd never be called hollow-cheeked, her face lacked its normal roundness. Even Barthuli looked worn, to the extent you could tell with Gerd.

"It'll take at least an hour to refuel," Carnes said, nodding toward the ramp. "Want to get out and walk around?"

Weigand shook his head. "I'll stick here," he said. "When I'm operational, I don't . . . well, anything else is a distraction. Besides, there's the suits."

In the C-141's bay, cardboard boxes were stacked and covered by cargo netting on seven wooden pallets. There were also two Conex containers, eight-foot cubes of corrugated steel for secure transport. One Conex contained the team's displacement suits.

In a barracks bag under Weigand's seat was an EMP generator. Weigand had built it before they left Chicago, mostly out of local materials requisitioned from Great Lakes Naval Station. The field expedient was a bulky, ten-kilogram device with its own shoulder stock instead of being a clip-on to other weapons. To power the unit, he'd had to cannibalize the power pack of one of the headbands. The result wasn't perfect, but Weigand knew he needed a tool that could take out hostiles wearing ARC armor before he got deeper in the danger zone.

"I'd like to go out also, Pauli," Barthuli said. "I'll be interested to see how much the base differs from its status in our timeline. It's the primary transshipment point feeding the war zone."

"Do you have all that information in your little computer?" Carnes said, bobbing a finger toward the bulge in the analyst's pocket.

The transport's bay echoed with the sounds of attendants and their equipment outside. A ground crewman walked past the trio, carrying a flashlight and chattering with animation into a walkie-talkie.

Weigand wondered if Air Force maintenance standards were collapsing as suddenly as central political control was. The Pacific was a very big ocean. If this plane came down in it, Nan's team was going to have to seal off the revision without help from Pauli Weigand.

"No," Barthuli said to Carnes. "That will have to wait until we rejoin the transportation capsule—or return to ARC Central, of course. But if I don't gather the information now, it'll be lost forever."

Carnes looked at Weigand and raised her eyebrow in interrogation. Weigand shrugged and made his decision as he spoke: "Sure, go see if you can find a canteen and bring me back something that isn't emergency rations. And something to drink, a liter if they've got it."

He flashed Barthuli a smile as hard as that of a statue's marble lips. "Rebecca," he said, staring at the analyst. "I want you to have him back here in an hour. If that means you knock him cold and drag the body back, do it. Do you have a problem with those terms?"

"No," Carnes said. She glanced at the analyst appraisingly. "I'd already decided I'd do that this time, if it was just Gerd and me alone."

"If it's a choice between you having a physical headache, Gerd," Weigand said, "and me having a figurative one, I'll make sure it's your problem from now until you're Nan's responsibility again. Understood?"

"Perfectly," Barthuli said. He didn't appear to be either surprised or upset. He linked arms with Carnes in a mimicking of the gallantry of a past age. Together they left the aircraft. They had to walk with care in cargo bay, because the deck plates were roller-side up for ease in moving containerized cargo.

The ground crewman was in the front of the aircraft, talking with one of the flight engineers. Outside, a red light threw rotating pulses across the concrete as a truck pumped kerosine into the C-141's fuel tanks.

Pauli Weigand had done everything he could do at this moment. When they reached Bien Hoa Airbase, Gerd would locate transportation for the next leg of the journey—either to Hanoi or to Son Tay directly, depending on what was available. Weigand would have the job of getting the team aboard by routing the necessary orders through the communications chain.

But until then, Weigand had no immediate task. Some people, perhaps most people, would have spent their time worrying about the unguessable future. Weigand simply turned his brain off. He didn't chat, didn't play solitaire, didn't even look out the window when windows were available—which they weren't on this strictly military transport.

Weigand remained standing, working out kinks caused by the fold-down seats. Discomfort was a normal part of being an ARC Rider; it didn't bother him. The danger this time was greater than it would be on a normal operation, but that was merely a difference of degree, not kind.

What froze Weigand whenever he let himself consider it was the fact that he was in charge of the operation. Putting Weigand in a situation like this was comparable to ordering an arachnophobic to care for a collection of tarantulas.

But nobody'd ordered anything. Pauli Weigand was here because of fate or luck or God, take your pick. He had to make the decisions because neither of his companions was capable of doing so. He'd sooner have stuck his hand in a fire, but that wasn't an option. Weigand would carry on until they'd succeeded or they'd rejoined the remainder of the team.

Or until he was killed, of course.

It was a good thing for Weigand that he *could* turn his mind off when he didn't need to think.

A car and a lowboy carrying a large gasoline-powered forklift pulled up at the rear of the aircraft. Five men in Air Force dress uniforms got out of the car. They wore dark blue armbands which Weigand didn't recognize, and the four enlisted men carried M16 automatic rifles.

A civilian started the forklift. The uniformed men spoke for a moment to the C-141's female loadmaster, then walked up the ramp with her.

Weigand moved aside. The loadmaster gestured to him. The officer, a full colonel, approached Weigand as the riflemen waited watchfully. "May I see your identification, please?" the colonel shouted over the forklift's snarling clamor.

Weigand's face was still, his skin cold. He handed over the leather bifold he'd gotten in Chicago.

Weigand's present ID stated that he was operating under the authority of the Joint Chiefs of Staff, and that his name and rank were matters of the highest security classification. The ID wasn't, in fact, of a type in use anywhere within the US establishment, but a query to a governmental database

citing the card's identification number would elicit a supporting response. Institutional secrecy was the imposter's
best defense.

The colonel peered at the card in the beam of an aluminum
flashlight. "Thank you, sir," he said. His armband had a five-
pointed star in a white circle. It wasn't the regular Military
Region 5 insignia. "You have two companions. Where are
they now?"

"You have no right to question me," Weigand said coldly.
The forklift drove up the aircraft's ramp. Echoes multiplied
the already deafening noise.

The airmen pointed their M16s at Weigand. His acoustic
pistol was in the side pocket of his tunic. He'd be better off
to chance his strength and speed, but even that was a sure
loser. Two of the riflemen were several meters back, far
enough that Weigand couldn't hope to dispose of them by
hand before they could fire.

The loadmaster detached the straps holding the team's
Conex in place. The forklift bounced forward over the rollers
and clanged its forks into the grip points welded onto the bottom of the container. The engine revved, spewing dizzyingly
thick exhaust fumes.

Weigand placed his hands on his hips and glared, arms
akimbo, at the officer. "Colonel," he said, "I don't know what
you think you're doing, but it's a bad idea. Trust me. It's a
very bad idea."

The colonel grimaced. "Sir," he said, "I'm carrying out the
orders of Lieutenant General Oakley—"

"The base commander here?" Weigand said, shouting to
be heard. The forklift backed away, carrying with it the
Conex. "Then he's out of his mind—and so are you if you
take his orders. Our mission *and* our equipment"—He jerked
his chin in the direction of the forklift; though Weigand's
body didn't move, he noticed one of the airmen's hands
twitched on his rifle—"are critical to the war effort."

"We understand the significance of what we're dealing with,
sir," the colonel said. "Believe me, we want to have you on our

side. We intend to have you on our side. Come with us, please. You'll have to come anyway, and it'll be better afterward if everything stays friendly now. But you'll have to come."

Weigand chuckled. "Yes, of course," he said. He strode calmly toward the ramp. The nervous airman hopped two steps back, keeping well clear of the grab for his weapon that just might have occurred had the fellow been less alert.

The team had screwed up, had overegged the pudding. Weigand, the man in charge, had screwed up. By suggesting on the manifest that the team and its hardware were a war-winning top-secret project, they'd aroused the interest of locals who had more immediate needs for weaponry.

Weigand was sure he could get clear before long, but time suddenly was a factor. As the US establishment fell under the weight of an unwinnable war, it became more and more likely that the collapse would crush the team as well.

There weren't going to be many more flights to Southeast Asia. While Weigand didn't recall the team's survey of the timeline precisely enough to know what was going to happen to Travis AFB during the spasms of civil war which completed the nation's destruction, he was sure it wouldn't be anything good.

The air outside the cargo bay was hot and dry and thick with the smell of jet fuel being pumped into the C-141's tanks. The Conex and forklift were being chained into place on the lowboy.

"If you'll get into the backseat, please, sir," the colonel directed. An airman held the door open for Weigand. Another airman got in on the opposite side. They were going to sandwich Weigand in the backseat, making it virtually impossible for him to jump from the car while it was moving.

"Pauli, we're auditing the situation," Gerd Barthuli said through the bone-conduction speaker in Weigand's headband. "Rebecca has you in sight, and we've taken precautions to avoid joining you for the moment."

"Gerd, Colonel," Weigand said sternly as he bent to enter the car. "I want you to know that I expect to be on that aircraft when it leaves here in an hour!"

"General Oakley will discuss matters with you in detail, sir," the colonel said. He didn't sound concerned.

Before the colonel got into the car's front seat, he drew a pistol from his belt holster and held it in his lap as he sat down. Whoever these people were, they seemed to be professional enough to be sure Weigand was going wherever they wanted him to go.

Weigand's only options were whether he chose to arrive dead or alive. The M16s were too awkward for use inside the vehicle, but the officer's pistol was not. Weigand didn't doubt the colonel would shoot him through the front seat if he had to.

"Pauli, all right," Barthuli said. "You're hoping to escape in time to leave on the present flight. We'll help from this side."

Another great transport staggered aloft, the roar of its engines dissipating slowly as it reached for altitude. Weigand wondered if it carried supplies and men to the war zone, like the aircraft his team had arrived on. The partial load on their own C-141 was another sign of how completely war had stripped the US of the matériel necessary to fight.

The lowboy turned cautiously and drove back down the access road by which it had approached. The colonel nodded; his driver brought the car around to follow. Only one runway was lit, and only occasionally did Weigand see another moving vehicle. Clumps of grass grew through cracks in the asphalt roadway.

The lowboy turned into the lit interior of a hangar nearly a kilometer from the transport's berth. The great doors began to slide closed even before the car was fully inside.

The hangar contained pallets, three light armored cars, and at least a hundred uniformed troops. There were no aircraft. The vehicles and personnel all bore the blue circle-and-star insignia rather than normal US markings.

The sedan pulled up beside a group of officers, all of them male. In the near distance, a siren howled for a few lonely seconds, then fell silent again. The airman to Weigand's right got out and ushered Weigand from the car. The colonel remained seated in the front seat, his pistol unobtrusively leveled.

A fat man wearing a white dress uniform rather than the light blue of Air Force personnel watched troops climb aboard the lowboy. The men carried tools, including a bolt cutter with lever arms nearly a meter long.

The man in white gestured Weigand to him with a crooked index finger. Other officers watched alertly.

"You're one of the specialists from DC, are you?" the fat man said. He turned his head to look directly at Weigand for the first time. "What's your name, then? Since we've got to call you something. I'm Oakley, and I fully intend to be President Oakley before the year's out. Do you understand?"

Oakley's voice was rich and assured. He would have been a powerful speaker in a setting with better acoustics than this echoing hangar.

"You don't need to call me anything," Weigand said flatly. "My business is on the other side of the ocean. It's your business, too, you know. Everyone's business."

The padlock dropped from the Conex, its hasp severed by the bolt cutter. Troops pulled open the container's triple doors.

"I think the Chinks can wait, don't you?" Oakley said. Both sides of his tunic front were covered with medal ribbons. "We'll get to them—never fear, we'll get to them. But the first order of business is to put this country back on a proper footing with a leader who knows how to lead!"

Oakley's eyes were gray and as hard as chilled iron. "There'll be places for all those who help me willingly. Places for you and your friends. Be very clear in your mind, though: you *will* help me."

He smiled. There was nothing amused in the expression. "Or if you manage to die instead, we'll figure out your secret weapon ourselves. So save yourself a hard time, why don't you?"

Men carried the displacement suits from the Conex. Oakley stared at the equipment, his eyes narrowing. "I've seen that sort of thing before," he said. "But where's the power supply? They are powered, aren't they? Otherwise . . ."

"Pauli," said Barthuli's voice in Weigand's ear, "we're outside now. Do you have your facemask?"

"Gerd," Weigand said, "I have a mask. What kind of transportation do you have?"

"We can transport them to where they're needed, if that's what you mean," Oakley said, irritated to hear a question rather than an answer to his own query. He didn't comment on *"Gerd."* Weigand needed the syllable to key his transmission to Barthuli.

"Pauli, the vehicle we have will barely carry the three of us," Barthuli said. "We'll have to leave the suits here, out of phase. I'm sorry, but there's very little time."

As if the analyst had to tell him that.

"I'll show you how the armor works," Weigand said, walking toward the lowboy at a steady, purposeful stride. He reached to his headband and pulled the membrane over his face as he moved.

Gerd and Rebecca must have retrieved the gas gun from the transport. The four rounds remaining in the magazine wouldn't fill as large an enclosure as this hangar, but it would at least panic Oakley's men. The effect of the gas would wear off completely in three or four hours, but the people who saw their fellows drop as if poleaxed wouldn't know that.

Oakley followed, a step behind. None of the officers surrounding the general had spoken since Weigand arrived.

"It is powered, then?" Oakley demanded. "The suits aren't just for protection?" He didn't appear to have noticed Weigand's facemask.

"That's right," said Weigand. "There's no integral weaponry, but the skin's rigidity permits the user to carry up to about 400 kilos. Hard to balance then, of course."

He hopped onto the bed of the lowboy. Oakley grunted. A brigadier general with iron-gray hair held out his arm as a brace.

"Pauli, ready," warned Barthuli's voice. The hangar lights went out.

Weigand dropped flat and switched his faceshield to enhanced thermal imaging. He drew the acoustic pistol from his side pocket.

"Watch the spook!" General Oakley shouted, reaching for his pistol holster. "Don't let the spook get into his—"

Weigand shot him point-blank, then shot the brigadier beside Oakley for good measure. They were the only people who'd been watching Weigand at the moment the lights went out.

One of the technicians on the lowboy switched on a flashlight. Weigand waited till the beam jerked toward the main doors, then shot the airman. The fellow pitched off the trailer as if sandbagged. His light spun to the concrete floor. The filament shattered in a green flash.

Somebody started the engine of one of the armored cars. The structure was almost as hollow as the body of a drum. Distinct from the shouts and mechanical noises pulsing within, Weigand heard the *choonk*! of a gas projector.

"Gas!" he screamed. "Nerve gas!"

An airman far across the hangar fired an automatic rifle wildly. His bullets disintegrated against the walls in yellow sparks.

Weigand crawled forward on all fours, staying low to avoid the random projectiles. They'd kill you just as dead as an aimed shot would. The technician carrying the bolt cutter ran into him and pitched screaming the few feet to the floor.

Weigand reached the nearest suit, opened it, and set the control board on the inside of the backplate. He chose an infinite sequence of seven days out of phase, punctuated by returns to the horizon of three seconds only. He moved to the second suit.

This location was about the last place Weigand would have chosen to abandon the armor, a busy and technologically advanced portion of the temporal horizon. He didn't think Oakley's personnel could accomplish much in the three seconds they'd have to deal with the suits, though. Anyway, it wasn't as though Weigand had a lot of choice.

Forty meters from the lowboy, an airman scanned the hangar through an image-intensifier sight attached to an M16. Weigand raised and aimed his pistol, though he wasn't sure how effective acoustics would be at that range—particularly because the gunman wore a Kevlar helmet.

Before the rifleman could fire—if that's what he meant to do—he slumped backward and lay without twitching. The gas shells had landed in the areas of the hangar where people were most concentrated. The rifleman had breathed a wisp of the gas. He'd awaken some time around dawn, feeling refreshed though stuffy. There might be holes in his memory, but no serious long-term damage.

When the shells burst, their pressurized contents cooled the air it spilled across. Through his facemask, Weigand saw blue waves spreading in a ripple pattern from where each grenade had gone off. Barthuli or Carnes must have fired the full magazine, though he'd heard only the first round.

The headlights on the armored car's front fenders carved bright swaths across the hangar's interior. The vehicle was four-wheeled and boat-shaped: its small turret carried a pair of machine guns.

The driver put the car in gear and turned slightly. Weigand recognized Barthuli and Carnes as the two figures in jungle fatigues crouching to either side of the personnel door at the edge of the headlights' illumination. They were probably safe as long as they didn't do anything to call attention to themselves, but—

The analyst held the EMP generator. If Barthuli aimed at the armored car while the headlights were on him, he'd probably get both of them killed. It wasn't just a matter of the vehicle's gunner, if any. Barthuli would be targeting himself and Carnes for everyone in the hangar with a weapon.

"Gerd, don't shoot at the car!" Weigand shouted.

"Pauli, of course not," the analyst said with a hint of inappropriate amusement in his voice. All right, he knew better, but how was anybody to *know* how the crazy bastard's mind was going to work?

The armored car drove through a layer of gas, invisible to the vehicle's occupants. The turn tightened because the driver dragged the steering wheel as he slumped back. Moving at the speed of a fast walk, the car collided with a side wall of the hangar. The seven-tonne vehicle bounced back and hit the wall a second time. This time the engine stalled.

The headlights continued to burn, though they dimmed visibly when they lost the alternator's output. The hangar wall reflected the light back onto the car, showing where the letters AIR POLICE had been painted over on the blue side when the new circle-and-star was applied.

"Pauli, Rebecca is loaded with tanglefoot now," Barthuli said over the commo system. If anybody but the analyst had spoken the words, he'd have been prodding Weigand to get a move on with the third suit of armor. That might not have been Gerd's intent, but the point was a valid one.

"Gerd, I'm coming," Weigand said as he sent the third suit into limbo with the other pair. He stepped from the back of the trailer and trotted toward his companions.

There'd only been the single burst of gunfire. Someone with a bullhorn was trying to restore order. The gas shells had already accomplished that by strewing at least 90 percent of the hangar's occupants unconscious on the floor.

The enhancement feature of Weigand's facemask made running through the dark almost as safe as doing the same thing in daylight. Unprocessed forward-looking infrared (and the same was true of unprocessed image intensifiers) gave a clear view of objects but no trustworthy way to judge relative distance. The processor in Weigand's headband modeled objects with false shadowing so that they appeared to be the distance from the viewer that they were in cold fact.

Carnes opened the door as Weigand joined them. A pair of guards with automatic rifles lay on the concrete outside the door where an acoustic pistol had dropped them. Canted nearby on its sidestand, already turned to head back in the direction of the C-141, was a large motorcycle.

"Rebecca knows how to drive it!" Barthuli announced with pleasure. He took the tanglefoot projector Carnes handed him, then passed it and the EMP generator as well on to Weigand.

Carnes swung her right leg over the stepped saddle with a grunt, then rocked the bike upright. The spring-loaded side-stand flew up when the weight came off it.

"The one useful thing I learned from my husband," she said. Her thumb stabbed a button. The engine spun and caught with an out-of-synchronous rumble. "I didn't think so at the time. Now get on *carefully*. Keep your feet up, I know there's not pegs for both of you, and lean when I do."

"I wish we didn't have to leave the suits," Weigand said as he boarded the motorcycle gingerly. If he stood on the pegs and braced his lower back against the sissy bar, there'd be—barely—enough room for Gerd to squeeze onto the seat between Carnes and Weigand.

"I wish I was five years old and home with my mother!" Carnes said. She revved the big engine, ripping the night with its double note. "There's no way I can carry all of us and the suits besides."

"Ready," said Barthuli. He reached behind himself to grip Weigand's waist rather than cling to the driver.

Carnes eased in the clutch. The bike wobbled forward, then stabilized as she gassed it.

The fuel truck was no longer flashing its warning light from the C-141. The transport was still on the turn-out apron, but it looked to Weigand as though the ramp had been raised. He didn't have a hand free to adjust this facemask's magnification.

Carnes shifted into second gear. Acceleration rocked Weigand back hard. Carnes caught third and the exhaust note boomed out behind them.

"Come to think . . ." Carnes shouted over the windrush, "my husband taught me not to marry drunks, too!"

The bike roared as she shifted into fourth gear, blasting across the dark runway.

Out of the frying pan . . .

Bien Hoa
Air Force Base

Timeline B: August 14, 1991

The mob surged around the aircraft even before the ramp was fully lowered. The mass of people pushing aboard prevented the passengers who'd come from the States on the C-141 from disembarking.

A US Navy captain wearing a short-sleeved khaki uniform knocked Rebecca Carnes aside as he cannoned toward the front of the cargo bay. The officer held a blue duffle bag in one hand and clutched the wrist of a Vietnamese woman in the other. The woman was strikingly beautiful, with ivory skin and high French cheekbones. The infant she carried in a sling on her breast had solemn gray eyes.

The loadmaster shouted to no effect against the uproar. The copilot came aft, the plug dangling from the headphones around his neck. "What the hell's going on here?" he demanded.

He spoke first to Carnes, then realized she was a passenger trying to leave the aircraft. He switched his focus to a master sergeant, also in khakis, who was transporting several *pounds* of gold chains by the expedient of hanging them around his neck. The sergeant had an aluminum briefcase in either hand. From the way the handles dug into his fingers, the contents were extremely heavy.

"What do you think you're doing?" the copilot shouted. "You could've been killed when you pushed through the barriers while we were still taxiing! Don't you know that? We could have run over the whole lot of you!"

The sergeant set the briefcases on the fold-down bench beside him without loosening his grip on the handles. He was fat and sweating, even more than the familiar muggy warmth of Vietnam justified.

"I'm going to Japan," he said hoarsely, speaking through his gasping intakes of breath. "That's where you'll refuel, isn't it? Yokota? Look, buddy, I'll make it worth your while, but don't think you're getting me off this bird! Do you understand?"

His voice rose shrilly on the final interrogative.

Weigand murmured "Stay close to me" as he stepped ahead of Carnes. He held his barracks bag on his left shoulder where it couldn't be stripped from him by the pressure of the crowd. "I'll make a path."

"We've got cargo to unload!" the copilot said, gesturing to the pallets and the remaining Conex.

"Then fucking unload it!" the sergeant snarled. "But I swear I'll blow this fucker up if you try to get me off it!"

There might be explosives in his cases. Carnes doubted it, but somebody in the cargo bay probably did have a grenade. Shrapnel might not destroy the C-141, but it would make the bird unflyable.

Carnes pressed her body against Weigand's back, stepping each time the big ARC Rider took a shuffling step forward. Barthuli was behind her, just as close. It was the only way they could proceed against the thrust of the mob.

"Will they be able to take off?" Barthuli asked curiously as the linked trio reached the ramp. "With such a load, I mean."

The crowd stretched back in a broad fan, a multicolored blotch on the concrete. There must be at least a thousand people present, desperate to leave the war zone. Rumors of the use of nuclear weapons in Yunnan must have gotten out. How many of these folk had an idea of what world they'd be returning to on the other side of the Pacific?

The master sergeant, the black marketeer, probably did. That's why he was heading for refuge in Japan, not the once-united States.

Weigand clenched his huge left fist and extended it like a galley's ram, cutting a path through the center of the refugees. If he'd taken a line closer to the edge of the ramp, the three of them would have been pushed over the way hapless boarders were in the team's stead.

"Fly?" Weigand said. He had an instinctive grasp of practical matters. The analyst could have answered his own question, but only by researching it. "Sure, you can't pack enough flesh aboard one of these to equal the weight of tanks and ammunition it's built to carry. Whether any of them will be able to breathe, though, that's another matter."

Carnes glimpsed a convoy of two military ambulances and a deuce-and-a-half truck loaded with stretcher cases beneath a canvas awning. The vehicles were caught at the back of the crowd. A female doctor in fatigues stood on the step to the driver's seat, bracing herself on the open door as she peered over the mob.

"That's Dr. Byerly!" Carnes said in surprise. "I knew her when I was with the 312th at Chu Lai two years ago."

"We need a local contact," Weigand said. "We'll join her. Is that all right?"

"Yes!" said Carnes, surprised at her own enthusiasm. She'd seen no one she knew since the orders transferring her to the 90th Replacement Battalion and abruptly reassigning her to command a battalion of Argentine mercenaries.

The people who hadn't reached the belly of the aircraft were dispersing, hoping to find another long-haul aircraft to board. Carnes wondered how often this drama had been enacted in recent days. How many planes and ships still arrived from the States to feed the meat grinder of this war?

Some of those excluded slumped in exhaustion over their baggage; a Vietnamese woman wailed in a high voice. The Air

Force colonel who'd accompanied the woman was talking in a threatening tone to the copilot at the foot of the ramp, pointing repeatedly at the eagles on the shoulders of his dress uniform. The copilot looked too tired and frustrated even to move away.

"Will it be the same all over, do you think?" Barthuli asked as the trio separated to a more comfortable interval. "The mobs leaving, that is. Moving against the flow could be difficult."

The humid air was doubly heated by sunlight reflecting from acres of concrete runway and laced with the gut-churning residues of turbine exhaust. Bien Hoa smelled like the anteroom of hell.

As it was in plain fact.

"These are Saigon commandos," Carnes explained with a bitterness she'd never tried to suppress. "The worst thing they've had to worry about in this war is a problem with the office air-conditioning or the price of drinks in the officers' club. The closer you get to the field, the less you see of that. The less you see of anything except blood and mud."

A pair of flatbed semis, one of them mounting a winch on the tractor section, drove up to the C-141 and stopped. Cargo handlers, stripped to the waist and wearing sweatbands rather than hats, got off the vehicles. They eyed the refugees packed into the cargo bay.

"If they leave them there a day or two," Weigand said, "perhaps they'll melt and run out the bottom."

He lifted his olive drab baseball cap and wiped his forehead with the back of his right hand. The ARC Riders' normal garb was climate-controlled, but Weigand and Barthuli were in jungle fatigues to avoid unnecessary questions. The only reason they hadn't discarded the coveralls entirely was the possibility that they'd want the camouflage abilities of fabric that could blend to any color or pattern.

The driver of one of the ambulances walked forward to join Byerly at the lead vehicle. He was an MD, though he was much younger than Byerly. The third driver, a slender Oriental—perhaps Filipino rather than Vietnamese—waited beside his ambulance.

"Colonel Byerly?" Carnes called, because the doctor had stepped down to talk to the ambulance driver coming from the other direction.

Byerly turned, shading her eyes with her hand. Her hair, cut short to keep it out of the way, frizzed in all directions from beneath her cotton boonie hat. "Carnes?" she said. "Major Carnes."

Byerly's face hardened into something close to rage. She pointed to the C-141. "You're part of that lot?"

"We were disembarking, Colonel," Carnes replied, deliberately using the anger she'd felt as well. "Though that mob of Saigon's finest made that pretty hard."

"Sorry, Rebecca," Byerly said. As if the anger had been the only thing stiffening her body, she sat down abruptly on the fuel-tank step of her vehicle. "I'm so tired, and it's no damned good, none of it."

"Look, Colonel," the doctor from the lead ambulance said. "Let me go talk to them. These patients have got to get to Japan if they're going to have a chance, the way our personnel situation is."

He gestured toward the refugee-packed transport. "They'll understand that, don't you think? Some of them?"

A nurse leaned out from the bed of the two-and-a-half-ton truck. "Look," she called in a rasping voice. "I'm going to start losing them any minute now if they don't get some fluids. If we can't board, get us into the shade, for God's sake!"

The nurse looked eighteen. Carnes wondered if Rebecca Carnes had ever been as young as that girl seemed. Maybe one time, a lifetime of war ago. . . .

"You want to put your patients on board the transport, is that it?" Pauli Weigand said. He continued to hold the barracks bag on his shoulder, as if the weight meant nothing to him.

Byerly looked at him from where she sat. The step had a punched nonskid surface, but she was obviously too tired to care. "That was the idea," she said. "I've even got movement orders from USARV, for what that matters."

She nodded toward the transport. "Like as not, some of the REMFs who signed off on the orders are right there now."

"Rear Echelon Mother Fucker!" Barthuli translated, delighted to have heard an idiomatic phrase in its normal context.

Byerly returned her attention to the other doctor. "No, Vincent, I don't think a single one of those bastards would give up his chance of escape in order to evacuate our patients. After all, most of our people are battle casualties, so they've got nothing in common with the pigs on the plane."

"But we've got to get them to Japan, Colonel," Vincent said pleadingly. "Or they'll die. And who knows when another plane will be available?"

Fatigue had stripped the layers of maturity from the young doctor's psyche. He sounded like a child reacting to an adult situation with complete disbelief.

"I can clean the plane out for you," Weigand said. "Make it possible for the interlopers to be removed, that is. If I do that, can you put us up while we find passage for Son Tay?"

"Pauli, I used all the gas shells at Travis," Carnes warned. If she'd understood correctly, the acoustic pistols were individual, not area weapons. If the three of them started shooting, no matter how nonlethally, at the occupants of the C-141, somebody was bound to shoot back within a matter of seconds.

Byerly rose to her feet. "There's a medical supply flight to the 96th in Son Tay tomorrow," she said. "If it leaves, at any rate. I don't promise that. But what can you do about . . ." She motioned to the aircraft.

Weigand winced and looked hesitant. "The fifth round in the magazine isn't tanglefoot, it's an acoustic grenade," he said to Barthuli, the only other person present who would understand his concern. "It's, ah—"

He met Byerly's eyes. "There's a risk of permanent injury to those who are closest to the grenade when it goes off," he said. "Besides rendering them unconscious. Maybe death."

Byerly snorted. "The only reason I haven't gone looking for a CS grenade to throw aboard that plane," she said, "is that I couldn't load my patients until all the gas was scrubbed out of the bay. The fact that half of those bastards would trample the other half to death while they were puking their guts out, that wouldn't stop me in the least. Do whatever you please."

"Gerd," Weigand said, shaking out of his momentary diffidence, "help me make sure that the aircraft's crew is out of the way. Rebecca, I want you to stand well to the side of the aircraft when I discharge the grenade. Gerd and I will be protected by cancellation waves. You don't have a headband so you'll be at risk if you're in line with the opening. The bay will act as a resonance chamber."

Carnes glanced at the baggage handlers. "I'll go grab those guys," she said, waving. "I'll keep them out of the line of fire."

She grinned. "I'll also keep them from wandering off. We'll need as much help as we can get to throw the REMFs onto the taxiway after you knock them cold or whatever you're going to do."

The six cargo handlers stood together in the thin blob of shade thrown by the cab and winch mechanism of the lead truck. The leader of the detachment was a black with a paunch, massive arms and shoulders, and a Spec 5 shield pinned to the front of his sweatband. As he and his fellows watched Carnes approach, his primary interest was in her gender. His eyes gave only the briefest glance toward the oak leaves on her collar before refocusing on her breasts.

"Your job's to unload the Starlifter there, Specialist?" Carnes said crisply.

"We're watching events develop, Major," the Spec 5 replied, his tone just short of insolence. He and his men stood with their shoulders and right boots braced against the vehicle. They didn't straighten up because of an officer's presence.

One of the men eyed Carnes deliberately as he took a packet of cigarettes from the cargo pocket of his trousers. The pack was marked in flowing Cambodian script and sported a marijuana leaf in green on the front.

Carnes nodded curtly. "What's developing is this," she said. "The persons who've forced their way aboard that aircraft will be rendered unconscious in a few minutes. I want you to move your trucks up under the aircraft's left wing so that you'll be out of the danger zone. You will then help the rest of us remove the bodies and the rest of the cargo, then transfer patients into the aircraft for transport to facilities in Japan."

Carnes knew what the risk was, but she took it anyway. She stepped forward and swung her right hand, slapping the pack of joints away from the soldier who held them. Filter cigarettes with a twist-closed end spun across the taxiway.

"Or alternatively, *soldiers* . . ." Carnes said in a voice that cut like a circle saw; her fingers burned as if bee-stung, "You can be rendered unconscious yourselves and wake up on a flight to Yunnan in the morning. I guarantee they need warm bodies there. Which will it be?"

The Spec 5 stared at her, then broke into a grin. "Whoo-ee, little lady!" he said. "We're here to move shit, right? If some of that shit's bodies, that's cool. Not the first time we moved bodies, is it, bros?"

All six cargo handlers were black. It hadn't escaped Carnes' notice—or theirs—that the vast majority of the officers and senior enlisted men who'd forced their way aboard the C-141 were whites.

"Then get these trucks out of the way," she ordered. "I'll ride on your running board."

Weigand had found the copilot, Barthuli the loadmaster. The copilot trotted around toward the cockpit hatch, avoiding the crowd. Besides the people crammed into the cargo bay, others stood or sat on the ramp. Apparently they hoped to squeeze their way on later, or perhaps be lifted to safety when the ramp rose to close the aircraft before takeoff.

The semis snorted as they drove forward beneath the C-141's high wing. Pauli Weigand walked casually across the apron. He'd left the barracks bag with the medical convoy and carried only the projector he'd brought from TC 779.

Some of the refugees on the ramp watched Weigand, but since his back was toward them and he was walking away, they didn't seem particularly concerned.

"This good enough, missie?" the Spec 5 called from the cab of the truck, speaking across the driver.

"Yes, this is fine," Carnes said. She had no idea, really, but she supposed Gerd or Pauli would have warned her if it wasn't a safe location. She didn't know exactly what was going to happen, but the implications of the word *grenade* were clear enough.

Colonel Byerly was in the back of the deuce and a half, helping the sole nurse with at least thirty severely wounded patients. The fact that two MDs, a nurse, and an orderly had to deal with the transport as well as the medical needs of so many patients chilled Carnes' soul. Bad as it had been with the 96th in Son Tay before she was transferred to a combat command, the situation in Saigon was still worse. The war was a tree, rotting away from the inside out.

Weigand turned, raised his projector, and took momentary aim. A major on the C-141's ramp stood up and shouted as he drew a .45 automatic.

Choonk!

The projectile sailed over the major's head and into the cargo bay. Carnes could track its silvery flight with her eyes.

For a fraction of a second after the projectile disappeared, nothing happened. The major pointed his pistol.

The blast was as sharp as lightning. It was so loud that a cloud of dust rose from the surface of the runway behind the C-141 and curled outward, forming double horns that framed Pauli Weigand as they passed. Everyone on the ramp collapsed forward, like a stand of dominoes slammed down by a gust of wind.

"You can start carrying out bodies now," Rebecca Carnes called to the Spec 5 as she stepped away from his truck.

Washington, DC

March 18, 1967

By the time TC 779 had been inserted directly into the safe house and was scanning for anomalies in the cellar around them, Grainger was up and running in his hard suit. He even reset his displays for standard visuals: there wasn't room in the safe house cellar for much in the way of hidden threat, not with the capsule in there.

Boxes and crates were scanned and pronounced harmless. The exterior temperature was 68 degrees Fahrenheit, a welcome relief. Aside from rodents, arachnids, and flying insects which could carry communicable diseases, the cellar held no threat at this moment.

His suit took the data feed from TC 779 and pricked him with at least half a dozen inoculations in quick succession. It felt as though his right wrist cuff were nibbling him. Then that stopped and Roebeck's voice said, "Ready?"

"Nan, I'll go first."

"Tim, age before beauty."

Chun said, "Nan, Tim: stable and holding," softly in his ear. She was Chun Quo, his team mate, his backup, again; not the Oriental enemy she'd never been except in his mind.

Grainger took a deep breath. There were times instincts could get you killed faster even than stupidity. He wasn't going to let that happen.

Nan Roebeck's suited bulk shut out his centerpunched realtime view of the cellar beyond the opening hatch.

Roebeck's voice said, "Chun, you hold TC 779 out of phase as a safeguard against attacks. We're going to get out of the suits once we've done a security check. We'll set them for two minutes every four hours."

"Nan, I wish you wouldn't—that could be just what we shouldn't do."

"Chun, it's SOP. If you see something you don't like out there, try to pop back in long enough to signal us."

Chun sighed. "Nan, I don't like this."

Roebeck was out of the hatchway, moving around on the floor. Grainger followed. When he was through the lock and down the ramp, he turned just in time to see TC 779 phase out.

Then they were alone in Timeline B, committed, armed to the teeth, and ready for anything—until they got out of those suits.

Grainger felt the phase out of the displacement craft like a physical loss.

Roebeck was stamping around, punching holes in crates and generally trying to arouse any enemy that might be lurking.

"Nan, there's an upstairs to this place."

"Tim, if nobody comes down, we're not taking the suits up."

He could only hear her breathing if she enabled the intercom by using his name. The rest of the time, if he wanted to hear more than his own breathing, he needed to be taking external audio.

So he did that, until the moment came when she said, "Tim, let's get out of these. Go first. I'll cover you."

He hadn't wanted to get into the damned thing. Now he didn't want to get out of it.

When he'd climbed out of his hard suit and finally sent it off to phase space, he felt as if he'd lost his best friend. He sat on a crate, watching Roebeck watch him, alert for revisionists. Her suit loomed larger in the dank basement the longer they sat that way. Eventually Grainger realized that the scant daylight from a high barred window was fading to night. Sirens yowled distantly, perhaps as the roundup of civilians continued, perhaps from nothing more than random city violence.

Roebeck stayed suited, visor down, fully armored and holding a heavy plasma rifle in a robotically assisted grip, for nearly an hour before she was satisfied that it was safe to dispatch the second suit.

Then they were adrift, for the next four hours anyway, in a 1968 as alien as Command Central had become. Grainger methodically checked all his sensory gear and his disabling weapons for the third time. They weren't here to hide in a basement. Every hour they spent in this time was an hour forever barred from them. If they found out later that this was the critical interval, they could do nothing, ever again, about whatever may have transpired elsewhere during the interval they spent hiding.

Finally, wishing he could have waited her out, he nearly pleaded, "Nan, let's go do it, can't we?"

"I thought you'd never ask," said Roebeck, and let him go first up the stairs into the deepening alien night.

Bien Hoa
Air Force Base

The man's jungle fatigues had been starched and pressed to hold a crease. His name tapes read REYNOLDS and US ARMY, and the black low-visibility oak leaves on his collar could have been either those of a major or a lieutenant colonel. The hair behind his high forehead was thin with a good deal of gray in it, though otherwise he didn't appear to be older than forty. Pauli Weigand lifted him with one arm and his duffle bag with the other.

Reynolds had been standing directly beneath the acoustic grenade when it went off. Trails of dry, black blood ran from his nose and ears, and he was just as dead as if Weigand had shot him through the head.

Colonel Byerly had said casualties among the refugees didn't matter to her, but Weigand didn't believe she meant that. Certainly they mattered to Weigand.

He tossed the duffle bag onto the concrete, then carried the corpse down the ramp and laid it gently beside the bag. He knew it didn't matter—baggage or dead meat, neither one could feel pain—but he did it anyway.

The acoustic grenade was simple enough that an equivalent device could have been constructed on the present horizon, though the available support technology would have resulted in something both larger and less powerful than what

194

Weigand had used. The grenade created an omnidirectional sound wave, only microseconds in duration but of enormous intensity, by detonating a few millimeters of osmium wire with an electrical pulse. Chemical explosives could achieve similar effects, but at lower amplitude than was possible with energy density available from the 26th century's electronic storage systems.

Weigand couldn't have safely used an acoustic grenade at the range he had—a hundred meters—without the protection of the cancellation wave his headband generated. The compression and rarefaction of the band's tuned pulse were 180 degrees out of phase with those of the grenade and were of precisely the same amplitude as the detonation wave when it reached the person wearing the headband.

The grenade delivered overpressures comparable to the muzzle blast of the largest naval guns. It was stunning at moderate distances and potentially lethal to those as close as the late Mr. Reynolds.

Weigand wished Nan were here. He hated to make decisions like that one even more than he hated to carry them out.

"C'mon, c'mon, c'mon!" the chief of the cargo handlers boomed from the pallets at the front of the bay. "Burnett, pay out the hook and let's get this fucker empty!"

All the refugees had been removed from the aircraft, carried or—in the case of those the cargo handlers dealt with— dumped to the concrete as if they'd been so many sacks of mail. Weigand and the C-141's crew had been more gentle, though none of them made much effort to amend the ground personnel's technique. It was hard to find sympathy for cowards who feathered their nests while sending better folk to bleed and die.

Rebecca was with the patients, able to be a nurse again. She looked more relaxed than Weigand had previously seen her, even at times when they were together in TC 779 and there was no immediate crisis.

Barthuli had been willing to help with the physical labor, though as he'd said, he'd "probably turn out to be as useless

as tits on a boar." Weigand told him to graze the commo net
and see what he could learn. There wasn't a risk of drown-
ing in the information flow, since Gerd's software preselected
items based on his uniquely excellent parameters.

The cargo handlers robbed the refugees as they removed
them. Weigand didn't know how much use the money and jew-
elry would be when the collapse of America and the war effort
became total in the next few weeks, but that wasn't Weigand's
concern. The men were doing their job well enough. Whatever
Rebecca told them had made a sufficient impression, perhaps
underscored by the effect of the acoustic grenade.

The copilot, sweaty and wan, walked over to join Weigand
as the ground crewmen fitted a harness to the Conex. The fellow looked down at the refugees, piled like cordwood to either side of the ramp. "Christ," he muttered. "Where's this
going to end?"

"That's out of our hands," Weigand said with gloomy
diplomacy. The airman seemed a decent man, brave or duti-
ful enough to make a flight whose risks he must have known.
Though perhaps . . . you didn't need to be able to visit the future of this horizon to be able to predict disaster for America
both here and at home.

"It's out of everybody's hands," the copilot said. "It's like
stepping outside at forty thousand feet without a parachute.
It may take a while to drop, but you're going to hit the ground
eventually."

He hawked and spit onto the ramp. "Sure wish we hadn't
taken that first step into Nam."

Some of the refugees were stirring now, especially those
who'd been outside the aircraft when the grenade went off.
Weigand was ready to use his acoustic pistol on any individual who tried to get back aboard, but he doubted that would
be necessary. Those the detonation wave had stunned would
be a long time regaining full intellect and motor control.

"I'll go forward," the copilot said. "Help Harry check us
out for takeoff. We'll turn her around as soon as your friends
get their patients aboard."

A cargo handler shouted. The winch whined, taking up slack for a moment before it started to move the Conex. The steel container raised low-frequency thunder in the cargo bay as it moved down the rollers in the floor.

"Have you been fueled?" Weigand shouted.

The copilot shrugged. "We've got enough in the center tanks to get us to Yokota," he shouted back. "Air traffic control warned us before we took off there that there wouldn't be any fuel for us at Bien Hoa."

He shook his head, grimacing. "They said there was a load of seriously wounded waiting. We took a vote, all of us, and decided we'd try. It'll be all right, I figure."

Giving Weigand a half-mocking salute, the copilot walked toward the cockpit. The ARC Rider watched the man's slim, stooped figure for a moment.

The Conex trundled past. Weigand swallowed and jumped to the ground, pitching his big body far enough outward to avoid the pile of refugees.

Everybody eventually died—brave men and cowards alike. Maybe it made a difference to them afterward as to how they'd lived their lives. Maybe it only mattered now, while they were living it. That was enough for Weigand, at least.

He walked toward the medical convoy. The attendants were preparing to shift the vehicles closer to the ramp as soon as the last of the pallets were offloaded.

Barthuli had been sitting cross-legged in the shade of the aircraft's drooping wing, his computer/recorder trained on the horns of one of the nearby microwave communication towers. He stood and strode to join Weigand with a bemused expression on his face.

"Having fun, Gerd?" Weigand asked as he adjusted the direction in which he was walking to bring him closer to the analyst.

Barthuli quirked a wry smile. "This is a unique experience for me, Pauli," he said.

The two men walked parallel for a few steps, then stopped in unspoken agreement, their eyes on the distant fenced horizon.

"It's an information-rich environment, of course," Barthuli continued. He nodded toward the communications towers. "Requests, orders, manifests—anything you could want, all open for you or even me to modify according to our requirements. A flight to Son Tay should be no difficulty."

"We've got a flight to Son Tay," Weigand said. They were standing on bare concrete, fifty meters from anyone else. Colonel Byerly got into the cab of her truck and started the engine. "We think we do, at any rate."

"Yes, that's what's interesting," Barthuli said. His words weren't agreement. "There's no record of that flight that I can find. And from what I can tell—I may be wrong, of course—"

"And pigs may fly," Weigand muttered.

"—but almost none of the electronic data I can access relates to anything real on the ground. Orders are ignored, or perhaps the people to whom they're directed don't exist, or don't exist at that location. Matériel isn't shipped from warehouses as directed, either because it's not there to begin with—stolen, I suppose, or simply misplaced in the confusion—or because the people directed to move it aren't informed, or don't have vehicles, or were transferred a hundred kilometers away last month."

"Some things are getting done," Weigand commented, looking over his shoulder at the trucks, now loaded. Carnes and the younger doctor were talking earnestly to the cargo handlers, apparently asking for help in carrying the patients aboard the C-141.

"The chance of that cargo going where it's supposed to is virtually nil," Barthuli said flatly. "There's a somewhat higher chance of it being used for a purpose more or less in line with US government objectives, such as they are. I can show you a hundred sequences of orders and messages following up orders, and none of it makes any difference. Any more than the orders to load patients on this aircraft to transport them to Japan made any difference."

"They're going," said Weigand.

"They're going," Barthuli said, "because of what happened here—because Rebecca knew Lieutenant Colonel Byerly, and because we needed something Lieutenant Colonel Byerly could provide."

The analyst's face froze momentarily in a smile. "Also because you cared, Pauli. And other people care. There's still a system of sorts, that works in a fashion—because individuals know one another and care, despite all. But it isn't anything we could tap electronically."

"I'm going to help move people," Weigand said. "Then I suppose we'll get out of here." He cleared his throat and added, "It's a good thing we've got Rebecca along."

"And it's a good thing you care, Pauli," Barthuli said. His voice sounded almost wistful.

Son Tay, North Vietnam (Occupied)

The membrane that Carnes had pulled down from the headband to cover her face didn't physically impede her breathing, but whenever she thought about it she felt her throat constrict. The canvas sides of the three-quarter-ton truck were half raised. When she peered through the opening out at the darkened rice paddies, she couldn't see any difference compared to the way the landscape had looked without the facemask.

"This is the spectrum control, Rebecca," Weigand said, guiding her index finger to a roughened spot on the headband just above her left temple. "Infrared, light enhancement, and normal optical. You can tell which is which—"

Carnes pressed the roughness. Water stood out from the dikes like a sheet of silver. The short rice stems were dark fur above the surface. Insects buzzed through the warm air as tiny fireballs.

"—by the dot on the upper left corner of the display for about three seconds, red, yellow, or white."

She pressed. The amount of contrast shrank abruptly. The scene had color, but the hues were of low saturation. It looked like a television picture taken at noon when the sky was heavily overcast.

"I can tell the difference," Carnes said, returning the view to the normal optical range of a tropical night when the moon was in its first quarter.

The road was four-lane concrete, built by US construction companies in the early days of the occupation. There had been very little maintenance in the past five years. Though the roadbed was a dozen feet deep, the alluvial soil shifted occasionally under its weight. The truck drove over a crack and dropped eight inches to the other side.

Weigand and Barthuli bounced high in the air with the cases of medical supplies which had flown to Son Tay with the team on a high-winged U-10 utility aircraft. Carnes took the shock on her braced feet, then lowered her buttocks to the wooden side-bench again. She was used to these roads. It was a horrible thing to realize, but she was.

The lieutenant on the passenger side in front twisted around and asked, "You guys all right? Should've warned you."

He was a medical administration officer. He had a thin, intense face and was probably strung out on something. Maybe just strung out with war and his nerves.

"We're fine," Carnes said. "I hope your supplies are cushioned well, though."

They probably were. Not that it made much of a difference, the way things were going.

A howitzer fired into the night from a battery position within the compound to the west. The white flash shocked the sky like heat lightning. The muzzle blast nearly ten seconds later was dull and muted.

"You get much enemy activity here?" Carnes asked the lieutenant. She raised her voice to be heard over the rattle of the truck bed. The vehicle had only one headlight. The pylons which had once held sodium vapor lamps at every hundred meters along the roadway were dark, had been dark for years.

The FM radio wedged between the front seats was tuned to a local armed forces station. The volume was cranked high to compete with the noise the truck made.

The lieutenant's head turned like that of a wasp, with quick, quasi-mechanical movements. "What?" he said. He thumped the butt of his M16 on the floor at his feet. "Don't you worry about dinks, Major. We're ready for them."

Carnes nodded, keeping her wince internal. She'd seen . . . hundreds? It seemed like hundreds. Hundreds of people come in wounded by accident. Because somebody did something stupid, like banging down a rifle with a bullet in the chamber.

On the other hand, the lieutenant was out here, at night, to pick up supplies which his superiors had convinced Colonel Byerly that the 96th Evacuation Hospital needed even worse than Byerly's clinic did. Carnes supposed you had to be crazy to function in a war zone, especially this war zone.

"Rebecca, to use the mask as a communicator . . ." Pauli said. His voice echoed oddly, received both in the normal way and through the bone-conduction speaker built into the headband. He was so close to Carnes that the difference between radio and sound propagation rates was almost imperceptible. "Key the sending unit to a specific person by leading with the name, or for a general broadcast say 'Commo.' "

"Pauli, I understand," Carnes said, obeying what she took as a request. Gerd Barthuli was doing something with his little box, so Weigand had decided it would be a good time to train Carnes in the use of the headsets they'd brought from the immersion suits.

Only two of the units were full-function now. Pauli had taken the battery out of the one Carnes normally wore to power the weapon he'd built in Chicago. The facemask had still protected her from gas, though.

"The headband can act as a display, also," Weigand said, speaking normally again. "Though for the—"

The brakes squealed, but the truck didn't slow with any enthusiasm. The driver slam-shifted to a lower gear without clutching. Carnes switched her mask to light amplification mode to see what was going on.

"—time being, I don't think—" Weigand said.

The feeder road to Son Tay Base met the highway at nearly a right angle, much more sharply radiused than civilian engineers in the States would have designed its equivalent. The truck was approaching too fast for its ill-adjusted brakes alone to slow it to a safe speed. The lieutenant pounded the steel dashboard with his left hand in rhythm with the music.

The driver grunted, leaning to the right as he dragged the nonpower-assisted steering wheel around. Son Tay Base a quarter mile away was encircled with a berm topped with barbed wire. The gate, a frame of steel X-members stretching concertina wire, glowed like a fireball. Carnes' mask amplified the light of the single incandescent light beside the bunker.

"—you need to worry about—"

A burst of shots from the turn's inside corner shattered the windshield and at least two slapped through the driver's chest. The man shouted. The wheel spun out of his relaxed grip.

The truck straightened and drove off the opposite side of the feeder road. It jumped high but didn't turn over.

Carnes bounced like a pool ball between the roof of canvas stretched on steel hoops and the sidewalls of the bed. For a moment she thought she'd be thrown out the open back. The truck's sudden halt, mired in soft soil, saved Carnes at the cost of being slammed hard against the cab. She didn't lose consciousness, quite.

The driver tried to shout but gurgled instead. The lieutenant bellowed as he kicked at his wedged door with the heels of both boots.

Pauli Weigand, holding the EMP generator, hopped out of the vehicle with the grace of a big cat. He seemed so awkward until something happened.

"Rebecca, come with me to shoot!" Weigand demanded. "Use thermal and shoot!"

Carnes jumped clumsily over the tailgate and plodded around the truck to the driver's side of the cab. She'd have given the facemask to Barthuli, but she didn't know where the analyst had gone. The ground was soft and covered with waist-high scrub, some of it thorny.

More gunfire came from the opposite side of the road. At least two automatic weapons were firing. Their tracers were red, US issue. Bullets snapped through the air ten feet above the stalled truck.

Carnes opened the cab door and caught the driver as he slumped out into her arms. The lieutenant stood on the other running board and ripped off the entire magazine of his rifle in a single burst. A few of his bullets ricocheted sparklingly from stones in the road embankment, but most of them sailed off into the night in high arcs to nowhere.

"Rebecca, come support me now!"

One of the bullets that hit the driver had keyholed, spinning most of the man's breastbone through his chest cavity. Both lungs were collapsed, and his heart had been chopped into hash. There was no carotid pulse. The FM radio, flung into the darkness through the disintegrating windshield, continued to make the night shimmer with a rap song.

Carnes swallowed and slogged toward where she saw Pauli hunching on their side of the road embankment. The acoustic pistol was buttoned into the side pocket of her tunic. She took it out as she moved, bending forward to stay as low as she could without crawling.

The lieutenant reloaded and fired again. This time he was shooting in five- or six-round bursts, but his fire was no more accurate than it had been initially. He was more danger to the team than he was to the enemy, though at least his tracers and muzzle flashes would draw the hostiles' attention.

Carnes reached the low embankment, then raised her head just to eye level. The night had a hazy clarity through her faceshield, as if the landscape were drawn with sticks of pale pastels. A third rifle fired from the rising slope across the road. The bullets slapped angrily against the truck's sheet metal. The lieutenant dived for cover beneath the vehicle.

The shooter was only a blur to Carnes, even though the muzzle flashes told her exactly where to look. She remembered Pauli had ordered her to use thermal imaging. She switched the faceshield to infrared, saw all three of the attackers clearly through the shielding vegetation, and pointed her pistol at the nearest of them some fifty feet away.

She pulled the trigger. The pistol quivered. The ambusher, unaffected by the acoustic weapon, continued firing at the truck. So did his two companions.

Carnes clicked her trigger twice more, then held it down for several seconds. The grip of the acoustic pistol grew alarmingly hot, but the riflemen shot without pausing.

"Rebecca, wait!" Weigand ordered. "Wait till I tell you when!"

Carnes crouched and looked at the big ARC Rider. He was struggling to make some adjustment on his EMP generator. She didn't see what good a magnetic pulse would do against nonelectronic weapons.

One of the ambushers got up and started to cross the road, firing his automatic rifle from the hip. Before Carnes could react, the fellow pitched backward unconscious from an invisible blow. Gerd Barthuli was still alive and clearly more alert than Carnes seemed to be.

"Rebecca, get ready," Weigand ordered. He lifted his torso over the embankment, his EMP generator shouldered. "Now!"

One of the ambushers let out a terrible scream and leaped to his feet. Carnes swung her acoustic pistol in a desperate arc as though it were a fly swatter, mashing the trigger down. The man grunted and doubled up.

The third rifleman shifted his stance and shot at Weigand. They were close enough together to throw rocks at one another.

Three spurts of rock in an asphalt matrix blasted up from the road surface; one of the bullets retained enough integrity to ricochet outward with a banshee howl. Then that shooter, too, screamed, turned, and tried to run away. Carnes aimed at the man's bent back and again held her trigger down. The ambusher flung his arms out and sprawled on his face.

The acoustic pistol burned Carnes' hand. She dropped it. It hissed on the damp soil.

Pauli stood, drawing his acoustic pistol. He held the EMP generator in his left hand.

Gerd was standing beside the truck. The lieutenant stuck his M16 over the hood of the vehicle to fire another blind burst. The analyst wrenched the weapon away from him.

The ambusher lying on the feeder road was a Caucasian in American fatigues. He was breathing stertorously. Carnes pried the M16 from his unconscious grip. The barrel was hot from continuous firing.

Carnes pushed through the brush to the other two ambushers, who were lying close together. Pauli followed her. "The acoustic pistols won't work through vegetation," he said. His voice was hoarse. "They converge at the first change in the refractive index in the line of sight, whether it's a leaf or a man's skull. I had to get them to jump up so that you could get a clear shot at them."

"EMP did that?" Carnes said. Her throat felt as though it had been sandpapered.

The other ambushers were blacks, again carrying M16s and wearing American uniforms. One of them was a Spec 4. He held his stomach and cursed in a desperate voice. Weigand kicked his head back with a jolt from his acoustic pistol.

"Not EMP," Weigand said. "I modified the generator so that it could also induce a mild current in human sensory nerves at a distance of fifty meters or so. It's quite harmless, but it makes you feel as though your skin's being dipped in acid."

Barthuli and the lieutenant joined them. "They killed Benji deader'n shit, didn't they?" the lieutenant said. "Jesus, Jesus Christ."

"They were Americans," Carnes said. "They are."

"Yeah," agreed the lieutenant. "Waiting for something with a Red Cross to come by. Hoped they'd get drugs. Morphine, Demerol, Percodan . . . Jesus, Jesus Christ."

He shook his head. "I guess we better take them in, hand them over to the MPs at the gate. Notice they didn't risk *their* sweet necks getting involved."

The lieutenant looked from Weigand to Carnes, the only one of the team wearing rank tabs, and added, "Or I suppose we could shoot them here, Major?"

"We take them in," said Rebecca Carnes. She wanted to cry, but her eyes were as dry as her throat was.

Washington, DC

March 17, 1967

The Old Executive Office Building was perhaps the most ornately beautiful structure in the entire district. In Grainger's time, everybody had called it OEOB, unless you worked there—then you called it the White House. That was what your business card said if you were on the National Security Council Staff, which was housed there.

Walking with Nan Roebeck through the wrought-iron gates and down the broad stone steps into the courtyard, then up more steps and into the foyer where three guards waited, Grainger experienced a déjà vu of unsettling proportions. In the marble-floored foyer, he walked her right up to the desk and presented his 1967 driver's license to the guard attending to visitors.

"Mr. Calandine. He's expecting us at 2100 hours," Grainger said softly. Out of the corner of his eye, he watched Nan Roebeck, in a period-correct skirt and blouse, fumble in her 1967-style huge handbag for her ID.

The ID check wasn't by computer, that was one difference from Grainger's memories. The guard consulted a list and then punched an office phone number on an archaic base unit with square buttons that lit when depressed. He spoke into the handset and then hung up.

By then, Nan's ID was on the high mahogany counter. The guard took it, checked it against his clipboard, and pulled out two clip-on badges with large *V*s for *Visitor* printed in red on them.

"Wear these. Step this way."

Now came the weapons check. It too was primitive, cursory. A hand search of Nan's purse detected nothing. They waltzed through an ancient security arch that was set for metal only and was unable to recognize any of Grainger's acoustic weapons as dangerous.

Once through the arch, the guard said, "Down the hall to your left. Take a right. The elevator's halfway down on your left."

And they were in. The elevator doors were painstakingly chased brass. The floor buttons were round and stayed depressed when you pushed them.

When the elevator doors opened onto the second-floor landing, the high-ceilinged corridor was empty. Doors on either side were closed, the moldings around and above them as ornate as were the stairs behind. Nan Roebeck walked over to the winding stairs and touched the wrought-iron and gold leaf and mahogany. "This is . . . beautiful."

"Best in town. The doorknobs here all have the original insignia of some service or office on them—"

Grainger heard footsteps and shut his mouth. The man coming toward them wasn't Calandine, but his stride was purposeful.

"For Mr. Calandine?" said the man, putting out his hand but not giving his name. He was six-foot-six, with a bushy black mustache and a huge helmet of curly black hair. "This way."

Grainger was getting the feeling he was in over his depth. Roebeck cast him a furtive look. There was nothing to do but follow along, down the corridor, around a corner, and through a door into an anteroom.

"We're meeting in my boss's office," said the tall guy. Grainger nodded without listening as a secretary was introduced and held out her hand, which he shook. Behind her desk was the eagle-headed seal of the Central Intelligence Agency, on a CIA-blue wall.

"Would you come this way?" said the woman, and: "Coffee? Tea? A cold drink?"

Through two double doors they went, and he heard Nan ask for coffee, so he did the same. "Black, please," to cover his consternation. They were, without doubt, in the CIA director's office in OEOB. The paintings behind the huge desk and beyond the football-field conference table were from the national collection, the furniture was historical, and the ambience was all power.

The tall guy said, "Take a seat," and motioned toward the conference table. The chairs at the table were dark blue, covered with leather hides of actual animals turned into furniture. Strange to be back in that sort of milieu. Their guide smiled, and the huge mustache quivered. "We have a couple more people coming, so let's wait."

The tall man didn't want to make small talk. Okay. Where the hell was Calandine?

The coffee came, in Lenox cups with the agency seal. Spooky wasn't the word for this place. This was someplace Grainger had never been, in any timeline, and had no interest in being. This was an abode of elephants. Elephants can crush you underfoot without even noticing.

Grainger kept his eyes on a painting of an ancient boat in sunset. Roebeck, beside him, kicked him gently under the table. The tall man sat down opposite him and opened a folder containing an empty legal pad.

You couldn't ask what was going on. You had to wait. He hoped to hell she knew that. Under the table, there was plenty of room to slide his acoustic pistol out of his pocket and hold it one-handed between his thighs. Shoot your way out of the NSC? From the second floor? Not likely. But he had to do something. . . .

"Mr. Calandine will be joining us?"

"Not necessary," said the black mustache, twitching above the tall man's lips like an animal in pain.

"I wonder if you could tell us—" Nan Roebeck began as the doors opened again and two more men stepped in, one florid-faced blond with a khaki suit and a briefcase, the second short and rotund in a blazer and slacks, with hair combed back from a pronounced widow's peak and a huge head with Germanic features.

"That's what we're here to do, ma'am," said the khaki suit, slapping his briefcase down on the table.

The tall guy nodded. There were to be no introductions, no cards exchanged, Grainger realized as the florid-faced man in khaki began to speak.

"The Soviets have a mind-control weapon and they're using it on the National Security Advisor," he said flatly. "We know it's portable, highly directional, and emits at probably around 11.5 cycles per second. What we don't know is how to stop it." He pulled charts from his briefcase and laid them out with grave precision, so that they faced Roebeck and Grainger.

Soviets? *Soviets* just means "friends," or some such. Grainger racked his brains, and then realized that the man meant the Russian-dominated USSR.

"How do you know?" Roebeck asked with more presence of mind than Grainger had shown.

"We know, young lady," the short rotund man said with patronizing cordiality, "because it's our job to know." His voice was grainy and cultured. Grainger was now sure that this was the senior officer in the room. Some very senior officer, given the room in question. "I want you to be very sure that we know." Twinkling eyes and the jovial, conspiratorial smile of a seasoned agent-runner took the sting out of his words.

Nan Roebeck flushed and sat back, grasping the blue leather arms of her chair hard with whitening fingers.

"Mr. Calandine," said the tall man with the mustache, "felt that you needed to have these specifics." He tapped the charts on the table. One was a map of DC. One was a credible drawing of an acoustic device that no Soviet or Russian or all the combined technological skills of the entire Union of Soviet

Socialist Republics could have made in this century. "Mr. Calandine felt that you might have some light to shed on how one counters such a device."

Fuck. Grainger was going to hang Calandine out to dry, first chance he got.

The three intelligence officers stared at Grainger while his mind raced. "Earplugs," Grainger said. Did they understand sound cancellation in the mid-20th century? Probably not. "A ... wet ... suit. Lead-lined baffles. Glass-sandwich soundproofing. Or ... let us handle it." He had to take the initiative. He was here as a representative of Los Alamos' super-secret national security and intelligence component, one of the nuclear lab's baddest bad boys. That was the legend that had gotten him this meeting. Need to know, especially technical need to know, was sure to extend to a rival intelligence service, even in these ancient times. So he stonewalled. "Give us some idea what else you have besides basic drawings and this map of . . . possible past incidents. . . ."

He pulled the map closer to make sure he was reading it right. That's what it was. Time- and date-marked points, all in the temporal past. "Give us some tracking data on the targets you've identified, or what you've got for site intel, and just stay out of our way." Any number could play this game.

"We can't have you running around town shooting possible perpetrators, not when we can't explain why we're doing it. This can't blow," said the rotund man. He tripled his chins and laced his stubby fingers. The cordial smile was gone from his face, but his hooded eyes still twinkled.

"We won't kill anyone," Nan Roebeck promised with more authority than Grainger could have mustered. "We'll take the device out of play."

"Tell me another one," said the khaki-suited man.

"No, let's assume they can do that. Calandine says they can. And my parameters on this are clear," said the mustache. "But we want the device."

"So do we," said Grainger, suddenly hoping against hope

that he understood the game. "But we can't guarantee it won't be destroyed."

The rotund man punted back to two chins and smiled his cherubic smile. "We can do something with the remains—of the device, of course."

Who could? Was there a Defense Science Board in 1967? Did Johnnie Foster run it then, if it existed so far back? And if not, was "we" the Directorate of Intelligence—the analysts? Because if that was so, then the short, rotund man was very probably the deputy director for intelligence himself.

"What can you give me, sir," Grainger asked, looking at the rotund man, "that will take this discussion out of the hypothetical?"

The rotund man looked at the khaki-clad man. The khaki-clad man looked at the mustached man. The mustached man nodded. Data-heavy sheets came out of the briefcase. Two photos were reproduced there, along with names, addresses, and general government tracking data circa 1967. The khaki-clad man pushed those over to Grainger. He had to put his acoustic pistol back in his pocket to take them with his right hand, but he didn't want to awkwardly grab the sheets with his left and advertise that his right was otherwise engaged.

Once he'd pocketed his pistol, Grainger swept the two sheets off the table as if he could care less. He got up. "If that's it . . ."

Roebeck rose with him. The rotund man rose suddenly and the khaki-clad man scrambled to his feet.

The tall man stayed seated. "What's the procedure for dealing with any collateral damage, exposure, and hand-over of people or matériel?"

"Whatever you recommend, within feasibility for us," Nan said in a yawning silence during which all Grainger could think of was that there wasn't going to be any collateral damage, exposure, or hand-over of people or matériel. He had what he'd needed and hadn't dared to ask for. He just wanted to get out of there alive.

"We'll expect a call from you," said the mustache, "to Mr. Calandine. Then this group will convene again. Please give us as much warning as possible if you think the wheels are going to come off this mission." The mustache lifted to reveal, for the first time, a full set of large, white teeth.

The mustached man held out his hand and Grainger recognized a Citadel ring as he shook it. When he let go, the other two men were already disappearing through the double doors.

"I'll walk you down," said the tall guy, herding them toward the door. "Good brief, everybody. The DDI bought it. Now all you have to do is make this problem go away—invisibly, if possible."

Before Grainger could stop her, Roebeck said, "Invisibility's our strong suit."

"Just make sure to bring me back whatever's left," said the mustached man. "He really wants that device."

Neither Grainger nor Roebeck answered. Their footsteps were loud on the marble as the mustached man escorted them in silence to the elevator and down, past the guards, where they handed in their *V* for *Visitor* badges.

Not until they were alone out on Pennsylvania Avenue did Roebeck say anything. "Just like a historical novel." She shuddered. "We're not really sure, though, if we can trust them."

"Why not? They want the same thing we do. They're not going to get all they want, but they'll get the most important part."

"You hope."

"I promise," Grainger said grimly. In a strange and sad way, he'd come home. The spooks in there were a lot closer to him intellectually and operationally than were the ARC Riders. Their allegiance was one he'd shared too long not to remember—or to honor.

The United States was a place he'd sworn an oath to protect, an ideal he'd lost when he'd been cut lose from his native time. A part of him was glad to have it back, even though that ideal and that place were grossly changed and more threatened than ever before.

Or since.

Son Tay Base,
North Vietnam (Occupied)

Timeline B: August 17, 1991

As Pauli Weigand swung his long legs out of the back of the jeep, he set his facemask to sweep the thermal spectrum for a half second every three seconds. That was a refinement of the headband's capability which he hadn't bothered to explain to Carnes.

Carnes started to get out of the front passenger seat. The driver, a nurse named Sendaisa with captain's bars, put a hand on her shoulder and said, "Becky, are you really sure you want to do this? We could sure use you as chief of nursing again. And don't worry about Saigon learning. Saigon can't figure out which direction the sun comes up, these last few months."

Carnes capped Sendaisa's hand with her own and squeezed. "Thanks Val," she said. "I'm on another job, now."

She got out of the jeep before Sendaisa could say anything further. Carnes was part of Weigand's team. Weigand wasn't sure why, but he didn't think it was as simple as the ex-nurse fearing to be left behind as her horizon sank into chaos and H-bombs.

Weigand was glad he had Carnes along. The one piece of good luck in the whole business was that Carnes and Barthuli were with him when he got separated from TC 779.

Sendaisa hesitated a moment longer, looking past the team to the compound where she'd delivered them over her protests. After the ambush, the MPs towed the ambushed truck from the soft ground with their armored personnel carrier. The damaged vehicle, only marginally drivable, had barely gotten them to the 96th. Carnes had found Sendaisa, an old friend, to run the team a kilometer across the base to where Watney stayed when he was in Son Tay.

The compound of the 504th Provisional Company was on the northern perimeter of Son Tay Base. It was encircled by a bamboo stockade interlaced with concertina wire and razor ribbon. Grenade booby traps hung from the wire, deliberately obvious in warning.

Barthuli had determined before the team left the Continental US that the 504th was carried on the books of the Army of the Republic of Vietnam. In reality, the unit was the personal fiefdom of Kyle Watney—Colonel Watney, though there was no evidence that either the US or Vietnamese governments had granted Watney rank of any kind. Watney had raised the 504th, staffed it with a combination of volunteers and the dregs of military prisons transferred to him to do with as he chose, and paid for the unit in fashions that didn't leave a ripple in the formal record.

Watney ran the 504th as if he were God. There were six human heads on stakes outside the stockade's gate. One was a skull with scraps of dried flesh still clinging; two were so fresh that the eyeballs hadn't yet sunken into the sockets. From the stories Carnes and Sendaisa had told, any or all of the heads could have belonged to members of the 504th who'd offended Watney in some way.

Weigand glanced at his companions. Carnes looked . . . perhaps tired, perhaps disgusted; not afraid. Gerd was his usual interested self, though he limped slightly from the bruise his left thigh had taken when he flew from the truck as it left the road.

Weigand shrugged. "Let's go, then," he said.

"I'll lead," said Rebecca Carnes, putting her hand on Weigand's chest to slow him to a half step behind her. "Watney knows me."

A bonfire in the heart of the compound swirled sparks into the night sky and glimmered through the interstices of the bamboo. There were no electric lights. Recorded music with a throbbing bass line played loud enough to be audible half a klick away. If any of the other residents of Son Tay Base objected to such noise at 0200 hours, they had better sense than to complain to the 504th directly.

The gate was of barbed wire woven on a bamboo frame. It hung ajar. A crossbar, a length of broken torsion bar from an APC, lay beside the opening.

"Hello?" Carnes called. She swung the gate fully open.

The guard was behind a curtain of dried grass. He showed up clearly when Weigand's faceshield swept the infrared spectrum.

The guard lunged from the darkness with a sharpened bayonet, thrusting at Carnes' throat. Weigand grabbed the man's knife wrist with his left hand. The fellow was short, strong, and spiked on drugs.

"I'm a friend of the colonel's," Rebecca Carnes said. She sounded as calm as a clerk taking inventory. "We're here to see Colonel Watney."

The guard writhed like a snake. The pupils of his eyes were shrunk to pinholes. He should have been virtually blind in the faint moonlight, but he'd seen Carnes' throat clearly enough.

"Colonel not here," the man said. His voice was husky; there was the dimple of a long-healed bullet hole above his larynx. "Go away or I kill you. I kill you anyway!"

He was amazingly strong. Weigand was afraid he'd break the guard's wrist if it was necessary to squeeze any harder to hold the man. The fellow wore a fully automatic Czech machine pistol slung like a lavaliere. The weapon bumped against the tattoos on his bare chest as he struggled. Neither he nor Weigand was using his free hand.

Gerd spoke to the man in a language Weigand didn't understand; Oriental, certainly. The guard stopped struggling, though he still held tense. He snarled back to Barthuli and spat on the ground at the analyst's feet.

Barthuli leaned forward within ten centimeters of the guard's face and shouted at him. The guard shouted, then dropped the bayonet. He stamped the weapon against the ground with his bare foot as he continued to curse Barthuli in broken desperation.

"Let him go," Barthuli said.

Weigand released the guard's wrist, giving the man a slight push as he did so. He wasn't going to second-guess Gerd, but it seemed at least as likely as not that the guard was going to try to kill them all as soon as he was loose.

Instead, the man turned his back on the team and squatted, wrapping his arms around his knees. He began to sway and keen.

Weigand glanced at Barthuli and asked, "What on earth did you say to him?"

"It wasn't really what I said," the analyst explained. "I told him we'd force all his female relatives to have sexual congress with hogs before we killed them. But my recorder had analyzed his speech patterns, and I was able to address him in the dialect of his home village. I think that was the important thing."

"Oh," said Weigand. His stomach turned. Not because of what had happened. That was a slick maneuver which avoided the physical violence Weigand had thought was inevitable. "Good job, Gerd."

The problem was that Weigand knew if the situation required (and allowed) it, Barthuli would have set women out to be raped by pigs with the same cool reason that permitted him to make the threat.

"He's from a village about seventy kilometers northwest of Beijing," Barthuli said. "Colonel Watney has recruited ralliers from the Chinese forces as well as Vietnamese."

"Let's go talk to the man," Weigand said. He worked the strain out of his left hand, clenching and spreading the fingers.

Ahead of them, music pounded the night and the sparks swirled high. The guard had slumped into a drugged stupor, but his eyes were still open. Weigand felt the needle-sharp pupils drilling into his back as the team walked onward.

Son Tay Base,
North Vietnam (Occupied)

Timeline B: August 17, 1991

Rebecca Carnes supposed she'd been that close to death at other times. The moment the Chinese soldier aimed his rifle at her in the middle of Firebase Schaydin, if not before; and probably before as well. Not from a knife, though, six inches short of her neck when Pauli caught the gooner's wrist.

She mustn't call them gooners anymore. They were all human, the way she herself was human; and thus capable of human weakness, like depersonalizing someone faceless in the darkness who'd tried to rip her throat out.

An armored personnel carrier sat on a trailer to the left of the gate. The APC seemed to have been abandoned. Both tracks were missing, and several forward road wheels on the left side had been blown off by a mine. She walked past the disabled vehicle, leading her two companions in the direction of the bonfire.

The wind shifted slightly. The APC smelled as though it were regularly used as a latrine. A fly lit on Carnes' wrist. She crushed it against the thigh of her trousers with a quick motion. She'd seen worse.

Carnes hadn't been afraid when the irregular at the gate tried to kill her. She hadn't really been afraid since the ARC Riders showed her the flash and mushroom absorbing Tampa,

Florida. The world Rebecca Carnes knew had died in that moment, and a part of her person had died with it.

A huge Sikorsky helicopter, a Sea Stallion, was parked in the middle of the compound. Its six rotor blades drooped like the branches of a young willow. When Carnes had seen similar birds they'd been in naval markings, frequently with the orange fuselage panels of the Air-Sea Rescue Service. This helicopter was painted flat black without even tail numbers to identify it.

Two men leaned against the dual landing-gear wheels, kissing and fondling one another's genitals. One of the men was Caucasian, the other Oriental. The joint of opium-laced marijuana they'd been smoking smoldered on the hard ground beside them.

Someone screamed in the near distance. Perhaps it was an animal.

"Do you think Watney might really be gone?" Weigand asked. She'd returned the headband with working commo to Barthuli. He had to bend close to Carnes' ear and shout to be heard over the thunderous music.

"Val says the 504th came back from an operation this morning," Carnes shouted back. "Watney was treated for a through-and-through puncture wound in the right calf muscle and released. They won't be out again so soon."

She thought for a moment, then added, "This is probably a victory celebration. I suppose victory."

Beyond the Sikorsky were two buildings and forty or more men around the bonfire. The buildings were roofed with sheet metal. The lower course was boards slatted outward to provide ventilation instead of being nailed firmly edge-to-edge. The upper portion of the walls was screen wire, though the fabric was ripped in many places.

The roofs and walls were chewed by hundreds of bullet holes. Many of them appeared to have been fired from the inside.

The buildings were side by side with about fifty feet between them. That was where the bonfire, built in a dozen 55-

gallon drums, flared wildly. Each steel drum had been cut off a few inches above the sand-filled base, soaked with diesel fuel, and ignited. Several pigs had been roasted above the oily flames on a grill woven from barbed wire. The bits that still remained hung toward the fire, burned to carbon.

Carnes thought of the National Guardsmen in Iowa and of the napalm victims she'd treated over the years. She supposed it was pork Watney's men had roasted this night.

Watney lolled on a couch covered by a tiger skin on the opposite side of the fire. The bandage on his right calf was red with fresh blood. Carnes knew from her own experience that Watney wouldn't stay in hospital if he could walk away—even if he had to walk with the aid of two of his scarred thugs, each of them armed like a fire team. Nurses who knew him didn't even bother to argue. Nowadays nobody had the time or energy anyway.

"You might wait—" Carnes started to say. She leaned closer to Weigand and repeated in a shout, "You stay here! He knows me."

Pauli nodded, though his impassive face didn't mask his concern.

Carnes passed close to the end of one of the buildings. A Caucasian man was making love to a Vietnamese woman on the raised porch. The woman still wore a brassiere, though her small breasts scarcely required being confined. Her eyes followed Carnes as the man on top grunted and swore softly.

The building wasn't a barracks, though it might have been built as one. The 504th was using it as an arsenal. Carnes saw quivering firelight reflected from machine guns, racks of rifles of differing design, shoulder-launched rockets, and crates of grenades, ammunition, and high explosives.

The one-eyed Vietnamese squatting beside Watney stood up and tossed a bottle into the nearest barrel. The flames puffed blue and settled back to their normal sluggish red.

The man wore a belt of machine gun ammunition across the chest of his black T-shirt. He lifted the ammo over his head and flung it into the bonfire also.

Carnes cringed and looked away. The belt, at least a hundred rounds, went off in rattling explosions. The noise was doubled by bullets and fragments of cartridge casings hitting the sides of the drums. Somebody screamed. Somebody else emptied an automatic rifle into the fire, flinging blazing sand in all directions. Drunken men laughed and hooted.

Sparks landed on the arsenal's riddled metal roof. Carnes resumed walking around the fire. Her right thigh, her wrist, and her ear all stung from bits of embedded metal.

Watney himself was the first person to notice Carnes, though she didn't think he recognized her personally—just as an intruder. Watney locked her in a wide-eyed stare as emotionless as that of a shark starting its run toward prey.

Watney's Vietnamese henchman followed his leader's gaze. The Viet reached behind him for the folding-stock Kalashnikov stuck into the ground by its bayonet. Watney caught the man's arm and used it as an anchor by which to draw himself off the tiger-skin couch.

The attention of most of those present turned to Rebecca Carnes, though there were some exceptions. On the side facing the building still used as a barracks, a black, a Caucasian, and an Oriental were seeing how far they could piss into the bonfire. Flames rolled up from the steam and spat a curtain of sparks. The black turned away, cursing brokenly. His urine continued to splash the ground. The other two men clung to each other and shrieked drunken laughter.

"You remember me, Colonel," Carnes said. She didn't know if he could hear her over the music. Maybe he could read her lips. "Nurse Carnes from the 96th? You remember me!"

Watney nodded slightly, recognition arriving with the tiny click of pins mating in a tumbler lock. Watney bellowed an order in the direction of the barracks. The music came from a boom box under the eaves. It was hooked to external speakers and an amp driven by an aircraft battery.

A naked Vietnamese sprawled beside the unit with a smile and open, glassy eyes. He didn't move when Watney spoke.

Watney's henchman wrenched his Kalashnikov loose and pointed it—toward the boom box or the stoned attendant, Carnes couldn't be sure which. Watney snarled "Slopeheaded bastard!" and pushed the muzzle of the automatic rifle aside.

The Vietnamese fired anyway. The three-shot burst slammed over the heads of several men still lolling beside the fire. A Caucasian laughed, but the stocky Oriental beside him jumped into a crouch and leveled his M16.

Watney jerked the Kalashnikov away and flung it toward the stockade behind him. He shouted again at the attendant who, now awake, lowered the volume as directed.

Watney eyed Carnes again. "Yeah," he said. "Yeah, I remember you. Come here to join us?"

He turned to look around him and swayed. He'd been drinking, in addition to fatigue, loss of blood, and whatever painkillers he'd taken for the wound.

"We're mostly guys right now," he said, slurring the words slightly. His henchman put out an arm to steady him. "But I don't have any prejudice, Carnes. You just have to want to die for the good old US of A, that's all."

"I'm here with some friends," Carnes said. "They'd like to talk with you."

She nodded across the fire toward Weigand and Barthuli. The analyst was picking up something on the ground at his feet. From Carnes' angle, the flames were as much a screen as illumination, but the object looked like a grenade—part of the insane jumble of lethal hardware that strewed the compound. She hoped to God that Barthuli himself wouldn't blow them all up.

Watney and his henchman both followed the direction of Carnes' glance. The Viet's muscles were rigid and trembling with fury. On his forehead was crudely tattooed SAT CONG—"Kill Communists"—a self-delivered death sentence if he were ever captured. The butt of a .45 automatic stuck out from the cargo pocket of his tiger-striped fatigue trousers.

"Are they suits?" Watney asked with a lack of affect which didn't deceive Carnes in the least.

"No," she said sharply. "Not the way you mean."

She eyed her companions more critically. The last thing she wanted was for this man to think she was lying to him. It was hard to know how to describe Gerd Barthuli; but he certainly wasn't an administrator from an air-conditioned office.

"One's a field operative," she said. "The other, he's a specialist. They're not suits."

Watney's henchman said something to him. Carnes had more than a smattering of Vietnamese, but she couldn't follow the passionate flood of language.

Watney smiled at Carnes. "Tak thinks you all should go away," he said. "He doesn't trust you. I think Tak's right."

Carnes took the chance she had to take. She smiled back and said, "They want to talk to you about what happened on March 31, 1968."

Watney's eyes opened a little wider. Carnes looked into them and through them, and all the way to the soul of a man in hell.

Watney smiled. The expression had a jagged look, like that of a jack-o'-lantern carved with a straight razor. "You're from . . ." he said. He lifted his chin, a slight gesture and one that could have meant anything, except to someone who knew the answer.

"I'm not," Carnes said. She flicked her eyes toward Weigand and Barthuli again. "They are, though."

Watney shook himself like a dog emerged from a pond. He wore shorts made from fatigue trousers, sandals cut out of automobile tires—Ho Chi Minhs—and a shoulder holster holding an inverted revolver. The surface of his body was covered with scars. Most of Watney's back was pink keloid from napalm, and the dozen dimpled bullet wounds across his chest looked to have been a certain death sentence.

Yet Kyle Watney still moved with strength and even a certain raw grace. The limp from the present wound would be unnoticeable in a few weeks. Chances were the same would be true of whatever damage he received in the next operation or the one after that.

"Yeah, I'd like to talk to them, too," Watney said. He spoke with no more expression than an oyster has sliding down a diner's throat. He started around the fire.

Tak grabbed Watney by the shoulder and spun him around. Carnes didn't see Watney's hand move, but when he faced the Viet, the revolver was pointed at the man's nose.

Tak shouted. Watney tapped the revolver muzzle on the Viet's forehead, between the words SAT and CONG. Watney said something in a voice as dry and lethal as the rustle of a cobra through grass.

Carnes had been wondering how a man with such open contempt and hatred for Orientals could lead a unit made up largely of Vietnamese and Chinese—many of them ralliers, turncoats from the Communist armies. She hadn't even been sure what Watney was fighting for. He didn't seem to have any political beliefs or even interests.

But now she understood. Kyle Watney was fighting in order to die, and to kill Orientals. He didn't care whether they died under the lash of his bullets or at his side, trying to execute his orders. And the men of the 504th were as mad and desperate as their leader. It was really as simple as that.

Tak tried to hug Watney to his chest. Watney slapped his henchman on the forehead, *hard*, with the butt of the revolver. The Viet fell to the ground.

Other irregulars shifted uneasily, watching the tableau. Watney holstered his revolver and turned, following Carnes to the shadows where the two ARC Riders waited.

Weigand's hands were spread on his thighs in plain view. Barthuli was examining a baseball grenade with the interest to be expected of an entomologist for a rare moth. Around the fire, men went back to their previous pursuits. The attendant turned up the music, then lapsed again into somnolence.

"Colonel Watney?" Weigand said. "I'm Weigand, this is Barthuli. We—"

"Where do you come from?" Watney said, as harsh and direct as an incoming rocket. Weigand's size brought out a hostile undercurrent that Carnes hadn't heard before in the smaller man's tone.

Weigand glanced at Carnes. She shrugged. "He knows," she said.

"We're from about three centuries up the line from you," Weigand admitted without hesitation. "Two and a half, perhaps."

Watney's henchman got groggily to his feet. He wiped his forehead, smearing blood from the pressure cut there. He glared across the fire with bestial hatred.

"You can turn this around?" Watney said. He gestured with a clenched fist. "Turn it *back*?"

"Yes," Weigand said simply. "With your help we can."

"All right," said Watney. "I'll help. I've been waiting—"

His face melted into a childlike wistfulness, utterly at variance with any expression Carnes had seen there before.

"Twenty years, I guess," he said. "I didn't mind that we couldn't go back. I'd been willing to die. Even then I was. But it was three years or so before I really understood what we'd done."

Watney began to cry with great wracking sobs that drained the strength from his legs. He knelt because he could no longer stand. Carnes squatted beside him, trying to comfort something she still thought of as a rabid animal; but an animal in pain, and therefore her responsibility.

Tak screamed, "I kill all you fucking fuckers!" He aimed an M16 across the bonfire. The fresh punctures caused by the belt of ammunition pursed like bleeding mouths. Other irregulars jumped up, reaching for weapons.

Weigand knocked the Viet backward with a jolt to the forehead from his acoustic pistol. Barthuli's arm swung in a long arc. That was the wrong way to throw a grenade. Carnes had treated a lot of men who'd forgotten to lob a grenade like a shotput, the way they'd been trained to do. The grenade was much heavier than a baseball of similar dimensions, and the man throwing it the wrong way was likely to chip bones and pull tendons by the excessive strain.

Barthuli hadn't had any training at all, but the bomb flew accurately through the open door of the arsenal building. "Incoming!" he shouted as he turned and ran.

Carnes lurched to her feet. Weigand picked her up bodily and followed the others, helped on his way by his light-amplifying facemask. Watney was already dashing toward the gate. The colonel's reflexes hadn't been slowed by whatever mix of hope and memory drove him to tears.

A thousand one, a thousand two . . .

Grenades had five-second fuses, Carnes remembered that. And remembered men who'd been brought in horribly mangled, because their grenade had gone off early, or because it had sprung back almost into their arms after hitting a springy cane of bamboo.

. . . a thousand three, a . . .

Weigand, as strong as a horse, carried her around the flank of the Sikorsky and threw himself forward with her in his arms. His elbows and belly took the shock rather than crush her. Despite that cushioning, the ground felt as hard as the top of a cast-iron stove when Carnes' buttocks slammed it.

. . . thousand f—

An irregular fired at them with a Kalashnikov. A green tracer ricocheted skyward from a stone only inches from Carnes' outflung hand.

The grenade went off. A moment later, the stacked munitions followed in a blast that turned the night white, then orange. The ground rose and hit Carnes harder than when she'd fallen on it a moment before. She gasped, throbbing with pain.

The helicopter staggered. The upper half of its fuselage ripped like tissue paper in a tornado. The ruptured fuel tanks ignited in a spreading, deep-red bloom.

Carnes got to her feet. Weigand tried to help her. She thrust herself out of his grip. She could see well enough by the throbbing light that projected her shadow across the disabled APC.

Burning jet fuel woke ruby reflections from the wire snaking through the bamboo stockade. The guard stood in the gateway, waving his machine pistol and calling out. Carnes wasn't sure the words were in a real language.

A mortar shell screamed from the night and landed directly at Carnes' feet. She opened her mouth to shout in final surprise. The bomb, its tailfins blown off by the explosion that sent it skyward, was part of the 504th's stored munitions.

It hadn't exploded when shells around it did. It didn't go off now, either.

Watney shot the raging guard twice in the face. As the man spun into a gatepost, Watney fired twice more into his back.

The Chinese rallier thrashed in death. His foot kicked Watney's wounded leg as the colonel limped past. Watney cursed and shot the dead man a fifth time.

The team stumbled through the gate. Sirens wailed. There was a white flash half a mile away and, seconds later, the *crump* of the explosion. Another mortar shell, thrown farther than the one that had narrowly missed Carnes, the fuse this time still in working order.

"Head for the 96th," Carnes directed. Her eyes hurt with the constriction of the tears that wouldn't flow. "We'll have to walk, I guess. Val will find us beds."

"There'll be emergency personnel in a few minutes," Watney said. He was reloading his revolver. "But if we stay by the side of the road they won't bother with us. They'll have enough on their minds already."

Carnes started down the gravel-surfaced road toward the hospital a half mile away. Another mortar shell went off in the distant night.

Behind the team, a pillar of fire rose above the compound of the 504th Provisional Company. Parts of the helicopter were magnesium, and their white glare blazed at the core of the burning fuel.

Washington, DC

March 19, 1967

The two targets were primarily a man named Geoffrey Alden Bates and secondarily a woman named Lucille Rhone. Their abstracted CIA dossiers gave no hint of how hard it would be to find them in the antique environs of Washington, outside of walking into Bates' office and confronting him.

Grainger had Bates and Rhone's home address, home phones, work phones, car license plates and descriptions, and no idea how to proceed without the superior data processing capabilities of TC 779 or even the hard suits. So they were out here in back of Embassy Row, where the expensive real estate was, staking out Bates' house as if they were two indigs or actors in a period play.

They had rented an internal-combustion auto with a standard shift called a Thunderbird or T-Bird, which was reputed to be state-of-the-art but had no telecommunications equipment whatsoever. In it, they had sat outside this house arguing for far too long, waiting for the man whose picture CIA had given them to show up.

Roebeck had her membrane down and was scanning for any sign of high-technology activity which would violate the parameters of the time period, either from Bates' house or anyone from Timeline B Central who might be surveying it.

The unaugmented EM band was unremarkable, at best, on this horizon. If anything significant was happening, it would stand out like a dinosaur in these environs.

Grainger had his acoustic pistol on the split seat between them and was monitoring for other telltales—even those of human activity inside the house. If he could just sight on Bates for seven heartbeats or seven respirations, he could lift a signature that was as unique as a fingerprint. Then the ARC Riders could track Bates at will, wherever Bates went, whatever he did that was within their equipment's range of 1,000 meters. It would be easy to keep watch on the perpetrator until the man was accessible. Grainger's millimeter wave target locator was carrying a bio-attuned microwave radar that fixed on the target's combined heartbeat and breathing pattern.

But he had to find the guy to get a bioradar fix.

You couldn't just break into that house and wait, not in this neighborhood. Especially because there was at least fifty pounds of canine animal in there, which Grainger's bioradar scanner had identified as completely conscious and alert.

If they couldn't get a fix on Bates tonight, they'd have to go to the guy's office, which was also too public a confrontation for Roebeck's taste. Grainger thought they could pull it off.

"Look, Nan, it's the dark ages. A virtual police state. Why don't we just show up at this guy's place of work tomorrow, put everybody we meet to sleep with tranks as we go in, and take his ass? Make him tell us where he's got the device stashed—"

"We've been through this, Tim. I don't want to scare him into running. He might run anywhere, or, for all we know, anywhen. We can't tag him well enough to follow if he can leave the temporal locus, and we don't know he can't. We've got time."

They were reasonably safe burning days here, so far before the critical March 1968 time frame. He hoped. Every time you lived through a temporal interval you locked yourself out of it. No revisitation was survivable. If somewhere else on this planet something critical was happening right now, Tim Grainger could never come back here again to fix it.

He thought about the DDI whom they'd met at the NSC, who wanted the remains of the equipment for analysis. If that happened, this timeline would go even more haywire. Tim Grainger understood the time-honed rules of his former profession well enough to realize that if he and Roebeck were out here hunting Bates, purportedly seconded to CIA from DOE, then at least one other homegrown agency team was out here looking, too. Perhaps more than one. You could have CIA, DIA, FBI, and maybe a half dozen other acronymous agencies all keeping Bates under surveillance and waiting to strike. Roebeck and he were probably risking interdiction by any one or all of them. So there were multiple undefined threats in this carbon-monoxide-laced night.

Grainger kept scanning through his membrane for any car he'd seen before, using enough light intensification to make sure he could recognize number plates if he saw them again, storing car colors and faces in his memory. Lucky it was a quiet street.

Then it wasn't so quiet, not for Grainger.

"Nan," he said, "I know it's real close to Embassy Row, but what do you think about a car full of Orientals coming around this block twice?"

"Interested in us?" Roebeck snapped to seated attention.

"Us or the house. Could be either. Could be neither."

"Get out of here. Key this thing, or whatever you do to make it go."

"Okay," he said with a grin. It was fun to drive the T-Bird, almost like visiting AmericaLand Theme Park. But the grin quickly faded as the Orientals in their black car drove slowly by, clearly looking at them with more than casual interest.

"Damn, we're being scanned. Move."

Grainger's membrane, in passive detection mode, was already corroborating Roebeck's words.

He slammed the clutch in and out, ground the stick into reverse, and tried to wheel the crude auto out of its parking slot. It took both hands.

The acoustic pistol was beside him on the seat. . . . Why didn't Roebeck grab it?

"Nan, don't wait to be sure—"

His eyes were aching. His stomach was cramping. He could barely feel his hands. He was filled with an over-whelming need to drop his head between his knees and puke his guts out onto his shoes. Then he needed to shit. Bad.

He couldn't let go of the wheel. He had to move the ancient automobile out of range of the Orientals. He slapped the clutch into a forward gear and grabbed, nearly deaf and blind, for his own acoustic pistol to counter the acoustic fire he was taking.

But Nan Roebeck knocked it out of his hand. "Go," she shouted in his ear. "Go!"

He wanted to shoot back, but he couldn't see. Anyway, both his hands were fully occupied.

He could barely make out the road's white dotted line through his tears. He headed for it, foot pressing the gas pedal to the floor of the car.

The auto leaped forward with a squeal of acceleration, hit something hard with its left fender, shuddered, and careened toward the intersection ahead.

His stomach twisted once more and he gasped for air. His body wanted to void everything he'd eaten or drunk in the last six hours from every appropriate orifice. He held on to the steering wheel to stay upright, nearly chinning himself against it, just driving forward.

Beside him, he felt Roebeck moving around, and suddenly the assault on his senses stopped. His ears and eyes cleared. His muscles unknotted. His intense need to void his bowels diminished.

He blinked. There was a terrible honking in his ears. Then he realized he was halfway into the intersection, blocking other vehicles, which were sounding their horns.

He continued on through, taking a left turn across two lanes of traffic, before he looked at Roebeck. She had a piece of brown paper in her hands. She was wiping vomit off herself and her equipment. The SOUND CANCELLATION ENGAGED light was blinking happily from her pocket terminal.

"We're going to be apprehended now," she said dolefully, wiping her mouth with the back of her hand.

"Where?" Then he saw it.

He'd thought she meant the Orientals, the Timeline B natives from Central. But she didn't mean that.

A police car with District of Columbia markings was flashing its lights at them. If the sound cancellation hadn't been engaged, its wailing might have been deafening.

"What now?" Roebeck said accusingly.

"I had a traffic accident. We ate some bad food. My girlfriend has food poisoning. I'm trying to get her to the hospital." He pulled over to the side of the road. "Maybe you and I know better, but you sure look—and stink—like a girlfriend who has food poisoning. Otherwise, I'd have dumped you out of the car by now. Wish we had 'Smell Cancellation.'"

"I just saved your ass, you ungrateful bastard. What more do you want?"

"I wanted you to shoot those sons of bitches. That was the plan, remember? Since this auto requires two hands, I was going to drive and you were going to shoot. Take out any emerging threats. Incapacitate them if possible. Kill for self-preservation if necessary. But shoot! Solve at least one of our problems, since you had a target of opportunity. But no. You've got to be nonviolent. If I'm going to face arrest and need to use my CIA-given clout, it ought to be for something more than smashing up some diplomat's automobile."

Roebeck didn't answer. Instead, she groaned and covered her mouth. Then she retched again miserably. She'd been closer to the infrasound device than he, the way their T-Bird had been parked on the one way street.

And then he had to roll down his window as the policeman came up with flashlight in hand. The smell of vomit billowed out the open window.

The officer took a step backward. "What's going on here?" he asked, wrinkling his short, broad nose.

As Grainger talked his way through their hastily devised scenario, he hoped to hell that the Orientals hadn't gotten more of a fix on him than the license numbers of this automobile. If they had a bioradar unit with them, he and Roebeck weren't going to be safe anywhere on this horizon.

Which meant to Grainger that, as soon as he got through with the local police, he was going to insist they call back TC 779 and debark for elsewhen.

They could still do this mission from another horizon, a week or a month or six months from now.

With those Orientals alerted, they were going to have to.

Son Tay Base,
North Vietnam (Occupied)

Weigand watched Kyle Watney with impassive concern. The revisionist lay on the steel springs of a bunk in a ward of the 96th Evacuation Hospital, disused for want of staff. There were no mattresses. Watney didn't appear to care or even notice the lack.

Weigand stood, his back to a partition wall. He didn't worry that Watney would lie to them. Weigand trusted his instincts to notice conscious deceit, even without Gerd's biometric analyses to support those instincts.

Beyond the row of beds were screened windows. The night rocked with the sound of small arms and occasional explosions. Tracers rose lazily into the air, a rope of red beads so far across the base perimeter that the sound of the machine gun firing them was indistinguishable from the background noise.

"An attack is reported," Barthuli said. He raised an eyebrow to show that he was asking confirmation rather than merely stating a fact.

"God knows what they're reporting," Watney said, his eyes on the darkness which the single hanging light bulb threw above the edge of its reflector shade. "There's no attack, though. Just scared people shooting at nothing because they think what happened at the compound was an attack."

"Ah," said Barthuli. "Though it was an attack of sorts. We were."

The problem with Watney was that he was completely insane. You couldn't trust anything he said, because what he believed and consensus reality were so different.

"There were six of us," Watney said to the ceiling. "Me and Krieghoff, sent here to Vietnam. Bates and Rhone in Washington, the District of Columbia."

The revisionist's tongue savored the words like a gourmet tasting a perfectly seasoned dish.

"He was the leader, I suppose," Watney continued in a tone of wonderment at himself and the world. "Bates was. Rhone never led anything but the way to the bar, and she led there often enough. Domini and Douglass stayed in Denver and sent the rest of us back."

"May we attach induction inputs to your temples to get physical descriptions of your associates?" Weigand asked politely. They didn't need Watney's agreement to hook him to the recorder/computer, but he had to be conscious for the system to work. Barthuli's equipment would only fumble across a subject's surface thoughts. Best that Watney be agreeable.

Watney looked at Weigand. "They'll have changed in twenty years. I didn't see any of them but Krieghoff since we were all together in Denver. Krieghoff's been dead almost that long."

"We're more interested in what they looked like in 1968 when the operation started," Barthuli said with a colorless smile.

"Oh, right," Watney said. "I forgot who you were. I—"

His face trembled with desperate misery. "I've prayed somebody would come. I know there can't be a God. But I've prayed every night despite that. And now you're here."

"We can attach the outputs?" Weigand prodded. "There'll be no pain."

Tim Grainger had been a hard man and an unhesitating killer when the team recruited him from his time. Weigand had never doubted that Tim was basically as clean and straight as an ash pole, though. Grainger's circumstances had bent him like a bow, but there was nothing crooked about the man's soul.

Kyle Watney was something else again.

The revisionist waved a dismissive hand. "Sure, do whatever you want to do." He snorted. "Pain doesn't matter anyway."

Barthuli stepped over to the bunk, holding the two tiny induction transmitters he'd taken from their storage flap in his device. As Weigand had said, the beads were painless in operation. They simply received the subject's surface thoughts and retransmitted them as clean digital signals to the processor.

Rebecca Carnes slept under, not on, another of the bunks. Her head was cradled on Weigand's barracks bag, although much of what was in it was hard as stone. If Carnes was formally recruited into the ARC Riders, she'd get anti-fatigue programming. Weigand was amazed at how long she'd been functioning already.

"Can you describe the apparatus that brought you to this time?" Weigand asked. Barthuli placed the beads, then moved them individually by slight increments. He frowned in concentration as he listened to the alignment signal from his computer/recorder.

Watney shook his head tiredly. Barthuli lifted his fingers quickly away. "Sorry," Watney said to the analyst. "I didn't mean to move."

Barthuli resumed his task.

"I didn't know anything about the technical side," Watney explained. He smiled bitterly. "Oh, I was necessary. Without my money, Professor Domini wouldn't have been able to pay the power bill, much less build the equipment."

Barthuli stepped back. "That will do, I believe," he said, taking his device from the side pocket of his fatigue jacket.

Watney sat up smoothly. His eyes locked with those of Weigand, the only member of the team whom Watney thought of as an equal. "I wanted to be here, you know. Here in Nam.

I called it *Nam* even when it was only history, archival recordings. I wanted to be part of the victory that cowardly politicians had robbed our great *nation* of."

Carnes was awake. "You wanted this?" she asked. The bed's wire matting cut the view of her face into rectangles. "You wanted to make the war go on?"

Watney hugged his arms to his trembling chest. "I'd studied it," he whispered. "It was a failure of will, that was all. We'd been afraid to win the war, and that was the beginning of the end."

"We?" Weigand repeated with minuscule emphasis. The shooting on the perimeter had died down, but he could see the glow of a fire that hadn't been a direct result of the explosion in the 504th's compound.

"America," Watney said. "The real America. Not just a province of a world state dominated by Orientals and Africans and *scum*!"

He glared fiercely at the men from his future and the woman from the present he'd created. He began to cry. "God help me, I thought we could win this war. *God help me!*"

"You thought America could win a land war in Asia?" Barthuli said. There was no hint of incredulity in his voice. Because the analyst was so obviously seeking clarification, the question wasn't insulting on its face as it would have been had Weigand asked it—let alone Carnes, one of the theory's direct victims. "Against Vietnam, and then China, and I suppose the USSR as well if matters had continued long enough?"

"I didn't know!" Watney shouted. "I studied the histories. I thought it was . . . pieces on a board, *Weltpolitik*. One nation keeps its nerve and the other collapses. A *game*."

Rebecca Carnes slid out from under the bunk. She looked in the direction of the revisionist, but Weigand wasn't sure what she was really seeing. Tampa devoured by a firestorm, he suspected; or perhaps the Chinese soldier preparing to shoot Carnes at the high-water point of American involvement in this war.

"I didn't know about the mud and the jungle and the Asians, so many Asians," Watney said in a broken voice. "Pieces on a board. And they wouldn't quit. No matter how many of them died, they wouldn't *quit*."

Barthuli sat on the metal frame of a bunk, looking at his recorder/computer. "Tell us about your associate Bates, please," he said.

Before Watney could speak, an image appeared over the device: a man in his forties, black-haired and handsome, though a little softer than Weigand thought was ideal. The image turned and smiled toward the company; calm, powerful, its face lighted by a wicked intelligence.

"Yes, that's him," Watney said. He lowered himself carefully back onto the springs. "Geoffrey Alden Bates. A man with a vision."

He laughed like a man choking. "Whereas I merely had a dream. I don't know about the rest of us."

He rubbed his eyes. "Or I suppose I do. Krieghoff and Professor Domini were concerned with the technical problems. I don't think they cared what the result was, so long as they achieved *a* result. Krieghoff cared afterwards, when he saw where the result left him. Douglass was really only a flunky. And Rhone—"

"Rhone," Barthuli murmured approvingly.

The image of a woman with aristocratic features displaced that of Bates. Her hair switched through at least a dozen styles and colors, each in an eyeblink.

"Lucille wasn't stupid," Watney said, still shading his eyes. "But you wouldn't have guessed that by the way she fawned over Bates. He owned her."

The image's clothing vanished. She knelt on all fours, her legs spread. She looked back over her shoulder at the viewer. Her eyes were empty of emotion and intelligence.

"Except when she was drunk," Watney said in a husky voice. "Then anybody owned her."

Weigand felt as cold as he had in the moment he saw Watney pistol the guard blocking his way. To treat enemies with ruthlessness was a human characteristic, however regrettable. To treat friends and associates in the same fashion was something altogether different.

"I understand that you're not a technician," Weigand said. "But can you roughly describe the vehicle that brought you to this horizon, this time? Was it a suit or a container of larger volume?"

Watney frowned at him. "It wasn't either," he said. "Nothing left the professor's laboratory. He mapped us, he called it mapping. And then he projected us into the past."

Barthuli nodded enthusiastically to Weigand. "That's how they slipped past Central!" the analyst exclaimed. "They came back as people rather than as spaces *containing* people. I very much wonder how the device worked. There hasn't been another case of that—"

He broke off suddenly with a smile, then added, "Well, perhaps there has, of course. On this timeline, though not on our own."

Weigand shook his head in exasperation with the analyst's refusal to focus on the job in hand. "That can wait for a follow-up mission," he said harshly. "Domini probably doesn't exist on this timeline he created. We've got to deal with the problem in 1968 before somebody worries about 2250 or whenever. Somebody else, I hope."

"Yes," agreed Barthuli. "But it's important to know that the device *could* have been detected if Central had been looking for that particular type of event. It's quite distinct from the vestiges left when you displace a volume, you see."

"You don't see the sunset when you're looking into a microscope," Carnes said. She sat on the floor with her legs crossed, staring at her ankles. Barthuli beamed at her.

"I knew something must be wrong when Domini didn't bring us back," Watney said.

"As soon as you succeeded in making your revision," Weigand explained, "your horizon and your associates there with it ceased to exist on this timeline."

Watney nodded. "I figured it was something like that," he said. "I didn't mind. I was willing to die for America. I couldn't think of a better time to live than when America asserted her dominance above all the other nations of the world."

He sat up, then stood as he spoke. Watney's voice took on the husky power of a man channeling a force greater than himself.

He met Weigand's eyes. The revisionist's face broke into the shattered smile Weigand had seen on it once before. "Oh, yes," Watney said softly. "I believed that. I really did."

"You had studied the horizon in order to operate in it effectively?" Barthuli suggested. "Money, current events—that sort of thing?"

"Oh, more than that," Watney said. "I'd trained, Mr. Barthuli. I was a rich man, I could indulge my whims. I was trained to be a soldier fit to serve in the army that lifted America to her apotheosis."

He looked at Weigand, and in this at least the two of them were alike. "I'm good at it, you know."

His fingers traced the line of bullet scars across his bare chest. "It was more than the skills, it was instinct. And it was . . . I *felt* superior because I came from the future. You understand that, don't you? The feeling that you're better than everyone around you, so they can't really touch you? You know!"

"A lot of Riders feel that way," Weigand said. "A lot of us."

Weigand had never understood that attitude, any more than he'd understood parents setting their infants to scream on Moloch's blazing altar; but he'd seen that, too, and a score of variations on it. He looked at the revisionist and tried to feel compassion rather than loathing. Weigand's face was as calm as a cold wax sculpture.

"They think I can't be killed," Watney said. "My men do. Sometimes I do myself. Krieghoff went to pieces when he realized we couldn't go back to 2257, that was where we came from. He'd finally decided he'd go to Washington and try to find Bates. I knew that wouldn't have done any good. And anyway Krieghoff was killed in an accident before he got to Saigon."

The shooting outside had stopped. A siren called despairingly across the night.

"Accident?" asked Carnes. She wouldn't look directly at Watney. Even in speaking to him, her jaw muscles stiffened.

"A cyclo hit him as he was crossing Highway 13," Watney said. "I had to identify the body. A cyclo carrying Coke girls. They were following a battalion of the 25th Infantry to a new area of operations."

Watney looked at the trio he hoped would rescue him from the world he had made. "It wasn't like training, you know," he said in his husky voice. "And it wasn't anything like the histories I studied said it would be. But that was all right, so long as I was fighting for a cause. It wasn't until I saw the changes in America, and that there was still more Asia, and more Asians living in it to continue fighting. . . . Then I started to understand."

Weigand felt his own authority riding on him like a crown of thorns. He had to make decisions and he wasn't ready to.

He swallowed. "Okay," he said. "We'll sleep. In the morning, we'll decide how we're going to return to ConUS and then to the 1968 horizon. But for now we'll sleep."

"Wait!" Barthuli snapped, his eyes on something in the air before him invisible from Weigand's angle. More politely the analyst continued, "A moment please, Pauli. Colonel Watney, who is 'Fern'?"

Watney frowned. "Yeah," he said, "General Fern. I think he gave me a first name, but I don't remember it. He's Air Force."

The face of the man whose name Barthuli plucked from the trash of the revisionist's surface thoughts hung above the recorder/computer. The word "return" had kicked up the recollection. A man of forty; hatchet-faced, with black hair cut short enough to be a mere shadow on his scalp.

"He tried to recruit me yester . . . three days ago," Watney said. "While we were saddling up, for God's sake. Some special operation."

He snorted. "As if I need the Air Force to task my boys! And stateside Air Force besides."

"Fifth Military District," Weigand said, the words coming out even as the image of a head expanded to head and shoulders. The patch on General Fern's left shoulder was that of MR 5, but with the blue star central boss of General Oakley's personal forces.

"Yeah," the revisionist agreed. He looked at the holographic image with a more critical eye. "Yeah, that's right. You knew about that?"

Barthuli smiled tightly. "Not until now," he said.

"The CO of Travis is gathering a private army for a coup," Weigand said. "He wanted real combat troops for the lead commando. People like your team. What did he offer you?"

"He didn't offer a damned thing," Watney snarled, angry because he was tired and unwilling to be pushed in what he regarded as a pointless direction. "I told you, we were saddling up. I told him to get out of my way or he'd have boot tracks on his face."

Watney grimaced, remembering that these were the only people in the world who could end the nightmare he and his accomplices had caused. "Sorry," he said to his hands. "Look, I mean to help, I just . . . I don't know. He's still here, though. Was this afternoon when we got back. He came in a DC-8 in Air Force markings, carrying a bunch of people he'd brought out of Yunnan. It's still parked at the west end of the airfield."

Weigand nodded, forcing his mind to work. "Gerd—" he said.

"The aircraft hasn't been refueled," Barthuli said before Weigand had the question out. The analyst must have been working on the answer from the instant he'd identified Fern; even so, it was fast work. "It took some fuel aboard yesterday. More, the necessary minimum to reach Kadena, is supposed to arrive by noon tomorrow."

Weigand looked at the revisionist. "Can you get us onto that aircraft, Colonel?" he asked. "As members of your unit?"

"If I say you're mine," Watney said in a voice like a dog's growl, "nobody in Son Tay, nobody in the *war zone*, will raise an eyebrow. They know me."

And I know you, too, Weigand thought, *you murderous bastard*. Aloud he said, "Okay, the plane's going where we need to go, back to Travis."

He permitted himself a quiver of a grin. Watney might think that a quick trigger finger was something to be proud of. Weigand could beat the revisionist as a gunman if he had to—a fifty-fifty chance, he'd beat the revisionist. But there was a lot more to real competence than that. "Whether or not the pilot plans to," he said, "that's where we'll land in ConUS."

Rebecca Carnes said, "Good to have a commanding officer like you, Pauli." The words were a slap at Watney; but they were the truth as she saw it, or she wouldn't have said them. Even though she was wrong, the statement gave Weigand a flash of hope.

Weigand felt some of the prickly weight lift from him as he stepped to the light switch. They had a long way to go—but they were heading in the right direction for now.

Travis Air Force Base

Mechanics were already clustered around the port outboard engine by the time Rebecca Carnes followed the rest of the team down the boarding steps. A lime-green crash truck parked facing the nacelle. Its headlights added to the illumination of a sky from which the sun had vanished while the DC-8 taxied wearily to its berth.

Half a dozen guides in blue-on-white armbands marshaled the passengers toward the nearby hangar. Carnes couldn't swear the structure was the one to which Weigand and the displacement suits were taken when the team touched down at Travis the first time, but that seemed the likelihood.

Behind her, a Samoan without rank tabs said to a staff sergeant whose scalp was half shaved, half scar tissue, "No, they'll fly on two engines. One out, that was no problem."

Most of the killers Fern had recruited from the war zone walked bent under the weight of duffle bags: loot, more general souvenirs, and the weapons and munitions they'd brought with them. As protective coloration, Weigand's team members carried firearms.

Carnes understood Weigand's order, but her submachine gun would probably be as useless as the revolver she'd tried to use in Yunnan. The acoustic pistol was a comforting bulk in her side pocket, though. Because it had no recoil or muzzle

246

blast . . . and because Carnes knew the result wouldn't be fatal, even to an enemy trying to kill her, she was a *nurse* . . . for those varied reasons, all of them psychological, she was confident of what she could do with the weapon from the future.

Pauli openly carried his EMP generator. It was unfamiliar to the remainder of the aircraft's 127 passengers, but they were all of them individualists armed with a wide assortment of weapons. The generator was attached to a rifle stock and *looked* like a weapon. The acoustic pistols looked like toys, and the sort of attention they might gather would be of an undesirable sort.

"That crippled pig fly on two engines?" the staff sergeant sneered. "You've got shit for brains! Brand new, maybe, but neither of us were born back when that was brand new. It's a fucking wonder we didn't fall right out of the sky when we lost the one."

The sergeant's tone made Carnes glance over her shoulder. The Samoan wore a bland expression. For the moment, at least, he seemed willing to ignore the insults as mere alcoholic nonsense. The shortest of the DC-8's three refueling stops had been 12 hours. The sergeant had drunk his way through each of them, and had brought enough booze aboard besides to last him to the next layover.

Still and all . . . the Samoan wore his own dried right earlobe on a neck thong. He'd explained to Carnes on the flight's Guam-to-Hawaii leg that he'd removed it from the mouth of the Chink who bit it off while the Samoan chewed through the Chinese soldier's throat. Being too drunk to be polite in this group meant either that you were very good or very lucky.

"Not that it'd have made more than a couple days difference," the sergeant added. "Whatever the fuck Fern's got cooked up for us, it won't be survivable. Back here in the World, for Chrissake?"

"Could be," the Samoan agreed in an equally careless tone.

Weigand motioned Carnes up to his right side. Watney was on Weigand's left, with Barthuli—who had the other communications headband—to Watney's other side. A guide looked over his shoulder but didn't interfere.

"This is the same hangar," Weigand said. "The suits will be coming into phase in ten minutes."

Barthuli said something Carnes couldn't catch. "Just under ten minutes," Weigand said, his lips pursing. "We're going to have to lock them in phase immediately, because it'll be a problem if we have to wait a full week."

"Will the people here recognize you?" Carnes asked. "General Oakley and his staff?"

Weigand shrugged. He was very tense but trying not to show it. "We'll deal with that if we have to," he said. "The light wasn't good, and they weren't really interested in me. We *can't* leave the suits. We'll need them to displace to 1968."

Then he added, "I wish I knew what Nan would do."

"We'll handle it," Carnes said.

They entered through the personnel door rather than the great plane-wide leaves closing the end of the hangar. Hundreds of three-high bunks had been set up against one of the sidewalls since Carnes previously saw the interior. Parked along the opposite sidewall were three APCs in addition to the wheeled armored cars, and more pallets of matériel were stacked in the rear of the hangar.

It didn't look like an army with which to conquer Washington. Oakley must be counting on surprise; though for that matter, Washington might not be defended by much at this point, either.

Only about half the overhead lights worked, too few to adequately illuminate the hangar. Carnes didn't notice Oakley. The general himself wasn't a commanding figure, but the dozen staff officers clotted about him should be pretty obvious.

The best hope the team had to retain control of the displacement suits was confusion and lack of a proper chain of command. If Oakley wasn't present, there was a fair chance things would work out.

A major with a bullhorn stood at the end of the bunks, facing the men entering the hangar. He spoke into the bullhorn.

The device groaned brokenly in response. The major snarled something to a lieutenant walking by with a clipboard. The lieutenant shrugged and stepped on past.

The major threw down the bullhorn and shouted, "Everybody from Flight 8734, come this way."

His unaided voice was almost extinguished by the hangar's surf of echoes. The passengers from the DC-8 shuffled closer anyway, directed by the guides. The major might have something useful to say.

"The people who just got off the flight from Hawaii, come this way," the major continued. He pointedly avoided referring to where the men had been recruited; not that anybody looking at the band of grizzled killers would have been much in doubt. "These are your quarters. You've got half an hour to choose bunks and strike your gear. Then you'll be taken to another building for briefing on your mission."

The major paused, then continued without making eye contact with the men in a semicircle about him, "And there'll be no weapons when General Oakley briefs you."

There was laughter and growls. "Want to bet?" a man bigger than Pauli Weigand said. He pointed a pump shotgun at the major's face from less than six feet away, then grinned and lowered the weapon again.

The group moved forward. Men streamed past the major to the bunk lines like the sea about a pebble. The men regarded the hangar as civilization. For most of them, even the cramped seats of the ancient DC-8 were closer to civilization than they'd been in months or even years. They were looking forward to running water, cooked food; in many cases women, in most cases liquor. Oakley's chances of holding a formal briefing in half an hour were even less good than the odds Carnes gave of the general becoming President of the United States.

Weigand murmured something to Barthuli. "The displacement suits will be arriving *here*," the analyst said, projecting three six-inch ovals of red light on the nearby concrete. Carnes couldn't tell the source of the light. "In three minutes, *seven*teen seconds."

The four members of the team formed a close huddle. The major was shouting to his subordinates, the guides who'd brought the passengers from the DC-8. He hadn't moved since the shotgun was aimed at him.

Men from the war zone, the bulk of their gear tossed onto bunks or simply on the floor, were sauntering toward the door. They might have some distance to walk or drive commandeered vehicles, but major military bases were effectively towns. They'd find what they wanted.

All of the returnees Carnes saw were carrying automatic weapons, as much in warning as by reflex. Air Force personnel kept out of the way.

"Okay," Weigand said. "When the suits appear, the three of us"—he nodded to Carnes and Barthuli—"will put them on and walk into the back corner, down one of those aisles of containers. While we're doing that, Colonel Watney will . . ."

Weigand's eyes met Watney's cold, empty expression. Weigand smiled with as little warmth and handed his EMP generator to Carnes.

"No," he said, "Colonel Watney will put on the third suit. There's nothing to it, Watney, just walk like you would normally. Rebecca, you'll watch the other people with the generator set to nerve stimulation."

Weigand turned the EMP generator on its side to check the setting. On the fore end was a sliding switch cut from a piece of aircraft spar, added at Son Tay after the dangerous minutes it had taken Weigand to reconfigure the device from EMP to nerve stimulation. The switch was in its forward position.

"I don't want you to call attention to yourself," Weigand added sharply. "Don't—"

"I understand," Carnes said, snappish in her present state to be told the obvious. "You intend to talk your way clear in the confusion. I'm to stay unnoticed and act only if someone starts using force."

The big ARC Rider bobbed his chin in agreement and apology. "Whatever happens," he said as he glanced sideways toward Watney, "I intend this to take place without our having to kill anybody. Do you understand, Gerd?"

"All right, Pauli," the analyst replied. He removed his computer/recorder from a side pocket. "I'm ready to lock the suits in phase when they appear."

"I won't tell you your job, Weigand," Watney said. The smile that tweaked his lips was almost a sneer.

Carnes walked toward the bunks. She wanted some distance between her and the trio of men, and her tropical battledress uniform was less obtrusive among the passengers from the DC-8 than it would be in the middle of Air Force personnel in stateside fatigues.

Weigand and the men with him stood ready, six feet back from the ovals the analyst briefly projected on the floor again. How were Oakley's people going to react to the appearance of the armor?

In the hangar were still at least a hundred men—mostly men; General Oakley must have a prejudice against women. Over 60 percent of the varied US-based military forces had been women even when Carnes was shipped overseas for the second time.

Carnes wouldn't necessarily have been given another overseas posting. What if she'd stayed in ConUS? Would she have been stationed in Tampa? Or Atlanta? Or—how many other American locations had been targets of American H-bombs? Barthuli had said a hundred and—

No, that was the number for the whole world on this timeline, this horizon. Still, many—

The refractive index of the air in front of the three men changed. Carnes remembered the distorted transparency as TC 779 appeared between her and the Chinese rifleman.

She turned her head, keeping her companions in the corner of her eye as she tried to spread her attention over everybody else in the hangar. The EMP generator was down along her right thigh, unremarkable in the lights' sparse vertical harshness. In this vast cavern, nobody could watch all the places that might be crucial to see in the next instants.

The three displacement suits appeared, so abruptly they seemed to have been present all along. Weigand stepped forward.

A mechanic was leaning over an APC's open engine compartment a hundred feet away. He blinked and called something to his assistant in front of the vehicle, handing up a wrench. An officer addressing a pair of airmen near a silent forklift stopped in midphrase and stood openmouthed.

The right gauntlets of two of the displacement suits held square-sectioned weapons larger than the ARC Riders' acoustic pistols and of obviously different design. Weigand, Barthuli—and an instant later Watney as one of the suits shifted aim—dropped like rice sacks.

No thrashing, no convulsions as shocked nerves fired when the bodies hit the concrete. It was as if all the three men's tendons had been cut.

Barthuli fell on his multipurpose device. The revolver Watney had managed to draw bounced beside him. Its steel barrel and alloy frame rang in separate keys.

One of the suits stepped forward. The suit that didn't hold a weapon remained statue still, harmless; *empty*. The other armed suit turned so that it was back to back with the first, covering the rear as the first suit bent down.

Weigand's head moved. The angular weapon twitched. Pauli flattened again like warm gelatin.

The officer who'd seen the displacement suits appear started to walk over with a perturbed expression. The enlisted men remained beside the forklift, staring after their superior with blank incomprehension.

Rebecca Carnes was thirty feet from the suits and her fallen companions. She reached down with her left forefinger and pulled her weapon's switch into the rear position. She deliberately kept her face turned away from the tableau behind her.

The officer—he was a captain—called, "Say, who—" and fell the way Carnes' companions had. The motion was almost as smooth as that of a fluid-filled balloon. She'd never seen anything like it in her life.

Carnes turned and squeezed the trigger as she swung the EMP generator. She didn't have any idea what the range or dispersion of the weapon's effect might be. There was no recoil. The stock and her flesh in contact with it quivered like a beehive.

The suit kneeling over Weigand's body froze in place. The suit that had just shot the Air Force officer fell frontward, though not exactly on its face. The pointing arm and gun hand, as rigid as those of a bronze statue, clanged on the concrete and held the figure like a flat tripod on gun muzzle, left toe, and the point of the left shoulder. The third displacement suit overlooked the scene with bland impassivity.

Carnes ran to her fallen companions, ignoring the presence of the other personnel in the hangar. Barthuli moved, Watney and Pauli Weigand moved; even the Air Force captain was blinking groggily in the hands of the enlisted men who'd shouted as they came to his aid.

It was as if the sun had risen over the soul of Rebecca Carnes.

Watney's right arm thrashed. Carnes thought the revisionist was in convulsions; then she realized he was groping at his empty shoulder holster. Watney was operating on reflex. Though his eyes were open, he didn't see the revolver he'd drawn and dropped in the instant the suited figure shot him.

Weigand's pupils were the same size and only moderately dilated in the interior light. "Rebecca?" he said.

"What's going on here?" demanded an officious voice.

"Get back, you damned fool!" Carnes snarled over her shoulder. "These men have received an electric shock. Who's responsible for these facilities?"

She didn't have any idea what had happened to her companions, though it wasn't electricity. Electroshock would have induced rigidity and convulsions. Instead, they'd relaxed. Utterly.

Gerd turned his head and softly patted his cheek with his right fingertips. He didn't try to move from the concrete. "I feel . . ." he said. "How very interesting. How interesting."

Watney found his revolver and gripped it in his hands. He rose to a squat, looking like nothing so much as a beast encircled by the score of Air Force personnel now clustering about the event.

Weigand's heart rate and breathing were normal. He didn't appear to be harmed, just disoriented. He frowned up at Carnes and said, "Where is . . ." He couldn't think of the words or—perhaps—the idea with which to complete the question.

"Are these suits radioactive?" the officious voice demanded, rising in timbre. "Is there a radiation hazard? Answer me!"

Rather than standing up, Gerd Barthuli crossed his legs beneath him and rose to a sitting position. He still held his computer/recorder. He began to use it as if oblivious of the noisy strangers around him.

"My God, the suits," Weigand murmured.

"There's no radiation!" Carnes said. Was there radiation? Would it help if she claimed there was?

She turned her head. The man asking the questions was a portly, middle-aged sergeant. The short sleeves of his khaki shirt were almost covered by the number of wavy, Air Force–style rank stripes.

"These men have nearly been electrocuted by somebody's negligence!" Carnes shouted. The jagged nervousness of her tone—emotions she let out rather than putting on—and the implications of what she'd said moved the spectators back abruptly.

Pauli stood, wobbled, and caught himself on the shoulder of Carnes rising beside him. "EMP?" he said into her ear.

Watney was standing. He checked the revolver's loads, then reholstered his weapon. He seemed to be pretending that he was alone in the great room, his face a mask of mindless tension. Watney was as dangerous at this moment as a grenade with the pin pulled; so obviously dangerous that even some of the REMFs noticed and moved out of the vicinity.

"Yes, I . . ." Carnes agreed. The generator was on the floor beside her. She picked it up and tried to return it to Weigand.

"Not now," Weigand said. He put his hands on the hips of two Air Force officers bending over the nearer displacement suit and moved them away with as much pressure as was needed.

"Pauli," said Barthuli from the floor, "it's been over four minutes of total shutdown. And it'll cause questions if you open the equipment now."

"Okay, I see that," Weigand said flatly. "The third suit, that's okay?"

"It was unpowered when the pulse destroyed the others," the analyst said. "It should be fully functional."

Carnes was still holding the generator. She slid the switch from EMP to irritant field, then slid it back. She didn't know what *had* happened, much less what she should be prepared to prevent in the next seconds or minutes.

"We're scheduled to leave for Washington, DC, on the same aircraft that brought us across the Pacific," Barthuli said. Carnes couldn't be sure whether the analyst was stating information or was pushing Pauli toward a particular decision. "Of course, schedules under the present conditions . . ."

"Okay," Weigand said. He hugged himself, then pointed to the senior sergeant who'd been questioning Carnes. "You," Weigand said. "I want these two pieces of equipment"—he tapped the kneeling displacement suit with his boot toe, then pointed the same toe at the suit frozen into a tripod—"packed in a Conex marked 504th Provisional Company, do not open. *Now.* And I want that piece"—Weigand gestured toward the undamaged suit with his left hand; his right didn't move far from the pocket in which Carnes knew Weigand kept his acoustic pistol—"boxed in wood, minimum clearances, also stenciled 504th, and delivered aboard the mission aircraft at once. The Conex remains here. Do you understand?"

There were about thirty people in the group around the team. Some onlookers had drifted away; others came over to see what was going on, whispering to those who'd been present longer.

One of the officers was a bird colonel. He remained in poker-faced silence, unwilling to interfere or even ask questions that would display his ignorance in the face of Weigand's forceful certainty.

The sergeant saluted. "Yes *sir*," he said.

The man was sweating. Carnes remembered his question about radiation. The military had forty-odd years of experience lying to its personnel about radiation dangers. Carnes' denial would do nothing to reassure the fellow, though her presence in the possible contamination site was a positive sign.

"You there," the sergeant said, pointing to a junior enlisted man. "Bring over that forklift. Cole—don't you move away, Cole, all you lot—"

His arm swept a group of airmen. The crowd of spectators began to break up under the sergeant's orders and the general feeling of tension. The colonel stepped toward the team and opened his mouth to speak.

"No, you do *not* have a need to know what's going on, Colonel," Rebecca Carnes said sharply. "This matter is in the hands of the 504th, and *only* our hands."

The colonel glared down from six inches of height and two rank steps over her. He looked at Carnes—and Weigand—and for an instant at the empty horror of Kyle Watney's face. The colonel executed a parade-ground about-face and marched toward the parked vehicles.

Barthuli got to his feet. The team moved a few yards away to where they could watch the sergeant's preparations without getting in the way. Even Watney's expression was returning to human norms.

"I destroyed the suits when I EMPed them?" Carnes asked Weigand quietly.

Weigand took the generator from her. "Yeah, thank goodness," he said. He checked the switch setting. "We're all right so long as one remains. The pulse doesn't affect the suits when they're shut down."

The forklift whined up. Besides the driver, it carried an enlisted man riding on the stack of empty pallets on the forks.

"Could I have saved the others?" Carnes asked. "Gerd said 'four minutes.' Do they—"

Weigand grinned wanly at her. "The armor was fried in the first microsecond," he said. "Don't worry about it. You did the right thing."

He cleared his throat. "What Gerd meant was the people inside the suits—our opposite numbers, this timeline's ARC Riders. Nobody else could've located the suits and waited for us in them."

"The environmental systems stopped functioning with the rest of the suit," Barthuli amplified. His tone was cool but for him kindly. "After four minutes, the occupants won't be . . . recoverable."

"Oh," said Rebecca Carnes. She swallowed.

Airmen began knocking the pallets into boards under the senior sergeant's direction, making an enormous clatter. The team backed a few more steps.

"I failed in my intention not to kill anybody, Colonel Watney," Weigand said. The words could have been apology or a challenge. The revisionist shrugged, his mind at a distance from the proceedings.

Outside the hangar, a jet engine ran up to a scream as it was tested. The sound throbbed through the building like the call of a beast of prey.

Baltimore, Maryland

March 1, 1967

This time, Grainger wasn't taking any chances. He'd get Bates and Rhone on this attempt, even if he had to kill them—if Roebeck gave him half a chance. The woods around the ARC Riders' second rental car were deep and somehow shielding as he drove Roebeck toward Washington on a gray day with just a hint of spring to it.

Roebeck wouldn't relent. No killing. Just walk up and use superior technology to preempt, interdict, and disarm any number of equally high-tech slant-eyed adversaries from Timeline B Central, or a revisionist enemy from somewhere else up the line who had no compunction about killing you—or both.

He'd tried to reason with Roebeck when they were safely back in TC 779, out of phase, and going through an agonizing hot wash. He'd partially succeeded. "Boss, we should go back down the line a week or so, to before we met Calandine. Maybe he tipped the gooks from B Central to us. We've got what we need—current tracking data on the targets, correct for the March One horizon as well as for the Ides. We find a new staging area. Fuck the safe house. It's B Central's safe house these days. Using it means risking running into them accidentally and/or providing them with a likely locus in which to act against us."

"Just exactly what is it you're suggesting, Tim? Lay it out for me. After all, you're our expert on old America and intelligence techniques," Roebeck said icily. All through that memorable hot wash, her discomfort at Grainger's manipulation of the local intel community had been painfully evident. To all of them.

"There's *no* expert in our ARC on *this* old America. I told you, we've got to preempt the Orientals—and whoever tipped the CIA to the mind control device. I swear it was nothing I said to Calandine." Roebeck clearly didn't believe him. They couldn't let the growing distrust and suspicion destroy their unit cohesion, especially not in a unit of two plus one Oriental. Chun increasingly gave him a bad feeling. Who had tipped the CIA, or the Orientals from B Central, to the ARC Riders' locus behind Embassy Row was still an unanswered question.

Grainger was willing to bet that the culprit was Calandine, under direction of the revisionists who had started this timeline rolling, but it was doubtful he'd ever be able to prove it. That was the way things went in the ARC. You fixed the problem, things straightened out. Very rarely did you get a textbook explanation to log in your after-action report, since there was no alternate history left to examine at your leisure. The only good thing about alternate histories, as far as Grainger was concerned, was that once you pulled the plug, they disappeared as if they'd never been.

Except in your own memories. Where they'd never disappear. Grainger couldn't get those Orientals out of his thoughts. At that moment, he was looking at one right across from him in the close confines of TC 779.

Chun had seen him staring at her. "There's plenty of forest out near the Baltimore flight line on this horizon. I can put you there and stay on the horizon with you if you like, Nan."

"No need to risk the capsule," Grainger had said hurriedly. Out of phase, the harm that Chun could do if she were a traitor was sharply constrained. Alone in the venue, with TC

779's capabilities at her disposal, she could be up to anything. Of course, there was no way for Grainger to tell whether she hadn't dephased while the other ARC Riders were hunting Bates and Rhone and sicced her kinsmen on him and Roebeck. . . .

"I still say we preempt," he insisted. "Go back to before we screwed up and preempt *every*body's action: the locals; the Orien—the B Central operators; everybody. We can *do* this—zero the targets and take them before the other side knows to look for us. Let's try again, same drill, earlier time, insertion at the Baltimore flight line—if the boss agrees." Grainger had looked hopefully at Roebeck.

"All right, but no unnecessary violence, Tim. And only if you can convince me how you're going to do without your local support base. If Calandine can't be trusted, then he can't be trusted. Not now. Not then. Not ever. Nor anyone from his orbit."

Grainger wasn't sure he could pull off a preemptive insertion without support from the local intel community, but he was sure as hell more ready to try a March 1, 1967, horizon than he was to battle it out on ancient streets with the guys from Timeline B's Central sometime after March 19, 1967. When they knew he'd be coming.

So here they were, rolling in Timeline B again. Before again. As the sun started to wane, it was getting cold as hell on March 1, 1967. The sky even looked like snow. The rented Lincoln Continental that Chun had prearranged for them to pick up at the airport didn't include fusion heaters or a routing computer, but they were making do in the drafty automobile with their coveralls' climate stabilizers and paper maps. He had what he really needed—fake ID, local currency, and targeting data on his quarry.

The rest, either his way or Roebeck's way, was soon going to be history.

His second rented car had been no problem to acquire despite his local ID, because the accident he'd had with his first one had been in this horizon's future—his fake driving record was as yet unmarred.

This time, he was going to make an appointment with Bates that Bates would have to keep.

And this time, he had an automobile with an automatic shift, so he wasn't forced to leave his personal security in Roebeck's slow hands. If there was reason to open fire, he wasn't willing to depend on her to do it. Not after last time.

The worst of the situation was that you couldn't drive around the country in your hard suit. The bulky suits wouldn't exactly fit in automobile's trunk, so the suits were again stashed out of phase. Roebeck had wanted to leave them with TC 779 and he'd flatly refused the mission if that were to be the case.

So there was open discord now. Chun knew he didn't trust her and there was no way to make up for that. Machiavelli had warned that you kept your friends close and your enemies closer. Overt hostility in an ARC Riders team couldn't be tolerated.

Roebeck had told them both so in no uncertain terms.

Not happy campers, this time out, not any of them.

Roebeck turned on the RF receiver and music poured out. Some female was singing something about baby love, in an impossibly childish voice. Roebeck spun the dial. There was no newscast that she could find.

She sighed and sat back, pulling her membrane down from her headband peevishly. The style of the day allowed for all sorts of strange headgear and clothing, which made utilizing their coveralls and basic commo gear less of a problem than it otherwise could have been.

Three hours after insertion, Roebeck was still so angry about the tone of the hot wash that she was talking to him through her commo link, despite the fact that he was right beside her.

"Tim, you've got to patch it up with Chun. That's an order. If you don't trust her, that's your business. Keep it your business. We're literally dependent on her for our lives—unless you want to spend the rest of yours here in the worst possible version of the next two weeks of 1967, or disappear with this horizon if we're successful."

"Don't think I hadn't considered that. I'm sorry. I told her. I apologized. I'm just jumpy." If Chun decided to leave them here—or him here—there'd be no recourse. And any ARC Rider would be in lethal trouble if one—or more—were still on this horizon when the calendar reached March 15, the day they'd first inserted. Staying here was a death sentence, whether or not the mission was successful. And Chun could decree them MIA/KIA by failing to retrieve them before that date.

It was interesting to know one possible date of your death. It gave things a singular perspective. He'd known the risks when he'd politicked for preemption, but he hadn't felt them until the capsule shimmered out of phase and he and Roebeck were on their own within such a severely circumscribed survivable timeframe.

"Tim, I'm sorry, too. You and Chun are both critical to this team. Let's go get this toad Bates and his girlfriend Rhone and be out of here before dawn. Then I'll forget the whole thing. You and Chun can prove each other's trust by succeeding. Do that, and life and the world as we know it can go on. All right?"

"Just what I had in mind," he said with real fervor.

In lieu of any more best-laid plans which might go awry, they were going to confront Bates at a Democratic fund-raiser he was known to have attended on March 1, according to Chun's data on the recent past of Timeline B circa March 15, 1967. The local newspapers had reported their names among the socialites gathered at the Hay-Adams Hotel to hear the President speak. Lucky Bates was political. Lucky Chun was such a good researcher.

Maybe too lucky. But Roebeck didn't want to think that way.

He couldn't talk to her about his reservations, so he said, "Nan, we've got to go somewhere to get the appropriate local clothes for this." Coveralls could do only so much. Over them, he was going to need black tie. Nan was in worse straits: you couldn't wear coveralls under most mid-20th century evening gowns. She was going to need something of the sort a Muslim woman might buy if required to attend a formal dinner in the West. Lucky this was Washington.

Grainger hated luck. He didn't trust it. There was too much of it showing up on this mission. The bell curve was going to catch up with them: all the bad luck they weren't getting might fall on their heads like an avalanche.

The matter of access to the fund-raiser had nothing to do with luck. It was a simple case of buying into power: you paid your money, you got your ticket. That was what fund-raisers were about. Chun had already registered both of them from TC 779 before she phased out, charging the door fee to Grainger's credit card. She'd been told that there would be an "opportunity to contribute further to the cause by check."

So now they had manual checkbooks: pieces of paper on which you wrote the amount by hand which you wanted debited, and the payee's name. Somehow, Chun had assured them, the name alone provided a destination for the debited funds. All without having to know the routing numbers. It was amazing that the local banking system kept things straight.

Chun had quizzed them on the procedure until they could write the paper debit creditably in the new checkbooks she'd made for them, which carried the appropriate numbers of a local bank to which actual funds had been transferred from some luckless bastard's offshore account by her manipulation. So the checks were good, at least for the next few weeks. After the 15th of March, it wasn't going to matter to him and Roebeck whether anyone caught the banking manipulation.

If they were still here on the Ides of March, they'd cease to exist before the end of the night.

Getting the proper clothes for a black tie fund-raiser was harder than Grainger had anticipated, and more costly. They used up nearly half of the checks Chun had given them doing it. When they had finally purchased tuxedo (alterations promised for later that day at an extra charge), bow tie (which he was taught to tie in the store), dress shirt, suspenders, shirt studs, collar stays, cuff links, socks, shoes, overcoat, long-sleeved and high-necked evening dress (so that Roebeck could wear her coveralls underneath), pantyhose (!), high heels, evening bag, and fur coat, they had visited five stores and raised their visibility considerably. Worse than that, it was getting late and Grainger hadn't yet collected his altered tuxedo.

His instincts were telling him they should get invisible, fast. He was exhausted from watching crowds and passersby for repeating faces and scanning every establishment they visited for possible traps.

He flat didn't want to go back to the store to pick up the dinner suit. He told Roebeck that. "Returning someplace at a scheduled time window? I just don't think we should."

"Well, you're not going to that fund-raiser dressed like that." Roebeck, now an expert on contemporary customs, looked him up and down critically. "You look like a hippie. We're lucky we pulled this off. Let's go to the hotel and send someone for your things, then."

It wasn't a much superior option, but Grainger agreed. Driving the big car without incident through early evening's impossibly congested traffic arteries to the hotel opposite the White House was about as much as he could handle right now.

The Hay-Adams was comfortable, antique even in its own time, and full of staff eager to please. As they checked in, Grainger held his breath. No problem. His local credit card worked fine. The receptionist agreed to send someone to pick up his tuxedo and deliver it to their room.

They had three hours to rest, dress in the complex clothing, and do recon on the site of the fund-raiser.

In the suite furnished with antiques, soft divans, and a four-poster bed, he nearly fell asleep to the sound of Roebeck enjoying an unlimited H_2O shower. At this level of society, people lived well enough to envy, even in 1967.

He turned on the television to keep awake, but couldn't find the news channels. He mastered the phone system and ordered coffee by voice from a person with a slow southern drawl. He swept the room for bugs and found nothing electronic whatsoever, not even a hotel-generated RF security scan.

Then the tuxedo and attachments arrived, and he was at pains to remember how to put all the pieces of the evening wear together. He was still struggling with the bow tie when Roebeck came out of the shower in a towel.

"You're not going to bathe?" Her hair was wet and she shook it at him.

"Is it part of my job?" He was dressed. He didn't want to go through all this again.

"It should be obvious to you that a bath or at least a wash would improve your ability to . . . blend in," she said scathingly.

Roebeck standing wet in a bedroom wrapped in only a towel was different from Roebeck his boss in uniform. He knew it and she knew it. They both needed to ignore it for the sake of the mission. He'd never realized how pale her skin was, or how freckled.

He said, "I'm going downstairs to get a look at the room." He had his acoustic pistol, his handheld scanner, and that was it. "You'll have to handle all the sensory sweeps." He ran a hand through his short-cropped hair. "I've got my gear inside my hat, but you evidently don't wear those hats indoors. When you're ready, come down in your coat and we'll go outside. Then we can come in again and take the opportunity to do a thorough spectral sweep."

Best he could do. He had to get out of there.

He wandered around the hall, found the elevator. In the lobby he drifted down the stairs into the dining room, and up another flight until he was stopped by a very polite waiter dressed just as he was, who told him this room was for a private party.

He said, "I know. I'm a guest." Just to make sure he wasn't mistaken for part of the staff.

"Staying with us, sir? I see. Well of course, if you wish to look around . . ." Now the waiter thought he was some sort of special security.

Grainger was unsure whether to take the opportunity to walk the room, and the concomitant chance that the waiter would mention it to someone, or to leave as unremarkably as possible. He had his hat in his hand so he could see the tell-tales of his commo system, and his overcoat on his arm to hide the bulge of his acoustic pistol against his thigh. Just in case. "Thank you, I'll do that."

He drifted around, turning his hat in his hands as unobtrusively as possible. The waiter ignored him. Maybe it would be all right. There wasn't an Oriental waiter in sight. The room was scanning pretty much as it should. . . .

Then two big guys in gray suits with hearing aids came up to him, one on each side, lighting the RF telltale jammed into his hat. He was willing to bet that 1960s hat bands didn't light up and blink at you. He flipped the disabling switch as if flicking a spot of lint, then looked up at them, hat held against his chest.

Before they opened their mouths he knew he was in trouble.

The President was going to speak here. The Secret Service advance team was on site hours before, even in 1967, on behalf of their soon-to-arrive "protectees."

"Can we help you, sir?"

"I was just looking for my name tag," he said lamely. "My wife likes to know where she's going to sit before she decides what jewels to wear." Did that sound like 1967 snobbery? He hoped so.

"And what's the name, sir?"

"Mr. and Mrs. Timothy Rainer."

One of the beefy Secret Service men stood in Grainger's way while another stalked off to check the seating list. He was going to have a real problem if Chun hadn't successfully gotten them on that list.

As it was, he didn't want to explain the hardware in his hat. He let the hand holding it drop casually to his side.

Just then Roebeck's voice called out, "Tim, dear, come on, *please*! You can talk to your friends later. I want to get a little air." Imperious, demanding. Just perfect.

The beefy Secret Service agent looked past him. Grainger looked, too. The woman in the fur coat and the evening gown was tapping her fingers on crossed arms.

"Guess you can go along, sir. I'm sure we'll—"

"Right here," called the second agent, pointing to a seat directly in front of the raised dais which held the head table. "Mr. and Mrs. Rainer."

"Thank you, gentlemen," said Grainger, and turned on his heel.

Under his overcoat, his hand relaxed on the pistol that had somehow slipped into it when he wasn't paying attention. When he reached Roebeck, he was sweating.

"I owe you one—darling." He pecked her chastely on the cheek and guided her toward the doors and the relative safety outside with one hand in the small of her fur-clad back.

As they were bowed out of the doors by staff, he wondered how many chinchillas had died for that coat. Outside, Roebeck asked, "What happened in there?"

"I met the Secret Service advance team." He shrugged. "At least I know who they are. And no, I didn't show any ID."

"Walk, damn it," Roebeck hissed. She put her arm in his and nearly dragged him along. Then he saw why.

A presidential motorcade was turning this way, flags on the front fenders, motorcycle escort, flashing lights, and all.

From nowhere, press was coalescing. The ARC Riders had to get out of sight.

This operation was sliding quickly into the dumper. Between sirens and motorcycles, you couldn't hear yourself think. He put on his hat and stepped into the shadows near the wall of the building so that he could slide his commo gear into position. "Nan, this isn't going to work."

"Tim, I'm getting that feeling, too. But—look."

He turned to look where she pointed.

The presidential limousine was pulling into the circular drive of the hotel. Secret Service swarmed the car and kept back press with cameras that still had flash attachments. The effect of the flashing cameras was nearly blinding until Grainger pulled down his membrane and enabled his eye protection. Then everything was murky, but he did see the President and his wife get out of their car. Those ears were unmistakable.

That car drove away. The next one held the National Security Advisor. After the advisor and his wife got out of the car, another couple followed.

Bates and Rhone.

"God help us," Roebeck groaned. "Chun didn't say they were *that* well connected."

"They're that well funded. You want to give up now, or you want the expensive dinner we paid for?"

"No, we'll go in. Maybe something will happen that will give us a shot."

"Give a big contribution, and make an appointment," Grainger said dourly. "That's the only shot, unless you want to let me take down a roomful of history-worthy locals with acoustics pushed to levels that may be indiscriminately lethal, or try breaking into Bates' house again."

Bates was better looking even than his photograph, tall, black-haired with bold, intelligent eyes that swept Grainger and Roebeck as a matter of course. The eyes didn't pause when they encountered Grainger or Roebeck, but Grainger had the feeling he'd been acquired and logged. Not as an enemy, only as a datum.

As planned, the ARC Riders toughed it out. They drank the cocktails, ate the shrimp canapés, and sat through the five-course dinner with attendant speeches.

The President was saying, "My dear friends, the Founding Fathers gave us a proud legacy. That legacy demands that we act to ensure the future of the United States for our children and grandchildren against an increasing threat to our national security. I'm telling you here today that the buildup in Southeast Asia cannot be allowed to continue. This war cannot be lost, or with it we'll lose our own freedom. And to protect that freedom, we need every one of you. Your contributions will help us fight the divisive factions in this country that want to give our future to the Communist enemy. Here at home, and abroad, a Democratic America must prevail." The President frowned, looked at his notes, and took a step back from the lectern as if he'd forgotten why he was there.

At the head table, Bates leaned back in his chair and flung an arm over its back. In his hand was a napkin. Under the napkin was ... something. Something pointed at the President.

The President took a step sideways, then forward. He rubbed his nose with his thumb and forefingers, and looked down again at his speech.

Then he continued reading from where he'd left off.

"That's it, Tim, did you see?" Roebeck leaned close and whispered in his ear. No hats in this place.

"I saw. What do you want me to do? Start spraying the head table with acoustics?"

"No, of course not. But now we know."

"Next move, boss?"

"Write that check you were talking about. See if we can get an appointment to see Bates in his office—he's deputy chairman of the Democratic Reelection Committee, isn't he?" Nan Roebeck leaned even closer and looked at him hard. "Nothing else. Nothing now. We can't risk it." There were strangers on both sides of them, listening to the President intently—or so Grainger hoped.

"So it isn't a suicide mission, after all? Thanks, Nan. I'm glad to hear it." He'd have done it, if she ordered. Right then and there. He didn't see any choice.

But she did. She kissed him softly on the cheek, for appearance's sake, and murmured, "We'll get a shot at them. You'll see."

At the head table, Rhone was sipping champagne and slipping her arm over Bates' shoulder. She was either drunk or pretending to be, while she tweaked whatever device Bates was holding. The President of the United States continued to read his speech.

Not until the President was done did Bates sit forward, putting both hands under the table before he raised them to clap enthusiastically. Neither of Bates' hands, nor either of Rhone's, held so much as a napkin any longer.

Over Northeastern
Virginia

"Well, my goodness, *that's* how they did it," Barthuli said. He beamed at Weigand in the aisle seat beside him. "The weapons that our counterparts used on us!"

Weigand nodded to show he was listening. The analyst had been working all through the long flight, but the flickers Weigand saw of the air-projected hologram display gave no hint of the subject. Weigand hadn't wanted to disturb Barthuli with a pointless question—Gerd would tell them if there was anything he thought they needed to know.

The other reason he hadn't questioned Barthuli was that Weigand had disconnected himself from the world he couldn't affect for the time being. If he engaged Barthuli, or Carnes, or even Watney on the other side of the aisle, Weigand's brain would cast over the decisions he'd made and would have to make in the future; knowing that he didn't have enough data to decide intelligently, nor enough resources to act with any reasonable hope of success. Deciding and acting anyway.

Better not to think. Best of all, never to have been born.

Barthuli had hoped for more enthusiasm at his announcement, but the analyst wasn't a man who depended on others for his pleasures. "Their weapons suppress acetylcholine production!" he said proudly. "The target's nervous system shuts down entirely because the messenger chemical isn't released."

"The guns inject chemicals?" Weigand said. He'd been so sure the weapons were electronic—and thus destroyed by the electromagnetic pulse as surely as the suits—that he hadn't bothered to appropriate one or both. A mistake, *another* mistake?

"Oh, no," Barthuli said. "That couldn't be or we wouldn't have come around so quickly when the stimulus was removed. Cholinesterase in the bloodstream would have taken some while to decay, hours perhaps."

Weigand couldn't remember the event precisely. He'd noticed the forearm of the displacement suit crooked toward him when it should have been straight, the gun that shouldn't have been in the hand. After that—white fuzz around the edges of his vision, *heat*, his skin flushing as though he'd been seared. Those were the normal concomitants of having fainted, as was the patchy amnesia regarding the few moments before and after.

Carnes leaned forward to catch Weigand's eye past the analyst. "We've been descending," she said. "My ears wouldn't pop until just now."

"Squad leaders, prepare your men," the PA system crackled. "Landing in ten minutes."

The old aircraft was noisy, and its speakers were so illtuned and rasping that you virtually had to know what was being said to understand it. That was all right. They did all know what was coming. Carnes' weren't the only ears to have felt the descent into the target area.

Watney, the team's nominal squad leader, stood up in the aisle and began checking his equipment. The revisionist carried a ten-pound charge of TNT, three light anti-tank rockets, an M16 rifle with a 40mm grenade launcher beneath the barrel—much the way Anti-Revision Command EMP generators clipped to fléchette guns, and *what* Weigand would have given for proper ARC weaponry at this moment—and bandoliers of both rifle and grenade ammunition.

Other men, all the other men, rose from their seats as well. This formerly commercial aircraft wasn't configured to unload an assault company in a hurry. Those aboard were aggressive, hard-charging men. Anybody slow getting through a doorway was going to be trampled if he wasn't shot first.

Barthuli eyed the jostling, hair-trigger mass of killers crowding the DC-8's aisle. "Odd, isn't it?" he said. "As if that would help us arrive more quickly."

Weigand slid the switch of his EMP generator back and forth. He wondered if he should wear the displacement suit, stored now across the two seats beside Watney. The protection and sensors would be useful for the entire team; but if the hostile ARC Riders were present, Weigand would be painting a bull's-eye on his forehead.

"The weapon's field causes a response in the emitter cells," Barthuli resumed, looking at Weigand again. "The same principle as the irritant effect your device"—he nodded toward Weigand's jury-rigged EMP generator; jury-rigged, but it worked, it had saved their lives—"causes, but more subtle if I may say so."

Weigand nodded, not really listening. The hostiles must track displacements, not arrivals or the course through nontime. They'd located TC 779 when Weigand's group left it, and they'd found the suits themselves at Travis when the equipment repeatedly displaced out of phase at the same geographical point. But the hostiles hadn't hunted down Weigand and his companions in 10K or the Midwest in 1991, because they hadn't made two displacements from the same point.

"The device acts in a manner opposite to that of contemporary nerve gas," the analyst said. "Nerve gas inhibits cholinesterase production so that the victim's nerves fire without remission until he dies. I wonder"—his brow narrowed in concentration—"if the same sort of projected field, beam, could inhibit cholinesterase?"

"Okay," Weigand said, making his mind up as he spoke. He got to his feet. "I'm going to wear the armor. Colonel Watney, please let me by."

Carnes was short enough that she could stand upright in front of the window seat. She rose when Weigand did and said, "What if it wasn't the same people who attacked the . . . the capsule, Pauli? This pair was . . . They didn't want to hurt you. The guns didn't do any permanent damage. Not like the others."

The conversation was of no interest to soldiers nearby. The others' minds were filled with immediate problems: would the airport layout be as described? When would the guards realize they were being attacked?

Weigand wondered how much it had bothered Rebecca to have killed the hostiles. She'd brushed off the slaughter of the Guardsmen in Iowa easily enough. That had made Weigand think she was as callous as most of those the Anti-Revision Command recruited from early horizons. But Carnes hadn't killed the victims that time, and that distinction clearly made a difference to her.

Watney with his packful of munitions was wedged too tightly to move in the aisle or even turn his body. He craned his head over his shoulder and said to the man behind him, "Back up and let my sergeant by, buddy."

"They were just trying to minimize the public disruption, Rebecca," Weigand said. "I doubt the way they deal with revisionists—that's what we are to them—is anything as complicated as displacing them to 50K."

"Fuck!" said the man, a cadaverous black whose fungus condition cast pink speckles across his skin. The black braced himself and thrust backward. "Get him by, then!" he snarled at the 15-centimeter gap between his chest and Watney's pack.

Watney pushed forward and Weigand slid between them, feeling constricted and afraid, afraid of making the wrong decision. If the plane exploded in the air, he'd never have to explain to anybody why he'd failed. . . .

"I don't think that was really their reasoning, Pauli," Barthuli said. He was still seated, almost the only person in the passenger cabin who was. "Their transportation capsule would have caused as much comment when they summoned it as a plasma discharge or two. I think our opposite numbers wanted to pick our brains because their preemptive attack on TC 779 failed."

Weigand had taken the displacement suit out of its concealing crate as soon as the DC-8 lifted from its last refueling stop, a civil airport serving Nashville. It was awkward now to clamber into the armor between the close-pitched seats of the aircraft, but the task gave him something on which to concentrate apart from the events coming in the next minutes.

"Maybe, Gerd," Weigand said as his right leg finally found the correct angle and slid into the armor. "But remember, a couple plasma discharges might have set off the whole hangar. A lot of those pallets were ammo and explosives. The hostiles don't dare do something that will change *their* past, however willing they may be to kill when they have the freedom to."

"This attack isn't going to succeed, is it?" Carnes said. She'd stepped over the analyst's legs and now stood in front of the seat Weigand had occupied. "Surely General Oakley isn't going to become . . . President?"

Barthuli chuckled. "President of what, you mean, Rebecca?" he said. "No, of course he'll fail. Analysis would tell me that, even if we hadn't seen the actual results when we surveyed the horizon looking for, well, for you. But to abort the attempt still in California, that sort of revision could cause any number of effects up the line. Pauli is right. An error by our opponents could divert their future, even if it doesn't bring ours back."

Weigand closed the plastron over his chest, but he left the faceshield open. He could see and hear better with the armor buttoned up, but it was bad enough to have to be in this packed passenger cabin without enclosing himself still tighter.

There wasn't any choice about which of the team would wear the suit: Weigand was the only one it would fit. He wondered if the reason two, not three hostile ARC Riders had waited to ambush the team in its own armor was that none of the Orientals was tall enough to wear Weigand's suit.

He still felt like a coward, protected when his subordinates were not. What would ARC Central and those up the line think of his decision?

The DC-8 had been repainted at Travis in the colors of Delta Airlines. It was a sloppy job, but there was a lot of bad workmanship around as America fell the last of the way into an unwinnable war. The plane would be landing some minutes ahead of the day's regular flight from Atlanta. National's runway wasn't long enough for aircraft of this size and vintage, but the pilot was convinced he could get them in.

The troops Oakley recruited from the war zone had the job of capturing National Airport. The briefings had used old airline magazine drawings of the airport layout with the recently added defenses—a missile battery and a number of blockhouses with dual-purpose automatic weapons—drawn in by hand. When that mission was accomplished, the remainder of the coup force and its vehicles could land unopposed in military transports.

The airport's defenses were manned by the Presidential Guard. Weigand doubted the troops' quality was any higher than that of Oakley's brassarded equivalent, but it takes very little effort to shoot down an aircraft on its landing run. The sight of six or seven lumbering transports—there'd have been ten if Oakley's spares and maintenance situation had permitted them to make a 5,000-kilometer flight—would fill the air above the runways with tracer bullets.

The PA system rattled something unintelligible. Buildings, then water, raced by beyond the scratched Plexiglas of Weigand's window. He closed his faceshield.

The wheels thumped. The men in the passenger compartment swayed as a single mass. The plane hit a second time. The pilot was coming down deliberately hard to shorten his run, but the tires were in no better condition than the rest of the aircraft. One of them blew like a bomb.

The plane slewed. Somebody screamed a prayer in Spanish. Another tire blew and a roostertail of sparks shot back from where metal abraded on concrete with a shriek that silenced all voices and all hope.

The pilot brought the nose straight, then made a deliberate turn to the right. Metal still rubbed, but the sound was petulant rather than triumphantly bloodthirsty.

Wind roared through the cabin. The Air Force officers acting as cabin staff were opening the doors while the DC-8 still taxied.

Brakes moaning like damned souls, the aircraft shuddered to a halt at the terminal. Weigand had seen only three other aircraft through his window; one of those was deadlined for repair, starboard control surfaces and engine removed.

"Go!" an officer shouted, but his voice was a poor, weak thing compared to the bellow of over a hundred killers heading into action down the emergency slides.

"Go, go, go," Watney mouthed. The revisionist was taut as an E-string, but he waited under Weigand's orders until the assault force cleared the aircraft.

Watney understood *their* mission had nothing to do with capturing the airport. So far as the team was concerned, the attack was merely a ride to Washington, necessary because the suits—the suit—couldn't displace spatially.

General Fern had tasked "Watney's Squad" to eliminate the blockhouse armed with 20mm cannon—aircraft guns on improvised ground mountings—on the roof of the building. Weigand had no intention of getting involved in a battle, on the roof or elsewhere, but anything that caused confusion was to the benefit of the team as it escaped from the area.

Weigand paused on the emergency side hatch, aiming his EMP generator. His three companions, Watney in the lead, went out the parallel hatch two rows back instead of waiting for him. That wasn't what he'd intended. The air glittered with muzzle flashes, tracers, and shattered glass falling in the noonday sun.

Weigand pulsed the three microwave communication cones he could see from this angle, then aimed at the airport radar antenna and gave it a full two seconds. The radar receiver would fail—and possibly explode—when it tried to amplify the pulse. The control staff would have enough to think about already, but a healthy fear of their equipment might delay them from summoning help by the channels that hadn't been put out of commission.

His companions were almost to the terminal. Carnes turned to check Weigand's progress. He jumped down an emergency slide which was already collapsing from a burst seam. The top half of the terminal exploded.

The assault force's gunfire had raked the upper floor where the gates had been in the days when the boarding bridges were in use. The blast blew the walls out and threw bodies, scores of bodies, as far as fifty meters from the building.

The shock knocked Carnes down, but she'd risen to her feet before Weigand reached her. Some of the bodies had been stripped by the explosion; others were wrapped in their own burning garments.

The disused floor had been occupied by folk who otherwise wouldn't have had a roof over their heads. The squatters cooked their food in narrow warrens partitioned with cardboard. One family had a stove with a gas bottle big enough to blow themselves and everyone camped in that gate area to kingdom come when a bullet hit.

All across the upper floor, smoke belched through bullet holes and the gaps where windows had been before the blast. Fuel, flesh, fabrics—sooty flames, gnawing the air with petulant orange teeth. Weigand supposed he should be glad. The smell and screams would increase the confusion still more.

Weigand led Carnes into the building. They had to get into the city proper. Going through the terminal was shorter and a safer bet than trying to go around the U-shaped building, chancing gunfire from the dozens of doorways and windows.

Watney and Barthuli waited inside. The analyst held his recorder/computer rather than an acoustic pistol. He hadn't bothered to bring the Kalashnikov "assigned" to him out of the DC-8.

The lounge was a charnel house. It had been crowded with would-be passengers—more people than aircraft the size of those serving National could have accommodated. They'd been pushing toward the doors to be sure of getting places on the outgoing flight.

To be able to fly in these final days, you needed some connection with power; and as always in chaos, power surely did flow from the barrel of a gun. Most of those in the lounge were wearing military uniforms. That might have been the reason, or at least the excuse, the assault force had for opening fire indiscriminately.

On the other hand, Oakley's shock troops were men only days back from jungle and the loess hills of Yunnan. They might not have thought they needed an excuse to kill REMFs like these.

The man lying in front of the door had silver hair and an aristocratic face. His uniform had been white and gold; now it was red as well. His hands were spread on his chest. The man's eyes were open and he wasn't dead yet, but it wouldn't be long.

One of his bodyguards was headless. A 40mm grenade had eviscerated the other, though he, too, was technically alive for the moment.

There had been hundreds of people in the lounge. They were mostly there still, where air-bursting grenades had killed them, or sprawled in windrows of three to a dozen as automatic rifles and machine guns raked their running backs.

A few survivors tried to hide behind the luggage carousels. Men in battledress shot them down, working in pairs like hunters driving squirrels around a tree trunk to one another.

"Okay," Weigand said, as a placeholder for thoughts that he couldn't permit himself to think. He pointed out the front of the terminal building, toward the parking lot and beyond it the city in which they would go to ground while planning the next maneuver. "Straight on through, me in the lead."

The entryway's marble floor was treacherous with slippery pooling blood. Weigand skidded twice, catching him-

self on cracks, but his balance was nearly perfect when the
adrenaline was flowing as now.

Half a dozen members of the assault force were ahead of
him. Apparently because the automatic opening mechanisms
no longer worked, the door slides had been wedged open.
Four of the attackers ran through one open doorway; their
two fellows used the next one to the right.

A 105mm high-explosive shell from a tank in the parking lot
hit one man of the pair. The shell didn't explode then because a
human chest didn't provide enough resistance to set the fuse.
Instead, the round screamed across the terminal, hit a concrete pillar in the far wall, and blew bits of its across the distant runway.

The man whom the shell had hit was a head and shoulders
poised above running legs. The center of his chest had vanished, and the air behind him was a fog of blood. The parts
of his body toppled as machine gun fire riddled the four men
in the next door opening.

"Down!" Weigand screamed, throwing himself flat. A second 105 round blasted through the terminal, in and out in a
shock of air. There was a huge explosion beyond and a gush
of orange flame lighting the terminal through all openings
on the runway side. The shell had opened up the DC-8 like
a plow through fallow land.

Bullets from two or three continuously firing automatic
weapons punched in from the front of the terminal. Machine
guns weren't a danger to Weigand in the displacement suit,
but 20-kilogram tank shells would kill him as dead as they
had the soldier who'd taken the direct hit.

Barthuli was saying something. Weigand tuned the analyst's words out. He didn't have time for answers that might
not be to the precise questions that mattered now. He had to
focus on his suit's sensors and artificial intelligence.

There were two tanks, bow on to the terminal building and
about a hundred meters away. They had diesel engines and
hydraulic controls. The only equipment an electromagnetic
pulse could affect were their laser range finders and radios.

The range finders didn't work to begin with and were need-less with the tanks firing at pistol range.

Kyle Watney extended the tube of one of his anti-tank rock-ets, arming the weapon. He rolled out from behind the pillar where he'd been sheltering. Weigand grabbed the revision-ist's ankle and pulled him back down.

Two more 105mm shells hit the terminal. One was aimed at the south end, from which somebody'd been shooting at the tanks. There was a red flash; a telephone flew from that wing of the building as a secondary projectile.

"I've got to get between them!" Watney screamed at the smooth surface of Weigand's helmet. "The LAW charge won't penetrate from the front, I have to hit them from the side! They'll shoot us to shit if we stay here!"

The automatic cannon on the roof opened fire. The wrack-ing 30-round burst terminated in a *whoomp*! as something went wrong.

"I'll go," Weigand said, taking the missile from Watney's hands. The revisionist didn't try to resist. "Give me the other two. You wouldn't get through."

The south wing ruptured in an oily blast. God only knew what had been stored there. The explosion wasn't caused by a tank shell, because the next pair of those streaked across the anteroom a half second later. The vehicles were firing armor-piercing arrow shot this time. One projectile drilled the pillar above Carnes and Barthuli in a blaze of green and scarlet light, sparks from the reinforcing rods and the tungsten penetrator.

Weigand thumbed his inner left wrist. Displacement's fa-miliar disorientation was a relief after the carnage of the ter-minal building. He couldn't have gotten through the alerted tanks, either, not with the certainty required. Pauli Weigand would have risked his life without hesitation, but he couldn't risk the operation that would fail if his displacement suit took a main-gun round.

The tanks weren't alerted, weren't even present, on August 4, 1991, when a man in bulky armor appeared in the termi-

· nal of National Airport. The figure pushed screaming travelers out of the way, lumbering through the front door and
across the sun-drenched humidity of the parking lot beyond.

Weigand had displaced back to a point one hour before he,
Carnes, and Barthuli had arrived in Iowa at the start of their
odyssey across this temporal horizon. If he was delayed in
the past longer than an hour, he was . . . dead, he supposed;
certainly vanished from this timeline. But only death would
delay him that much anyway.

A pair of guards with submachine guns patrolled the front
of the terminal building. They shouted at Weigand—shouted
at his back, because he ran by without pausing. The grid of
lines on his helmet were centered on the spot in the pavement
where he needed to be when he returned to August 24. That
was all that mattered for the moment.

A helicopter was moving slowly up the Potomac River.
Sound reflecting from the water's surface syncopated the
clop of the blades.

One of the guards threw his weapon to his shoulder,
shouted another challenge, and fired. Three or four of the pis-
tol-caliber bullets hit Weigand and bounced off with bitter
whines. Protected by his armor, Weigand heard but couldn't
feel the projectiles.

Maybe this was why the tanks were waiting in front of the
terminal when the force from California assaulted it. Three
weeks earlier an armored figure had burst from the terminal
carrying anti-tank rockets, had run into the parking lot—and
there vanished, an enigma and a threat. That could easily have
spurred the authorities to shift a pair of tanks from the
Pentagon garrison.

But if the tanks hadn't been present on August 24, Pauli
Weigand wouldn't have displaced to outflank them in time.
Maybe Nan understood these things, maybe those up the line
did. For now . . .

Weigand checked the cocked anti-tank rocket, checked his
location; both were correct. A dozen more submachine gun
bullets spanged and sparked from his armor.

Weigand returned to August 24 and the middle of a fire-fight.

Fire had fully involved the terminal's upper floor. The lower level of the building would be uninhabitable in mere minutes if it wasn't now. Ten meters of the south wing had been blown to rubble. In the bay at the back of the terminal, hotter flames from the DC-8's jet fuel mounted fifty meters in the air.

The tanks were fifteen meters apart, firing into the building with both cannon and machine guns. No one aboard the vehicles noticed that Weigand had appeared between them, but an automatic rifle in the terminal raked him with its fire. The bullets didn't have enough energy to hurt *him*, but they could damage the rockets he held if he didn't use them promptly.

Weigand aimed at the side of the turret of the tank on his left. The bow slope and the front of the turret were thicker armor than this small missile could penetrate, but the sides were less of a problem.

Weigand pulled the long trigger. The rocket fired with an angry *thow*! and a gush of orange flame from the back of the tube. The missile hit the turret exactly where Weigand had intended. It ricocheted skyward from the curved armor without exploding and struck again a good five hundred meters distant. This time it went off, blasting a divot from a sparsely traveled roadway.

Weigand swallowed. It hadn't occurred to him that the weapon would be a dud. The mean time between failure of Anti-Revision Command equipment was comparable to that of granite.

"Pauli," said Gerd Barthuli in the instant that Weigand's mind, blank with catastrophe, was capable of hearing the voice in his ears. "Colonel Watney says that the arming distance of a LAW is ten meters. You're too close to the target."

Weigand strode ten meters farther from the tank as he extended the tube of the second rocket. The shooters within the terminal stopped firing at him when they saw him attempt to destroy the tank, but the clang of the missile hitting the turret had aroused interest within the vehicle. A head emerged from the open cupola hatch.

The armor of an M60 tank was as impervious to rifle and machine gun fire as Weigand's displacement suit. The men of the assault force were primed and ready for a target they could not only hit but hurt. At least three marksmen blew simultaneous holes through the tank commander's head.

Weigand aimed the notch-and-post sight of the second launcher at the same point as before. He pulled the trigger. The missile tracked straight and went off against the side of the turret with a white flash.

The *crack*! of the warhead was almost lost in the *clang*! of beaten metal. The shaped charge's metallic lining hit the turret armor as a gaseous spearpoint, piercing the steel and ripping on through the tank's fighting compartment. Ammunition went off inside. A blast and fireball lifted the loader's hatch, belching a ring of black smoke skyward.

Weigand walked toward the tank he had just put out of action. He didn't run, because he was extending the launcher of his last rocket. His armored grip was so strong that he might well have smashed the fiberglass tube and rocket motor if he'd been too hasty.

The second tank's 105 fired as Weigand turned. The muzzle blast lifted dust from the asphalt and rocked the heavy vehicle back on its suspension. The crew within were unaware that their consort was burning 15 meters away.

Weigand aimed, squeezed, and watched the third missile strike home to detonate. The smoke from the warhead dissipated on the breeze fanning the flames of the terminal building. There was a red-rimmed smudge on the turret side. The coaxial machine gun beside the main gun fell silent, but for a few seconds there was no other sign that the missile had been effective.

The tank blew up with a shattering roar. The turret leaped five meters skyward, spun, and crashed back down on the blazing hull, upside down and with its long cannon cocked to the side.

Weigand got to his feet. The displacement suit had protected him from injury, but he would have needed ten times the mass not to be knocked down by the shock wave. Figures ran from the terminal—Carnes, Barthuli, and Watney, but other members of the assault force as well.

The building was fast becoming an inferno. Most of the men in the north wing had already abandoned it for the captured gunpit on that end. Those in the south wing were surely dead.

The air between Weigand and Barthuli shimmered and took on the appearance of translucence rather than transparency. Carnes and Watney, five meters to either side of the analyst, were still as clear as before in the spark-shot, smoky atmosphere.

TC 779 locked into phase with the temporal horizon, hovering above asphalt that was beginning to bubble from the heat of the burning tank. The capsule's outer hull was scarred by sealant sprayed on to replace plates melted during the attack in 50K.

The hatch opened. Chun Quo stood in the hatchway screaming, "Quickly, they're going to use a nuclear weapon!"

Weigand was already running for the hatch. The unprotected members of his team ran also, in a blue ambience beyond which the world moved in slow motion.

Quo had thrown the immediate vicinity slightly out of phase. The team would be all right if the damaged capsule's systems could maintain phase with absolute precision despite the high-energy shock of a thermonuclear explosion.

Weigand was two steps from the hatch, pausing to let Carnes enter ahead of him. All his electronics failed simultaneously. The displacement suit became a lump of metal as dead as an anvil, with Pauli Weigand at the center of it.

He wasn't in doubt as to what had delivered the electromagnetic pulse that had overwhelmed his suit. As his suit froze, he'd seen an image that he knew would remain with him for the minute or two before he died: a second transportation capsule hovered over the fire-wrapped parking lot beside TC 779.

Washington National Airport

Rebecca Carnes thought she was seeing a mirage—the ARC Riders' time vehicle mirrored by a side effect of the process which slowed down motion beyond the immediate bubble of blue haze.

Differences struck her like a hammer of ice: the second vehicle's hull was as smooth as a knife blade, and its hatch was closed. This wasn't a double of TC 779 but rather the enemy that had ripped the wounds in the capsule of Carnes' friends.

Weigand fell forward, overbalanced by the arm he'd thrown out to gesture Carnes into the vehicle ahead of him. He hit the asphalt and rolled onto his right side with no more control than a sack of groceries has. His suit was dead. Shortly Pauli would be dead also, like the suited enemies Carnes had EMPed in California.

She knelt beside Weigand. Her short hair lifted and began to spark purple in a building static charge.

Gerd shouted something, one hand on Watney's shoulder and the other pointing toward the hostile vehicle. Chun Quo had vanished from the hatch of TC 779. Huge sparks popped soundlessly between the vehicles and the asphalt.

The displacement suit's external latch was beneath the right armpit. Carnes tried to push it open from the back and failed. To get a better angle, she jumped over Weigand's body as though it were a vaulting horse. The surface of the armor was hot, hot enough to blister.

The world beyond the blue ambience went white in a flash that Carnes knew now to recognize. An opalescent cloud, light tangible and more hideous than the face of a corpse lain three months in a shallow grave, swept at a snail's pace across the airport. Everything it touched dissolved.

The displacement suit clicked. The chest plate opened only halfway, blocked by the ground itself. Carnes grabbed the gauntlet of the outstretched arm and used it as a lever to lift the suit. She gained two inches, a third, using her thigh muscles against the stiff weight.

"Gerd!" she shouted as she started to slip, but it wasn't Barthuli's hands that suddenly aided her and flung the dead mass on its back. Pauli had gotten an arm free. He pushed against the asphalt with strength doubled by desperation. With the front fully open, Weigand threw back the helmet and clambered from the suit. Carnes braced herself to anchor his brutal grip.

Watney pulled the friction igniter of his satchel charge and flung the bomb against the side of the hostile vehicle. The charge bounced back. The vehicle drifted in the other direction as though the two were of equal mass.

Weigand started for the satchel charge. Carnes grabbed his arm and swung the big man enough that he tripped on the legs of his rigid armor.

"I've got it!" Watney cried as he scooped up the ten-pound charge again by its carrying strap. He put his free hand against the hull of the hostile capsule. It drifted like spider silk, but the revisionist walked after it in constant contact.

The nuclear shock wave had expanded beyond the limits of the airport reservation. Objects drifted in the vacuum glowing behind the wave front. The only thing Carnes could recognize was a fragment of pierced steel girder, probably part of the terminal building.

Barthuli clambered into TC 779. Weigand tossed Carnes aboard like a sack of rice and jumped in after her. The capsule's insubstantial outer blister and the inner door shut more quickly than visible motion.

Chun sat at the front of the vehicle. Bars of vertical red light danced in the air before her, obvious warning signals. The inner bulkhead was an unbroken display of the scene beyond the hull.

Watney followed as the capsule fled, like one magnet pushing another across the surface of a fluid. A line of thin gray smoke trailed from the satchel.

"A pyrotechnic fuse," Weigand muttered. "If he'd used an electronic delay, it wouldn't have worked in the stasis field."

Chun turned her head toward the others. Her face was still. "Is he—" she said.

The satchel charge went off with the smoky red flash of TNT, a *huge* flash. Watney vanished.

The hostile vehicle skittered from the explosion. The membrane of blue light above the hull collapsed downward, sucking with it the outward hellrush of secondary compression waves rebounding from ground zero.

Superheated gas touched the vehicle. The solid matter of the hull sublimed with the speed of glass shattering.

The remnants of what had been a transportation capsule spewed out into the firestorm, as dead and glowing as everything else within a mile radius.

Rebecca Carnes hadn't prayed since her first tour in Vietnam. She looked at the fiery expanse where Kyle Watney stood a moment before and whispered, "Christ have mercy on his soul."

Chun Quo's face was a death mask. She touched a control without speaking. TC 779 displaced from the heart of hell.

Washington, DC

March 2, 1967

Grainger was so frustrated he would gladly have hosed down any number of federal buildings, or, better, the business high-rises on K Street among which Bates' office was situated.

The team had a roomy briefcase now, the legal sort with an accordion bottom, and Grainger had bought a pilot's case which had even more room. Enough room for a tanglefoot device.

Armed to the teeth, they were about to make a serious try for their prey in this urban jungle with its plants in pots on concrete sidewalks.

It felt good to be doing something real. Last night in the elegant hotel room, it had taken all of his self-restraint to avoid trying something way too real, like hitting on his boss.

He'd taken a very long H_2O shower instead, trying to estimate the number of gallons he was turning into wastewater. Even in his time, the overage charge for that water would have meant a month's salary. In Roebeck's milieu, such luxury was not available even to the very rich: there was no such thing as a constant stream of available water for cleaning your body. You cleaned your body with bracingly abrasive dry chemical particles sprayed from heated air jets in a dry shower stall. Water was for drinking, cooking, and the rest belonged to the environment's flora and fauna by international agreement.

They had appropriate day clothes, now, at Roebeck's insistence: blue blazers, rep tie, khaki pants for him; a gray suit with flare-legged pants for her. Headgear was still a problem, so Grainger had yet another hat and so did Roebeck. She looked really grotesque with the round hat pulled down over her hair, which was brushed forward as much as possible to cover her equipment, and her pants legs flapping around her booted feet.

He supposed he looked no better, and yet they seemed to be attracting no undue attention. It was, after all, the sixties.

In Bates' building, you walked up to a guard presiding over a free-standing desk. The front of the desk was a glass-topped list of who occupied what floor. You then asked for the floor and the person. The guard called ahead to confirm that you had an appointment.

Then you were waved on, to a bank of marble-clad elevators with no attendant. You were, virtually, on your own.

They were alone in their elevator, but there might have been surveillance cameras installed above the false ceiling. They didn't talk. They didn't check their gear.

They were going to bag themselves a couple revisionists, or else.

When the elevator opened, Roebeck checked her hair, which just covered the membrane pushed up on her forehead. "Ready?"

She stepped out first.

"Yes sir." He followed.

The suite numbers on the door didn't immediately tell you which direction to take. They went down the hall a bit, turned, and came back the other way.

At the very end of that hall was a pair of mahogany-colored doors with a brass plaque on one. As they neared it, one door opened, and a man with an overcoat and a briefcase came out.

Grainger tensed. The man drew no weapon, but held the door open, smiling distractedly.

Roebeck paused, then walked straight toward him, shoulders squared.

Of course, Grainger realized, the gentleman was holding open the manually operated door for a lady.

Good thing he hadn't shot the guy down.

Roebeck said "Thank you," and the stranger said "My pleasure" and then headed for the elevators, leaving Grainger to fend for himself where doors were concerned.

The carpet was a rusty orange inside the office. The chairs were upholstered in brown hides. More dead animals turned into furniture.

A receptionist at a horseshoe made of the same mahogany received Roebeck's announcement that they were ". . . here to see Mr. Bates. We have an appointment at fourteen hundred hours."

The receptionist looked at her curiously. "I'll just tell Mr. Bates you're here. Please take a seat."

She should have said "two o'clock," Grainger realized. By then, so did Roebeck.

You couldn't anticipate every difference in custom. Maybe it would be overlooked. The receptionist had a huge curly black hairdo which made her look like a mongoloid child. Her skin was the same color as the desk. The desk was made of more mahogany than Grainger had ever seen outside of 50K or in a museum.

No wonder there had been no mahogany trees left in his own time. There were paper periodicals all over the glass table before the reception area chairs, too. Tens of them. Made of heavy, glossy stock with multicolor printing that made it nearly impossible to recycle efficiently. The prices for the periodicals were a pittance compared to the price for so much real first-use paper in Grainger's time.

This was Timeline B, after all, he reminded himself. Timeline A was sure to be more environmentally conscious, once they reinstated it. History made a point that environmental responsibility had started in the sixties. Still, he felt as if he were in a center of corruption par excellence. And he was probably right. His instincts were usually pretty good.

Roebeck didn't want to talk. Her breathing was very slow and shallow. He concentrated on syncing his respiration to hers. Always a good exercise before a team went into action. Synced breathing and body language provided a functional edge when conscious coordination was critical to mission accomplishment.

She noticed him, and nearly smiled. She took her own pulse, and mouthed the results: "Sixty-eight."

He brought his own pulse into line as best he could, getting it down to sixty-nine before someone came to get them. Women always ran cooler before action.

The greeter rubbed her hands together. She was wearing a close-fitting jacket with buttons that had little crossed *C*s emblazoned on them. She teetered on impossibly spikey heels.

"Please come this way. Mr. Bates will see you now." She tottered away and they both followed. Over her shoulder she asked them if they'd care for some refreshment, coffee or tea, perhaps.

They both said "No," perfectly synchronized.

The woman cast a glance backward and then faced front.

Bates' office was at the end of a long straight corridor. No problem getting out of here in a hurry. When its doors opened, Grainger was startled to see a huge corner window that showed a panorama of the buildings across the street and beyond, toward a little park and OEOB beyond it.

Bates wasn't in there, yet.

"Mr. Bates will be right with you," she assured them as she tottered out through a side door, closing it behind her.

"Now what?" Roebeck whispered, jostling him. He was already getting out his weapons. One way or another, this was going to end here and now. These revisionists, their flunkies, the Orientals—whatever came through that door was either going to come quietly with him or be acoustically subdued or tranked.

Or go headfirst out that conveniently placed window to the street below.

He just laid everything out in plain sight. He opened his case. He primed his acoustic pistol, extended its antennae to provide full directionality at close range. He set it for a ten-hertz pulse to be delivered at a point of impact two centimeters wide. He held it in one hand while he locked and loaded his tanglefoot launcher and slung it on his shoulder—in case there were more people than Bates waiting to come through that door.

"Tim . . ."

"Nan, just be ready to follow through. Call Chun now and tell her we're go for extraction."

"You're that sure?"

He was that desperate. "You know I am."

She got out her fléchette gun and chambered a round. "Backup," she said needlessly.

Then the side door opened and Bates came through first, with Rhone close behind him, laughing as she shut the door with a wriggle of her butt.

The laughing stopped abruptly.

Aboard TC 779

**Displacing from August 24, 1991,
to August 30, 1968.**

"We couldn't afford to be surprised again," Chun Quo said. By watching the images reeling past on the display she avoided having to look at her companions. "Not after the damage the capsule received in the first attack. Nan and Tim are operating from the safe house, while I kept the capsule out of phase."

She wiped her eyes by brushing against her shoulders, one and then the other. She couldn't use her hands because she was holding the control wands. "We can join them now that the danger has been removed."

"I'd like to apologize to him," Rebecca Carnes said. "Watney. I—after he shot his own man back at the compound, I . . ."

Weigand was covering her scrapes and burns with gel that soaked in as soon as it was applied, leaving the surface tacky to the touch. The goo tingled mildly as it went on, as though Pauli were bathing the wounds with carbonated water. Her itching and ache vanished immediately, and Carnes found she had normal feeling again in her blistered fingertips.

Barthuli glanced back from a display focused for his eyes only. "There's nothing to apologize for, Rebecca," he said. "The colonel was exactly what you thought he was. He would have been the last to deny that."

"We enlisted Watney because I thought we needed him," Weigand said with a harshness Carnes didn't expect from him. "That was true. I was just wrong about what we were going to need him for."

"Ruthlessness isn't a survival characteristic for the individual," Gerd Barthuli said. Carnes wasn't sure who the analyst was speaking to, or even—quite—sure who he was speaking about. "But it may be for the larger body, for the race."

Carnes had become used to the images cascading on the main display. They formed a montage of objects juxtaposed in time rather than in space. It was only rarely that a scene meant anything to her on a conscious level, but the ripple of forms and colors soothed rather than rubbing a jagged edge against her nerves.

Chun was conning TC 779 manually. Despite her skill at preprogramming displacements, she lacked the instincts for manual control that Nan Roebeck had. Under Chun's direction the capsule moved in a series of unfelt jerks that even Carnes could notice on the display. She suspected that for Chun, the frustrations of manual control absorbed her cancerous anger at being involved in the death of Watney and the crew of the hostile transportation capsule.

"I saw W-w—your suit, Pauli, displace," Chun said. The image paused long enough for Carnes to see a lioness rubbing her shoulders against a concrete tree in some zoo or other. "Nan—and me, but it was Nan's idea—had set our navigational probes to detect suit displacements when we realized that the other parties were able to do that. I checked what was going on, and . . ."

"And saved our lives," Carnes said loudly.

"Let me check your buttocks," Weigand murmured. "You tore the back off your trousers, I suppose when you came down the slide from the aircraft."

"I forgot the other parties might investigate also," Chun said. "I'm not . . ."

Not used to operating against opponents so sophisticated, Carnes thought. *Not somebody who automatically thinks of ambushes and kill zones, the way the Kyle Watneys do.*

Carnes walked to the front of the capsule while Weigand was in mid-daub. "You saved our lives," she said, her hands resting lightly on Chun's shoulders. "You and Watney saved . . . everything you care about. He acted and you acted. Without your separate actions, we'd all be—"

Probably as dead as the pair of hostiles in California.

"—failed. But don't take Watney's actions on yourself. Don't ever do that."

"I've been thinking about Jalouse," Barthuli said unexpectedly. "When we correct the revision here in 1968, all chance of releasing him from this timeline's ARC Central ends. We can't do it because we were already there—"

"Gerd, we know that," Weigand said tautly. "Rebecca, let me finish covering your scrapes. God knows what germs were going around that airport."

"And of course another team of ARC Riders can't be tasked to the mission," Barthuli continued, "because it isn't possible to displace from our timeline to the revised one."

"Barthuli, we know that!" Pauli Weigand shouted, his face blotched with rage and sick failure. "Look, if you want to run on about this to Nan, fine! But don't tell me it's a mess I can't fix, because I know that!"

"Yes," Barthuli said calmly. "But there's something you may not have considered, Pauli."

Washington, DC

"They're at the safe house," Chun said, looking back at Pauli Weigand with a face whose very openness implied the frown of concern she tried to hide. "I wasn't expecting to find them here. I was just using it to make sure we hadn't lost our temporal zero."

"They left their armor behind," Weigand said as he leaned forward instinctively to bring his eyes closer to the display. "Those are just the empty—"

The two figures in the basement of the safe house moved. They weren't empty suits. "No, I'm wrong."

Why on earth were Nan and Tim wearing armor at this juncture? Had the hostiles made an attack here before—*before* in terms of their personal timeline as well as that of the sidereal universe—they engaged TC 779 at National Airport?

"Bring us—"

Did he have the authority to give orders to Chun? Was that the right order anyway?

"Yes," Quo said. "I thought we should . . . I'll dock us now."

Weigand wasn't sure he'd ever been so glad to see anyone as he was now to see Nan Roebeck. As soon as she was aboard TC 779, Pauli Weigand could return to being just the guy who obeyed orders.

Nan carried a fléchette gun with attached EMP generator,

the latter a tidy package less than a tenth the bulk of the unit Weigand had cobbled together on this horizon. Still, the makeshift had worked. Weigand was glad it was slung to Rebecca's back when he tossed her aboard. His unit had worked, and he'd worked as team commander; though neither of them was as slick as the real article.

"Fifteen seconds," Chun warned as TC 779 initiated its final approach sequence. The gelid shimmer of the air in the basement center warned the suited ARC Riders. They stepped quickly to either side of the unfinished room.

There was nothing odd about Nan with a fléchette gun, but Tim Grainger held a gas/tanglefoot projector. Tim's displacement suit was unmistakable because the right knee joint had been replaced after a previous operation. It still had a distinctively new gloss.

Weigand couldn't think of a time Grainger had picked a projector when there were lethal weapons to be had, but the choice might have been on Nan's orders. The team commander was ultimately responsible for every decision a member of the team made. The decisions Tim—Tim's reflexes, really—could make before anyone stopped him weren't always the sort Nan would be comfortable remembering in the hours before dawn.

TC 779 shuddered. The safety mechanisms lifted the capsule a centimeter before they permitted it to lock into phase with the horizon. "Not bad," Weigand said, though he could have done a good deal better himself.

Quo gestured with her control wands, opening the inner and outer hatches together. Gerd frowned but didn't speak whatever thought was on his mind.

"Nan," Weigand said as he stepped to the hatch to greet his fellows. "We met and destroyed—"

The figure he thought was Tim Grainger fired at Weigand's chest. The projectile knocked Weigand backward, slamming the air from his lungs.

He gasped involuntarily, so the gas that filled TC 779's

cabin when the shell ruptured froze him an instant before it got the others. Chun held her breath, but it didn't matter because the skin-absorptive formula reached her nervous system through her face before she could get her mask down.

Weigand's muscles went rigid, though he was still fully conscious. He bounced like a wooden dummy off a bulkhead and to the deck. To keep from rendering the transportation capsule uninhabitable, the hijackers had used a short-term paralyzing agent whose effects would wear off in a few minutes.

As they boarded TC 779, the armored figures dropped the weapons they must have captured when they took the displacement suits. From the suits' storage pouches they drew angular handguns like those the pair at Travis used on Weigand and the men accompanying him. Weigand knew this time to expect his mind to dissolve into white static.

As it did.

Washington, DC

August 30, 1968

He didn't know who he was. He couldn't move and he wasn't sure why, maybe because he was a disembodied head floating in a prickly white mass that—

"Oh!" shouted Pauli Weigand as a rebuilt acetylcholine supply repaved his nerve pathways. He curved up from the burning fog that wrapped him.

The hostile ARC Riders were getting out of the displacement suits they'd appropriated to ambush TC 779. "Watch him," one said. The words weren't in Standard English. The capsule's internal systems automatically translated them. "He's big."

Both hostiles were male, both of Oriental ancestry. The speaker aimed the acetylcholine inhibitor that was his equivalent of Weigand's acoustic pistol.

"He could be a hydraulic jack and he still wouldn't be able to stretch his restraints," the other hostile said. "Relax. Unless you want to kill them now?"

"No, Central will want them," the first speaker said. "Who knows how many more there may be? And if we miss one capsule?"

He made a cross-cutting gesture at the base of his rib cage.

The hostiles must have been extremely uncomfortable in the hijacked displacement suits. Neither of them was as tall as Roebeck, and Grainger was a good four centimeters taller yet.

They weren't mirror images of one another, though, any more than Chun and Barthuli—both mumbling in their bonds beside Weigand—were. The one who'd spoken first was slim, fine-boned, and of a lighter complexion than his stocky companion.

Stocky eyed Weigand speculatively. The Oriental was obviously strong and proud of it, but if he really thought he had a chance of taking Pauli Weigand hand-to-hand, he was a fool.

Not so great a fool that he'd taken any chances with the bonds, though. Weigand's hands were lashed to his ankles behind his back, and from there attached to an eyebolt mounted for the purpose at the rear of the cabin.

Many revisionists had ridden here after the team's previous missions. If the hostiles had used TC 779's restraint tape, the whole capsule could have been lifted on a strand of it. If they'd used their own, Weigand didn't imagine the material was significantly less strong.

"You've lost," Weigand lied. His voice was a croak. He hacked, clearing the phlegm that had accumulated while he was unconscious. "We blew up your capsule already."

The slim hostile shrugged. "Mishima and Goto were no loss," the console said as his lips spoke syllables of a wholly different rhythm. "As for the capsule, this one will do quite well. Central will be pleased at the intelligence value."

He and Stocky seemed at home in TC 779. Stocky was programming a displacement, using the control wands Chun favored. Weigand wondered again at timelines that could be so close technically while utterly distinct in culture.

Chun gagged as she regained consciousness. She twisted violently. Even if she'd been able to spin like a top, she couldn't have affected her bonds. Barthuli was alert also, but his mind had surfaced as silently as the nostrils of a manatee coming up for air.

"Ready," Stocky said.

Slim sat down where Grainger normally would. He nodded. Stocky's wand initiated the displacement sequence.

"Where are our friends?" Weigand asked. The form of his question avoided giving the hostiles any information they didn't already have.

"The man and the woman are back at the safe house," Slim said with a smile of deliberate cruelty. "Oh, yes, we have you all, now. Fools not to realize it was *our* safe house also!"

"And if you think Calandine might free them—" Stocky said. "We thought that, too, so he's immobilized with them. They were sleeping when we arrived. Trusting a phase-locked chamber against us!"

"Yamaguchi wanted to interrogate them immediately," Slim said. He smiled. He had the look of a man who preferred his food to be alive when he ate it. "I told him that could wait—we needed to be in the displacement suits when their friends came back for them."

He smiled at his companion. "But I'm sure Central will permit him to conduct the initial stages of the process when we return."

Interrogation by Weigand's Anti-Revision Command could leave the subject with a headache, but nothing worse occurred. Slim's operation had comparable technical skills, so the methods implied in Slim's smile must be a matter of taste.

TC 779 trembled on the verge of meshing with the horizon. "You have the con, sir," Stocky—Yamaguchi—said with unexpected formality.

Slim concentrated on his individual display. Like Yamaguchi, he used control wands, but he held them between thumb and forefinger at the balance.

The main display hovered momentarily above the east lawn of the White House, then swooped forward with a smooth grace that Nan Roebeck would have been hard put to better. Walls, furniture—a house servant in formal attire— blurred through the viewpoint. Slim was holding the capsule out of phase, viewing the temporal horizon from a point that was no more than a dust-mote shimmer in the air.

The display steadied on a darkened room with six people present. Four of them were flaccidly unconscious. The President of the United States was upright in his armchair. An alert man had swathed him in transparent wrapping like that which had immobilized the military advisor in Quang Tri a matter of hours before.

The woman wearing a face-covering helmet squatted before a 23d-century mind control device. Its antenna was focused on the President's forehead.

"Pauli?" Chun Quo said. "What—Oh."

Yamaguchi looked back at her, grinned, and returned his attention to the main display.

"Don't talk," Weigand said. "Don't say anything. It'll make it worse."

The woman in the room of the White House took off the helmet and spoke to her companion. She folded the antenna into its carrying case. The man freed the President, then coiled the fine cord into the separate power unit while his companion finished packing the device itself.

Each carrying a case in the left hand, the pair of revisionists opened the door and strode down the hall at a deliberate pace. The pair of guards outside the door had laminated IDs clipped to the lapels of their suits; they wore the cards with the photo and data against the cloth. The guard's eyes were unfocused, and the men made no sign as the revisionists walked past.

23d century technology was light-years beyond the defense capabilities of this horizon. Weigand supposed the pair had drenched the hallways ahead of them with a medium-term hypnotic gas, but there were other alternatives.

"We'll take them when they exit the building," Slim ordered harshly. He was keyed up though not necessarily nervous. His wands adjusted the controls.

Yamaguchi rose and drew his acetylcholine inhibitor. "Can't leave revisionists wandering around loose," he said to Weigand. "Even if they did accidentally do us a favor."

His teeth and his smile were as perfect and false as a silicone breast. Chun looked at Yamaguchi with the perfectly blank expression of a mongoose for a cobra.

TC 779 quivered. The display hovered three meters from an exterior doorway. Slim stood beside Yamaguchi. He aimed his pistol toward the closed hatch.

The door of the building started to open.

Weigand looked at his companions and said, "Nan, Tim— these two hostiles in TC 779 are going to shoot the revisionists when they walk out of the White House."

The door swung back. The guard there in the hallway was as glassy-eyed as his fellows at the President's door. TC 779 locked in phase and both hatches opened. The man and woman in the White House doorway triggered their acoustic pistols.

When Weigand warned them over the intercom, Roebeck and Grainger dropped the cases they were carrying. The sections of mind control device were still falling when the two fired.

Nan Roebeck was faster than Weigand had imagined. She hit Yamaguchi only a heartbeat after Tim Grainger shot the stocky revisionist. Of course, Tim's first acoustic pulse had already knocked Slim back from the hatchway unconscious.

Washington, DC

The basement of the safe house smelled slightly of damp and of ozone. Normally the latter would have made Nan Roebeck worry about TC 779's condition, but not now. A few of the capsule's circuits were arcing beneath the temporary insulation? Big deal. They'd do their job a little longer.

Pauli Weigand came down the stairs. He looked much harder than he had when Roebeck last saw him at 50K. "Calandine's in the phase chamber with the revisionists Bates and Rhone, Nan," he said. "The hostiles put them all under with a storage drug. It's probably the same as ours, but if it's not—I don't know what kind of side effects our antidote might have."

Roebeck tossed him a medical pack. Pauli had lost his with the displacement suit at National Airport. "Try it on one of the revisionists first," she said. "If it works, then bring Calandine around. I'd like to leave him in place if we can."

"Right," said Weigand as he went back upstairs. "We'll see if Bates goes into convulsions. Watney said the business was mostly his idea."

There was a tone of satisfaction in Weigand's voice that surprised Roebeck slightly. There hadn't been time for a proper debriefing, but she didn't need to be told that Pauli had been through a lot on this operation.

Chun Quo came out of TC 779. "I've put them under for twelve hours," she said. She cleared her throat and added, "What are you going to do with them, Nan?"

"Our opposite numbers, you mean?" Roebeck said. "We're going to strip their memories with a red dose and drop them in 50K, just like we're going to do with the revisionists who started the whole business."

Chun nodded, in understanding rather than agreement. "Central . . ." she said. "And perhaps those up the line. Might want to, ah, talk to those persons themselves."

"Yeah," Roebeck said. "The only possible thing they could gain from that exercise would be a way to communicate between our timeline and the other one. That's why you and I are going to wipe all the navigational records from the vehicle before we return from 50K to Central. So nobody can ever find these people after we've marooned them."

She turned so that she was face-to-face to Chun. "Do you have a problem with that?"

Chun looked away. In a voice tiny with embarrassment, she said, "Nan, if you hadn't said that, I was going to give them a triple red dose. Enough to be sure they'd never wake up."

Roebeck hugged the shorter woman to her. "No need for that," she said. "Besides—I'm leading this team."

Barthuli was watching them from the vehicle's open hatch. Quo broke away awkwardly and said, "I'll go help Pauli and Tim." She skipped up the stairs without looking back at the analyst.

"You seem to have come through well enough, Gerd," Roebeck said. The analyst, now that he was back in ARC coveralls, didn't appear to have changed at all.

Barthuli gave her a smile that was either wry or sad. "Unlike Pauli and Quo, you mean?" he said. "They'll want some support when we return, but I don't think there'll be any . . . disabling scars. Nothing the therapists can't put right."

"But not you," Roebeck said, making the implications of her previous comment explicit.

"I don't think the varied experiences of the current operation have warped my psyche, team leader," Barthuli said. He wasn't laughing at her. There was no emotion in his voice at all. "But it would be a little hard to tell, wouldn't it? In any case, I think you'll continue to find me a satisfactory analyst."

He looked toward the ceiling. Condensate beaded the bare I-beams. "Why did you decide to carry out the revisionists' mission in a changed format rather than aborting it?" he asked.

Roebeck nodded. "All right," she said. She squeezed her arms tightly around her chest, then realized what she was doing and forced herself to stand loose again.

"Gerd," she said, "I kept coming up with a less than 12 percent chance of the President announcing tomorrow that he wouldn't run for reelection if we simply eliminated Bates and Rhone as I'd planned. I—"

Barthuli was looking at her. She met his eyes. "The . . . our opposite numbers' existence . . . it depended on a revision at this nexus. But I think our timeline, our existence . . . that depended on a revision, too. Tim and I went into the White House with the equipment we'd taken from Bates and Rhone, and we used it to influence the President to step down."

She flashed a false smile. "I really wish you'd been around to do the analysis instead of me, Gerd."

He shrugged. "You'd have checked my results, wouldn't you?" he said. "You'd still have made the decision yourself?"

"Of course," Roebeck agreed.

"I checked your results," Barthuli said, "and came up with a less than 3 percent probability that the President wouldn't run again without your intervention."

He grinned with more real humor than Roebeck remembered having seen on the analyst's face before. "And the results of the President winning a second full term would be

. . . You'll want to go over my extrapolations, Nan. So will the people at Central who no doubt think they have the right to second-guess field agents. Quite interesting, in the sense of the Chinese curse."

Barthuli chuckled. "I don't believe there'll be any negative repercussions from the decision you made," he said.

"I—" Roebeck looked away and blinked. "Yeah, I was thinking about what was going to happen when Central went over my report," she said. Holding her voice very steady, she added, "You know, Gerd, if you *really* didn't care what happens, you might be happier. But you'd be no good to me. No good at all."

Quo came down the stairs. Behind her came Pauli, with Bates slung over one shoulder and Rhone over the other. Tim Grainger brought up the rear, his fléchette gun held with an attempt at casualness that deceived no one who knew him.

"Bates came around fine," Weigand said. "So I gave him another hit. It won't kill him, but he'll likely have a headache when a sabertooth or wolves do the job."

"Anchor the revisionists to the bolt next to our opposite numbers," Roebeck said. "We've gotten a full load between the two groups."

"Despite attrition," Grainger said mildly.

"Oh, Pauli?" Roebeck added to the big man's back. "I haven't had time to thank you for warning us about the ambush."

"My pleasure," Weigand said. He paused in the hatchway and turned so that he could look at Roebeck past his comatose burden. "Slim had already let us know the sort of time we were in for if we stayed in their hands."

"Their communicators are earplugs, not headbands like ours," Chun said. "They didn't recognize what Pauli was wearing. But if Pauli hadn't stayed so calm . . ."

"Then it would still have come out the same," Weigand said as he disappeared into the vehicle. "I've seen Tim draw. They hadn't."

"Thanks for the compliment," Grainger said dryly. "But you know, sometimes an extra tenth of a second comes in real handy." He followed Weigand aboard.

"I think we're ready, Nan," Chun Quo said quietly. "I've programmed the initial displacement to 50K."

Roebeck slammed upright with a sudden awareness of failed responsibility. "Major Carnes!" she said. "Did we . . ."

The tip of her tongue touched her lips. "Did we lose her as well as Watney?"

"No we did not, Nan," Gerd Barthuli said. This time his expression would have lit a room. "I had an idea, you see. Pauli, Quo—and Rebecca—worked out the details of how it could be executed. We'll show you."

He bowed and gestured Roebeck to the hatchway with full 18th-century formality.

Epilogue: ARC Central

Jalouse dropped his plasma weapon. He spread the fingers of his right hand before his face while he tried desperately to latch his helmet with the other. A screaming man stretched over the desk and fired with the muzzle of his machine pistol touching the gauntlet.

Three bullets struck Jalouse's palm, flinging the arm aside, the hand numb within the armor. At least a dozen rounds ricocheted from the curved front of the helmet, howling like wasps the size of eagles. The multiple impacts did what Jalouse had failed to do: latch the faceshield despite the tag of joint sealant that had come adrift when the ARC Rider grabbed at his visor with desperate strength.

The gas shell hit the forehead of the man leaning over Jalouse. The projectile weighed 220 grams and was moving as fast as the hoof of an angry mule.

The shooter hurtled backward, knocked unconscious by the impact. The contents of the shell sprayed across what should have been Transfer Control Room Two, volatilizing before the droplets reached the far bulkhead.

Civilians folded up, their muscles unable to obey the commands of fear and hatred that still glared from their eyes. A machine pistol slipped from nerveless fingers and fired a last shot into the ceiling.

The armored figure who'd followed Jalouse through the airlock slung the gas projector and said in an unfamiliar female voice, "Hold me! We're displacing in ten seconds!"

Jalouse thrust his arms out. His right hand wouldn't close properly, but his left gauntlet twined fingers with hers and they hugged, chest to chest.

The room's inner door opened. The hall beyond was filled with figures in displacement suits with an odd shoulder flare. The leader aimed a plasma weapon as the whole scene faded into the darkness outside of time.

Light. Chest-high grass, clouds too scattered to dim the bright sun, and a warm breeze on Jalouse's face as he threw his visor up again.

"What the *hell* happened?" he gasped. The other figure opened her helmet also. He'd never seen her before. "Who *are* you?"

"My name's Rebecca Carnes," the woman said. "Can you help me out of this suit? I think we got the legs two different lengths when we put it together out of the spares in the capsule."

"But what happened?" Jalouse repeated. He was shaking, but feeling started to return to his right hand as he reached for the latch of Carnes' armor. "I've never seen you before."

"Your friends couldn't go fetch you from . . ." she nodded, upward, a direction in time. "From there, from that Central. Because they'd been there when you were caught and couldn't go back. But I could."

She stepped out of the suit with Jalouse's support. She was wearing loose garments of a style he wasn't familiar with. Her trousers had been shredded by whatever she'd done before suiting up. What the *hell* had been going on?

"Are they . . ." Jalouse said. "Is . . . are they all right?"

"Everybody made it," Carnes said. "Everybody's going to go to the real ARC Central together. Including you."

The air above the sun-drenched prairie trembled, then solidified into an Anti-Revision Command transportation capsule. Jalouse's breath caught when he saw the damage to the hull, but Nan Roebeck's smile from the opening hatch was all the proof he needed that things really were under control.

DAVID DRAKE was born in Dubuque, Iowa, in 1945. He graduated Phi Beta Kappa from the University of Iowa, majoring in history (with honors) and Latin. He was attending Duke University Law School when he was drafted. He served the next two years in the Army, spending 1970 as an enlisted interrogator with the 11th Armored Cavalry in Viet Nam and Cambodia.

Upon return he completed his law degree at Duke and was for eight years Assistant Town Attorney for Chapel Hill, North Carolina. He then drove a city bus for a year and, since 1981, has been a full-time freelance writer.

Drake has a wife, a son, and various pets. He lives in a new house on 22 acres in Chatham County, North Carolina, where he feeds sun-flower seeds to the birds.

JANET MORRIS is Vice President of Morris & Morris, a private consultancy specializing in new defense technology and non-lethal warfare. She is a Fellow at the Center for Strategic and International Studies in Washington, D.C. She has participated in several unprecedented U.S./Russian technology exchanges. in collaboration with David Drake, she has written *Active Measures* and *Kill Ratio*, among other novels. With her husband, Chris Morris, she has written *The American Warrior* and other titles. She is also the author of the *Tempus* series.